Heal My Broken Heart
A Gold Coast Romance – Book Two

By Elle G. Mraz

Copyright

Heal My Broken Heart
The Gold Coast Romance Series – Book Two

Published by Elle G. Mraz
Distributed by CreateSpace
Copyright © 2016 Elle G. Mraz
Cover Design © by Elle G. Mraz
Cover Photo © by Elle G. Mraz

ellegmraz@gmail.com
www.ellegmraz.com

First Edition: May, 2016
First Printing: May, 2016
Printed in the United States of America

ISBN (eBook) 978-0-9966947-3-5
ISBN (paperback) 978-0-9966947-4-2
ISBN (hardback) 978-0-9966947-5-9

Acknowledgements

Thank you so much to my friends and coworkers who would casually, then more incessantly, ask if book two was ready yet. Writing this book was a lot easier than writing the first one because the story was already there. But I never would have sat down to write it if I hadn't thought people might actually want to read it. I love to write; and what a difference it makes knowing there's someone out there who really wants to get lost in your imagination with you. It's an honor and a privilege, sharing my stories. Thank you so much for your continued interest in them.

And again, thank you, Anna. I do believe the bulk of the data on my phone is dedicated to the text messages we share. Thank you for responding to my mindless dribble, day or night, at work or home, swamped or free. It always comes through at the exact moment I need it.

A portion of this book's proceeds will go directly to the South Florida nonprofit, Future 6 Helping Hand, specifically: For the Love of Surfing — an organization that makes my heart full and forever grateful to be surrounded by such awesome people. To learn more about this wonderful nonprofit that supports children with special needs and at risk youth by getting them involved in surfing, skateboarding, or other various community activities, please visit their website: http://f6helpinghand.org/surf-camp/

For Jason

Prologue

The expansive warehouse — converted to a massive rave club — swallows Anson whole just as it's so expertly done nearly every night since coming home to her, dead. But tonight, the vibe is beyond the previous dark and despondent drive. He desperately needs to be numb.

He thumbs a pill on the bar, contemplating its purpose, his purpose, or whether there is a purpose to any of it. He ignores call after call from his brother; instead choosing to study the alcohol rings bleeding through the autopsy report opened up on the counter — until he can no longer take it. Before a stray thought of reason strikes, he pops the pill and chases it down with his glass of blended scotch.

"I've been watching you the last few weeks," says a smooth, male voice just off to the side of Anson. "But tonight: something says you want this to be your last. Tell me: what's changed?"

"The fuck?" Anson barks, turning to face the man.

"You're not our typical patron; yet, night after night, you dance."

"Hey, listen man: I come here to forget. Not to be bothered by someone collecting social behavior stats," Anson growls, now eager for the effects of the pill to kick in.

"No one comes here to forget. Especially someone who plays doctor at a Houston hospital several hours away. You come here to feel alive. If you truly don't want to kill yourself in the process, let me know. I could use a man like you in my fleet."

"Who sent you here? How do you know that about me?" Anson asks brusquely, turning his whole body toward the man.

"I own this place. It's my business to know. And I recognize talent when I see it. You've got something. If you want to make people truly believe there's something worth living for, call me when you're ready to be something more than just a doctor." The man puts a business card down on the autopsy report and disappears into the cloak of club patrons.

Anson glances down at the card, now amused by the strange man's invitation.

Xavier LeBeau
XL Messieurs
Your Dreams. Our Reality

He laughs — so far he's only destroyed dreams. He stares suspiciously at the flashing lights bouncing off the dancing bodies. Slowly the defining edge of every person begins to liquefy. The colors wash over his now medicated vision, enticing him to join the massive blanket of sensuality and rhythm.

He places the card in his pocket and staggers into the blur of dancers. The body heat envelopes him as his tormented heart erratically races to keep up — until it can't. He surrenders his control: the rhythm of the bass the only thump in his chest; the collective breath of the crowd the only air in his lungs.

He never wants to leave.

He never wants to live — beyond the moment.

Chapter 1

Florida's Gold Coast (synonymous with South Florida) stretches for miles, beginning in Palm Beach County then straight down to Miami-Dade — all along the southeast coast of Florida. People often attribute the name to the glitz and glamour of oceanfront living — high-rise condominiums and expansive estates saddled right into the history of railroad tycoons and drug cartels. Or, they see its Great Gatsby beginnings rooted in the Spanish gold that has been found along the coast from sunken treasure ships centuries ago. Regardless, the name had always been synonymous with home for Kendall Matthews.

Through all the storms she'd weathered here (and the ones still building offshore), she never had any intentions of calling another coast her home. In this particular moment, ripping through the rapid turquoise current of the Gulf Stream on Dan's Sea Fox Voyager — the glint of the sun on the ocean spray like a shower of diamonds scattering through the air — Kendall had never felt more alive.

Finally, she felt home again... sans Dan.

The speed of the boat, however, matched the speed of her thoughts. This particular Saturday morning fed the adrenaline junkie she housed within. Gabriel's 30th birthday party would be incredible — she had no doubt. Their mom, Elena, pulled out all the stops: a starstudded gallery birthday party for the socialite crowd of South Beach. Ariel and William were sailing swiftly through the last few weeks before their own extravagant event: their wedding, to be held at the Biltmore in Coral Gables — nothing short of opulent perfection. Then there was the phone call she'd just received from her realtor. Dan and her quaint humble abode (the 1955 concrete block home of Sandalfoot Lane) already had its first showing booked, after only one day on the housing market!

But all of these exciting thoughts paled in comparison to the one resounding echo of the morning. The most powerful adrenaline rush of the day definitely belonged to the moment Dr. Anson Allaway held her face in his hands and said: Kendall, I'm in love with you.

She hadn't been able to speak. He'd been keeping so much secret: his past with Grace, his business with Xavier outside of Gold Coast General, stripping, the plethora of sexual partners he'd had between the time of Grace and Kendall... The list seemed to have no end.

But when it came to how he felt about her; what her presence in his life meant to him — suddenly Anson was an open book of love and unashamed to say so. Kendall could not help, but be swept up in the whirlwind of emotional release that washed over her.

"So why did he really come over?" Ariel asked, elbowing Kendall as she stood in front of the captain's seat steering the boat.

"What?!" Kendall shouted back, pretending she hadn't heard her as their hair whipped wildly in the salty wind.

"Dr. Sex? Why did he stop by this morning?!" Ariel asked louder.

Kendall smiled, shaking her head at Ariel. She knew her blatant dismissal of Anson's surprise pop-over would not go unnoticed by Ariel. There had to be more. There was always more.

"Come on!" Ariel shouted again, jabbing Kendall in the ribs.

Kendall assessed their situation. Gabriel and William sat securely behind them, Ariel and Kendall taking up the pedestal seats. She worried anything shouted might sail right into the open ears of both men. She eyed Ariel and mouthed the words: He loves me.

"Are you kidding me?!" Ariel squealed.

"Shhhh!" Kendall hit her, glancing back to the boys again. "That's what he said."

"O. M. G," Ariel mouthed back. "Did you say it back?"

"No! It's too soon!"

"But you feel it, don't you?" Ariel boldly concluded.

"Let's talk about this later. Besides" —Kendall rolled her eyes in William's direction— "I don't think he's too keen on him."

"Anson doesn't like Will?" she asked, perplexed.

"Shhhh! No!" Kendall gripped the steering wheel tighter with frustration.

"Then what?"

"William. Does. Not. Like. Anson," Kendall mouthed very clearly.

"Why the hell not? Did he say that?" Ariel questioned, turning back to William who was oblivious to their conversation.

Ariel had noticed William hadn't said much since meeting Anson, aside from when he'd privately mentioned their wedding was already busting at the seams with guests, why include yet another

4

stranger — referring to Ariel's impromptu wedding invite to Anson at the house that morning. Ariel had found that comment strange.

She shrugged, stumped by Kendall's assessment. The conversation would definitely have to be picked up back on land.

***

"So who's coming to this tonight?" Ariel whispered, tiptoeing past a sleeping Gabriel on the La-Z-Boy recliner. Hours out on the ocean in the scorching South Florida sun with wind-burned cheeks definitely called for a nap before being the guest of honor at his party that night.

"My mom's invited all of South Beach, I think," Kendall said, rolling her eyes. "I swear; this boy gets everything. What the hell did we do for my 30th?"

"Did you even have a 30th birthday party?" Ariel asked, feeding into Kendall's sibling rivalry as she sat down on the couch.

"Exactly!" Kendall said, vindicated even if it was only in jest.

"Dan did that surprise sunset yacht cruise in the Intracoastal for you," William piped in, fresh from his shower. "I remember because that was one of my ideas for proposal. But then I nixed it. Didn't want to be unoriginal."

"Oh my goodness! You're right. I totally forgot," Kendall remembered, her memory of happier times fogged out by her burgeoning pessimistic view of the world since Dan's death. "That was a good time. A really good time."

"You were going to propose on a boat?" Ariel asked, turning to look at William. "When have we ever been on a boat aside from Dan's?"

"I don't know, it seemed unique," William responded, shrugging. He then bent over the couch and kissed the top of Ariel's head. "But proposing next to Georgia's Amicalola Falls just as the sun was rising was pretty perfect, if I do say so myself."

"Yeah, another thing I don't do: hike," Ariel said, laughing. "But I'll give you that. It was pretty romantic." She craned her neck back beyond the edge of the couch to kiss him upside down.

Kendall rolled her eyes as she pushed off the cushions. "You two are cute — if you like that gag factor."

Ariel swatted Kendall's butt as she walked by. "I do believe you're the one with the boyfriend who drops by just to say he loves you. 'I just called. To say. I love you,'" Ariel sang out, mocking her.

5

"You two that serious?" William suddenly chimed in, concern evident in his voice.

Kendall shrugged casually, wanting to avoid an Anson debate.

"And what if they are? You know something we don't?" Ariel asked, jumping to Kendall and Anson's defense. "Love is inevitable when you've got such good chemistry."

"No," William dismissed the notion quickly. "It just seemed sudden to me. I'm not knocking you, Kendall. I'm happy for you. Really. I just got a vibe."

"A vibe?" Kendall asked, now intrigued, knowing Anson was indeed hiding something. Getting an outside man's perspective could be beneficial.

"Like, maybe he's a player," William said. "I don't want you getting hurt."

Kendall and Ariel looked at one another, bobbing their heads around as they absorbed William's assessment. Anson had been an unapologetic playboy and they both knew it.

"Well, there's definitely truth to your vibe," Kendall admitted. "And I do appreciate your concern. But don't worry: I'm keeping my head about me with him. Sometimes too much." She looked off reflectively for a minute. "I truly believe he has my best interests at heart. And he's not seeing other women. I trust him with that."

"I doubt he is either," William agreed. "But sometimes we hurt others despite all our best intentions."

Kendall was taken aback by William's uncharacteristically poignant statement. She looked at Ariel who simply offered up a sweet smile and a shrug.

"Well, thank you," Kendall said, pausing to think if she should open it up any further. "I'm going to take my shower now. When Gabe wakes up, tell him he needs to take one as well."

Following her shower and preparation for the party that night, Kendall exited her master bedroom to a deafening silence. She quickly ascertained that Ariel and William had been engrossed in a heated argument. Gabriel sat stunned on the recliner.

"What? What just happened?" Kendall asked, breaking the awkward silence.

Ariel glared at William. She turned to Kendall.

"Is there something you're not telling me about Anson?" Ariel asked hesitantly. "Because if there is, that's your business. I won't push you to say anything. But if you don't know everything there is to know about him, then there's a problem."

"What do you mean? What am I missing?" Kendall asked, her eyes darting between Ariel and William.

"When Anson was here this morning, did he say anything about Will?" Ariel asked, probing deeper.

"What do you mean? Why would he? What the hell is going on?" Kendall asked defensively. "Will: I'm sorry you don't like him. I know he's not Dan. But Dan is dead. And I have to move on. And for right now, I'm choosing to do it with Anson."

"Kendall: You've got this all wrong," William interjected. "I just think you're taking things a little fast with this guy. Maybe you should first get to know him better."

"Are you kidding me? What is this Ariel?" Kendall shouted. "Why are you just standing there like that?" Her eyes narrowed in on Ariel with discontent.

"Hon, you know I'm on your side with this," Ariel answered, her heart now racing as every fairytale image she and Kendall had conjured up that morning as they discussed the evolution of Kendall's relationship, seemingly evaporated before her eyes.

"Well, then what is this?! This attempt to steer me away from the man that loves me!" Kendall shouted, tears threatening. "Why do you want to take that away?!"

"No honey. That's not it at all. I just…" Ariel looked at Gabriel, then over to William. "What should I say?"

"Kendall, has Anson ever told you about an Xavier LeBeau?" William asked regretfully.

Hearing that heavy-laden name from someone other than Anson nearly knocked the wind out of her. She stared vacantly as she reviewed the last month with Anson. Her drained expression racked Ariel. Kendall plopped down onto one of her dining room chairs and envisioned the seedy life of a male stripper and all that might accompany it.

"Kendall, hon? Are you alright? You don't look so good," Ariel remarked, approaching her.

Kendall was far from prepared to hear whatever William had to say. Not now. Not in front of Gabriel before his big birthday bash. She stood up abruptly from her chair to finish getting ready. But all the adrenaline ran dry from the rampant pounding in her chest and her blood plummeted to her feet. Her brain went offline.

Kendall hit the floor with a thud.

***

"Hello?"

Kendall's voice echoes off the barren walls of the dank stairwell, which seems to be expanding at an exponentially rapid pace.

She sees a shadow slip behind the wall to the next flight of stairs above her.

"Is someone there? Dan?" she calls out.

She sits alone at a mile-long dining table — something out of Alice's world in Wonderland. She's definitely beyond the looking glass.

"Wait. What just happened? Where am I? What's going on here?" Kendall searches frantically about the room.

Again, a shadow streaks across the end of the table, but she fails to see the body attached to it. Or is it Peter Pan's lost shadow? Her confusion begins to spiral out of control. Her anxiety chokes around her neck as the vast size of the empty room overwhelms her.

And his hand touches her. There. Between her legs. Anson. Anson's hand. His skilled fingers. She can feel them. But she's alone, staring at the streaks of their impassioned love-making like trailed grease across the monstrous table. And entrails. And death.

She attempts to bolt but the stethoscope around her neck snags, holding her securely to the chair, choking her. And not a single heartbeat can be heard.

"Kendall! Kendall," Ariel tirelessly repeated, shaking Kendall's shoulders.

"What happened?" Kendall asked groggily, attempting to sit up, only to be held back by two sets of hands.

"Kendall, you just collapsed," Ariel explained, pressing a cold towel to Kendall's brow. "William caught your head before it hit the floor."

Kendall blinked several times, restoring her focus. She was on a pillow on the floor outside her bedroom, Gabriel and Ariel hovering closely over while William paced with his phone ready in hand.

"That's strange. I'm sure I'll be fine," Kendall said, easing her way to a sitting position. "Whoa. Okay, so I'm a little woozy. Gabe, grab me some orange juice please."

Gabriel jumped up and headed into the kitchen.

"Kendall: What's going on?" Ariel whispered.

"I don't know. Here: help me up," Kendall replied, Ariel assisting her to the chair. "I just had a weird vagal response. A pain in my gut or something." Kendall looked up at William, his expression alarming her more than her situation. "Will, please put your phone down."

"I'm not sure what a vagal response is, but I don't like how you look," William said. "Should we at least call your mom and—"

"What? No!" Kendall immediately rejected his suggestion. "No, everything's fine and we'll be heading out as soon as Gabe gets showered." Kendall accepted a glass of orange juice from her brother. "Okay, Gabe? Go ahead and shower so we can get ready for your party."

"Are you okay?" Gabriel asked, deeply concerned. "Why did you fall over like that?"

"It's called fainting. Too much sun, too much excitement, not enough food and water. That's all, bud. Nothing to worry about. I've fainted before and I'm just fine. So, go ahead and get ready so we can go see what Mom's planned for you, okay?"

Gabriel hesitated, watching Kendall drink back her orange juice. She looked up at him, motioning for him to go, and he obliged. The minute Gabriel closed the guest bedroom door, Ariel looked straight at Kendall.

"Kendall, I don't like this. As far as I can recall, you've fainted only two other times in your life and you're certainly not running a marathon right now," Ariel said sternly, looking Kendall over. "Girl: are you pregnant?"

Kendall let out a long sigh, cradling her head in her hand, her arm propped on the table. "The possibility crossed my mind this morning. I've been feeling off. But it just doesn't make any sense with the IUD. And it'd be so early. Seven weeks ago max is when we first got together."

Ariel looked up at William who was seriously stressing, pacing in place.

"Does the asshole even know?" he suddenly blurted out.

"William!" Ariel reprimanded him.

"Well does he?" William asked again. "Kendall, I hate to burst your bubble, but Allaway is not the knight in shining armor you think he is. And you've got to get the full picture before you make any longterm decisions about him. Especially if you're pregnant with his baby."

"I know about the stripping," Kendall confessed, needing to nip the whole thing in the bud. "I thought it was in his past, but I guess he's still involved. I don't know how you know and I'm not sure I want to at this point. But, he came over today because he clearly needed to get some things off his chest. I'm guessing that's part of it. So for right now, let him tell me what he needs to tell me. Okay?"

"Kendall, there's more to it," William began, but Ariel stood up from her crouched position in front of Kendall and held up her hand to him.

"Stop," Ariel demanded. "This is not the place or time. She's got bigger issues right now if she's actually pregnant."

"I just know he's not worth her time," William mumbled as he returned to the living room to pack his bag.

Kendall shook her mind clear.

"Well, I don't even know if I'm pregnant," she said, taking control of the situation. "So, one thing at a time here. Ariel: run to the pharmacy on the corner and get a pregnancy test. If it's positive, I'll get it all checked out Monday. If it's negative, this has been a whole lot of drama for nothing.

"With regard to Anson's sordid past," Kendall continued. "Again: *I* will take care of that and get to the bottom of it all and draw my *own* conclusions on whether or not he's worth my time.

"And in a half hour we're going to Miami like none of this ever happened. Tonight is all about Gabe and I don't want a single look, pat on the back, or any questioning of how I'm feeling. As of right now, everything is perfect. Fucking perfect."

Kendall stood up, feeling much stronger, and marched back in her room to finish getting ready for the night.

Chapter 2

Elena Reyes-Graham pulled out. All. The. Stops. at Gabriel's *Dirty Thirty Birty* — as scripted across the invitations as well as the banner over the gallery in shimmering glitter paint (a name Kendall vetoed from day one, yet lost control over once Daniel heard it and ran with it, considering he was the event's main coordinator). It was unparalleled even by SoBe standards. Daniel, Elena's gallery director, promoted the event like an A-list art show and the people of South Beach did not disappoint.

Gabriel's infectious personality was well-known in Elena's circle of South Beach, reaching well beyond it simply through the stellar reputation of *Galerie Gabriel*. The gallery was lit up, showcasing stunning oversized photographs of Gabriel out fishing, strolling along the Art Deco district, dining out at various landmark restaurants. Black and white, full-color, close-up portraits, landscapes — everything featuring Gabriel in his element along South Florida's Gold Coast. They were beautiful, breath-taking, and overflowing with joy.

"Mom!" Kendall exclaimed as the four friends walked through the gallery doors right around 7:30pm, the party scheduled to begin around 8 o'clock.

"So? You like?" Elena teased, her arms held out as she spun, addressing not only the gallery, but her sparkling black sequined gown.

"Holy shit! I had no idea *this* is what you were talking about when you said pictures of Gabe. This is incredible. And yes! You look amazing!"

Kendall embraced her mom affectionately and stepped aside as everyone greeted her. Kendall continued to take it all in, mesmerized.

"I had a photographer follow Gabriel around from time to time. Some are already sold. It's all going to his trust," Elena explained proudly.

"Wow," Ariel managed to say, also in awe of how spectacular it all was. "So, I know who will be planning my 35th."

"I'm famous!" Gabriel announced loudly, looking ever-so dapper in his navy suit vest and silk coral tie.

The event was fully catered and featured a live DJ. Before it even got started, the room hummed with the positive vibes of excited energy. But by 9 o'clock, the gallery was packed: Jimmy Choo and

Versace all on full display, champagne and Black-Eyed Peas popping continuously (Gabriel's favorite band), and photograph after enormous photograph sold to the biggest names of South Beach and Coconut Grove with plans for prominent displays in lobbies and business offices alike; not to mention private home collections. The night was surreal and Gabriel ate. It. Up.

They all did.

Kendall gravitated to the section of photographs with both Gabriel and Dan. She had no idea her mom had been planning this party for nearly a year. Elena had pointed out the print she'd already purchased for Kendall prior to the party starting. Gabriel and Dan were on the boat. There was a series of them out on the SeaFox. But this one was a black and white portrait. Dan broadly smiled, looking down at his lure as Gabriel howled with laughter — his head thrown back, eyes squeezed shut, the creases around them deep and inviting. Gabriel's arm held onto Dan's shoulder, something Gabriel often did even though he was a good foot shorter than Dan. The blurred background of the Atlantic appeared calm and clear; a billowing, puffy cloud pinned in the sky above them completed the picture of exceptional whimsy. Time very much stood still in the photograph and Kendall couldn't take her eyes off of it.

It was beautiful, pure, and honest.

As the hour approached eleven, Kendall, William, and Ariel settled into a corner high top. They'd had their fill of hors d'oeuvres, libations, and dancing, but the lively sport of people-watching was still in full force. From where they sat, they enjoyed a voyeuristic view into the classic photo-booth set up. The barely-there curtain could not hide the questionable props and expressions of its models, at one point nearly ten people cramming in for a session and requiring Daniel — who remained quite the professional emcee the entire night — to step in and break up the boisterous crowd.

Gabriel seemed to never tire: circulating the crowd, enjoying cake slice after cake slice, and proudly posing with his pictures and their buyers. Kendall felt she just might burst with how happy she was for him.

Once Elena began to slow, drawing out her small-talk for lengthier periods of time at their corner table, Kendall knew the party was nearing its end.

"What time is it?" Kendall asked, her mom actually pulling up a seat next to her this time around.

"After midnight," she answered, exhausted. "But look at all of them. They're still here. And Gabriel! He's still going. I can't believe it!"

Kendall leaned over and kissed Elena's cheek. "You outdid yourself, Mom. This was beyond awesome."

"Thank you, baby." Elena smiled. But then her expression relaxed as she looked Kendall over.

"What?" Kendall asked hesitantly.

"Gabriel told me you fainted."

Kendall rolled her eyes. She knew he'd say something. It was impossible for him not to.

"We'd just gotten back from the boat and I was dehydrated. Not a big deal," Kendall said dismissively.

"Well, you're not eating enough then," Elena concluded, holding up a truffle dripping in decadent ganache. Kendall accepted the mouth-watering morsel, opening her mouth for her mom.

Elena looked around, exhaling with satisfaction. The opening of the gallery door caught her eye as more guests walked in. "Oh, I got to go stand over there to turn people away, otherwise the lights will continue to attract the SoBe moths."

She winked at Kendall and patted Ariel's hands as she walked by. Ariel looked ready to pass out, leaning up against William as he leaned against the wall. It'd been a very long day.

"Dr. Johnson?" a male voice called out over to them, making them all perk up momentarily.

"Yes," William answered hesitantly, eyeing the well-groomed Latino man suspiciously. And then all of a sudden he stood up, Ariel nearly falling off her chair as her back support dropped away from her. "Angelo," he said, his memory fully jarred. "Good to see you. It's been a long time. This is my fiancé, Ariel, and her friend Kendall, sister of Gabriel — the guest of honor," William quickly spouted off.

"I know Gabriel. We all do at the club. He's a legend," Angelo commented, squeezing Kendall's hand affectionately.

"Oh. What club is this?" Kendall asked with curious delight.

"A Miami-based club," William quickly answered, his eyes aggressively darting at Angelo.

"An entertainment club," Angelo offered smugly, winking at Kendall.

Kendall lowered her eyebrows at both of them. "You better not be talking about a strip club. If you're telling me Gabriel's well-known at a strip club, I'm done for the night."

Angelo laughed heartily. "No, no. Not like a patron. He's only been there during off hours. He helps with our fish tank."

Kendall and Ariel shared a collective sigh of relief. Gabriel often assisted with the local fish tanks that his employer, Gold Coast Reefs, maintained.

"Well, I hope the ladies are fully clothed during those hours," Kendall commented, now looking beyond Angelo to see if party-goers were finally getting the hint that the party was over.

Gabriel suddenly appeared, slapping Angelo on the back. "Hey Angelo! What's up my man?"

"The man of the hour! Gabriel has hit the big three-O. When you going to get up on stage at XL and give the ladies what they want?" Angelo joked, Gabriel falling into a fitful of laughter.

"Oh god. I think I need to exit this conversation," Kendall said, laughing and sliding off her high-top chair.

"Only if you go up there with me, Angelo!" Gabriel egged him on, still laughing.

"My day is over, my man. I only manage now. Gotta get more young bucs like you."

And Kendall stopped in her tracks. "Wait– What? Male strippers?"

"XL Messieurs. Male entertainers. We're the best around! All over Texas, N'awlins, Hotlanta, and right here in SoBe, baby!"

Kendall stood still, looking over at William who slowly shook his head, *no*, reading her every rapidly evolving thought.

"Do you know Anson Allaway?" The question was out before she gave it a second thought.

"Of course. He's actually down here right now with Xavier. But we don't see him much at the club. He's more of a silent partner. Why? You interested?" Angelo offered, oblivious to the wildly uncomfortable tension building between William, Ariel, and Kendall.

"Interested in his...? What– services?" Kendall squeaked, then gulped, wondering if she'd pushed it too far.

"Kendall's already dating him," Gabriel suddenly announced, following along in the conversation flawlessly. "He's a doctor at her hospital."

"Oh. Well then," Angelo said, backing up to slowly scan Kendall from head to toe with a cunning grin. "You know him better than I do. I'll let him know you were thinking of him."

Kendall just stared at him with disgust, Angelo recognizing he'd overstayed his welcome.

"Well, it was good to see you fine folks," Angelo announced. Then he looked over at William who was still stone-faced as if he'd just watched a horrifying accident unfold in slow motion. "Doctor by day, escort by night. That's not a gig I'd give up anytime soon, but uh... I guess every dog has his day, am I right?" He squeezed William's shoulder, giving him a jolt, then walked off.

Their jaws dropped.

"Wait– what?!" Kendall blurted out.

"What's an escort?" Gabriel asked, looking quizzically between all their blank stares.

Kendall stood stupefied, her eyes locked on William's. And he simply stared back, unable to formulate a single word to refute a single thing she'd just heard.

Escort.

Escort.

Escort.

The word just kept exploding over and over in her head. She couldn't shake it and wondered to god how she hadn't put two and two together earlier. *Doctor by day, escort by night.*

It all made perfect sense.

"Kendall?" Gabriel prodded, shaking her arm. "What's an escort?"

"Wh-what? What, bud? A *what*?" She fumbled foolishly over her words, suddenly unsure if she'd heard anything at all. Maybe she'd imagined the whole conversation. Maybe she did hit her head when she'd fallen earlier in the day. Her brother couldn't actually be asking her to explain what an *escort* was? *Could he?*

"An escort. Angelo said Alltheway was a doc by day and escort by night. What's an escort?" Gabriel repeated.

"Allaway. It's Allaway," Kendall stated, beginning with the basics, the things that made sense in her mind. "And an escort is simply someone who walks people around. Like at a wedding. Remember Anna's wedding? You were a type of escort. You helped

15

walk guests down the aisle. That's all. A friend for someone so they don't have to walk alone."

"It's a wrap!" Daniel shouted excitedly, snapping their heads to the front door. He locked the door with an accomplished sigh. "We did it! Dirty Thirty Birty has come to a close. Happy Birthday, Gabriel!!"

But Gabriel's face was nowhere as exuberant as it'd been moments ago.

"Whatever Barbie," Gabriel mumbled, knowing his understanding fell short.

And the picture became ugly, tainted, and horribly dishonest.

Chapter 3

"Ow!" Kendall jumped in her seat.

"Oh, sorry! Some jerk just cut me off," William explained, glancing at Kendall through the rearview mirror as she sat behind him in the back of the Audi.

Ariel turned to look at Kendall. It was late afternoon on Sunday, the escort bomb-drop and birthday bash behind them... the wedding and Kendall's well-being still ahead of them. The three were on their way back to Palm Beach County from Elena's condo.

"No, not you. I was zoning out and startled or something. The seatbelt kind of dug into me," Kendall commented, rubbing her shoulder. She looked back up and was met by Ariel's warm, umber eyes peering over the passenger side seat.

"Ariel, stop looking at me like that. That's the exact look you gave me when Dan died. No one died." Kendall averted her eyes from Ariel's concerned expression. "Not yet, at least," she muttered under her breath.

"Are we going to talk about it at all?" Ariel asked. "I mean, we successfully ignored everything just like you asked. But I really don't want to ignore it for the next few weeks and then suddenly — *bam* — the whole thing erupts at the wedding."

"It'll be fine. Your wedding will be princess-fucking-perfect," Kendall responded thoughtlessly, staring out the window at the southbound traffic.

She felt miserable, the pit of her stomach in a vice of twisted knots as her thoughts stewed in the fetid scenes of Anson's secret past. Movie reel after endless fucking movie reel compulsively played out like some forbidden torture tactic in her brain. Was this really true about the man she'd fallen for after Dan?

After all, it was an enviable lifestyle, according to stud wannabe, Angelo — *the little fucker.* And there was her technically true definition of an escort. But Gabriel felt duped; at the very least knowing he couldn't completely follow the conversation.

She hated making him feel so small. She felt like the ultimate bitch-sister.

Then there was that ever-so delicate detail of having a positive pregnancy test and lying about it to Ariel and William just so everyone would get off her back.

She could see her medical record now: *Gravida 5, para 0. Nothing but death.*

Ariel faced forward, hurt by Kendall's comment. William held Ariel's hand, but her expression remained stiff. Only then did Kendall notice she wasn't the only one in pain.

"Ariel, I didn't mean it like that," Kendall finally said. "I'm sorry. Your wedding will not be affected by this and that's a promise. I really need to get out of my head... Or at least shake this G-string-wearing gorilla off my back." Kendall forced a laugh, but Ariel remained quiet. So Kendall shifted gears.

"Yes. We do need to talk about it. I just don't know what I'm ready to hear yet," Kendall said through an exhausted sigh. "And I guess, in a way, I need to hear it from him first. I need his side. Yes. I have a million questions swimming around for you. For Will. But, I know getting those answers will never change anything. Because you are my family. And I love you no matter what."

Ariel's shoulders relaxed as Kendall continued.

"But Anson? His answers? I don't know," Kendall said honestly. "So, I need to go in as blank as possible. Does that make sense?"

Ariel turned to face Kendall again. "Sure," she said softly. "So let me know when you're ready to talk." She gave Kendall a small smile.

"I will," Kendall agreed, reassuringly. "I promise."

Really, it was all too much to digest; denial and avoidance her only friends when it came to the decisions she'd made since Dan's death. Kendall reached down to adjust the backseat air-conditioning controls, needing to feel a breeze against her face.

"How are you feeling? You're looking pale again," Ariel commented.

William looked up at his rearview mirror.

"Do you think you might faint again?" he asked.

"I just need to get home and I'll be fine," Kendall said, resting her head back against the seat cushion. She had to take care of this on her own. She couldn't monopolize the charitable concerns of her family any longer.

But Ariel and William weren't buying it.

"Kendall: be honest. What did that pregnancy test say?" Ariel asked, having had her suspicions since Kendall never showed her the negative test result.

"I have a fucking IUD. I can't go through this again." Kendall cried, burying her face in her hands.

"Call him," William said to Ariel. "I'm taking you to the hospital, Kendall."

Ariel reached back and found Kendall's phone in her purse. She called Anson.

"Anson? — No, this is Ariel Duval. I have Kendall's phone. Listen, are you still in Miami? — Oh, good. You're just north of us. You'll get there before we do. Go straight to Broward County Hospital. Kendall's not doing well. William and I are with her and we're taking her there — Well, I can't be certain, but I think she's having a miscarriage."

Ariel had been staring at Kendall the whole time she spoke, watching her breathe, Kendall's brow furrowed as her face grew paler.

"Honey, lie down. Hurry, Will. She doesn't look good," Ariel said, remaining calm.

Kendall consciously slumped down along the back bench, processing everything Ariel said to Anson.

"Anson, stop. Listen to me," Ariel continued, her voice staying strong. "She's still awake, but I can tell she's hurting. Just listen for a minute. Yes, Kendall's pregnant. And she's got issues in that department, so this could be serious — Anson? Anson? Did you hear me?"

Kendall began to hear that familiar ringing in her ears, knowing the cloak of darkness that accompanied the tune would be closing in shortly. She closed her eyes and listened to the world through the singular note.

She heard William angrily curse at traffic surrounding them as he exited I-95 toward Broward County Hospital, her body rocking like a ragdoll on the bench seat to every jerked turn. She heard Ariel directing Anson over the phone, calming him. Ariel would then repeat Kendall's name over and over again, telling her to hang on, that they were almost there and everything would be alright. She then felt the phone press against her ear and she heard his voice.

"Kendall? Baby, it's me. It's Anson. I'm here at the hospital. I'm waiting for you. Can you hear me? Kendall?"

"Hey, Anson," Kendall answered softly.

"Hey, Kendall," he replied, her voice instantly calming him. "Are you okay? Is it true? Are you pregnant?"

"Afraid so. But it doesn't last. It never does," Kendall responded, her voice now a haunting whisper.

Ariel pulled the phone back, putting it on speaker.

"Anson, we're a block away. I see the ER entrance sign," Ariel said and then looked back at Kendall. "Honey, we're here. They're going to fix everything."

"It hurts so bad. I think I'm dying," Kendall exhaled, the ring drowning out the voices around her, the darkness ready to swallow.

"Oh god! Baby, no! No!" Anson shouted through the phone. "You're not dying! I love you. Goddammit, Grace! I love you. I should have married you!"

And then Anson went quiet, dazed by the words in his stream of conscience. Ariel looked at William dumbfounded.

"I'm sorry," Anson whispered, his words choked. "I never... I never wanted to hurt you."

"I know. And so did she." Kendall's words slipped away like the last burning sliver of a Key West sunset into the Gulf of Mexico.

Then silence. No more ringing. No more pain. No more light.

Kendall needed emergent surgery and a unit of blood for a ruptured fallopian tube due to an ectopic pregnancy. Elena and Gabriel joined the three others, arriving to the hospital after Kendall had already been transported to surgery.

They all anxiously paced the surgical waiting room, continually looking up to the large monitor that tracked the progress of patients in the operating rooms. No one uttered a word during the wait, not even Gabriel; the agonizing look of his mom's face frightening him as she clung tightly to his hand.

Fortunately, not even an hour after being taken back, an OR nurse emerged and delivered the highly awaited news of a very stable Kendall after a successful open salpingectomy and oophorectomy. The cloud of stress silencing their voices instantly lifted as they all began to finally move within the confined space and breathe with relief.

They settled back into the waiting room seats, finally able to speak candidly. But before Anson took a seat, Elena approached him and formally introduced herself, having only exchanged looks of concern since meeting him earlier when Ariel had brought Elena and Gabriel up to speed on Kendall's status.

"So you're the man who helped save my daughter's life. I'm Elena, Kendall's mom," she said, extending her hand to Anson.

"Anson Allaway. But, uh, that was Johnson and Ariel. I wasn't there when it all happened. They did everything. I just showed up. But thank you. It's a pleasure meeting you, although I wish it was under different circumstances," Anson replied, smiling. He nodded his head at Gabriel, shaking his hand as well.

"Actually, you were *there* when, well, *it* all happened," Elena said, the twinkle in her eye making Anson downright blush, his beautiful blue gaze dropping to the floor. "And although we are here right now — by no fault of your own — because of *it*, and all that accompanies it, my daughter found a new purpose. For that, I am grateful to you."

Anson questioned Elena with his eyes. He locked onto the richness in her hazel gaze, her soothing, welcoming nature reassuring him.

"*Love*," Elena stated matter-of-factly. "It's a powerful lifesaver."

Anson swallowed, his heart swelling, and he smiled.

"Thank you. You have an incredible daughter. You must be very proud," he said.

Elena held his hand and squeezed it tight, too clutched to speak. She simply wanted to remain strong and see Kendall fully healed. She took a seat and collected herself.

"I hear you're a neurosurgeon? Impressive," she commented, settling into small talk.

Anson nodded. "Yes. I work with Kendall at Gold Coast General."

"That's nice. Makes work actually more enjoyable, I'm sure," Elena continued in her commentary. "Always something to look forward to while there."

"Well, we don't get to see each other much at work," he said with disappointment. "And I'm guessing it'll be even less if she actually does go back to night shift like she's considering."

"Oh? Night shift? She hadn't mentioned that to me," Elena replied, looking over at Ariel to see if she'd known.

"She's only mentioned it in passing," Ariel said. "She'd get paid more and be able to save money faster."

"But right now the only things I'm allowing on her to do list," Anson added, "are resting during the day and sleeping at night."

Elena nodded with a smile. "Good. She needs that right now."

But after a moment of punctuated silence, Gabriel spoke: "Well, now you'll both work at night, right Doc? Angelo said you're a doc by day and escort by night."

The perpetual spin of the Earth faltered momentarily, interrupting the very automatic rhythm of Anson's heart. He froze.

William and Ariel jerked to attention, their eyes bulging out of their heads as sheer panic surged up again, but now from a completely different direction.

"I... I..." Anson stuttered, looking at Elena, his eyes full of terror and mortification.

Until she began to laugh — hard — her face flushing into a royal red as tears pricked the corner of her eyes. Gabriel joined in, feeling satisfied in his unintended joke. William, Ariel, and Anson all took in a collective breath, as they seemed to telepathically communicate between one another on what the hell just happened.

"Oh my goodness! Anson, I'm so sorry," Elena chuckled, trying to catch her breath. "You have to forgive my son. I never know what dribble he's going to pick up from our South Beach crowd."

Anson remained speechless, probing the faces of William and Ariel for answers, knowing he definitely missed something since Saturday morning.

Elena sighed, her smile settling into a more refined and reflective state. She didn't dare look back at Anson, now experiencing her own wave of mild embarrassment. Although, admittedly, she loved the humor in it all, thinking how Kendall would have responded if she'd heard that little line of Gabriel's.

"Well, Gabe," Anson said, eager to put a playful spin on the whole situation. "I guess I know what your sister sees in me now."

Elena erupted in embarrassed laughter again.

"I guess it's because Kendall doesn't like to be alone," Gabriel concluded, now feeling like he understood Kendall after all. "So when we're not around, you can walk by her side."

"I couldn't have said it any better myself," Anson said, smiling broadly.

Chapter 4

"Family for Matthews?" a nurse called out from the surgical waiting room door.

All five from Kendall's entourage stood up, eager to see her.

"Just her husband right now. She's asking for you," the nurse clarified, pointing at Anson who she'd seen when they first took Kendall back.

"Oh, uh, we're not married," Anson said with disappointment, knowing Kendall's mom was first in line in terms of healthcare laws. "Is it to sign something?"

"No, not at all. She's been through a lot and the meds don't seem to agree with her. She just keeps asking for her husband, Dan, so I assumed she meant you."

Everyone's face went blank, Anson actually stepping back, rocked by the request. The nurse — puzzled by their reactions — began to back track and Elena immediately stepped forward.

"I'm her mother. I'll go in. She had a similar reaction to the anesthesia when this happened" —Elena glanced between Ariel and William— "seven months ago now? We almost lost her. Her husband passed away suddenly seven months ago and then she lost their baby, so her recovery — well from everything — has been pretty rough."

The nurse's expression sank, the tragedy of the situation exponentially increasing. Elena, Gabriel, and the nurse disappeared behind the door.

Anson could barely breathe.

"This happened *after* Dan?" Anson asked in shock, abruptly spinning around to see Ariel.

"If you didn't know, I'm not sure it's my place to say anything," Ariel replied hesitantly.

"She had alluded to miscarriages," Anson continued, lost in thought. "I knew that scar wasn't that old, but I never..." He shook his head in disbelief. "Was it his or–"

"Of course it was!" Ariel barked back, angry Anson would even suggest something otherwise. "She was already in her second trimester when it happened. They saved both her ovaries but took one tube and a bit of the uterus. That's why she extended her leave. She couldn't cope." Ariel's face suddenly softened as she realized Kendall's fate. "Now she only has one ovary left and no tubes. She can't have a baby."

Anson remained quiet, disappointed he never asked her to open up about the events around Dan's death, yet conflicted since she clearly never wanted to. Defeated, he walked back to the row of chairs along the wall and sank into a seat.

"I knew she'd extended her time," Anson said, reviewing their conversations in his head. "But I assumed it was all because of losing Dan. I knew none of this. Nothing at all."

"Kind of like what she knows about you," William added, crossing his arms and leaning back in his chair.

Anson glared at him. "This isn't about that. I love her. And I haven't been active since we decided to be together. It's totally different."

"How can you say that when you haven't told her anything *and* you've gone to Miami twice since Dan's birthday?" Ariel asked, her restrained anger now boiling over.

"Dan's birthday? What are you talking about?" Anson asked defensively.

"The stupid FFN. The night before Dan's birthday," Ariel whispered harshly, now wondering if he and Kendall talked about anything outside of sex. "I knew I should have stopped her, but I thought it'd help her somehow."

Anson stared reflectively, now understanding so much more of Kendall's warped vision going into their relationship. It *was* supposed to only be a one-night stand. And he pushed for more.

"That's why she wouldn't sleep over..." he said dazed, analyzing everything from their short, yet passion-driven interlude from reality. "It was all just an escape. I was an escape." Anson's voice was low. His heart sank even lower.

"How can you say you love someone and still betray them? Kendall can't stand a liar. Clearly you don't even know her. But I guess you can't expect much from a desperate womanizer," Ariel hissed, William promptly grabbing her hand to remind her where they were.

Anson's eyes burned into her furiously. But the root of it was his own self-hatred.

"I asked her to come this weekend to tell her everything and be there when that side of my business officially dissolved. What exactly was said at the party? In front of Gabe, no less?!" Anson demanded. "I can't believe you'd talk about it in front of him. And Angelo? That fucking prick is done!"

Ariel kept quiet, stone-faced with anger, as Anson's eyes viciously darted between her and William.

"At least someone's talking to her about it..." Ariel muttered.

"This is complete bullshit," Anson snapped, abruptly getting up from his chair. "Especially coming from you!" Anson pointed his finger right at William. Then he looked at Ariel again. "You might want to make sure you know all the facts about him, as well, before saying, *I do.*"

William swiftly stood, squaring off with Anson. Anson's glare remained locked for just a second, then he exited the waiting room.

Elena and Gabriel returned, catching only the back of Anson as he left. Elena questioned Ariel and William with her eyes.

"He was called to the hospital emergently," William quickly offered to squelch any further questioning. Ariel eyed him from the side, her blood boiling.

"Oh. That's too bad, but understandable," Elena commented, taking a seat once more. "I'm sure you all will keep him informed, as will Kendall when she's feeling better."

"How is she?" Ariel asked, angling her body away from William.

"She's hurting, emotionally and physically," Elena explained. "But she calmed down. They're going to bring her to the ICU soon, just to watch overnight considering the previous surgery in that area and the risk for re-bleeding. They said we could see her for a few minutes after they get her settled in, but then to return tomorrow morning during visiting hours. After having a chance to speak with the surgeon, I feel confident she'll do just fine."

Ariel nodded and smiled at Gabriel. She wanted to focus on the moment and not her swirling thoughts of paltry pasts.

"You doing alright, Gabe?" Ariel asked, his uncharacteristic hardened stare somewhat unnerving.

"Did Alltheway hurt Kendall?" he asked, startling all of them.

"Oh goodness. No honey," Elena said, patting Gabriel's leg. "These things happen sometimes, whether we want them to or not. It's no one's fault. Life is unexpected and sometimes hurts. We've unfortunately seen too much of that this past year and I believe wonderful things lie ahead for Kendall. For all of us."

***

Kendall grimaced, attempting to reposition herself in the hospital bed. Her room was dark, just the glow of the dimmed ICU lights behind the drawn hospital room curtain guiding her in the foreign surroundings. She glanced upward, the red and green squiggles from her telemetry monitor above almost bizarrely unrecognizable to her, as if merely a prop on a medical television drama she'd ordinarily poke fun of — the data streaming across them now foreign to her. She reached for the side rail to adjust the head of the bed. The mechanical jerk against her battered body made matters worse and she whimpered softly.

Anson, asleep in a corner chair, immediately moved to her side. "Hey. You need pain meds?" he asked quietly.

"Anson? What are you doing here? What time is it?" Kendall asked, feeling around in the bed for her phone.

He grabbed a hold of her hand and brought it to his lips, kissing it. Without warning, the emotional adrenaline of the afternoon's events finally caught up with him. Anson dropped the top railing of the bed and leaned over, clutching her hand to his chest as he kissed her forehead — a kiss filled with deep sorrow and protective love.

"Hey, hey," Kendall said softly, consoling him as she attempted to run her fingers through his hair, her IV tubing dragging and snagging in the sheets of the bed. "I'm okay. I'm going to be okay."

Anson suddenly sucked in through his wet lips, only making the restrained cry more audible. He drew in a few more breaths, controlling his response, and released the grasp around her hand. He stood up, wiping his face, and then tenderly kissed her soft lips.

"I'm so sorry," he finally spoke, reclaiming her hand. "I'm so very sorry. I never meant to hurt you." He methodically massaged each finger, every so often planting soft kisses along the back of her hand.

"Anson, please. This isn't your fault. You can't throw yourself on the sword for something you had no control over."

He let out a disgruntled groan and shook his head. "Even when you're laid up in an ICU, you're going to try and tell me what to feel?"

Kendall smiled and then grimaced.

"I'll get your nurse for pain meds," he said, giving her a little space.

"No, please don't. Not yet," Kendall requested. "I don't like the side effects of them."

"Kendall, I'm not going to watch you suffer here. It's been a while since you've had any anyway."

"When did you get here?" she asked, remembering her phone. "Wow. It's nearly one AM. Don't you have to work in the morning?"

"Let me worry about that," he said, pulling up the corner chair next to the bedside. "I got here a little after eleven. The nurse told me you'd just fallen asleep after getting some meds."

"They let you in? Unless the patient's dying or a hospital employee, we don't let people in this late at GC General," Kendall commented.

"It helps when I wear my surgical scrubs and badge." He smiled, raising an eyebrow.

"It helps when you've got that mug melting the hearts of all the nurses."

Anson laughed, kissing her hand again.

"You really need to get some sleep," he said. "You'll have even more pain tomorrow."

"Haven't you learned yet: I've got a high tolerance for pain."

Anson's smile faded. "How long did you know you were pregnant? You were ignoring the symptoms of this, weren't you?"

Kendall looked away from him, staring up at the dark ceiling.

"I only found out this morning," she explained, going through the timeline of events once more. "I thought the pain was the IUD, like that's just how they felt or something. Turns out the little fucker wasn't even in there anymore. Apparently it can fall out without being noticed and it's more likely to happen on someone who hasn't had a baby yet. I don't even know why I agreed to it after all that happened last September."

Anson sighed. The breadth of ignorance between them visible for the first time.

"I wouldn't have hidden anything like this from you," she said, reassuring him. "Ariel told me how worried you were, how you carried me from the car into the ER, and pulled every doctor card you could to get information."

Anson watched her closely.

"She also told me you know about my other ectopic pregnancy." Kendall paused, waiting for him to confirm this.

"Why wouldn't you want me to know that?" he asked. "Kendall: That changes a lot of things in terms of your state of mind."

27

"Exactly! That's why. It changes everything. I hate all this fucking change. I get enough pity from people for being a widow. If everyone knew I lost a baby at the same time and nearly died myself... How do you recover from that? I still can't wrap my mind around it and I can barely handle the panged look in the eyes of those who know.

"You have no idea how my mom and Ariel fawn over me. Like I'm some delicate flower now. And I can do no wrong. No one says no to me. I couldn't bear to get that from you, too. And I pushed you and pushed you, yet you're just so goddamn perfect, loving me no matter what...

"I'm angry, Anson. I just want to wallow in rage and fuck it all up. Everything's so fucked up but people look at me like I'm some saint for having a dead husband and dead fetuses and working as a nurse. I hate it! I wanted you to just want me and take me and fuck me hard so I wouldn't feel any of it anymore!" Kendall sobbed, then cried out in pain, Anson immediately pressing the call-light and flinging open the curtain to flag down a nurse.

"Get her some fucking fentanyl now!" he called out, then looked back at Kendall doubled over in pain, fighting against her natural inclination to pull herself into a fetal position. Her muffled cries tore his heart.

"Baby, it's okay. Shhh, don't think about any of it. I'm sorry. It's okay. Shhhh, it's okay," he murmured, stroking her hair. But the wait for some relief felt like forever. "Damnit! Can someone do their fucking job already and get the hell in here?!" he shouted out, further fracturing the rhythmic beeps and buzzes of the ICU in the quiet of the night.

A few moments later, Kendall's night nurse entered the room and drew up a syringe of Dilaudid. She administered the med, speaking softly to Kendall, soothing and reassuring her.

"I'm s-sorry, he sh-shouted," Kendall apologized, trying to slow her crying. "He's just wor-worried."

The nurse smiled sweetly at Kendall and turned to her computer.

Anson fisted his hair, pacing in the corner of the room. "Baby, don't speak. Just try and relax." He stopped at the foot of the bed, looking over at the night nurse who was quietly typing. "I'm sorry. I hate seeing her in pain. I apologize, nurse...?"

"Chandra," the nurse answered, her back still to Anson.

"Chandra. I'm sorry. You're great. I'm an asshole."

Chandra saved her computer work and then turned around to look at Anson.

"I know and I know," she replied smartly. "And I'm going to ask you to leave now."

"Oh, no. Come on. Don't do that," Anson protested. "Chandra, you look like a reasonable woman. I'm sorry I lost my temper. It won't happen again."

"You're right. It won't. Because you won't be here," Chandra retorted, crossing her arms over her ample bosom and knocking Anson down more than just a few notches. "Now this angel here was resting just fine until you got to talking. She doesn't need your stress working her over right now. I know you care for her and that you think you know what's best for her, but I've been nursing as long as you've been alive and I'm telling you right now, the drama you've brought in has no place but outside this ICU room. Let the woman sleep and recover in peace. You can see her in the morning. I'll be right out this door all night long."

Anson had nothing. He looked over at Kendall, also a bit surprised, but admittedly relieved.

"I'll be fine. Go home and get some rest," she said, agreeing with Chandra.

Anson let out a heavy sigh. "Call me if you need anything," he urged Kendall, leaning over and kissing her forehead. "Anything. Even if it's an hour from now. Same goes for you, Nurse Chandra. Anything happens: I want to be the first one called."

"We'll call her mother. Then you," Chandra clarified, her crossed arms tightening, the look on her face saying it all.

Kendall rolled in her lips, biting back her smile, the interaction between Nurse Chandra and Dr. Allaway far too entertaining for a middle of the night exchange.

"What do you like, Chandra?" Anson asked, the charm and swagger coming out in full force. "You a Starbucks gal? Dunkin Donuts? I'll have breakfast here in the morning. How do you take your coffee? Cream? Sugar? You like whipped cream?"

"I'm diabetic," Chandra said bluntly, awarding Anson no leeway.

"Okay, okay. I'll have something special just for you," Anson replied with the lift of his eyebrow.

"Mmhmm," she hummed, directing Anson to the open door.

Anson looked back at Kendall and smiled. "I love you, babe. I'll see you tomorrow as soon as I can. Remember: Call me if you need anything." Anson stepped to the doorway, Chandra standing guard like a sentry. "Have a good night, Chandra. Take good care of her."

"I always do," she said.

Anson left the unit.

Chandra looked back at Kendall who shrugged apologetically.

"Sorry about that. He means well. He really isn't an asshole," Kendall said.

"They never are… until they're in here," Chandra replied. She turned off her computer and then turned back to Kendall, holding her hand. "You rest, baby girl. This is your time to heal."

Chapter 5

KM: **I'm getting lots of thank you's for your breakfast delivery, you charmer you.**
AA: **Nurse Ratched loosened up yet?**
KM: **Hey now. I would have said the same thing.**
AA: **How are you feeling this morning?**
KM: **Like I lost a game of chicken with a train.**
AA: **Need me to head down?**
KM: **Aren't you at the hospital?**
AA: **Doing clinic right now. But you're my priority.**
KM: **Only come when you're all done.**
AA: **I always do... after my lady of course.**
KM: **Anson!**
AA: **I'll be by later this afternoon. :) Love you.**

Kendall read over those last two words several times. *When did love get so complicated?*
KM: **XOXO**

Her current condition definitely complicated things — and delayed decisions. The daunting conversation of past professions and future aspirations, however, permeated her every thought. Sometimes it was like a nuisance: an irritating scent of incense that comes on too strong when walking through the doors of a new age store, but eventually settles into a forgivable state. Other times, however, it downright choked her like a polluting cloud of exhaust and she found herself gasping for clarity.

Saving her heart from Anson's grasp was becoming increasingly hard as time ticked on. He caressed her just right; his healing touch like no other.

Ariel visited Kendall early afternoon following her lectures at Gulfstream University. They lightly glazed over everything: the tragedy of the past year, the need for dancing the night away at the wedding, how incredible next year would be purely based on the teeter-totter of fairness in the world. It *had* to be. They laughed and smiled, adding another Band Aid to the arterial bleed of Kendall's emotional hemorrhaging.

"Well, I'm going to head out and let you rest," Ariel said, sitting on the edge of the bed, her hand resting on Kendall's leg covered by the hospital linens.

"My mom and Gabe will be here in a little while. And then Anson. It's like a gravy train of love," Kendall said, smiling.

Ariel remained quiet, offering up a small smile.

"What?" Kendall asked, or rather, insisted.

Ariel let out a long sigh. "I don't know," she said, shaking her head. "Maybe I'm just too close to the situation. Too close to you."

"What do you mean?" Kendall pushed.

"William doesn't want me to talk about it; saying I'm dredging up too much of our own buried conflicts. And I understand. Everyone's got a past. I know what we have because we already hashed out everything we needed to years ago. But I don't think this is the time for you to do that with Anson." Ariel took in a deep breath. "Kendall, he's helplessly in love with you. And he doesn't even know you. Besides: Loving you right now is like hugging a cactus."

"What the? I thought you were protecting *me* from *him*. Not the other way around," Kendall said defensively.

"Well, of course I'm protecting you. But... you've been pushing him away since it all started. Before you knew about Xavier. And I don't think he's really understood why until yesterday, but it's like he can't walk away now. You're in the freakin' hospital. I know you're quite taken by him and all, but if your conversations never make it past pillow-talk–"

"You're certainly assuming a lot there, for not knowing him at all."

"Well, how well do *you* know him?" Ariel shot back. "Because at this point, I'm guessing I know a lot more about his past than you."

"Ariel. That's not fair. Not everyone talks to death about everything like you do and has to know every fucking detail about another person to make their mind up on whether they're worth their time or not."

"Okay. This was the wrong time to say anything," Ariel said, getting up from the bed and reaching for her purse on the table.

"No! You have something to say? Then say it," Kendall demanded. "You think this is all my fault?"

"No! I didn't say that," Ariel stated firmly.

"You think I've lost it! That I've become careless and don't give a fuck who I hurt in the process. That I've been wallowing in a sea of self-pity and this is just another way to keep it all going. That's what you think, isn't it?"

"Well you're not doing yourself any favors."

"What? You think I wanted another miscarriage? That *that* was the plan all along when I came up with the FFN?"

"No! Of course not. But I don't think you're thinking clearly. You don't seem to care if anyone gets hurt in the wake of your destruction. How it's not just *you* going through all your tragedies or whether dying along the way would affect anyone outside of yourself."

"Oh please! You think I'm trying to kill myself?" Kendall hissed, rolling her eyes. "If I wanted to fucking kill myself, I'd have done it already. And newsflash: I shouldn't have to care about what other people think."

"Newsflash: Not all suicide ends in death."

Kendall stared at Ariel; the truth behind her words struck Kendall dumb.

Not all suicide ends in death.

"And of course you don't have to care what others think," Ariel continued. "That's just something *considerate* human beings do."

They stared at one another for a brief moment. Then Ariel unleashed.

"Maybe we've all been too easy on you, letting you walk over us with your snide comments and cutting tone because we've been giving you the benefit of the doubt. Waiting for your heart to heal and finally move on. But I'm not going to do it anymore! You need to own up to your behavior and stop dragging others into it.

"Like you said: we're family, so I'll get over this. But people like Anson, your coworkers, people who only know the side of you that you *want* them to know: *those* people, they won't forgive you when this is all said and done after you've strung them along for so long. And I'm not saying this because I'm on Anson's side. Far from it. But at some point one of you has to decide to let the other go so you can actually be normal functioning people instead of enablers of your own fucked up mourning process!"

Ariel breathed laboriously and then burst into tears, slumping back down onto the bed and crying into her hands. Kendall's eyes welled up as she watched Ariel sob.

"I'm sorry," Kendall whispered, her lips quivering. "I'm so sorry, Ariel."

Ariel moved up the bed and buried her face into Kendall's neck, the two clinging to one another as much as the confines of Kendall's state would allow. They remained silent for several moments, at one point a nurse checking in to see if there was an issue that needed to be addressed.

Ariel suddenly drew in a rapid, deep breath, the pillow smothering her slightly. She sat up straight and wiped the wet skin beneath her eyes blending any streaks of running makeup.

"You know I look like shit when I cry," Ariel commented, her sinuses now all clogged as she pulled her makeup compact out of her purse to assess the damage.

"You know you're the only one who can say something like that to me and get away with it," Kendall replied, wiping her own tears.

Ariel groaned. "Well someone had to tell you the truth. Shit." She sniffed and began smoothing out the splotchy streaks with the pressed powder. She looked herself over in the handheld mirror and shook her head. Then she looked at Kendall and mumbled: "Bitch."

"Yeah. But I'm a patient in an ICU," Kendall said cheekily, her subtle smile emerging.

"You get *one* widow card and *two* near-death-experience cards. No more. I'm done," Ariel jeered. She took in a cleansing breath and shook her head at Kendall. "And I don't even want to *talk* about your overuse of the miscarriage card." Then Ariel looked at Kendall sympathetically. "I'm sorry. I'd be certifiable if I was in your shoes. I already feel that way just sitting here with you."

Kendall smiled, Ariel caving and smiling back. Ariel then groaned and flung her hands up, letting them flop back down.

"I'm pregnant," she suddenly revealed.

"What?!" Kendall sat straight up and abruptly regretted the move, gingerly easing her way back into the bed.

"Careful!" Ariel reprimanded her. "Don't hurt yourself further. I'm serious about being done with your death cards. You're going to have to live forever."

"Ariel!" Kendall exclaimed, her eyes now welling up with tears of joy.

Ariel groaned, giving in to Kendall. "I just found out. I'm not even eight weeks. I wanted to tell you Saturday, but then... well, *this* all happened. You know I wanted to have a baby pretty quickly. So I went off the pill a couple months ago thinking it all has to regulate out or something for several months. Not true. Boom: I'm pregnant. You mad?"

"Are you out of your mind? I'm ecstatic! Ariel! I'm going to be an auntie!" Kendall squealed.

"Shhh. We're not telling anyone yet. Not even my parents. Hopefully my Vera Wang will still fit for the wedding. I've already gained weight. And the nausea is starting. And I'm a hormonal mess. A hot, hormonal mess."

"No, leave that title to me. You, my love, are beyond perfection," Kendall gushed, tears now free-falling once again. "I can't believe it. I'm over the moon. Over. The. Moon. Best news of the day. Of the year!"

"Thank you. But it's early; so, you never know…" Ariel said quietly.

"That's my bad luck. Not yours. This baby?" Kendall placed her hand on Ariel's belly and smiled proudly. "She's got future world leader written all over her."

"*She*? What makes you say that?" Ariel asked, smiling skeptically.

"Because," Kendall said, her eyes gleaming with delight. "It'll be Will's lot in life to be surrounded by strong-willed women."

***

Anson walked briskly down the Broward County Hospital hallway. Kendall had been moved to a general surgical floor, her condition stable and no longer requiring ICU monitoring. He waited impatiently in front of the elevators, eager to be by her side once again.

The doors opened and out stepped Elena and Gabriel, taking him by surprise.

"Hello there. How's our patient?" Anson asked, hoping to make the exchange friendly, yet brief.

"She mentioned you were coming," Elena said, smiling. "We're just heading out. She looks better today."

"I hope you're not leaving on my account," Anson replied, allowing the elevator doors to close as he fulfilled unspoken family formalities.

"We've been here for over an hour already. Time for a new visitor." Elena glanced down at the bouquet of long-stem red roses Anson held at his side. "Remove the baby's breath," she suggested thoughtfully. "Kendall never liked the smell of them."

"Thank you for the tip," Anson said appreciatively. He reached over and pressed the elevator button once more.

"Well, have a good afternoon," Elena said, turning to walk away with Gabriel. But then she hesitated, needing to say more... even if it wasn't her place.

"I realize this hasn't been the ideal way to meet *the mom*," Elena began. "And perhaps meeting me was never part of the plan." Anson opened his mouth to refute the idea, but Elena stopped him. Now he knew where Kendall got it from.

"Kendall once mentioned you personally know her heartache. I'm very glad she found you and I can see you have her best interests at heart. But..." Elena paused for a moment, carefully plotting out her words. "She has been in survival mode and everyone else's interests outside of her own have taken a backseat. Know that it's okay to walk away should she push you away. I'm not saying I want that at all. As I said to you last night: you've helped her more than you know. And I know she'd be lucky to have you stick around. But this is now her third loss in a year, her second hospitalization, and she's already in her bulldozing mindset of moving on."

The elevators had opened and closed again during Elena's monologue, Anson remaining still. He struggled to come up with the right thing to say, as if back in high school in his girlfriend's living room getting the evil eye from her father. What struck him odd, however, was Elena protecting *him* from Kendall. And it bothered him.

"With all due respect: I don't plan on being just another loss. I know the armor she wears all too well. I see the person she is beneath it and I intend to support that person as long as I can. And you're right: in the end, she may push me away completely. But I'll handle that when the time comes."

Elena smiled, nodding her head. She pushed the elevator button for Anson.

"It's not your fault," Gabriel then added. "Kendall can't have babies. It's sad, but true. She couldn't even have them with Dan. It's just the way her body works."

Anson immediately felt a clutch of emotion wrap around his throat.

"We were" —Elena gestured to the elevator, indicating the direction of Kendall's room— "just talking about that. About babies and family and the future." Elena shrugged. "Just the various thoughts that swim through the mind after events like this."

Anson nodded.

"You're still a good match: a doc and a nurse," Gabriel said, chuckling to himself. "Together, you take care of sick people and that's good. Dan took care of people too."

"I appreciate you saying that, Gabe. More than you know."

The elevator chimed, the doors rolling back granting Anson an escape.

"Well, that's my cue," he commented, stepping onto the elevator. But he held his hand between the doors preventing their closure. "Hopefully the next time we meet it'll be outside the hospital."

"That'd be nice," Elena said in agreement. "Perhaps we can plan a little get together for Kendall's birthday next week. A nice dinner. Maybe a night out on the town."

"Oh, um..." Anson stalled. "I planned to take her down to the Keys. You know: for a little *R & R*. But if you already had something in mind..."

"No, no. Nothing at all," Elena said. "A trip to the Keys is right up her alley. It's always been a favorite escape of hers. Have a good afternoon."

"See ya, Doc," Gabriel said, smiling.

Anson smiled back, letting the doors close on their conversation.

After plucking the white budded stems from the bouquet, Anson entered Kendall's hospital room: a semi-private room that she shared with a 78-year old appendectomy patient.

"You got the window," he said, announcing his arrival as he stepped past the dividing curtain.

"Hey," Kendall cooed, his striking stature always a beautiful sight, especially after the not-so-subtle family conversation suggesting she let him down easy. "Oh. Thank you!"

Anson set the roses down on her bed and bent over, kissing her softly. He pulled up a chair and settled in.

"So how ya feeling?" he asked, his whole body instantly relaxing.

"Better. Obviously, I'm seriously sore. I'm not gonna lie. But if I don't move too much, it's tolerable."

"You look better. More color in your face."

"You're looking pretty good yourself. No surgeries today?" Kendall asked, her eyes taking in every sculpted inch of his suited physique.

"One. But I stopped at home before coming down here," Anson explained, then smiled playfully. "Had to get ready for a hot date with a hot nurse."

"Oh well, don't let me keep you from her," Kendall joked.

"Ran into your mom and brother when I came in," Anson said, segueing the conversation completely. "I think your mom likes me." He waggled his eyebrows.

"Oh really? What makes you say that?" she asked skeptically.

"Just got this feeling." He gave her that cunning smirk that'd always made her pounce multiple times before.

"I was hoping they'd make it out before you made it in," Kendall confessed. "You know, just so you wouldn't feel awkward or anything."

"It's not a big deal. But I wish *this* wasn't what made us all meet up. I am responsible, even if it wasn't intentional. I'm guessing they'd have a different view of me if we'd first met at the wedding." But then he thought about it — curious how much the entire family knew about his life outside of being a surgeon. He wasn't exactly sure what even Kendall knew.

"I understand where they are coming from," she said. "But that doesn't mean I agree with all their opinions. Don't worry about it right now. It'll work itself out."

Anson searched her eyes, hoping she really meant that. But then they shared their own awkward pause, now both curiously aware they were discussing a lot more than their individual conversations with Elena. Anson decided to nix any further probing of the minds.

"So, when do they think they'll release you?" he asked, looking about the room and eyeing the large bouquet of flowers on the window sill from Ariel's parents. "What was your hemoglobin this morning?"

"Um, I'm not sure. I didn't ask. I'm guessing it wasn't bad since they moved me out of ICU. One of the residents that rounded this morning thought tomorrow morning was feasible for discharge. But the surgeon hasn't been in yet, so I guess it'll all depend on what she says."

"Tomorrow? Really? You just had the surgery last night," Anson responded skeptically.

"I didn't have brain surgery, Dr. Allaway. Most of my recovery is just recuperation, which I can easily do at home. They know I'm a nurse and I have family support. I'm pushing for discharge tomorrow."

"Well, you're not going back to your home. You'll stay with me." Anson's voice left no room for argument.

But of course she tried.

"Anson, I have to be at my place to get things ready. Ariel and my mom both agreed to take care of the cleaning for me; the house has a showing this week and–"

"What? What do you mean: *a showing*?"

"I thought I told you... Um, I put my house on the market last Wednesday. Well, officially it happened Friday."

"You weren't exactly speaking to me last Wednesday," he said, slighted.

"Oh. Right," she said quietly. "Gabe's birthday. I forgot. A lot has happened since then, hey?"

"So you're definitely selling and going to school come fall," Anson concluded, bowled over by all the information that's flooded his brain the last two days regarding Kendall's private life and the event it took to get it all out.

"Yes."

"Where will you live?"

"I'll rent a place," she said. "My mom thought perhaps I'd stay with her to save money, but I don't want to do that. I couldn't. It'd make me crazier than I already am." Kendall crossed her eyes and stuck out her tongue.

"So, selling the house is for tuition and board?" Anson asked, not amused by her antics.

"Yes," Kendall answered, now feeling guilty. "You knew this was a possibility. And now it's happening. What do you want me to say, Anson?"

He frowned, reluctantly succumbing to the reality he hoped to avoid. "I said I'd help with your schooling. You shouldn't have to give up your home to make that happen."

"Yes, *I* have to. *I* need to do this on my own. Independent of you, independent of my mom. Completely independent. I need to know I can do this and do it well. Survive on my own, so-to-speak."

"That's just your pride talking. No one gets to where they are completely independent of everyone else."

"Anson."

"It's true. Even if it feels that way. Someone has always helped that person succeed. I know this to be true in my own life."

"And it's true in mine, too," she argued, not wanting to enter a full-blown argument. "I've been helped by countless people, including you. I'm not discrediting that. But at some point the baby bird needs to leave the nest." Kendall smiled at her clichéd line, Anson's facial expression softening.

"Well, I'll keep a bird's eye view on you, then," he said peevishly.

Her smile broadened and Anson rolled his eyes at her.

"I'll have Manuela, my cleaning lady, stop by your place tomorrow," Anson continued. "She'll have the place market ready in no time. She's used to tackling my home; she certainly can take care of your place."

"No, don't–" Kendall attempted to refuse, but Anson shushed her.

"You don't get a say in this. When you're discharged, I'm taking you home to my place. You'll recover there until I decide you're ready to go. It's not time for school yet anyway. So I plan to keep you dependent as long as I can."

"You're such a bossy boyfriend, Dr. Allaway," Kendall teased.

"Damn right I am. And I only come down harder if you're a noncompliant patient, so this conversation ends here."

"Yes, sir," she said, saluting him like a drill sergeant.

"What'd I ever do to you to deserve your constant mocking?" he asked, shaking his head in amusement.

"Hey, you're the one who decided to go and fall in love with crazy. I had no part in that."

"Something tells me you did," he replied, kissing her several times in a row, Kendall's smile sealed beneath his lips. "Loving you, Nurse Matthews, has been the best thing for me since… I don't know when."

Chapter 6

Unfortunately, due to her hemoglobin level dropping a point Tuesday morning, Kendall's surgeon kept her over night with two more blood draws on Wednesday to make sure everything stabilized. They granted her a late discharge and Anson arrived as soon as he got the word. Ariel had dropped off an overnight suitcase at the hospital for Kendall earlier in the day to take back to his place. Although the hesitation regarding Anson and Kendall's relationship remained, Ariel agreed it was best for Kendall to stay with him until fully recovered.

Anson's Delray Beach home was pitch black and eerily quiet when they entered. It smelled of clean counters and floors. Kendall shuffled around, feeling for a light switch along the wall.

"It's over here," Anson said, stepping in behind her and flipping on the light. "You can always tell when Manuela has been around; every single light is off."

"Oh. It definitely smells freshly scrubbed," Kendall commented, slowly walking up the steps.

"I asked her to swing by and do a spot check of surfaces. She'll be by Friday to really do her deep cleaning. She cleaned your place today."

Kendall smiled, now oddly reticent in the moment.

"It's strange being here..." she admitted quietly, watching Anson put her suitcase in the room behind the kitchen — a room she'd never actually been in. "You know," she continued, when he returned. "Knowing I'm sleeping over, but there won't be any sex." She shrugged, satisfied in addressing *one* of their many elephants.

"I never thought I'd hear myself say this, but uh, I'm happy about that," he replied, a subtle grin upon his face.

They stood and looked at one another, as if seeing the other for the first time — almost like the first night together out on his driveway. They never could have guessed how far that night would take them. That one night: the night of unleashed and unchecked emotion; of self-discovery and chemical combustion; of never going back. Where passion gave way to fate and fate gave way to reality and reality gave way to truth — and the truth became too much to bear.

God, she's beautiful. Anson took in an audible breath.

"So it's late," he said, clearing his throat and taking charge of their next move. "I want you using the elevator to get upstairs. We'll

41

head up and get you settled in my room. I know you want to shower. You sure you're not hungry?"

"Maybe a little," she said. "The fish dinner at the hospital didn't look too appetizing."

"Okay, so while you shower I'll get something ready for you to eat. What are you in the mood for?"

"Canned soup?" she suggested, shrugging. "Nothing big. Maybe some water?"

"Soup it is. I'll have to see if I have any water. That might be asking a bit much." Anson winked and stretched out his arm to her. "Come on over here. I'll show you the elevator."

Ariel had packed Kendall a long nightgown, figuring anything cinched around her waist would ultimately be uncomfortable. Kendall felt matronly, especially wearing her granny panties and a bulky pad as her insides recovered from the failed pregnancy. She analyzed her look in the large mirrors of his master bath, a hazy fog clinging to the image from her hot shower. This was not the look she ever planned to have in Anson's presence.

"I look like I'm ready for the nursing home," Kendall commented as she exited the bathroom.

Anson was lying down in his boxer briefs on the bed after setting up a small table near her side with soup and a glass of water. Of course, he looked hotter than hell. *Fucking eight pack.*

"I hope I'm in your nursing home someday," he said with a sly smile, putting down his phone.

"Whatever, Casanova."

Anson laughed, propping up the pillows on her side, then patted the bed for her to join him.

Kendall eased her way onto the bed carefully, every stretch of her bruised abdominal muscles causing her to cringe and halt in her movement.

"Have you taken anything yet?" Anson asked, getting off the bed.

"After I eat a little. I have no idea how people get addicted to these pills. Their side effects are worse than the actual pain."

Once she relaxed into a more comfortable position, Anson brought a wooden bed tray over her lap.

"This is really sweet of you," she commented, as he arranged the dishes on the tray and even added her phone to the set-up. "I think I'm bringing out your inner nurse."

Anson moved back to his spot on his side of the bed and smiled proudly at the arrangement he'd created for her. He picked up his phone once again and began scrolling through various news stories.

"You're not going to eat anything?" Kendall asked.

"I ate before I picked you up at the hospital."

"Oh." She dipped down her spoon and quietly slurped up a bite of the chicken and wild rice soup. It was lukewarm. "You never watch TV in bed?"

"No. I'm distracted enough usually. Sleep is hard to come by. I shouldn't even keep my phone nearby. But if you want me to pull the one on that side over here, I'll do that. It's not a problem."

"Goodness no. I don't need it. Just an observation."

"I'm guessing you'll make a number of those over the next few weeks," Anson commented, looking at her from the corner of his eyes.

"Oh I can't imagine I'll be staying here *that* long."

"You will if I have anything to say about it." He raised an eyebrow at her.

They were now as middle ground as they'd ever been — without any hint of a dramatic exit or mind-blowing orgasm on the horizon. It felt different, yet okay... But not exactly right. After a while, Anson set down his phone and snuggled up close to Kendall's side.

"Let me know when you're finished," he said, resting his head as close to her as possible without it being in her lap. He closed his eyes.

"I'm sorry. I'm done," Kendall immediately said, attempting to push the tray back.

Anson sat up quickly. "No, don't rush. I'm just beat and can't focus any longer. I got called in last night for a bleed."

Kendall sighed, her shoulders sinking. "Anson, you're exhausted. The last thing you need is to care for someone outside of the hospital as well."

"Kendall. Trust me on this. This is where you need to be. Where *I* need you to be."

He leaned over and kissed her, then moved her tray off the bed. He helped her get positioned into the bed better, then turned out her nightstand lamp.

43

"You comfortable?" he asked, the room now completely dark.

"Yes. Thank you, Anson. For everything."

"My pleasure," he answered. "I'm all yours, Kendall. Don't ever think I want you anywhere else, but here with me. I love you."

***

"Oh my goodness. Who do you belong to?" Kendall asks in delight, although completely surprised to see a newborn infant crying on the bed. "You're freezing! Come here."

She picks up the naked baby and quickly swaddles it against her — skin to skin — providing that necessary heat and nurturing contact. She looks around the room and sees no one, still baffled as to how such a beautiful baby suddenly appeared out of nowhere.

She then feels a sharp tug on her nipple.

"On my goodness! You're trying to nurse! No, no, little one. I'm not your mommy," Kendall says sweetly, prying the baby's hungry lips from her breast. But the stimulating sensation grips her along her abdomen and everything begins to hurt. She cries out in pain.

"Oh shit," Anson whispered. "I was half asleep..."

Kendall blinked several times and finally remembered where she was: Anson's bed. She looked over at him, the silver glow of the night lighting up the room and his eyes.

"What?" she asked, baffled.

"I was half asleep and wasn't thinking," he said softly.

"It wasn't you. I was dreaming."

"Oh. Well, you said, '*Baby,*' and grabbed my arm, so I thought maybe you were wanting me to... Then you pushed me away. Sorry."

They looked at one another in the serene quiet for a moment longer.

"You doing okay?" he asked.

"Yes," she answered, realizing he was not familiar with her sleeping patterns... at all. "You should know: I have crazy dreams. And sometimes act them out. It's nothing you did."

They laid quiet a little while longer, Anson's blinks eventually slowing until he closed them again. But then he felt the quiver of her body as she tried to stifle her cries.

"Kendall?" He sat up and attempted to pry her hands from her face. "Kendall, look at me. What's wrong?"

She buried her face into his bare chest, soaking his heated skin with her tears as she sobbed. Anson stroked her hair, his own heart aching.

"Baby, tell me what's wrong," he whispered again. "Are you in pain? Is it the miscarriage? You have to talk to me."

Kendall slowly backed away from him, wiping her tear trails off his chest. "Sorry."

"Don't worry about that. What's going on? Talk to me."

"I'll never... have... a baby," she cried, barely able to finish the sentence.

Anson held her close, kissing her head as he continued to comb her hair with his fingers.

"Aww, babe. Did you still want a baby? Even after Dan?" he asked and then grimaced, wondering whether it was an appropriate question.

"I always thought I would someday," she said through her sniffles, lying back down onto her pillow. "I mean, I still had the equipment to. But now..."

Anson held her hand in his, his thumb strumming her knuckles as he studied her features in the dark.

"You still have one ovary. You still have a uterus. It wouldn't be the old-fashioned way, but if you wanted, you could still have your own baby," he said thoughtfully, donning his doctor hat. "You're young–"

"This is my fifth miscarriage," she added before he went down any roads of miscarriage explanations.

"Oh."

"I know. You'd think I'd be used to it by now."

"No. I'd never expect that," he said quickly. "Kendall, I'd resided in the fact long ago that I'd never have kids, even though I'd always pictured myself with at least one. And when Ariel said you were pregnant over the phone, I'll be the first to admit: I wanted it to be true. The possibility of an actual family after all these years felt right. But everything immediately shifted when I knew you were in danger. I just wanted you safe."

Anson shifted over her, making sure she saw him in the dark.

"I'm so happy you're safe. Nothing else matters right now. Just you, *here*. With me."

Anson leaned in and kissed her briefly. He gave her a small smile.

"I'm sorry to burden you with all of this," she said.

"This isn't a burden. It's just that... well, we're learning a lot and going through a lot simultaneously. Don't ever apologize about this."

"Not how you ever imagined this night to be like, hey?" she whispered.

He looked at her quizzically.

"My first time sleeping over," she clarified. "You never thought it'd be like this, did you?"

He kissed her deeply, yet gently. "I have to get up in just over an hour. Let me enjoy this first sleepover a little while longer."

Kendall smiled and Anson nestled in right next to her, closing his eyes.

"You would have been a good dad," she whispered, her eyes glistening with the threat of another wave of tears.

"With you by my side," he replied, nuzzling into her hair and dozing off to sleep.

Chapter 7

By Friday, Anson and Kendall had rolled into a polite routine of playing house… and doctor with a side of nurse. Their affection for one another and his adoration of her were very apparent, yet often oversaturated for Kendall. However, the overriding theme quite notable to both of them — although purposefully ignored — was *denial*. Neither addressed the riptide current fraying the edges of the fiber that seemed to bind them together.

Their relationship was founded on sex. They couldn't have sex. And one of them had just given up sex as a side job.

This had been the focus of the phone conversation between Ariel and Kendall that morning while Anson was at the hospital working. The blind eye to all that had boiled over *prior* to the ruptured tube, Ariel aptly named *juvenile denial*. The term did not go over well with Kendall. In fact, she hated it. Even if she enjoyed its catchy rhyming quality.

Kendall's muscles cramped from the long walk along the beach while she'd been on the phone, so she sat down in the sand to take a break. Nothing, however, soothed the ache of how she ended the call. Although to be fair to herself, Kendall had warned Ariel: if she uttered *juvenile denial* one more time, she'd hang up her. And well, Ariel had; so Kendall did.

With the wedding two weeks away, Kendall had to figure out a way to make things right, but it seemed impossible while in recovery mode at Anson's place. Her mind throbbed with overrun chaos.

"Hey Kendall! Kendall… Kendall?" Anson called out as he approached her sitting in the sand behind his house. He tapped her shoulder. "Hey beautiful. Where are you?" He smiled beautifully, sitting down next to her in his suit pants and pale blue button down.

"Oh, sorry," she answered, pulling her earbuds out and wrapping the cord around one of her hands. "I didn't hear you."

Anson leaned over and kissed her. "You okay?"

"Yeah. I'm just listening to some music, watching the water. I did quite a bit of walking earlier. The sand definitely makes it a work out."

"You hurting? Have you taken anything yet today?" Anson asked, concerned.

"No. I'm fine. Really. Just sore. I'm not taking anything anymore." Kendall smiled at him. His endearing expression should have been just as captivating as the cadenced lapping of the tide upon the beach; but she couldn't bring herself to get lost in his eyes like she wanted to.

"Lake Atlantic today, hey?" Anson commented, gesturing with a nod at the serene surface of the ocean. "Not missing out on any surfing, that's for sure."

"Yeah, after you left, it kind of called to me from your bedroom this morning."

"You've been out here since then? That was nearly five hours ago," Anson said, glancing down at his watch.

"Well, not the *whole* time. It's just that, Manuela was cleaning and I didn't want to get in her way. I'm more comfortable out here."

"Baby, the last thing I want is for you to feel awkward here. I want you to feel as if it were your place, too."

"Anson, it's not my place. I'm your guest. And that's okay."

The South Florida sun was uncomfortably hot against their faces now as midday fast approached. Anson took a hold of one of her hands, examining it like a rare jewel, then kissed it. He waited; searching for the right words.

"What if you weren't just a guest?" he asked.

"Anson," she immediately responded, needing him to squelch his thought.

"Seriously. What if this was your place, too?" He looked directly at her.

She looked down at her feet buried beneath the cool, damp sand and wiggled her toes out.

"You could feel the sand between your toes every morning if you'd like," he continued, his eyes following her distraction. "If you moved in–"

"Señor Anson! Señor Anson!" Manuela shouted from the deck back at the house, waving her arms excitedly. "There's someone very special here to see you!"

Anson and Kendall both turned to look behind them and next to Manuela was a dark-haired, devastatingly handsome man, whose striking build resembled that of Anson's.

"Talon? No shit," Anson said with baffled excitement, as he got up from his seat in the sand.

"Who?" Kendall asked, accepting his assistance to stand.

"My brother. There's only one person Manuela gets all gaga over and it's him." He laughed and the two slowly made their way back to the house. "What the hell is he doing here?"

"Where does he live?" Kendall asked.

"Out in California."

Anson picked up his pace as the exuberant expression upon Talon's face became clearer. Anson took the deck staircase by twos and the men hugged boisterously, laughing out loud as their brawny chests clashed with a thud against one another, delighting Manuela immensely.

"What the hell, man? What are you doing here?" Anson asked, his smile lighting up his face as he jostled Talon. "Why didn't you call?"

"What? I can't fly in for a surprise visit? I had to see if my house was still standing after having *you* live in it for over a year," Talon said, pushing him back. But then his animated look softened as his gaze shifted over to Kendall who was methodically making her way up the stairs.

Anson quickly backed up to her, wrapping his arm around her waist, and pulled her in close to his side with possessive pride.

"Talon, this is Kendall Matthews. Kendall, this is my brother."

"Wow. It's great to meet you, Kendall," Talon said, extending his hand. "Really great. I've been waiting a long time to meet you." Talon appeared star-struck, his genuine pleasure in meeting Kendall almost unnerving.

"Uh, thank you," she responded. "It's really nice to meet you as well."

"Okay, okay," Anson said, breaking their handshake.

Kendall questioned Anson with her eyes, the two men clearly sharing an inside joke. Talon arched his eyebrow wickedly — evidently the smirk was a family trait.

"Here, let's go inside," Anson said, wiping his brow, and directed everyone through the sliding glass doors.

A small black rolling suitcase stood near the front entryway with a herringbone gray suit jacket folded over the handle. It matched the pants Talon wore. Anson pointed at it as he opened the refrigerator, then pulled out a Heineken, offering it to Talon.

"You moving in as well?" Anson asked, popping the beer cap.

"Just for the weekend. Unless" —Talon looked back and forth between Anson and Kendall— "this bachelor pad has finally become domesticated." The twinkle in Talon's deep Pacific blue eyes as he winked at Kendall packed a punch of salacious sorcery all its own. And the man had dimples — dimples to die for.

"Oh no," Kendall answered with a nervous laugh. "No, I'm not moving in. I'm just here a few nights recovering from a little surgery."

"Oh," Talon said, taking a swig of his beer and looking directly back at Anson.

An awkward vibe now surfaced between the three and Anson moved quickly to squash it.

"Hey, so should we all go out to lunch? I've got some time to kill before heading back to the office. You can fill us in on what you're doing here, Talon. What do you think, babe? You hungry?" Anson asked, looking over at Kendall.

"Um... Well, why don't you two go and catch up? I'll just be a drag. I'm a little tired from my morning walk. I think I should lie down for a while anyway." Kendall finished the glass of water that Anson had poured for her. She looked back at Talon and reached out her hand. "It was a pleasure meeting you. Hopefully we'll see each other over the weekend."

Kendall smiled at Anson, then walked to the stairs, ascending each step carefully. Anson and Talon exchanged looks and hushed words across the counter before Anson followed after her.

"Hey Kendall, do you need some help?" Anson called up to her, Kendall stepping onto the second floor.

"No. I'm fine. Really. I just overdid it this morning, that's all," she answered, continuing in her slow ascent to the third floor loft.

"Why aren't you using the elevator like I told you to? The last thing you need is–"

"Anson," she said firmly, stopping in the middle of the steps and turning around to look back at him. "The last thing I need is you doting over me. I'm okay. Really. I've been through this before." She stopped, looking down at the floor, not wanting to be an angry, bitter, and defensive griever any longer. "Just know, I'm going to be okay, okay? Thank you for your concern, but please: go be with your brother."

Anson took in a deep breath.

"I'm trying to help. I want to be here for you, Kendall. But I can't if you're shutting me out already." Anson stepped up and rested his head against her chest, gently leaning into her.

Kendall inhaled the earthy scent of sage that clung to his clean, silky hair and acquiesced. She draped her arms around his neck and kissed the top of his head.

"I want to make this right," he whispered.

Her body further relaxed and Anson took one more step up, now eye level with her. He paused, but Kendall willingly closed the gap and met his waiting lips.

For a moment, their lips barely touched, hesitant to give in. But the rapid rush of Kendall's heated breath against his lips as the adrenaline he supplied sped up the rate of her heart, pushed them both over the edge.

Anson sucked her lip in sharply, all their exchanged kisses since the surgery having been almost platonic in nature, their sexual tension dormant in the wings. But this kiss ignited the passion they'd been blatantly missing. And his tantalizing kisses still carried a direct current to her groin. Kendall whimpered against his mouth, his tongue slipping between her parted lips. He slid his fingers beneath her shirt — his caress so careful, so gentle, almost resistant as he avoided excessive pressure to her mending muscles. But he ached for more and Kendall could feel his sense of urgency surge through his veins.

She combed her nails across his scalp and pressed her breasts into his chest. Anson found his favorite spot along her neck and worked up to her ear. He tickled her soft lobe like a nipple and Kendall's body quaked against him.

"Anson." His name, barely a puff of breath upon her lips as the true cry came from her body calling out to him.

"God, I've missed every part of you," he groaned earnestly, trailing open-mouthed kisses down her throat, moving below her collarbone, then up the other side of her neck. He squeezed her breast over her bra, caressing her with a clear ardent desire as he nipped her sweetly. She bit down into her bottom lip — hard — suppressing her vocal response.

The sensation was oversaturated with want, yet confounding to say the least. It was tender, yet tortuous; restrained, yet explosive; stimulating, yet stunting. There was so much pent up between them. So much that still needed to be said, explained, and conquered. There was too much current passing through in this single exchange between the second and third floor. Too much emotion to explore in this chance moment while Anson's brother casually drank a beer downstairs and Manuela scrubbed the entryway toilet. There was simply too much weight behind Anson's touch — and a fleeting stairwell kiss was far too defenseless against the tsunami of desire crashing over them.

Anson's tongue flicked at the supple flesh of her other earlobe as he simultaneously pinched her nipple through her bra. But this time Kendall actually moaned — an angelic punctuation of sensual sound peaking — and Anson could no longer fight it.

"Marry me," he pleaded into her ear, his voice raspy with need. "Stay here forever."

Kendall abruptly pulled back and looked at him wide-eyed, his Caribbean blues glistening.

He was serious.

And now, she was speechless; breathless — symptoms far too close to *scared shitless*.

"Uh... I didn't mean it like that. I meant... Well, down the road. Maybe. I know: It's too soon," Anson said, scrambling. "I'm thinking out loud. Actually, I'm not thinking. Don't over-think this, Kendall. I'm heading out with Talon and then I'll see you tonight after work, okay?"

Kendall slowly nodded, still in shock from his weighted confession.

"Okay," Anson answered for her. He pecked her open mouth and quickly descended the stairs.

With her breath still held captive, Kendall audibly exhaled and stared half a minute longer. Now each arduous step up to his bedroom carried considerable more weight; her mind a calamity of jumbled thoughts, her thighs soaked in conflicted desire, her stomach a frenzy of flitting butterflies, and her heart — her battered and broken heart — erratically racing, fueled by only an adrenaline kick that Anson knew how to administer.

Chapter 8

"So obviously I'm fucking it all up," Anson concluded, grabbing the last gulp of Johnny Walker and knocking it back. "I don't even know why I get like this."

Talon let out a heavy sigh, slowly sipping his beer as he signaled to the cocktail waitress to bring his brother another round. Anson called the office on the way to the sports bar claiming family emergency. He'd never done that before and Talon took note.

"Well *I* do," Talon finally divulged, eyeing the waitress with a sultry stare as she set down another glass of whisky. Anson ignored the flirtatious exchange between the two.

"Why?" Anson asked gruffly.

"Why what?" Talon absently replied, returning his eyes back to the table and the heavy-laden conversation that was sprawled out upon it.

"Why do I get like *this*?!" Anson looked down at himself in disgust. "This love-struck pussy blind to every fucking caution sign thrown his way. I'm so fucking desperate, it's humiliating."

Talon rolled his eyes and leaned in. There wasn't even a year between them, but in this moment Talon felt like their oldest brother, Garrison, who had ten years on them.

"One word: Joice." Talon sat back, proud of himself.

"*Joice*? What the fuck is that supposed to mean?"

"Joice," Talon said again. "When did you and that tart fuck around? Five years ago now? Maybe more?"

"Don't call her that. She was a client," Anson said angrily. "Well, a partner. A friend. It doesn't matter. I hardly think she changed me into this."

"She was a bitch who managed to rip your fucking heart out and make you break your own cardinal rule of not getting attached." Talon crossed his arms, his smug expression the final nail in his argument.

"I... It was... The whole situation was fucked up. Maybe it's all women," Anson suggested, swirling the smooth, amber liquid around in the glass.

"Uh, no, bucco," Talon sat up again, realizing he needed to spell it all out for Anson. "It's not *all* women. It's all *pregnant* women. Or possibly pregnant women. The minute Joice said she was pregnant, a switch flipped. It was like Grace all over. You don't remember?"

"What are you talking about, *a switch flipped*? I was trying to do right by her, make a go at it. We'd known each other for years. She knew everything about me already, so... I owed it to her."

"*You owed it to her*," Talon snorted under his breath. "You didn't fucking *owe* her anything. And you knew that first hand. Plenty of people have a kid together without being together. Look at our niece, Maddie. She's perfect. Gary and Jen had the sense *not* to try and make it work. And that worked out best for all parties involved. You have to stop doing this to yourself, man. Nothing you do will bring Grace back."

"Fuck you!" Anson snapped, slamming his palms down on the table. "This. Isn't. About. Grace!"

"It's always about Grace. Own up to it already," Talon replied, barely flinching to Anson's outburst. "Look at you. You're losing it all over again. You think you knock up a girl and then–"

"Stop! This isn't anywhere near the same situation as Joice. I'll admit: I went a little overboard before I found out it was all a lie. What does it matter anyway? She didn't mean anything. Not like that, at least.

"But with Kendall," Anson eased back into the booth and took in a deep breath. "It's totally different. She's... she's everything. And I felt that way before the miscarriage."

Talon shook his head at Anson's forgone look.

"Dude, you're still trying to save her. Now even more so, knowing Kendall's a widow and she's lost babies. I get it, man. It's fucking tragic and my heart goes out to her."

"I'm not trying to save her. Believe me, Kendall's very independent that way."

"Not Kendall," Talon corrected, shaking his head with frustration. "*Grace!* Shit, A. You never get it, do you?"

Stunned, Anson remained speechless and stared blankly at his brother. Talon leaned far over the table and spoke directly to Anson, his voice low and calm.

"There will be no baby you can father that will ever make Grace's pregnancy realized. There will be no woman you can save from her own troubles that will ever make you forgive yourself for not saving Grace from hers. There will be no love you can experience that will ever bring Grace back. You'll never. Make it. Right."

For a brief moment, Talon felt that for the first time ever, Anson finally understood what everyone else around him had seen for years. But the crack of Anson's fist crushing into Talon's jawbone as a flash of bursting stars shot across his west coast vision, definitely said otherwise.

Fuck.

***

"I punched out Talon," Anson announced as he tossed his keys on the kitchen counter, jolting Kendall up from her position on the Italian leather sofa in the living room where she'd been reading a book.

"What?!"

"I hit my brother," Anson repeated matter-of-factly, then chugged back a full glass of water. "I had a bit too much to drink (and that was his fucking fault). And he pissed me off (the way he does). So, I snapped."

Kendall stood up from the couch and walked into the kitchen.

"Uh…" she hesitated, glancing at the keys on the counter, curious if he was drunk now.

"This was hours ago. I've sobered up since," Anson added, noticing her wary expression. "We worked it out. Always do."

"Oh." She looked back at the front door where Talon's suitcase remained with the jacket still neatly draped over top.

"Don't worry about him. He found a warm body for the night. Always does. Cocktail waitress."

Kendall studied Anson's expression as he rapidly changed her perception of the man she'd met earlier in the day.

"He'll be by tomorrow sometime," he continued. "You ate some dinner, right?"

Stymied by the sudden bizarre disruption to her quiet evening, Kendall faltered again, until finally nodding, *yes.*

"Good. It's after ten anyway. Let's go to bed," Anson said, placing his glass in the sink. He walked to the end of the counter with his arm outstretched to her. He assumed she'd join him so they could ride the elevator up together.

"Wait… What just happened?" Kendall finally strung two words together. "I gather you never went back to work…"

"Baby, it's been one hell of a day. I'm off tomorrow. But I'll have to swing by the office and hospital to make up for today. So, let's hash it all out this weekend."

"No, Anson. Don't *baby* me when the last thing you said to me was '*Marry me.*' Then you bolted. And now you stroll back in saying you got in a fist fight with your brother — *no big deal, let's sleep on it?* What are we? Seventeen?"

Anson groaned, his patience with all things now gone. He desperately needed a do-over and felt every irritating wrinkle would iron itself out if they could just be together, side-by-side, skin-to-skin, in his bed. He walked over to her.

"No," he said, shaking his head. "We're not doing this now. I won't."

Bowled over by his austere expression, Kendall fell speechless once again. Anson took a hold of her hand and turned around to head back into the room with the elevator, leading her away as if she were a small child resisting bedtime.

"What the hell, Anson?" Kendall shook her hand free and stopped just outside the back room. "Talk to me! You serious about marrying me one day? Because here's a tip: married people talk to one another. I deserve to know everything going on with you right now."

"Fine!" he barked. "You stay here! I'm going to bed." Anson zipped past her and headed straight up the stairs, leaving Kendall alone.

About an hour later, Kendall tiptoed past a sleeping Anson and entered the bathroom. Adding fuel to the fire hadn't seemed worth it with both of them so drained. She knew the weekend's conversations waited in the wings giving them plenty of things to absorb then.

She decided to give him his space, planning to test out the guest bedroom downstairs, when she heard a sudden, '*Hey,*' as she quietly snuck by after exiting the bathroom.

"You scared me. I thought you were sleeping," Kendall commented, turning back to him.

Anson pushed himself up and leaned against his headboard.

"Where are you headed?" he asked.

She couldn't see his expression, her eyes still not fully adjusted to the dark. But he saw everything — the cloudless night with its reflecting stars along the ocean's surface lit up her face as if torch lights were shining in. She looked torn as she glanced back in the direction of the stairs.

"You leaving?" he asked, his sadness unavoidable to mask.

"No. Not at all," she refuted, sitting down onto the edge of the bed next to him. "Anson, I was simply giving you a night alone. You're stressed out and I feel like we're imprisoned in a purgatory of politeness."

Anson scoffed at her choice of words.

"So that's what this is," Anson said. "Kendall. It's real simple: I want you." He scooted down the bed to be next to her, his hand gently cupping her face as the other found its position on her hip keeping her close to him.

Kendall took in a deep breath, the smell of him filling her completely as his lips eventually danced down below her chin. He knew just what to do. Every. Single. Time. A soft flurry of light kisses landed upon her shoulder like snowflakes and — without fail — her thoughts derailed.

They'd never had sex in the dark, always some source of light available to highlight the show. But now, with sex off the menu and the day only a constant reminder of postponed conversations, night took on a whole new meaning. Without the light, all those hidden truths blended together as if nothing stood between them; getting closer to him seemed like the most enlightening move she could do. Kendall closed her eyes, resting further into the security of his touch.

"I wasn't mad," she whispered, her lips quivering as the delicious chill of his kisses scattered across her skin delivering a sensual shiver all the way to her toes.

And then his lips brushed hers, hushing her.

Oh god, how desperate they both were, to feel that mindnumbing electrical current that coursed through them when physically locked in. It'd been far too long since they'd made love; far too long since they'd felt the heat of one another; far too long since they'd feasted on the very carnal table of their relationship foundation. Maybe it was all sex: all heat, all passion with nothing left for downtime. But now it became a necessary impulse to be fed. That common ground had to be revisited if they had a chance in hell of moving forward.

Anson lifted her nightgown over her head, dropping it to the floor. His mouth met her nipple and she gasped; the heat of his breath against the tip of her tit melted everything internally. Her head fell back, languishing under his touch — the strength to make sense of anything that'd happened earlier beaten away with every flick of his tongue. He sucked her in hard.

"Ahh," she cried out, the ache in her breasts growing stronger as she longed to feel the weight of his chest against hers.

"Get into the bed," he quietly commanded, his husky voice in her ear sending another shiver down her back.

But common sense bubbled up, rearing its inconvenient head.

"Anson," she panted. "Babe, I... uh... we still need to–"

"Tomorrow," he pleaded against her neck. "We'll get it all out tomorrow. Let me just love you tonight."

"We can't have sex. You know that, right?" Kendall asked cautiously.

Anson pulled away from her and looked at her quizzically. Now Kendall could see him, her eyes taking him all in.

"Ever again?" he asked.

Kendall nearly laughed. "It hasn't even been a week and the norm is to wait 4-6 weeks. Please tell me you knew that."

Anson rolled his eyes at her, his delectable smile pulling at the corner of his mouth. "Yes. Kendall. I was aware that we would not be having sex tonight," he said dryly, kissing her forehead. "What happened to good ol' fashion making-out?"

They both shifted around in the bed, Kendall in her underwear and Anson in the buff, something Kendall hadn't realized until lying next to him.

"I'm not so sure I know how to *only* make-out with you," she humorously confessed.

"Well, we'll have plenty of practice if you intend on waiting the recommended period," Anson commented, turning to fondle her breasts. "Although, I am rooting for noncompliance in that department."

"Seriously, though," Kendall began, placing her hand on top of his, halting its exploration. "Before we blissfully ignore this day in, day out (like we do so much else), what happened today between you and your brother?"

Anson laced his fingers behind his head and let out a long sigh.

"If you want to give us a real shot," Kendall said, pushing him further. "We have to start talking like a real couple."

The serene stillness of the large loft cradled them — all the details outlined in crisp silver ribbons of light and soft blankets of cool gray. Here, *together*, they were safe; protected.

Anson fisted his hair, his rapid respirations suddenly audible and shallow. He sat straight up, the weight he bared too heavy to heave from his chest. He swung his legs over the side, his whole body tensing as if sinking into a frigid mountain lake.

Then he spoke.

"I said something to Grace a few days before she died that I believe is the reason she died. As if I killed her."

Kendall propped herself up, not ready for that level of conversation. In fact, she hadn't expected any mention of Grace. She thought for sure they were headed down *Escort Alley*. She studied his posture, the knotted muscles of his back tensing sharply. The glacial wave of his warped reality washed over his body like a baptismal shower and she knew: This was his story's beginning and the only point from where he could move forward.

"Grace had an exceptional energy about her. It was vibrant and magnetic. People gravitated to her. She was just one of those people that when in her presence, you were amazed by how positive she was.

"You should have seen her classroom. It was incredible. In her short career, she was voted teacher of the year *twice*. And it was never one of those things where people were jealous. She genuinely deserved every good thing that came to her and was so humble about it. I never knew what she saw in me."

Kendall moved against the headboard, processing every word he said in great detail as Anson continued to open up to the vast darkness of the loft.

"But those last years, she struggled with bouts of depression. Her grandfather had been bipolar and an aunt battled depression, so the terms were thrown around on several occasions. She was never diagnosed with anything and I'm not sure she really met the criteria, but it weighed on her.

"I felt it was more *my* stress causing the strain; telling her things would all be fine once my residency was over. But she insisted it was because we hadn't started a family; saying I was keeping her from fulfilling her life's mission. She wanted four kids. I knew this from the get-go. She was 27 — I was 26 — so I guess it was a good time to start. But *I* wasn't ready."

Anson paused for a moment, drawing in a couple of cleansing breaths. Kendall slid down the bed toward him, curling her arms under his and resting her chin on his shoulder; the warm curves of her chest now pressed into his back. Her embrace initially startled him, as if he couldn't accept such affection with the taste of guilt still coating his tongue.

But she stayed.

"A few days before she died, we'd gotten into it again about the wedding and having a family. I was sick of the same argument, stressed out and exhausted, not really hearing what she was saying or wanting to. It was a Saturday. Actually, all week she'd been giddy and energetic." Anson sighed with amusement as that last week drifted into his vision with sharp clarity.

"I remember her being horny. Like wanting kinky sex and shit." Kendall smiled on his shoulder, allowing Anson the freedom to relive it all. "I loved it. She had rambled on about eloping that weekend or heading back to Boston to see family. But I dismissed it all as her typical *in the moment* chatter.

"It was when she told me about this whole plan of flying out that night; gathering the parents and getting hitched Monday morning at the courthouse in Boston, then returning Monday night so we'd both only miss one day that week, that I flipped out on her. I told her she'd lost it; that she was manic and selfish. I remember our final exchange that day as clear as my words are now.

"She said, '*What if I'm already pregnant?*' and I told her: '*With your epilepsy meds and the fact you probably should be on lithium, the thing doesn't stand a chance.*' Then I just left the house for the rest of the day."

He leaned far forward, his head held in his hands as he quietly sobbed — his choked inspiration as his body shuddered the only sound to his despair. And as the epic silence resounding around them reached seismic proportions, Anson abruptly stood and escaped to the second floor.

Kendall fell asleep while waiting for him to return. When he climbed back into bed hours later, she turned to him still ready to talk should he want to. But his back was to her. She debated whether to wait until morning; but there was still something freeing about the night that she clung to. This was when the body restored itself; when the mind found peace and when all wounds seemed to heal. She gently pressed the palm of her hand against his back.

"I want you to know that I love you," she said softly, Anson's head angling closer to her as he listened. "That I fell in love with you against all my better judgment only because I was too afraid of experiencing it again, not because I was afraid of you. And what we have is real and powerful. I don't know how far this will take us, but I do know: I don't want to move forward without you."

Anson positioned himself to face her, his fingertips tracing the flow of her hair behind her ear. He gripped her neck, pulling her in close, and kissed her deeply. When he let go, rolling to his back and leaving her breathless, he sighed heavily.

They both stared through the darkness, even the grooves in the ceiling above now highlighted in detail. There was no place to hide. No place to escape. Only truth.

"Grace called in sick the following Tuesday and I found her later that night. I've been holding my breath ever since. Waiting, I suppose. For what? I'm not sure." Anson turned his head to look at her again. "Just waiting. Until I met you."

Kendall remained silent as his eyes searched hers.

"I want you more than anything and I'm scared shitless of fucking it all up; of driving you away the minute you see me for who I really am," he said to her. He looked back up to the ceiling, searching for an escape and coming up empty-handed. "I've been this way for so long, I... I don't know how to be anything different now."

Silence.

"You know about the escorting, right?" he finally asked, not an ounce of overriding emotion.

"I do," she answered, all their closeted walls razed.

He grimaced, almost in anticipation for a battery of questions to follow.

"But love is blind, right?" Kendall added quietly.

Relieved, he turned to her. "No. Not with us. Not anymore."

She gently stroked his roughened jaw.

"Anson, I see you. All of you. And I love you."

Chapter 9

Just before waking, when the fog of sleep lightly lifts its cloak of darkness, yet hangs overhead in such a forgiving manner, providing a few more precious minutes of lazy rest; separating the real world from the dream world a second more — the twilight of the human experience where the conscious state exists in limbo; where the rigid boundaries of the senses blur just a bit longer affording the existential truth of being *who one is* to take on a vast and freeing definition before the outside perspective confines it — that specific moment: that moment of blissful uncertainty, of countless possibilities, of perfect peace — *that* moment had been the greatest gift for Kendall since Dan's death. She relished in the pleasure of not knowing, or rather, forgetting; or perhaps, simply not caring about all the stress that assaulted her the second she woke up aware that she existed... without him.

During this perfect state of tranquility Kendall felt his fingers begin to explore the bare skin of her body beneath the cool sheets. She did not register to whom the fingers belonged, just simply that they were there, stroking her along the sloping curve of her waist and then up the arc of her hip bone, gliding down her thigh, then returning to the crested peak once again. The tenderness expressed in his touch finally filled all her senses and she drew in a long, revitalizing breath. The rays of morning welcomed her to a new day.

Now, fully aware that they were Anson's fingers, not Dan's; the sorrowful strain against her abdomen the result of a fling, not a husband; and the revealed side job that of escorting, not Uber driving — with all the truth flooding in — even then, her stress remained beyond the curved horizon of the Atlantic, granting her a generous extension of respite.

Anson moved in closer, sensing the acceptance of his touch. He molded himself to her inviting curves, bending his knees behind hers as the heat of his chest melted into her bare back. His one arm stretched beneath her pillow, cradling her head, and found her hand tucked away. He intertwined his fingers with hers and draped his other arm gingerly over her side, his hand cupping her breast.

"Is this okay?" he asked — their morning slumber now fully roused.

"Yes," she whispered, her voice far breathier than she'd intended. Her brain immediately listed off all the possible risks of a clitoral orgasm following gynecological surgery.

Anson remained motionless behind her, as he drew in the scent of her hair. She relaxed further, leaning back against him, soaking in as much of his touch as possible, wishing he'd explore some more. Primed, she gently rotated her bottom, just to test the waters, and Anson's morning wood sprang into action, growing thick with anticipation. Kendall reveled in the probing pulse against her ass.

This was how she knew him best.

He immediately fulfilled her request for more and inched his body even closer. He began to fondle her breast, rolling her peaked nipple between his thumb and forefinger and licking his lips slowly — tasting the memory of her perfect tits. But it wasn't enough; the temptation of her vanilla-sweet skin making it so hard — *so fucking hard* — to resist. He planted a series of molten hot kisses along the back of her shoulder desperate for a fix.

Kendall grabbed his hand on her breast and brought it up to her mouth, sliding his index finger inside — the warm, wet walls feeding his appetite. She began to suck; her sweet moan sending more than just a reverberated hum through his hardened bones. Her tongue swirled and flicked, working his finger over as if it was his most delicious dick. She took his middle finger in as well, and Anson played right along with the visual, thrusting his fingers further into the moist folds of her mouth.

Kendall felt his breath rustle through her hair as his respiratory rate picked up. But he held off on his burning desire to get off, wanting to control the sexual impulse he experienced day in and day out when with her. She continued her slow, temptress push, rubbing her cotton covered bottom against him fueled by the wet tip of his hard-on as it soaked through the back of her panties.

Anson repositioned himself, letting his cock push between her pressed, wet thighs. But it wasn't enough; his erection painfully throbbed until he instinctively wrapped his one leg over her, tightening his grasp in need of a firm pushback against the sensitive tip.

Kendall grimaced as a painful zing shot through her abdomen, the weight of Anson's leg causing an uncomfortable pull to her side —

the side of her lost tube and ovary. She tried to control her reaction, but it was too late.

Anson immediately sat up bringing the sheet down, Kendall rolling onto to her back. With the small incision exposed, he examined her closely — the deeply blackened-purple bruise stretching further every day as it drained internally along her side (the absorption of the old blood an unflattering process).

"Fuck. Are you okay?" he asked panicked, his eyes poring over her flesh no longer as her lover, but like the surgeon he was.

"Babe, don't worry. I'm fine. It just got pulled in a sensitive spot, that's all. It's fine," Kendall said reassuringly.

Anson dropped back down onto the bed, releasing an exasperated sigh. He grabbed Kendall's hand next to his in the bed and stroked her knuckles with his thumb.

"I'm so sorry, Kendall," he said again, completely defeated.

"What are you apologizing for? Anson, I'm not going to break that easy. It's okay. I liked what we were doing. I really liked it. I wish it could lead to more," Kendall said, turning her head to look at him.

Anson stared straight up, the clear fury raging within evident in his clenched jaw.

"Not just that," he said. "For everything. For what I blurted out yesterday and dumped on you last night. For pressuring you into this: into our relationship. For losing control and not protecting you, resulting in all of this: nearly killing you and then trying to fucking seduce you when you can't do a goddamn thing about it. It's just so fucked up. I'm fucked up. I don't even recognize myself around you." Anson shook his head with disgust.

The two lay on their backs, holding hands, Kendall studying him as he fought his personal demons. She recognized how undeniably comfortable she felt with Anson; this level of intimacy and her own vulnerability now acceptable even when navigating the middle ground. She didn't need a reprieve — if anything, she needed his beautiful blue eyes to fill her heart and mind with new memories, new love, and new life without Dan. The need to know everything about his past was suddenly absent. There was only this present moment and in it, she needed him.

"Anson," Kendall said softly, returning the squeeze of his hand. "Anson, look at me."

Anson turned his head to face her, his eyes now dark and thunderous like the Atlantic Ocean caught in a category 5 hurricane. Kendall's gentle massage against his hand and her tender expression eventually soothed his internal angst. The distinct crease between his eyebrows eased as the eye of the storm brought its eerie calm.

"Nothing's changed since last night. I love you. I know this without any doubt. I am very much in love with you."

Every last crease instantly disappeared from his face.

"And I know you love me and would do anything to protect me," she continued, bending his arm up closer to her heart. "Because of this, you feel all out of sorts. It's been too long for you. And you're terrified of making the same mistakes… I am too.

"But you didn't pressure me into this. If anything: I wanted to be pressured. I wanted to be in this relationship with you. I wanted you to fall in love with me. I needed it all. Anson, I've never been alone. Even before Dan, I've always had some boyfriend, or Ariel, or Gabe, constantly at my side. And I'm not sure if that's a healthy thing or not, but it's my reality. I guess I thought I could control how deep it got. But you can't control these things."

She studied his eyes for a minute, Anson quietly listening as they both saw each other. She then exhaled in amusement and raised an eyebrow. "And you, Dr. Allaway, get in deep."

Anson smirked and rolled his eyes. He pulled her hand to his mouth, kissing the back of her fingers.

"Thank you," he finally said.

"We'll just figure this all out our own way, okay? Don't worry about what others think."

"I can agree to that." He smiled. Then, with a jolt of energy, Anson pushed up and leaned over her, the tip of his nose just above hers.

"I, however, *fucking* love you. Your sweet ass and these… these perfect tits!" he exclaimed, apparently never too old for motorboating. "This will be the end of me if I can't fuck you into next week for three more fucking weeks!"

Kendall lost it in laughter, Anson like a maniacal madman, peppering kisses across her face and neck. He, then, quite suddenly and exhaustively, reclaimed his spot next to her.

"Or *five* more weeks," Kendall teased.

"Fuck!" Anson blurted out, clearly in jest.

66

"No one said *you* couldn't get off," she commented, her smile impossibly large as the sunrise filtered through the entire room.

"It's not the same. By any means," he retorted petulantly, although clearly satisfied with his successful rerouting of the morning mood.

"Well, what if I helped?"

"Thank you, Kendall," Anson said, sighing. "But contrary to popular belief, I will survive. I'm not making you do any of that."

"No, not *me* do it. You'll still do it to yourself, taking the brunt of the physical effort. I'd just be your muse, if you will."

"You want me to jerk-off in front of you?" he asked, now propping himself up to look at her.

"Well, yeah. Why not? Maybe I'll touch myself while you touch yourself..." Kendall bit her lip suggestively.

"Goddamn. I love you more and more every day," he announced, passionately kissing her.

Anson quickly got lost in the sweetness of her lips as Kendall slowly rubbed her hands up and down his chest. She palmed his pectoral muscles then glided her hands further down his sculpted physique, working him over. He moved his body above hers, stiff as a board in plank position, and continued his delicious drive into her mouth, making her salivate for more.

She stroked him; the long, firm shaft of his cock the only bridge to overcome in the gap between their bodies. Anson dropped his head and groaned with pleasure under the pressure of her grip as she squeezed and caressed every hot, tempting inch.

"This'll be quick," he said regretfully, the anticipation having done most of the work already.

"Kiss me," Kendall whispered, Anson immediately filling her mouth once again. But she shook her head. "No. Kiss my body."

Anson looked at her, Kendall's bedroom eyes besieging him. He straddled her and began to worship every exposed square inch of her skin with his skilled mouth. He sucked in one nipple gingerly, then the other, increasing in fervor. He nipped the soft curves of her breasts and the tender skin just below them, Kendall's body arching and relaxing like a rolling wave. Carefully he moved over her abdomen, placing one petal soft kiss over her bruised skin.

Every hitch of his breath — the delectable muffled moans he made as he got drunk on the very essence of her — warmed her heart to the core. Anson adored her, actually *adored* her, and her soul sang. She needed to feel more. To heal more.

He moved straight to her toes, tantalizing her with more succulent kisses. Kendall giggled uncontrollably and pulled her legs away from him, making Anson snarl back with his wicked grin. He trailed up her calf, moving at a tortuously slow pace. Finally, he made it to the creamy, soft skin of her inner thighs and drew in a full, enriching breath.

"God, you smell sweet," he said through a sigh. But then he saddled himself over her, his balls tighter than freshly picked pears.

"What? No kisses here?" Kendall whined, shimmying out of her underwear just a smidge. "I'm wetter than the 'Glades during rainy season, Anson. You have to give me something."

Anson smiled — one that reached the light in his eyes and set her inner flame ablaze.

"Baby, I'd like nothing more than to eat you for breakfast. Denying me the pleasure of your pussy is probably more punishment for me than it is for you."

"So get that filthy mouth of yours a little dirtier. Just a taste?" Kendall purred, her seductive tone and batting lashes doing their jobs flawlessly.

"Kendall! You're killing me. I wouldn't be able to pull back until I heard you come. And you know you can't right now."

"Not even a clitoral orgasm? I won't let it build. I'll just have a quiet one. Just a tiny release. I'm no longer spotting or anything. Please, Anson," she begged. "You turn me on so much. I'm sure it'll be okay. If I have the least bit of pain, I'll stop you."

"Yeah, but I don't know if *I'd* stop."

"Please. *Pleeease*," she begged. "I need this. I need you. Baby, please. Love me."

And that was the final argument he could not deny. He obliged with both reluctance and indisputable eagerness, carefully placing himself between her legs as Kendall grabbed a pillow and pulled it over her head.

"Don't hide. I want to see you," Anson said before he got started.

"Not this time," she answered, her voice muffled into the pillow. "You'll mistaken my *O* face for a pain response or something and then stop. I'm not risking it."

Anson laughed and shook his head. He slowly pulled down her underwear, then lost himself in the sinfully sweet aroma of Kendall Matthews.

"Oh yes! Like that! Oh god, I'm going to come!" Kendall announced minutes later, removing the pillow from her head as the trapped heat became unbearable. "Fuck! Ow! Shit! Owww!"

Kendall winced as the orgasm traveled up, causing uterine contractions to rhythmically pulse inside her; her muscles reflexively tightening and twitching, tugging at the internal stitching.

Anson sprang up, cock in hand and vigorously stroked himself over her chest until literally exploding all over her chest; the quintessential money shot if there ever was one.

"Holy fuck!" Anson exclaimed, panting. "Goddamn!" He collapsed down onto the bed next to her and lay spent. "Shit. That's the best time my dick's ever had not being inside of you. Holy hell that was hot."

Kendall looked down at her chest and then over to him. "You're not kidding."

Anson laughed. "Damn! That was a heavy load to be carrying around. So? You good?"

"Uh... No. Definitely won't be doing that again anytime soon."

"Shit. Are you hurting?" he sat up immediately with worry.

"Yeah, orgasms from you involve a bit too much internal muscle flexing and I have a feeling I'll be paying for that later," Kendall answered.

"Should we get you checked out?"

"No, no, no," she said, vehemently shaking her head. "I don't think anything popped. I now actually understand the reason behind a 4-6 week wait. But I'm not saying I didn't enjoy it. Because I did — until I didn't. So how 'bout you help me with this cum-fest."

"On your perfect chest?"

"Covering my left breast."

"Because you are the best?"

"Don't become a pest."

Anson laughed and kissed her sweetly. "I love you, Kendall Matthews." He then got up and retrieved some supplies from the bathroom.

Chapter 10

The morning unfolded with incredible ease after properly reducing the size of *that* towering elephant — becoming reacquainted with the sexual spark between them. Kendall headed into the kitchen to prepare some breakfast while Anson got ready to do rounds at the hospital.

She planned to connect with Ariel today before letting her fester any further. She also owed a call to her mom. She was confident she could assuage both their concerns with practicality and a bit of whimsy. Despite feeling like she'd taken another punch to the gut, she felt alive again.

"So, maybe I can have Ariel come over here while you're at the hospital?" Kendall suggested from the kitchen. "If you don't mind of course. Or I could have her pick me up instead if that's better." She poured some milk over her cereal, then chomped on a spoonful.

Anson appeared out of his study, sure to make some hearts flutter since he often wore jeans to work on Saturday. Kendall bit her lip as she remembered all the hushed catcalls of a few fellow nurses when Dr. Allaway would hustle by them on the weekends. When it came to eye candy, her sweet tooth definitely had the winning golden ticket.

"Of course I don't mind. Call her up now," he answered happily, jolting her from her reverie.

He set his keys and white lab coat on the foyer table and headed into the kitchen. Expectedly, he wrapped his arms around her, holding her from behind, and nibbled just below her ear.

"I could get used to this," he said softly as Kendall closed her eyes and leaned back into his touch. "Making love to you–"

"Not exactly," she corrected.

He smiled against her ear. "Fine. Making-*out* with you before work, having you here with your girlfriend during the day…" He slipped his hand beneath her tank top, pulling the one cup of her bra down and plucking her nipple out over the rim. His tongue skated along the edge of her ear and he huskily whispered: "Titty-fucking you in the shower."

"Anson!" she shrieked, whipping around and hitting him on the shoulder. "You're so crude and you know it, don't you?!" She shook her head, failing miserably to keep a straight face.

"And you love it," he said slyly, pulling her in close while waving the tip of his tongue in a lewd fashion.

She laughed, pushing him away again. "Sometimes I wonder which one of us is older here."

"Hey speaking of that," Anson began, shifting gears completely as Kendall picked up her bowl of cereal to eat at the table. "Your birthday's next Friday, right? May first?"

Kendall sat down at the end of the long, wooden dining table. The morning sun warmed her skin as she curled her legs up onto the chair. She felt stronger today. She looked stronger. Her eyes traveled down the slab of timber to *the* spot where they think she got pregnant. Anson deemed it, *the hot spot.*

"Yes, but I really don't want you planning something — or anything for that matter," she mumbled through a mouthful of cereal. "I think this is one of those birthday years I'd rather forget."

"Nonsense. I'm taking you down to the Keys," he announced, filling up his travel mug with coffee.

"Anson, I can't. Not that I don't want to, but really, I can't. It's the weekend before Ariel and Will's wedding and–"

"Invite them along. We'll do one of those couple weekends, if you'd like. Anything you want."

Kendall dragged a milk pathway through her cereal with her spoon, absentmindedly staring at their spot. *Had he cleaned my ass imprint or was it Manuela?* So much changed right there on that spot.

Lost in her thoughts, she hadn't noticed him approach.

"Okay, the idea doesn't thrill me either," he confessed, taking the seat adjacent to her. "I'd rather have you all to myself."

She gave him a chastising smile. That wolfish grin could charm the panties off a nun.

"Well, William isn't even here," Kendall said, now fully engaged in the conversation. "He's in Atlanta until next weekend. Ariel and I had plans to do a sort of girls' weekend. You know, my birthday, her bachelorette party–"

"Bachelorette party?" Anson perked up. "You do know: I know a thing or two about bachelorette parties. That is, if you wanted an awesome one." He grinded his ass into the chair, working it like a paying lap.

"Are we having this conversation now?" Kendall asked reluctantly, a cloud conveniently blocking out the sunshine — sure one elephant was smaller, but there were plenty of others to cast a shadow.

"No," he answered abruptly, ending his adolescent antics. "You're right. I mean, we will. But not right now. Later. Much later." He leaned in and kissed her, her eyes scolding him. "I'm kidding! Okay! Today. We'll talk today… Tonight. Maybe tomorrow morning?" He winked, getting up from his chair while squeezing her shoulder reassuringly.

But then he paused before walking away. "Actually, I might regret this but, uh… What exactly do you know?"

Kendall froze. They *were* going there now. In broad daylight. Over a bowl of soggy bran flakes. The same hour as being titty-fucked in the shower.

"You know," he said far too casually, working hard to keep the mood light. "So I know where to begin… when we talk later."

She took in a controlled breath.

"I know about your boss or business partner, Xavier LeBeau. Or should I just call him what he is? Your pim–" But she stopped short, desperate to just deliver the facts without her overriding tone of judgment. She collected herself — her voice once again calm and neutral. "I looked him up on the Internet. Read about *XL Messieurs*. Huge empire. Very successful adult entertainment business."

Anson slowly took his seat again, the fear in his face rising as the blood drained. *She really knows.*

"I know you and Will worked together briefly at some point. But he met Ariel at that time and left the business. I don't know the beef between you two or if it's all just wrapped up in some territorial pissing contest." The words couldn't fall out of her mouth fast enough. She had to get it all out before she chickened out. "I found this website, A-A-X-L-S dot com, linked to the XLM site but I needed a password to enter. I didn't try emailing the contact to get it. But I'm guessing you're profiled on it… offering services of sorts."

She hesitated, her voice now small and meek as she looked down at her cereal. Anson watched her intently. Then she met his eyes — those pools of inviting waters that reflected so much love with depths deeper than the Mariana Trench. And now his secrets were all surfacing, the pressure too much to handle.

"So that's what I know. And of course I have any number of questions, but the only one, I suppose, that has bothered me since finding it all out... well the one I really don't get is: Why wouldn't you share this with me before you asked us to become something more?"

The sincerity in her voice nearly crippled him.

Anson averted his eyes momentarily. He knew the question was fair game; prepared to answer it after working up to it — maybe over the next few nights. But he assumed every initial question would revolve around how he got into the business. *Why an escort when you're a doctor? Aren't you risking your practice? If it's not about the money, why do it at all? You could get women anywhere!*

But this was Kendall. And she went straight for the jugular.

"Well," he awkwardly said through a laugh, trying to rid the room of the pungent smell of regret. "I thought I was ready to just get it all out there, but uh..." Anson leaned back, rubbing his face with both hands. He dragged them over his head, fisting tight clumps of hair as he paused to sort through his thoughts — somewhat clumsily. "I asked for it. I know. And I commend you for still sitting here with me," he said, struggling to know where to begin. He brought his forearms onto the table, folding his hands in front of them.

Kendall remained quiet, giving him a chance to respond without cutting him off at every turn. She glanced back down at her unappetizing breakfast bowl then back up at him, the worry buckled up between his eyebrows as lumpy as her flakes.

"We don't have to do this now," she offered, extending her hand over his balled up fists.

He sandwiched her hand between his and sighed.

"I just don't think there's anything I can say to make any of this right for you," he confessed, his eyes fixed on their pile of hands. "It's been destroying me: trying to figure out how I can explain everything without changing the way you look at me. But if you want, I'll tell you whatever you want to know."

"Well," she said, taking command of their situation before he crumpled up into nothing right before her eyes. "I don't expect you to apologize for years past, or even for the way it all played out between us. Nothing's going to change that now. I know this is something you've done for years — before I came into the picture — and now you stopped it all. Maybe you liked it, maybe you didn't. But you gave it up for me. You changed for me. That's huge."

His face relaxed as the spotlight of the sun returned to the scene. No place to hide.

"I'm not sure I'll ever understand your desire to be an escort"
—There. She said the actual word— "even if you explained it to me.
But that's not really important. Rehashing our pasts is not something I
hoped to do with *this*," she said, reaching her other hand over and
placing it on top of his. "You and me: together. How *we* feel. How *we*
work. That's why I'm here. It's *us* I fell in love with, Anson. And I want
to keep moving forward. With you. Anson and Kendall."

Anson looked at her with disbelief, the corner of his mouth
tugging back, genuine awe replacing all his fear.

"How do you do that?" he asked, lost in the soft glow that now
surrounded her.

"Do what?"

"Love me with such grace and humility?"

Kendall's cheeks blushed like cherry red roses as her eyes
dropped from his gaze. She smiled; her heart full and her mind clear.
The feeling was far too precious to rush past; the euphoric sensation
fleeting, yet completely satisfying when present in the moment.

And they were both very much present.

"You and I... We both just *know*. We know," she said, giving an
endearing shrug of her shoulders, her sweet smile mirrored in his.
"And sometimes knowing together — it's enough."

Anson eased back into his chair, staring reflectively out onto
the deck.

"I like that. So, what do you see happening next?" he asked.

"We kiss and make it better," she suggested playfully, leaning
in for the kiss.

He met her lips; the tenderness of the exchange and the
suppleness of her lips quickly igniting his unending desire within. He
pushed off his chair, his hands locking into her hair and holding her
close as he moved in front of her. She moved to stand with him, but he
stopped her.

"I'll never leave if you get up," he whispered, his hands still
clasped around her face. "Just answer me this: Did you ever think it
could feel this good again?"

Kendall looked into the inviting pools of his turquoise eyes. He
was lost in her; lost in them; lost in the moment. She marveled at how
much peace her heart did find in his embrace — his very skilled,
trained embrace. How many women had he made feel that way? Yet
only *she* could make him feel it in return.

"Honestly, I never thought I'd feel anything ever again," she said. "You must have that magic touch, Dr. Allaway."

He smiled. "I'll check in with you later. Love you."

Just as he opened the front door to leave, Kendall called out to him.

"Hey. Maybe I'll pick out curtains today," she teased.

"Don't get my hopes up," he warned.

"So you really want me to consider moving in?" she asked sincerely.

"I may not be too keen on talking about the past with you. But a future together? I've never felt more ready."

Chapter 11

After some groveling and a few pre-wedding day promises, Kendall convinced Ariel to meet her at Anson's place. She paced about the house, analyzing his home from Ariel's perspective. Kendall loved the place. Not only was it aesthetically pleasing — no doubt a point of pride for Talon as the architectural mastermind behind it — but it complimented Anson so well. Mirrored him, really:

Crisp, sleek, chiseled lines that drew the eye up and down with such ease, you didn't even know you were staring. Colors and tones, curves and edges that punctuated the journey, seducing your mind even further into a full sensory experience. The open design that just put it all out there, making no corridor too private to explore — it was welcoming, comforting, alluring...

Just a few more weeks, she thought, laughing at her own desire to be a noncompliant patient.

Ariel would raise an eyebrow at the glass three-story high raindrop installation. She'd fall in love with the kitchen, yet comment on how Kendall doesn't even like to cook. The exercise equipment and swank lounge would irritate her — the indulgence of it all rendering her jealous, even if it was what she grew up with.

The invitation to live with Anson would be brought up. But now Kendall felt prepared for the conversation.

"Wow," Ariel began upon entering the foyer.

The South Florida weather — hot and on point that late April morning — infinitely increased the pleasurable experience of stepping into the cool air of Anson's home. Plus, the first floor showcased light like the glass lens in a lighthouse. It truly was breathtaking.

Ariel arched her neck back and literally gasped at the installation piece.

"Chihuly?" Ariel asked.

"No. I thought the same thing," Kendall said, walking up the steps to begin the tour.

"So, uh... is he looking for any additional roommates?"

Kendall's muscles all entered into a collective sigh, her shoulders and guard dropping as Ariel maneuvered slowly around the room taking it all in.

"Yeah, I've only really gotten to appreciate it these last few days," Kendall commented, taking a central seat along the kitchen counter as Ariel explored a bit. "Honestly, I never really came here during the day."

Ariel's eyes narrowed, but she kept quiet.

"Well, this is definitely the way to recover," Ariel said, staring out at the beach. "It's like the ultimate vacation home, isn't it?"

"There's a gym upstairs," Kendall boasted, unable to resist, now that Ariel was captivated.

"You haven't been working out, have you?"

"Goodness no. Not at all. I'm just saying." Kendall smiled — too suggestively.

"Don't tell me you're actually considering moving in." Ariel's chastising tone increased half an octave as she bee-lined it back to Kendall.

"Well…" Kendall stalled, cursing her need to brag about the gym. "Not really moving in, per se… just prolonging my stay. It's temporary anyway. I'll be in Miami by August."

"Yeah, but that's some four months away. Living with someone for four months changes things, don't you think?"

"Not any more than dating someone for four months would," Kendall countered. "If it works, it works. If it doesn't, it doesn't. But I'd be moving to another city if it didn't work so, that's a plus."

"And if it does work? And you say yes to his panicked proposal? Don't be so cavalier about this."

Ariel had to go there. Kendall groaned, getting up from the stool. She moved to the couches and Ariel followed.

"I'm not marrying him, Ariel. And I texted you that as a friend needing a friend, not for you to throw it back in my face. You never even responded."

"You hung up on me yesterday. And I *am* being a friend by telling you I think this is all blown way out of proportion if you actually want to go there with him now."

Kendall's glare bore deep into the large flat screen ahead. Her jaw clenched. She turned her icy expression to Ariel.

"I'm not fighting with you on this. You were all pro-Dr. Sex until I became pro-Anson. Now you want us as far apart as possible and I don't think that's being a friend at all."

"Kendall: Listen to yourself. You just experienced something very scary together and now you're making life decisions based on it. His wife died some ten years ago and–"

"Fiancée."

"Whatever," Ariel said dismissively. "Ten years is the point. And he's just *now* dealing with those issues? Your *husband* died months ago and he expects you to just be ready to move on?"

"I can't answer for him, but I feel at least ready to move forward and leave the tangible mourning behind."

"How can you say that when another tragedy just struck?" Ariel asked forcefully. "How can you possibly be in the right mindset to decide future things when all this shit keeps coming your way *after* Dan? You still haven't had a moment to breathe from it all."

"That's *when* you make life decisions!" Kendall sounded back louder than she'd wanted. "Something goes wrong and it changes you. You can either embrace the chaos or act like it never happened. And *finally*, I'm deciding to go with it. *I'm* different, Ariel. And Anson gets that. More than anyone else, he gets it."

Kendall sunk back onto the couch breathing heavily, her hands balled up into fists at her sides. Ariel studied her posture and dropped her head in defeat.

"I didn't come over here to piss you off again," Ariel said quietly. "I want us to get past this, but I don't think we can if I feel like you say one thing to me, something else to your mom, and something entirely different to Anson."

Kendall's hands opened up and she placed them in her lap. For a good minute she simply looked around at the large living room as Ariel watched her.

"Do you think I should have Gabe over here for a weekend?" Kendall asked seemingly out of the blue.

"What?" Ariel asked, not following.

"Gabe," she said, looking back at Ariel. "He was going to stay with me this weekend at my place. You know, before all of this happened."

"Oh... Well, when you're all healed up, I guess. But here?"

Kendall turned her whole body toward Ariel.

"I wanted to keep all of my worlds separate: my relationship with Anson and my relationship with you all. And well, that obviously blew up in my face." Kendall hesitated briefly. "When I see you, my mom, or Gabe, I think: grieving Kendall. I think: Dan. I think: What can I say to make you all think I'm okay?

"But when I'm with Anson: I'm just Kendall. Actually, I'm new Kendall — to him at least. I'm someone exciting. And the attention he feeds me?" Kendall smiled reflectively, her eyes glossing over. "Ariel... It's addicting. I'm not going to lie. He weaves his way in like a drug and I'm gone. The best kind of high."

Ariel relaxed, the buzz of endorphins bubbling out of Kendall difficult to dismiss. She hadn't seen that sizzling spark radiate from her since the first year with Dan. Kendall was definitely in love — honeymoon stage.

"But then I return to my reality," Kendall said, her expression sinking and Ariel's following suit. "To my home. To my routine. To you, my mom, and Gabe. The absence of Dan. And I'm angry at myself for wanting to escape back to Anson where I don't think of any of it. Where I don't care what happens. Where Dan never existed. And miscarriages never existed... until now."

Kendall's voice cracked and she looked high above, willing back her tears. She took in a deep breath and shook her head.

"It's not like life with him would be perfect. Anson has been acting more like you all do. Treating me like I'm broken. Because, once again, my personal tragedy had to take center stage. And there's this whole escort business — yes, we've made headway in our conversation about it. Then my decision to sell the house and move to Miami come fall; school and not working at GC General anymore; you moving to Georgia... with my niece in your belly!"

Ariel laughed, a tear breaking free from her own choked back emotion.

"I think of all this and say: just hold onto this slice of heaven a little longer. There's no rush. Bad times will keep on coming, so why not hold onto something good a little while longer? And if I can be that Kendall Anson saw in me before... well, I want it as long as I can get it."

Ariel nodded. "I get it," she said softly.

"And so does Anson," Kendall continued on, relaxing further into her thoughts. "I don't know: maybe he *would* agree to marry me on the spot and set me up like a princess in his palace. Sounds tempting, right?"

Ariel immediately fake-gagged, rolling her eyes at the thought of Kendall as a doctor's wife turned socialite.

Kendall laughed. "I know. I'd play pretend for the summer and then go bat shit crazy. I'm not letting myself be that naïve. But I am giving myself some leeway right now. I guess the whole, *stop and smell the roses* mentality."

"Well, sure. That works for *you*. But what about him? What happens at the end of *his* summer?"

"I don't know."

"But," Ariel began, scooting to the end of her couch cushion. "Don't you think if he's ready for long-term commitment now and you're thinking summer love with the rebirth of Kendall Matthews come fall... well, don't you think you're going to break his heart?"

"I knew you were pro-Anson deep down." Kendall said, smirking. "I'm not planning to just suddenly break up with him because I'm off to school. When you and Will decided you were going to date and he went back to Georgia, you worked it out. If we want to make a go at it, knowing the only big commitment on *my* radar is CRNA school, then we'll do it. But, if it puts too much of a strain on us, then I guess we'll cross that bridge when we come to it.

"Ariel, I just know: I can't live in fear of the future if the moment I'm in makes life worth living."

"Hear, hear! Bravo!" A male voice echoed out behind them, sending shots of adrenaline to spike inside Ariel and Kendall.

Ho-ly. Hell. It was Talon.

The women jumped to their feet and faced the front door, their jaws literally dropping.

Anson's brother — dripping with sex-on-a-stick and recently fucked confidence — stood at the top of the foyer steps, practically shirtless as the crisp lavender business shirt he'd had on yesterday hung wide open, displaying a billboard of gym success... and then some. The two women noticed glints of light reflecting off his torso of permanent ink — Talon's chest merely a canvas for a mesmerizing maze of tattoos. The tattoos of temptation snaked around a pair of studded nipples. The man had nipple piercings. Nipple. Piercings. And where the tattoo ended was anyone's guess as it dipped deep into the waistband of his gray wool pants that hung dangerously low — the black leather belt an apparent piece of accented fashion, not function.

"Talon! It's Talon, right?" Kendall scrambled to find her voice as she blinked rapidly.

"Like a bird claw?" Ariel questioned, still in shock.

"Exactly like it," Talon answered, his face lighting up as the ladies' cheeks heated to a warm glow. He then pulled back one side of his shirt and displayed a tattoo on his hip. "My first tattoo: a griffin. High school mascot. I was a wide receiver and adopted the name. I caught everything."

Including every STD?

He ambled over to the stunned women and extended his hand to Ariel.

"I'm Anson's brother, Jameson. But people I like call me Talon."

"I'm... I'm Ariel," she answered, or more like tripped over. "Kendall's friend."

"Ahh, yes. The one getting married soon." His grip was smooth like satin as he held onto her hand. Then he *tsked*. Actually snapped his tongue and tsked as his eyes traveled the full length of Ariel's body. "Another one bites the dust. Such a shame."

Kendall's mouth fell back open as her eyes burned into Ariel, desperately demanding one of Ariel's sharp, witty comebacks to drop like napalm on his ass. But Ariel could not break her trance; frozen stiff in Talon's grasp.

"And she's pregnant," Kendall blurted out.

"Kendall!" Ariel snapped, her hand dropping away from Talon's.

"Ariel." Kendall sharpened her glare.

Ariel smiled back at Talon out of embarrassment, Talon clearly entertained by the little exchange. The two women shifted their weight awkwardly from one foot to the other, Talon as cool and collected as the moment he walked in. Finally, Kendall broke the triangle and hurried into the kitchen.

"Anson moved your suitcase to the entryway closet if you're looking to change or anything," Kendall broadcasted, clearing the electric air. She poured two glasses of orange juice, holding the one up to Ariel. "Did you want something to drink, Talon?"

"Got a Heine?" he asked, following Ariel to the kitchen counter.

"Excuse me?"

"A Heineken," he clarified.

And there was Anson's smirk, but on his brother's face. Quite immediately everything about him was grievously irritating.

"It's not even eleven o'clock in the morning. You want a beer?" Kendall asked disdainfully.

"Sure. Why not? Hair of the dog," he said. In any other setting his demeanor would have been irritatingly irresistible. Right now, Kendall only found it irritating.

Ariel had hopped onto one of the barstools and sipped her orange juice quietly. Engaged or not, this man was a force to be reckoned with and she had no intention of missing the show. Talon glanced over at her and gladly took the seat next to her.

"So, what were you two ladies discussing as I walked in?"

Kendall clunked down a Heineken with a thud.

"Thank you. I can see that feisty spirit Anson's told me about," Talon commented, then enjoyed a long swig of the beer. "Ooh, that's good."

Kendall groaned through an eye roll, then looked at Ariel who was trying to suppress the humor she saw in it all.

"What was it? *This moment* — here in Anson's house I assume — *makes life worth living*?" He boldly broke open the conversation and looked directly at Kendall.

Kendall's eyes filled her face as her skin burned lava hot.

"So, Anson and Jameson," Ariel finally spoke up, drawing Talon's full attention. "Family trend? Any sisters?"

"Nope. One older brother. Garrison — Gary."

"And you don't go by James? Jamie?" Ariel questioned.

"Sure. If we're keeping it formal. But uh, *Talon's* got that bite, don't you think?" He waggled his eyebrows at her, Ariel's expression unchanging.

"Sure. In that *college-glory-days* kind of way. And you're, I'm guessing, the– what? Middle child? So pushing forty," she continued now fully recovered from her faulty start.

"You're good. But Gary's got us by a decade. *A* and I are like Irish twins, so not much of a middle child. Why?"

"Pierced nipples and tatted torso. It's always that middle child who runs a little buck wild. Isn't it, Jameson?" Ariel practically purred.

Kendall. Was. Floored.

"You a wild child?" Talon asked, swiveling his whole seat to face her now. He had an impressive arch in his eyebrow as he checked her over once more.

Kendall was ready to erupt. But Ariel held up her finger to silence her.

"Nope. An only child. But *your* type, I can read like a book. The tattoos you've probably been collecting for years. Those nipple rings, though? I'd hazard a guess that they're new. Maybe within the last year. Midlife crisis variety."

Talon turned back to face the counter, bored with her assessment, and took back another sip of beer.

"And I bet it followed a particularly poignant breakup," Ariel continued, leaning further in as she gained her confidence.

Talon looked at Kendall as if to ask: *What's up with your friend?*

"So now you've sworn your heart off to women, seeing every one of us like we're your next lay."

Talon actually looked rocked by her words, pulling his shirt closed and chugging back his beer with a bit more force.

"When really you're just like everyone else: scared shitless of being alone, all doughy on the inside. Looking for love. The real kind. The kind that will last a lifetime," Ariel concluded with pride.

"So, she's the shrink in the friendship, I'm guessing," Talon said to Kendall.

Kendall finally smiled.

"Is that what you do when you meet someone? Try to strip them down to nothing? And I'm not talking the way you'd like to do to me right now," he said smugly.

"Isn't that what you just did to me?" Ariel was on a roll. "Except I used my words, not my eyes. And, even though we're both still clothed here. I do believe: only one of us is sitting here stripped."

Ding, ding, ding, ding!!!

"Anson talks too much," Talon concluded, his sails of cockiness flailing.

Ariel beamed. "No. Anson and I haven't had any heart-tohearts."

Talon looked back at Kendall, questioning her with his eyes.

"No! I knew nothing about you," Kendall said apologetically through a laugh. "If I'm being honest, Anson and I are still getting to know one another... well, outside of the biblical sense."

"Yeah, there's nothing biblical about how you two know each other," Ariel quipped.

"You're quick," Talon said, laughing at Ariel's jibe. "Okay. So truce. How'd you break that all down about me?"

"So it's all true?" Ariel asked excitedly.

"Well, I got pierced a few years back. But I'd say the rest is fairly accurate. Although, I wouldn't say I'm a total womanizer."

"You flew in yesterday?" Ariel asked.

"Yes."

"And you didn't have time to change a shirt missing all of its buttons?" Ariel asked, gesturing to the dangling threads down the opening of his shirt.

"Uh... they fell off last night?" He laughed sheepishly. Then his eyes grew dark. "What can I say? The woman wasn't the type to keep the wrapping paper."

Ariel and Kendall simultaneously groaned.

Although still amused, he actually blushed. "It's all an act, ladies. No need to burn me at the stake." He shook his head. "A'll love hearing about this. Allaway swagger is our specialty. But, it's just to protect our sensitive hearts from warrior women like yourselves."

"Warrior women?" Kendall asked curiously.

"Strong women," he offered as an alternative.

"Is that a bad thing?" Ariel asked.

"No. Unless you're the type of woman who makes it known you don't need a man, yet decides to trap one anyway and watch him squirm."

"Trap one?!" Ariel and Kendall asked in sync.

"Well, clearly I'm outnumbered here... considering you're both satisfied with your supposed sperm donations."

His last line fell short, however — way short — and the massive room shrunk into a stifling silence.

"I'm not pregnant," Kendall said, hurt. "I had a miscarriage. And I would *never* trap a man like that."

"So, I gathered. The pregnancies always seem to disappear after the promises are made, right?" Talon straightened out in his chair carelessly unaware of the actual events of the last week.

"The surgery I had? It was because of a miscarriage. A ruptured tube, asshole," Kendall angrily explained through gritted teeth. Talon looking up at her doubtfully. "Why did you fly into town unannounced anyway? I thought it was to offer support for your brother."

"Wait a minute... What? Are you serious? You had an actual miscarriage?" He glanced over at Ariel who was eyeing him with the same set of seething daggers. "Hold up. I thought he said that happened after your husband died. I assumed you were recovering from some bullshit procedure like lipo; the miscarriage incidentally around the same time."

"Are you fucking kidding me?" Ariel snapped. "What the hell kind of brother are you?"

Talon shifted in his seat uncomfortably, now desperately trying to recall his conversation with Anson yesterday at the sports bar.

"I apologize. I thought... Well... I *am* here for Anson. I didn't want him to lose his head."

"Assuming he was making some rash decisions because I was threatening him with pregnancy?" Kendall's level of disgust made even Talon's stomach queasy. "No wonder he punched you out last night!"

"Shit. You have to understand: I was going on some bizarre text messages he'd left me–"

"You didn't even know *why* you needed to be here for your brother?" Ariel asked incredulously. "So: you came for yourself, didn't you? To make yourself the hero."

"Hey," Talon said sharply. "You have no idea what he went through when he lost Grace. The reasons why you do something aren't always clear. You just know you have to do it."

There was a marked maturing of their conversation; the three recognizing that nothing could be summed up in simple bytes of information. Layers of reasoning could always be infinitely divided into another level of understanding.

And they all understood: the truth varied, depending on the eyes.

Chapter 12

KM: **I've experienced the entire range of emotions with your brother today.**

AA: **He has that effect on people.**

After hashing out Talon's misconceptions of the past week, Kendall, Ariel, and he took to Atlantic Avenue in Delray Beach for lunch. Anson, however, was unable to join due to multiple cases hitting the Trauma ER that required his assistance every time he tried to head out. He owed his partner after leaving him high and dry the day before.

KM: **Missing you. I'm like a third wheel with Ariel and Talon.**

AA: **What are they bonding over?**

KM: **Mocking our blind love.**

AA: **I'd say it's better than 20/20.**

KM: **Is that our problem? ;)**

AA: **Perfect vision?**

KM: **Leaves little to the imagination I suppose.**

AA: **I'm imagining what I want to do to you just fine.**

By the time they returned to Anson's place, Talon more than successfully made it into both women's good graces. His charm continued into late afternoon as he showcased his surfing skills while they watched from the shade of Anson's deck.

KM: **Do you surf like your brother?**

AA: **The fucker's surfing now? Which board is he using?**

KM: **He's quite good too.**

AA: **I'm better.**

KM: **Never seen you surf. Can't compare.**

AA: **You've seen my moves. The skill translates.**

KM: **So... You saying Talon's talented in the sack?**

AA: **You trying to piss me off?**

KM: **XOXO**

Anson, far removed from the trio's freshly crafted inside jokes, rubbed his knuckles, still tender from yesterday's punch. He trusted Kendall implicitly, but he knew Talon. And their sibling history had left a permanent scar. Kendall's peppered commentary of the day was not helping the situation.

KM: **How'd you miss the tattoo/piercing parlor growing up?**

AA: **Talon's always been the peacock.**

KM: **Never seen a Prince Albert before...**

"Someone's eager for me," Talon remarked with cocky confidence as his phone blew up with texts in rapid succession. He pulled up a seat next to Kendall and Ariel in the shade of the deck after finishing surfing. "What are you giggling about over there?"

"What'd he write?" Kendall asked, laughing.

"What'd who write?" Talon grabbed his phone to read his messages.

AA: **The fuck is going on there?**

AA: **Did you seriously get your dick pierced??!**

AA: **Answer me asshole!**

"Damn! You trying to get me killed? What the hell are you typing over there?" Talon asked, opening up a beer.

"Just making home sound more interesting than the hospital," Kendall said, winking.

"You have no idea. Anson's always been a bit wary of me around his women. Old, old feuds. No longer a thing, but uh... I still tread lightly when I'm teasing him about a lady friend."

"What: Are you saying he's worried I'll jump your bones? Because if that's the case, then he really has some low expectations of me," she said dryly.

"Not that you'd do it, but that I'd try to trip you up somehow. We're only ten months apart, right? So, I was the oldest in our class, he the youngest. Then he skipped some meaningless grade and was a year ahead of me. Absolutely sucked in middle school because people assumed I failed. But in high school, I clearly held my own, making a name for *Allaway* through football. It was like he hit puberty late, but really, he was just younger. And admittedly, I was a dick.

"Both his junior and senior year prom dates found their ways to my bed. If we hadn't gone to separate colleges, I'm not sure he'd ever have gotten over it. Grace was the first woman he'd met that paid no attention to me. I remember when he brought her home that first Christmas, she never took her eyes off him. She was gone. And so was he. After that we finally leveled out as brothers."

"Oh," Kendall said, falling silent for a moment. "I'm glad you guys worked that all out. So, uh, alluding to a Prince Albert appearance might be a bit much?"

"Damn! You kidding me?" Talon sat up at attention, letting out a nervous laughter. "Not cool. Well, it was nice knowing you ladies, but uh…" Jokingly, he half stood as if plotting an escape.

"Seriously, though," he said, sitting back down in his seat. "I've met women he's been with since Grace and we've had this running bet. I'm not saying it's kosher, but it's what we've done. If I'm in town, I have free range to try and steal his *dates*" —he made air quotes— "away from him. You know, make the night even more exciting for them. And I've succeeded. Twice! And that says something because he ain't cheap." Talon smiled proudly, but then faltered. "Not comparing you to that, of course."

Kendall and Ariel glanced at one another wide-eyed, their uneasy energy tipping him off.

"There are no secrets between Anson and myself," he continued. "And I already know you both know, so no sense in pussyfooting around it. Hell. It's kind of sweet how two BFFs both fell for escorts, isn't it?"

Their jaws dropped open, only stunned silence escaping. They barely wanted to incriminate themselves to one another, let alone an outsider. Talon typed away on his phone to respond to his impatient brother.

TA: **Keep your head about you.**

AA: **Keep your dick in your pants.**

TA: **It's unpierced and flaccid. CTFD**

He chuckled to himself and set his phone down.

"When did you first know about me?" Kendall asked, curious as to how much the two shared.

"Obviously we talk, but we don't keep tabs on each other. Before his cryptic messages from last Sunday, you'd been brought up only a handful of times since last year."

"Last year?" Ariel questioned doubtfully.

"That's when he — your husband — passed away, right?" Talon asked Kendall hesitantly.

"Yes, September. But Anson and I never really connected until the very end of February. March really."

"Oh," Talon said, stopping short. "Well, yeah. But that's when things shifted."

Talon dropped his legs and leaned in, looking at the women head on. His expression was one Kendall had seen before on Anson —

89

one reserved for patient family members before telling them things didn't look good for their loved one.

"Anson likes his world outside of the hospital. It's so much more than what you might think. And I don't say this to make you uncomfortable or jealous. Quite the opposite really. *I* might be pining for *the one*, but not Anson. He'd had it. He'd made his peace with it. Well, sort of... Anyway. He adapted a new lifestyle and thrived in it.

"But he noticed you, Kendall, before it was, shall we say... appropriate. After you lost your husband, he wanted to connect with you. *He* wanted it. He said he could help you forget. And to be honest, I thought he was trying a new marketing strategy: widows."

It was like hearing a gunshot fire in close range. Suddenly the business-like agreement of how they began screamed in her head. *Anson* had been in control.

Kendall sneered, cutting Talon off.

"If he sees me as just some fucking client to fix–" she hissed.

"No, no, no," Talon quickly objected, holding his hand up in protest. "Fuck. No, not at all. Shit. He'd flip out if he knew this was the topic of our conversation." He wiped his face with his hands — another Allaway mannerism — and looked back at Kendall determined to get it right. "*I* thought that. *Me*. Not Anson. He simply had an interest in you and it turned out you had one in him as well. So, it was kind of perfect for him."

Talon shifted uncomfortably in his chair, collecting his thoughts as Ariel and Kendall stared at him with icy contempt.

"I was always jealous of Anson. He was smart, driven, and well, since he looks like me, clearly he's a lady killer," Talon joked, raising his eyebrows at the women, yet coming off too desperate to turn the mood around. "Uh, anyway... What I wanted the most was his ability to relate. He just got people. Kinda like you, Ariel. Can't hide much around people like you and *A*. And after Grace, he overcompensated and wanted to fulfill those desires or alleviate those fears he'd notice in his clients. He's served women for years now, as if it were some moral obligation."

"Moral obligation?" Kendall asked with repugnantly. "You're not making our relationship sound any better."

Talon took in a deep breath, silently cursing the depth of the hole in which he sat.

"But with you, it's different. Completely different," he continued with conviction. "Except one thing: Anson's need to make sure your every need is met; forgetting his own needs. This'll destroy him. And probably you as well. Is that the level of commitment you're ready for?"

"Talon, I hate to break it to you," Ariel said, jumping in. "But that's what happens when a man falls in love. They're helpless. Maybe you've just never been willing enough to be that vulnerable."

Kendall sat far back in her seat to mull over Talon's words. A line of pelicans caught her eye as they glided effortlessly across the blue sky. She'd marveled at the natural occurrence a thousand times before. Today, however, the streamlined vision inspired her and she wanted to mimic their direction: Forward.

Picturing the escort lifestyle in anything other than a seamy, dank light was not what she wanted to do. Talon, however, managed to concoct an image of Anson as a life-saving doctor by day and a women's shelter counselor by night. She turned to Talon, annoyed, yet receptive.

"I know what you're saying is coming from a place of concern. You want to protect your brother from heartache again. And guess what? So do I. So, please, understand: I won't try to trap him. But" — she held her hand up in dramatic pause— "I don't want to be trapped, either."

Talon nodded his head respectfully and then added: "It's Anson, however, that will do the trapping. He'll trap himself."

A second later, all their attention turned to the opening slider.

"Here's where show-*n*-tell is going down," Anson announced as he walked toward the group, smacking Talon upside the head as he passed by him. He flaunted his commanding presence and grabbed a seat. "Ariel. It's good to see you again," he said warmly, although the curt nod of his head revealed their unresolved tension.

Anson's hair was wet, having showered at the hospital. He looked confident, sexy, and as his gaze settled on Kendall, he looked focused — very focused. Every nerve-ending in Kendall crackled to life as they locked eyes, the headiness in his stare only reserved for her.

"Hey, Kendall," he said quietly, a deliciously subtle smile transforming the entire atmosphere of the deck.

"Hey," Kendall said softly, the pleasure of his presence almost too much, allowing her mind to wander.

"Well," Ariel said, suddenly standing up. "I should get going." She looked at Kendall, waiting for her rebuttal, but was met with only an absentminded nod. "O~kay then."

"Oh! Umm... Unless you want to stay for dinner," Kendall quickly offered, disconnecting from the Double A charge.

"I don't think anyone would enjoy having dinner with you two right now," Talon added, also standing. "If you give me a minute to change, I can take you out to dinner, Ariel."

"Wait, what?" Anson asked, confused. "You do know she's getting married in a couple of weeks, right?"

"Uh, yeah," Talon answered, irritated. "And that she's pregnant, too. We've been through this."

"Oh? I wasn't aware. Congratulations," Anson quickly recovered, baffled by how much he missed in a day. He glanced back at Kendall who shrugged with a smile.

"I apologize, Ariel. I forgot *A*-hole, here, is outside the triangle of trust," Talon commented wryly, winking at Ariel. She laughed, making her way past everyone to head back inside.

"No worries," she said, patting Talon's defined tricep, a few salty water droplets still clinging to his toned curves. "Thank you for the dinner invite, but I think I'll pass. Our triangle here needs more scandal like your closet needs more button-less shirts."

Talon boisterously laughed, pulling Ariel close and hugging her against his bare chest. She squealed, feigning repulsion over his cold studded nipples pressing against her forearms folded up against him.

"It was great meeting you," Talon gushed, releasing his embrace. "All the best with the wedding. And the baby. I'm still holding out for Jameson Johnson."

Kendall decided to walk Ariel back inside, both laughing at Talon. Anson, however, remained cold; irritated by the interaction between Talon and Ariel.

"What was that all about?" Anson asked the minute the slider shut.

"What? With Ariel? She's great. Sharp tongue. Like your lady. Both of them. Had me laughing all day," Talon said, his smirk growing as he remembered the number of zingers they'd served so skillfully.

"The fuck, man," Anson said sharply. "She's Kendall's *engaged* best friend. Marrying Johnson. Johnson from AAXLS. And apparently pregnant. Keep your dick in check."

"Hey asshole!" Talon snapped back, actually hurt by his brother's comments. "I've been hanging out with these women all day and I'm sorry to say it, *bruh*, but: Wake the fuck up! At least I'm real with these women, which is more than I can say so for yourself."

Talon marched inside the house just as Kendall stepped back out onto the deck.

"Everything okay?" she asked, her eyes looking between the two men. But Talon ignored the question, disappearing inside.

"Come here," Anson said, sliding his hands over his lap. Kendall willingly obliged.

The minute she lowered herself onto his muscular thighs and he buried his face into the heavenly scent of her hair, they forgot everything.

There was only Kendall. There was only Anson. Nothing else mattered.

"I've been thinking of you all day," he whispered, nuzzling and caressing her neck with his lips. "Come upstairs with me."

"Your brother's here now," she answered, kissing the top of his head in an attempt to placate him.

But his hungry hands traveled higher up her back, his fingers looping their ways around her soft, golden strands. He pulled them back just enough to expose her neck even further.

"Regrettably," his voice a soft growl of desire, "I won't be making you scream. I just need to get a fix."

Anson's lips followed the curve of her throat up to her chin and found her mouth panting with want. His lips grazed the surface of hers, sending a shiver down her spine. His touch — she'd never have enough.

"Okay. Let's go up," she whispered, ready for more.

Chapter 13

The healing power of touch — no one denies it's efficacy and in the nursing profession, touch is encouraged. A nurse will go through thousands of gloves in a year, often wearing a pair for less than a minute before switching them out. But when appropriate and safe, nurses use skin-to-skin contact to supply a potent ingredient to a patient's cocktail of drugs that no prescribed medication will ever replicate.

And that's only the power of touch in its simplest format.

Both Anson and Kendall reveled in the insurmountable high experienced from their skin gliding over the other's. It was what kept them locked in above all else. There was love. There was understanding. But nothing beat the power of their physical relationship.

Until too many other outside elements came into view.

Kendall stiffened under Anson's probing fingertips, a sharp silence falling upon them. Xavier had just called twice in a row, Anson's designated ringtone for him unmistakable since that unforgettable night several weeks earlier. Anson ignored the calls, but then a text message alert followed, taunting Kendall.

"I thought you were done with all of that," she finally said, pulling the sheet over her bare chest.

"I am. Well, as an active escort," Anson said regrettably. He groaned as he pushed himself off the bed and retrieved his phone from his pants on the floor. He fought with his boxer briefs and stumbled back to the nightstand. "You have to understand that this *was* and *is* very much a business. I'm financially invested in it as well. Ending that side of it is not so cut and dry."

"How can I understand any of it when you don't tell me about it?" she asked.

Anson picked up the blackout shades remote control and shaded one half of the loft. He took a seat in front of his computer, turning on the desk lamp, and opened up several files with spreadsheets. He navigated his desk with impatience, tersely rifling through papers. He then tapped away on his phone, returning the text.

Kendall's eyes traveled down the sinuating lines of his masterfully cut back. As an objectified man, he was ideal. And distant. And never noticeably flawed.

He had designed it this way.

"You miss it, don't you?" she asked weakly, her voice choked.

"What?" Anson asked in surprise, turning his whole body to her. "Miss it? Being an escort? Kendall." He went to her, seeing the pained expression on her face, and nuzzled his nose against the sheet along her side. "No, babe. Not at all. There's nothing to miss. I've got you and you're everything I've been missing my whole life."

Tears threatened, pooling up beneath her emerald eyes. Anson crawled up higher in the bed, bringing her into his arms. He stroked her hair as she fought back her desire to just cave to his touch.

"I haven't been fair to you," he began. "I've been reluctant to talk about it, but I realize not knowing seems to do more damage to you than actually knowing."

Kendall pushed up and leaned into him.

"It's *knowing* I don't know. It's not the same as *not* knowing. But I don't want details, really," she said, building her strength. "It's just that... when I picture you as a... well, I just don't know what to picture. And I'm still a hormonal mess, so it's not making it easy."

He gave her a squeeze, kissing the top of her head.

"Okay," he announced, sitting up taller. "Here it is." He drew in a cleansing breath. "Yes, Xavier is a mogul when it comes to nightclubs. That much you know. He's been in the business some thirty plus years. I met him right after Grace died. I was a mess and he capitalized on it. But it was good for me. I firmly believe that. In many ways, I owe him my life."

Kendall pushed off of him, needing to see Anson face-to-face for this. She reached down to the foot of the bed and put her shirt back on, much to Anson's dismay.

"Okay. I'm listening. Lay it on me," Kendall said bravely.

"So, even though I was already a resident doctor, I doubted everything: my entire future and whether I was even worthy of a career in medicine. I'd always gone to clubs and danced — before Grace and with her — so it was a natural escape. *X* handed me this opportunity to create an escape for others. A fantasy. I literally began as a planted club dancer. Simply someone there to invite others in and get them dancing. Before I knew it, I had regular nights and routines that club guests picked up on. The routine of it helped me focus in residency. I had no other distractions except this one scheduled obligation and people seemed to really respond to it; respond to me, like I was something they'd been looking forward to all week.

"*X* had been building up XLM during this time, but it hadn't taken off. After about a year, he asked me to help manage the entertainers. But in order to manage them, I really needed to know what it was to be one of them. So I transitioned from club dancer to an actual male entertainer. The extra money on the side was unbeatable. People in my program had family. For me? Career and club; nothing more."

Anson spoke frankly as he delved into his shielded past, but the look in his eye could not be masked. The turquoise water of his captivating blues downright sparkled.

"You really liked it, didn't you?" Kendall asked, a reticent smile emerging.

"Babe, you have to understand. It was a high I'd never known, especially after losing Grace. My whole approach to it was about the women. I already had a career that I knew would be lucrative, respected, and hopefully life-saving. But this was pure fantasy. And sometimes that seemed to be more necessary to someone than anything practical in medicine."

"But you were getting paid. It's not like some volunteer service for women," Kendall said, recalling the annoying, holier-than-thou image Talon had painted in her mind.

"Getting paid as a nurse doesn't make your job any less compassionate and self-sacrificing, does it?"

"Did you just compare nursing to stripping?"

"Kendall," Anson said, laughing softly. "Listen for a minute. The point is: it kept me going because I actually felt like I was helping people in some small way. And I had a great time doing it. I never worried about killing someone while giving them a lap dance."

Kendall eyed him scornfully, but his smile only broadened.

"Fine," she said, digressing. "But how'd that lap dance become sex? What'd Xavier say to lure you into that? At some point you had to think, this might not look so good as a neurosurgeon. How blurred are the legal lines between prostitution and escorting anyway?"

Anson let out a long sigh.

"Escorting isn't sex. It's *time*. Time might lead to sex, but that's not guaranteed. And I was single, going out on my own free time. The way *X* and I operate, we're fairly discreet. But as for how I got lured? Well... AAXLS was my idea."

Kendall's expression flattened. "*Axles?*"

"The website you found. For services. A-A-X-L-S," he clarified. "AAXLS. My site for our escort services."

"*Your* site?"

"Yes. I came up with the concept and Xavier backed it all financially."

Oh. His ongoing investment in it suddenly gained some bright light — a very migraine-inducing light. And her vision was too crystal clear.

"I didn't want to get attached again," he continued. "So I had to be unobtainable in one way, yet completely available in another. It made sense. The same way dancing did. I was providing a fantasy service that catered to a woman's desires, and ultimately, her needs. But I didn't need to be at the club to do it. And well, it worked with my schedule." He studied Kendall's stone-faced expression. "Kendall, I'm not going to sugar-coat it. I enjoyed it. But it was all business. And now? It really is. I run it."

Kendall swallowed the bile bubbling in her gut. Slowly, she got up from the bed and headed into the closet where her clothes were being stored.

"Kendall?" Anson called over to her concerned, now picking up his jeans from the floor.

"I'm a little hungry. Maybe we should go out to eat or something," she suggested, sorting through her clothes. "What's Talon doing? He's awful quiet down there."

"Kendall," he repeated, joining her in the closet. Of course he was still shirtless. But in the moment, his stealth, sexy approach made her feel cheap. Maybe if she'd paid him that first night, they'd both be moving forward in their own productive ways.

"Don't," Kendall snapped, shirking the touch of his hand against her waist. She stepped out of reach and visibly relaxed. "Please don't," she said softly this time, staring blankly at his hung shirts. "Not now. I need a minute to process it all. It's like hearing about the exes, yet exponentially worse. And you still have to keep in touch with them."

"Kendall, they aren't exes. Never did I date any of them outside of the business... Well, except one. Sort of. Not really. I'll tell you about that later. The point is: I never cared for them like–"

"Anson stop," she said firmly, turning to face him. "Of course you did. Maybe not like you do for me, but you still cared for them. As valued clients. Like you do your patients. And if what we have has been built on sex, then what you had with these women is a direct threat to us; whether you like it or not. And they *paid* you for your time. It can't get any more flattering than that. And that's the *only* thing I didn't do.

"I bet you anything your abrupt departure from *AAXLS*, or whatever it is, has created some sort of cluster among your regular clients, hasn't it? Is that why Xavier, or *X*, or whatever you call him, keeps calling? Or is it really all business? Because something tells me he doesn't need help balancing his budget."

Anson rustled his hands through his hair, then hung them on his hips. He couldn't deny how true her comments were. Perhaps better than 20/20 was not the remedy he'd thought it'd be.

"Okay. Let's get some dinner," he regressed, taking half a step forward. But her expression hadn't softened. He looked around his closet, resting his hands on top of his head. "I have never been more flattered than that night you came to me. I still feel that way. Please." He held out an opened hand to her.

She analyzed his stance: his eyes locked on hers, his hand eager, yet patient, his chest bare and like a fucking god. But still immortal. Still healing.

And she could help.

She reached for him.

***

"Mom! I took care of all that last week. I'm out of PTO but I can return as soon as I get medical clearance. I *am* being smart about this."

Kendall mindlessly wandered around on the darkened driveway of Anson's home as she talked on her phone. She and Anson had decided to eat in once they realized Talon had left the house. But before finishing their meal, Kendall stepped out to answer her mother's third call of the day.

"Well, how about tomorrow?" Kendall asked, trying to wrap up the twenty-minute phone call. "We can meet at my place and that'll give you a chance to see for yourself how *fine* I am. What's with the third degree? I thought you liked him enough."

"Let's just say *Pretty Woman* is only a movie. I don't have bail money," Elena answered curtly.

"Mom! *What* are you *talking* about?!"

"Do you remember a man named, Angelo, from Gabriel's party?" she asked, finally getting to the meat of the matter.

"I met a lot of people that night," Kendall said, attempting to circumnavigate around the name. Angelo's famed *doctor by day, escort by night* comment still burned.

"Well, he's a manager at an adult entertainment club down here and he seems fairly familiar with your doctor friend."

Kill me now.

"So are you saying Anson frequents strip clubs?"

"Ha. *That* I could probably stomach," Elena said dryly. "Kendall: Are you paying Anson for his services?"

"WHAT?! You can NOT be serious right now, Mother!"

"That is not an answer."

"NO! Of course not!"

"So he *does* get paid for *services*?" Elena prodded.

"Don't we *all* get paid for services of some sort?"

"Don't get cheeky with me, Kendall."

"What do you want me to say, Mom? That Anson leads a double life as an escort? That I'm using a sex worker as an escape from my grief? Who — might I remind you — also happens to be a brilliant neurosurgeon. Or are you simply looking for me to admit that I'm getting what I deserve for being so reckless since Dan died?" Kendall argued.

There was a long pause of silence.

"He loves me, Mom. And I love him. It might not be conventional, but it works. For us. For now."

Kendall could practically hear the pounding pulse of her mother's carotid against the receiver. But not a word.

"Unconventional doesn't make it wrong," Kendall added.

Another pause.

"Mom?"

"I just never imagined..." she answered, her voice sorely deflated.

"Neither did I. And I'm guessing, neither did he. I'm sorry I'm disappointing you. But can we talk about this tomorrow?"

Kendall said goodbye a few moments later and stood still — lost.

"So *that's* how that conversation would go," Talon announced, appearing out of the shadows as he wandered his way up the curved edge of the driveway. He was going for sympathetic ear, but Kendall was not buying.

"You know it's rude to eavesdrop, don't you?" Kendall jibed, turning back to the house and walking away from him.

"Wait up," he called out, picking up his pace. "I swear: I just happen to have awesome timing when it comes to you and your confessions. So: Mom knows. Hard pill to swallow, I'm guessing."

Kendall groaned, pausing for Talon to catch up.

"You have no idea," she said, walking up the pathway.

"What tipped her off? Our own mother doesn't even know. Well… as far as I know."

"My mom knows everyone. *Everyone.*"

They approached the front door, but then Kendall stopped Talon in his tracks.

"Hey. So, where were you tonight? Please say you didn't go out with Ariel. Did you?" she asked, worry wrinkling across her forehead.

"Why? You think there's a chance?" he asked, a brilliant smile lighting up his face in the dark.

"No! Goodness no. Not at all. I was just curious," Kendall spouted off quickly, reaching for the door.

"Well, tonight I dined alone at Dolphin Bar."

"What? No cocktail waitress looking for a big tip afterward?"

Talon raised an eyebrow at Kendall and opened the front door for her.

"So my mom knows," Kendall announced immediately upon entering the house. Anson had been watching television in the living room.

"What?" he asked, muting the news and looking back at them. "Knows what?" He eyed Talon suspiciously.

"She knows about *you*," she said with annoyance, walking over to her plate of food on the counter. She looked over the leftovers, mild revulsion washing over her, then dumped the whole thing in the garbage.

Talon grabbed himself a beer and whistled his way up the stairs.

"Where was he?" Anson asked, joining Kendall in the kitchen. "Eating at Dolphin Bar… *Not* with Ariel."

"So you told your mom about AAXLS? Why?" he asked.

"She figured it out. I wouldn't be surprised if she knows Xavier."

"She mentioned him?" Anson was impressed now.

"No, but she knows all big business owners down south. She runs a business as well, remember? And the business of fine art tends to be a rich people thing. Case and point," Kendall said, sweeping her arm across the spans of his home.

"Now I make too much money for you?"

"No. I didn't say that. I'm just saying... You know what? It doesn't matter. I'm done arguing for today. I'm going to bed." Kendall pecked Anson on the lips and went upstairs.

The next day, while Anson and Talon bobbed like buoys in the early morning surf, waiting for their next ride, Kendall drove Anson's black Mercedes G Class to Sandalfoot Lane. She hadn't been home in just over a week; but it might as well have been a lifetime.

Chapter 14

AA: **Where'd you go?**
KM: **Had to take care of some things at my place. Borrowed your Benz. XOXO**
AA: **Talon's flight leaves around 6.**
KM: **:(Say goodbye for me please.**
AA: **You won't be home by then?**
KM: **I think I'll stay at my place tonight.**

Kendall's phone rang.

"Hey," Kendall answered. "Can I call you in a little while?"

"What's going on?" Anson asked.

"I'm just out right now and I'm sorting through stuff at the house."

"Out where? You can't be lifting boxes right now anyway. Talon and I will head over shortly–"

"No," Kendall said curtly. "Just... Let me call you back in fifteen minutes. Okay? I love you."

Kendall ended the call, then took a sip of her orange juice. Slowly she looked across the table.

"What?" she snapped defensively, Elena's eyes boring into her.

Elena, Gabriel, and Kendall were eating Sunday brunch at one of their local favorites, *John G's*, in Lantana. Their dining experience, however, had been grossly unfamiliar. And Anson's phone call could not have interrupted them at a more inopportune moment... at least from Kendall's perspective. For Elena, his ring was the final nail in her argument.

"He's making sure I'm okay. There's a difference," Kendall said, stabbing into a slice of French toast.

"Alltheway is a *booty* call?" Gabriel asked, laughing. Whether he actually understood the meaning behind it, he didn't care. He'd heard the reference in enough contexts over the years to find it humorous. Besides, *booty* had always been fun to say.

"Great, *Mother*. See what you've done?"

"Gabriel. Don't be rude," Elena began, but Kendall jumped in before she could finish.

"Well, you certainly are. So, what you're saying is that you'll condone booty calls, but not from escorts. And you'll welcome grandchildren out of wedlock, but not from booty calls. So if I want anything to continue with Al-LA-way, *Gabriel*, I better prove to you somehow that I've not hired him for booty calls and that he's definitely not using *me* for them?"

Elena glanced nervously around. The restaurant, notoriously popular on Sunday mornings, didn't falter in the least. She relaxed somewhat and leaned in.

"I'm still wrapping my brain around it, Kendall. I think you can appreciate that. Let's just talk about something else for now." Brunch could not end soon enough.

KM: **I was eating with my mom and Gabe.**

AA: **Would have been nice if you mentioned it.**

KM: **I'm sorry. I needed a day with them, okay?**

AA: **Call me later.**

KM: **I love you.**

Kendall didn't hear back from Anson, but didn't overthink it. By evening, Elena and Kendall had settled into a place of understanding. Their mother-daughter boundary had been firmly reestablished and focus had returned to the future: Kendall's future.

"Are you sure?" Elena asked, doubt in her eyes.

"Mom, don't be silly. Of course. Gabe's a groomsman. He should do something with all this wedding planning anyway."

"I will be the cake tester!" Gabriel announced from his regal spot of La-Z-Boy comfort.

"That's already been finalized, bud," Kendall said from the front door as she walked their mom out. "But maybe they'll have some samples to share."

Elena headed back to Miami, Gabriel staying behind with Kendall for a few nights in her Lantana home. On Monday, Kendall planned to run some wedding errands with Ariel. Tuesday would be a day with the realtor. Wednesday, Gabriel was going to go fishing with some crew from Station 9. Thursday, Kendall had a post-surgery check-up appointment. She hoped for work clearance. Then Friday was her birthday; the perfect beginning to Ariel's bachelorette weekend. Kendall felt she was gaining some control again. She sent a text to Anson and called it a day.

KM: **I'll call you tomorrow. Going to bed. Love you.**

By morning, Kendall awoke to the sounds of a foreign ringtone.

She blindly reached for her phone on the nightstand quickly realizing it wasn't hers. She looked back behind her, Anson fast asleep in her bed, and saw his phone buzzing away on Dan's nightstand.

"Hey, Anson," she gently called to him, stroking his arm. "Babe, your phone."

The ringing stopped and he suddenly woke, looking at Kendall in a daze then directing his attention to his phone.

"Hey Lori," he groggily answered. He sat up, listening intently for a minute. He sighed with grief. "Yeah. Thanks for calling. So, Thursday... Okay. And what's my earliest today? Good. Block the times before that. Got in late from an emergency call... Thank you, but I'm at Kendall's place... She's doing well. I'll let her know. See you later."

He returned the phone to the nightstand and dropped heavily onto the pillow. He reached for Kendall, pulling her in close like a security blanket.

"Hey." His raspy voice whispered into her hair gave her a wave of loving chills.

"When did you get here?" she asked, spooning in closer.

"Little after midnight. Had to stop at the hospital."

"Who was that on the phone?"

"My office manager. One of our patients died over the weekend. Funeral's Thursday. She also sends you her best."

"Oh. Thank you." But then Kendall stalled, hoping to not come off nosy. "So, did she want to stop by your place this morning?"

Kendall could feel Anson smile against her ear. He could never hide it: he loved hearing her a bit insecure.

"She offered," he said cryptically.

"Why?" Kendall turned over to face him now.

"Because she makes the best cup of coffee and drops off paperwork at my place if I can't make it in early."

Anson kissed Kendall's nose and got out of the bed.

"Speaking of which, would you like some coffee?" he asked, smiling and completely naked. Kendall admired his morning physique, his eyes and stature rising beautifully with the sun. "Then, maybe you'll help *me* wake up a bit more?"

Kendall rolled her eyes and laughed as Anson opened up the bedroom door. Then it dawned on her and she sprang into action.

"Oh wait!" she called out a moment too late.

"Gabe!" Anson announced upon seeing Gabriel at the counter eating a bowl of cereal. With lightning speed, he stepped behind a dining room chair. "Hey man. I didn't know you were here."

Kendall rushed out of the room, Anson's boxers in hand, and ushered him back behind closed doors. She proceeded out into the kitchen.

"Hey bud," she quickly began, covering Anson's tracks. "Good morning. So, uh, Anson stopped by last night. Didn't even know it until this morning when I woke; that's how tired I was."

Gabriel looked up at Kendall, chewing on a mouthful of cereal, completely unimpressed with her rambling state.

Anson reemerged from the room, fully clothed, and stood next to Kendall on the opposite side of Gabriel.

"Good morning, Gabe," he said confidently. "Sorry to stop by unannounced. Just wanted to make sure Kendall was doing alright. But I guess you're already here taking care of things."

"Good morning, Doc. Yeah, I'll be here with Kendall this week. Feel free to stop by if she needs a *booty* call." Gabriel answered with a great big grin.

"GABRIEL!" Kendall shouted.

Gabriel's expression sank with remorse.

But Anson laughed. "Hey, you're keeping it real. I respect that," he said, defending Gabriel. "I suppose it does look that way."

"No. That is way out of line and he knows it. It is *not* okay."

Anson shrugged at Gabriel, offering his apologies.

"Sorry, Kendall," Gabriel said ruefully.

"Thank you. You need to watch it, though. Anyway. It's after seven, so I'm going to take a shower now. You need to get ready soon, too, Gabe." Kendall looked over at Anson. "We're doing some wedding stuff with Ariel today. Go ahead and get some coffee. Eat whatever. Don't treat him like a child even though he acts like a twerp brother." She turned back to Gabriel. "Behave."

Kendall closed the bedroom door behind her, leaving the two men in the kitchen.

"So," Anson began, wasting no time. "Booty call, hey?"

Gabriel eyed Anson suspiciously. "My mom called you Kendall's booty call. I know what that is."

"So, you think that's what I really am?"

Gabriel thought about it for a minute. "Don't know. Don't care."

"Well, it's your sister," Anson reasoned with him. "You probably care a little bit."

"Yeah," Gabriel agreed quietly through a bite of cereal.

"I want you to know: I care about her more than anyone. I really do love her. And I'd never hurt her."

Gabriel stopped eating, allowing a small disgruntled sigh to escape, annoyed with the breakfast interruption. But he strived for politeness.

"Kendall said she loves you. So, Mom said that's what matters."

"But what *you* think matters to your sister. If you and I can't be friends, I don't stand a chance with her."

Gabriel smiled.

"You're in luck, Doc. *Friend* is my middle name."

Anson smiled and poured his own bowl of cereal and milk.

"I bet it is," he said, feeling like he'd made it into the winner's circle. He'd never wanted someone to like him so badly.

"No, that's just a saying. My middle name is Garrett."

"And your last name is... Graham, right? Gabriel Garrett Graham."

"Three G's. Super force," Gabriel smiled proudly. "Dan always said the force was strong with me."

Anson laughed. "I like that. Mine was never that cool. It's bad enough when people call me Double A. So, I think it's worse to be Triple A."

"Triple A? Like the small battery?" Gabriel asked, unimpressed. "Not much force there." Then he began snickering. "Or you tow cars," he said, barely getting it out before he busted a gut laughing. "At least that's a big truck!"

Anson enjoyed seeing Gabriel completely let go, unsure of what it'd really be like to hang out with him. He'd never spent time with someone with Down syndrome and was relieved to find out it wasn't all that different than getting to know anyone else. Small talk was Gabriel's specialty and something Anson always excelled in as well.

"Anson Alltheway. All-away," Gabriel corrected himself. "I keep messing that up. Kendall hates that."

"Meh. It's close enough."

"So what's your middle name?" Gabriel asked.

"Well, now that's a secret. How are you at keeping secrets?" Anson asked.

"Terrible." Gabriel's smile nearly touched the upside-down crescents of his eyes.

Anson laughed. "Hey, at least you're honest."

"Always honest," Gabriel said truthfully with a nod.

"Well, try and keep it to yourself since I don't let anyone except people really close to me know it."

"I cross my heart. Kendall knows it?"

"Actually, come to think of it: No. She's never asked."

"Well, I won't tell her. I promise."

"It's Axel."

"Like an axle on a car?"

"Sort of. Little odd, isn't it?"

Gabriel shrugged. "It's kind of cool."

"I like it on its own. But all together? It's way too much. Anson Axel Allaway. I don't know what my parents were thinking."

Gabriel laughed and got up to clear his spot at the counter.

"Hey, so, what do you think Kendall would like to do for her birthday?" Anson asked, not ready to end their conversation. "I bought her a gift yesterday, but I want to take her out."

"She likes running," Gabriel suggested. "We go bowling together. And we play Scrabble."

"Bowling? Really? I never pictured her as much of a bowler." "She's good... for a girl," Gabriel said, chuckling.

"Well, I was thinking of taking her to the Keys for her birthday. Think she'd like that?"

"She loves the Keys. She went there for her honeymoon. Dan gave her a ring down there, too. She doesn't wear it anymore, though. She stopped wearing it for the New Year. It's 'cause he died."

Anson sat quietly for a minute, processing all the memories that could surface for Kendall if they were to go to the Keys together. The idea lost its luster quickly. Especially if she'd gotten engaged down there.

"Is she into fishing like you?" he asked Gabriel, moving the conversation along.

"Nah. Me and Dan were the fishermen. She's the fisherwife." Gabriel started laughing heartily, but then stopped suddenly. "Well, she's not a wife anymore."

Anson felt a knot begin to develop in the pit of his stomach. He was crashing hard.

"I'm really sorry about Dan, Gabe. I know what it's like to lose someone very close. I wish I could say it gets easier over time, but I'm not sure that it does. I think, instead, you just get numb to the pain."

Gabriel looked at Anson closely, then nodded his head. He fiddled with his fingers, not sure how to respond.

"Hey, so… maybe you and I can take the boat out sometime. Do you think Kendall would be up for that this weekend? I'd love to get out there and fish with you."

"She sold it," Gabriel said sullenly. "But Bob said I can go on it anytime I wanted with him. He's keeping it docked here until she sells the house. He works at the firehouse. We're going fishing on Wednesday."

Damn. Anson really needed to start asking more questions.

"How about the house? She sold that yet?" he asked further, now on a hunt for information.

"No. But she said people came and saw it. She doesn't know them. More people are looking this week. That's why she wants it clean."

"So when it sells, where will she go?"

"Miami," Gabriel answered matter-of-factly. "That's where her school is. And I live there. My mom is finding her a place."

"But her job is here," Anson said, keeping his cool despite his blood beginning to simmer. "And school doesn't start until August."

"She'll quit her job as soon as the house sells. And the house *will* sell. My mom said so. Kendall priced it right."

"So, did Kendall say anything else about me yesterday?" Anson boldly asked. However, he felt like a D-bag the second the question was out, knowing he was taking advantage of Gabriel's honesty… and naivety.

"My mom and Kendall went for a walk around Lake Osborne," Gabriel answered, offering up a shrug. "That's their girl time and I never go along."

Anson frowned; but then Gabriel reached out to pat him on the back with sympathy.

"Us guys got to stick together," Gabriel added, smiling so broadly his eyes were perfect rainbow slits once again. "That's what Dan always said."

"Well," Anson began. "The next time Kendall is having girl-talk, you give me a call. I know plenty of places we could go to have our own fun."

"Okay!" Gabriel agreed, immediately handing over his phone to Anson so he could enter his contact information. "I have to go get ready now. Here" —Gabriel handed Anson a banana— "give this to Kendall. My mom said she should eat smalls things more often if her belly is still bothering her."

Another thing Kendall hadn't mentioned anything about.

Chapter 15

Anson pushed open the bathroom door and found Kendall fresh from her shower. He leaned up against the doorframe and took full advantage of the free peep show, Kendall barely acknowledging him. She dropped her one leg from the counter and propped the other one up, lathering the leg with lotion.

"So is that why you smell so damn edible?' Anson asked, marveling at the unintentional seduction involved in her regular morning routine. "What do you use? I've been missing that smell." Kendall glanced back at him, noticing the banana.

"Is that a banana in your hand...?" she asked flirtatiously, continuing her liberal application of the lotion.

"Gabe thought you'd like it — so you don't get an upset stomach. Have you been queasy?" he asked, placing the banana down on the counter and picking up her beauty product container.

"Just post-op stuff, I suppose," Kendall answered dismissively.

"*Body butter*," he read, taking a big whiff of the thick, white cream. "Nice. Sounds edible. Guess that explains why you wore it that first night."

"It's just a body lotion," Kendall said with a smile. "And how do you know I wore this our first night?"

"It says *butter*— clearly it's meant to serve you up like a sautéed slice of heaven. And believe me: I remember your smell that night. How come you've only worn it a few times?"

"I don't know. It's like a perfume. I don't wear it to work and we've really only been on a handful of planned dates." Kendall finished rubbing the lotion onto her arms and took the container back from him, placing it into her bathroom cabinet.

"So what's the occasion today?" he asked, his gaze lingering lustfully over her curves.

"Nothing. Just wanted to feel put together."

"Well, bring that stuff back to my place. I could watch you butter yourself every day."

She eyed him in the mirror, picking up the banana. Predictably, she peeled it back with playful precision.

"You want me to butter your banana?" she asked coquettishly, slowly bringing the tip of the banana to her mouth.

He laughed, moving in behind her, their eyes locked into one another through the mirror. "I'd like nothing better, baby."

"You're an incurable nympho," she concluded, taking a swift bite of the fruit.

"And you're my drug of choice." He kissed her neck, his hands freely exploring her silky smooth skin.

Kendall rolled her eyes and wriggled out of his grasp. She put on her underwear and bra, Anson frowning in disapproval.

"Hey, what's your middle name?" Anson asked.

"My middle name? Oh, did Gabe tell you about his G-Force?" Kendall asked, laughing.

"Yeah, we bonded."

Kendall smiled sweetly at Anson through their reflections. "It's Graham."

"Your maiden name?"

"Yeah. It was Elena, but I legally changed it when I got married."

"Oh. That didn't upset your mom?"

"Not sure. I never told her I legally did it," Kendall said, smiling. "Garrett was my dad's name. Guess that was their thing. What's yours?"

"Mine? It's a secret."

"A secret?"

"Yes. A secret," he said, grinning.

"Well," she said, putting down her makeup and walking slowly over to him. "I bet I could work it out of you pretty easily."

"I'd like you to try," he said, licking his lips in anticipation of hers.

But then she turned on her heel and sashayed back to her spot in front of the mirror, Anson shaking his head with irritated amusement.

"So don't you have surgeries today or something?" she asked, continuing in her routine.

"No. Mondays are mainly office hours." Anson sat down on the edge of the bathtub and watched her.

"It's almost eight."

"Yeah and I don't have an appointment scheduled until 9:30. You trying to get rid of me?"

"No," she said, leaning far into the mirror as she concentrated on the application of her mascara. "But it's kind of strange: you sitting there and watching me get ready for the day."

"I find it fascinating. And I look forward to seeing it every day when you move in with me." He said it so clearly, without hesitation.

Kendall's rapid upward stroke of her mascara wand against her lashes halted momentarily. But then she carried on as if nothing had been said. She looked herself over in the mirror.

"Do you think I should get a boob job?" she asked jokingly, pushing her breasts together and looking at them from different angles. "It would have been far more convenient for me if you were a plastic surgeon."

"Oh please."

Kendall shrugged indifferently.

"'*There's a shortage of perfect breasts in this world. 'Twould be a pity to damage yours.*'" He smirked proudly.

Kendall laughed. "Where's that from again?"

"Come on! *Princess Bride*. Isn't that like every girl's favorite?"

"Ahh, yes. Lots of great quotable lines in that movie. But alas, I am no damsel in distress. *GI Jane* is more my speed."

Anson looked at her doubtfully. "Then why ask my opinion?"

"Fishing for a compliment, I suppose," she admitted and took another bite of her banana.

She left the bathroom to grab her clothes.

"I'm still waiting," he said, following her out.

"For what?"

"An answer."

"I don't remember you asking me a question," she answered smartly.

Anson crossed his arms.

"What?" she asked with guilt. "So, I don't want to talk about that right now. Another time. My brother's waiting for me. Ariel's probably going to get there early. It's just not the right time to discuss your fairytale dream."

"*My* fairytale dream? Why does it only have to be *mine*?"

"Because you're the one who wants it so badly. I never suggested anything like moving in or getting married. These are *your* fantasies."

113

Anson stood in silence, Kendall hardly noticing as she moved about the room, gathering accessories and a pair of sandals.

"Is that what you really think of this?" he asked, the hurt evident in his voice. "That I'm simply filling an unfulfilled fantasy of my own."

For a moment the room stilled.

"Anson," she said softly. "You're in such a hurry to rush past all our unknowns and plow into a new life together. You already know I love you and that I want this between us to grow and get stronger. But let's just let this grow naturally. Like it was. Before everything got so damn complicated."

Anson shook his head and collected his things from the night stand.

"What? What are you doing?" she asked. "You mad now?"

"No. Not mad. Just disappointed."

"Disappointed I'm not shouting *yes* and telling you to *put a ring on it*? Really, Anson? It's all a little rash, don't you think?"

"No; disappointed to know where I stand with you and that my rank won't be changing anytime soon."

"What do you mean, *your rank*? Because I'm hanging with Ariel and Gabe today?"

"Because you spend *one day* with your mom and the next day I'm out. *Yes*. A lot has gone down in the last week. A lot of grief. A lot of revelations. But they were *ours*; yours and mine, together. And I think we're handling it all very well. But now you want to stay at *your* place again. Live *your* life again. And keep me out. Keep things separate once again as if we are not together. It's hard to keep pace with you."

She didn't know how to respond.

"*GI Jane*," he muttered. "You're not kidding. Maybe I *am* looking for a damsel."

Just then, Gabriel knocked on her bedroom door. "Come on Barbie. It's eight o'clock and Ariel said 8:15." Kendall sighed, looking to Anson.

"Go," he said. "I'm going to stop by my place before heading into the office anyway."

"I don't want to fight," Kendall said softly, walking over to him.

"We're not fighting," he replied. "We're talking. Something I realize we *do* need to do more of."

Anson wrapped his arms around her, Kendall snuggling against his chest.

"Maybe *you're* the damsel," she suggested sweetly. "My damsel."

Anson drew in a deep breath. She smelled incredible; edible.

"I'd appreciate it if you didn't emasculate me in front of me... Unless, of course, that's your way of asking *me* to move into *here*. Turns out: your bed's pretty comfy."

Kendall kissed him. "I'll call you later today, okay?"

"Sure."

As she opened up the bedroom door, a thought occurred to her: "You know? Maybe you're not an incurable nympho, just an incurable romantic."

"You might have something there," he agreed, putting his arm around her waist as they walked out of her room. "Our hearts tend to weep a little longer."

"Like a non-healing diabetic wound?"

"Geez, Kendall. Nice imagery," Anson scoffed.

"Sorry," she said, laughing and leaning further into him.

"Finally!" Gabriel exclaimed with a huff. "It's time to go."

"Hey Gabe," Anson said, as they all walked to the front door.

"Yeah?"

"Can you say you've ever heard of a story where the damsel in distress was a guy and the knight in shining armor was a girl?" Anson asked, Kendall immediately rolling her eyes.

Gabriel looked at him quizzically. "I don't know what you're talking about."

"Exactly," Anson said proudly, looking over at Kendall.

Kendall and Gabriel climbed into Anson's Mercedes, Kendall agreeing the ride was smoother than her Jeep, hence easier on her still healing belly. Anson kissed Kendall through the window frame.

"We'll talk later," Anson said with a telling smile. "Take care of Barbie for me Gabe."

"Hey Gabe," Kendall said quickly, before Anson could step away to his Porsche.

"Yeah?"

"Who takes care of Barbie?" she asked, never taking her eyes off of Anson.

"Ken does," Gabriel answered with a sigh, clearly a line he'd had to answer umpteen times before.

"And who am I?" Kendall continued.

"Ken-dall."

"So who takes care of Barbie?"

"You do," Gabriel answered.

"Exactly," she said with satisfaction.

"Touché," Anson said, shaking his head with a smile. "Love you."

"Love you, too, *sweetums*," Kendall called out the window, blowing Anson a kiss as she backed out of the driveway.

Chapter 16

Tuesday afternoon, Kendall stormed her front door with eager excitement.

"Gabriel!" she shouted upon opening the door. "Gabe, I'm home and I've got big news." She rushed in and out of rooms, each emptier than the last, her excitement quickly fading. "Gabriel: where are you?" She grabbed her phone and it began to ring in her hand.

"Oh my god, Anson!" she answered in a panic. "My brother's not home!"

"That's why I'm calling," he said, his smile evident in his voice. "Don't worry. He's with me. It's funny; I just asked him if he remembered to let you know and–"

"Holy shit! Don't ever do that again! You can't just pick up my brother and not say something!" she yelled into the phone. "What the hell! He's not your brother!"

"Kendall, calm down. That's why I'm calling. He's fine. Everything's fine," Anson quickly rattled off, trying his best to assuage her fears. "He called me earlier and I agreed to come by, but he forgot to let you know."

"*He* called *you*?" Kendall asked doubtfully.

"Yes. *He* called *me*. Why is that so hard to believe? It'd appear that not all *your* people think I eat shit."

"Put him on," Kendall demanded.

"She wants to talk to you," Anson said. "I don't know, man. You might be in the doghouse tonight. I feel for you. Not a fun place to be when it comes to your sister."

Kendall audibly groaned through an eye-roll.

"Hi Kendall," Gabriel said kindly. "Sorry I forgot to call."

"Gabriel. I can't *believe* you didn't tell me where you were going. You know you can't just leave the house without checking in. How'd you get Anson's number, anyway?"

"He gave it to me. You were taking too long to come home."

Aggravated, Kendall groaned again. "Put Anson back on."

"So all is forgiven?" Anson asked lightheartedly.

"Don't. You. *Ever*. Do that again," Kendall said sternly.

"I'm sorry," he answered sincerely. "I actually thought you were aware. I called as soon as I realized you weren't. Gabe mentioned you keep track of him on his phone anyway."

"I do. Well... I usually do. But this afternoon I was busy and I hadn't checked it, so..."

"So, everything's fine," Anson concluded. "I swung by your place after work and we're at my house. Okay? How'd the realtor go?"

Kendall relaxed. "I'll tell you all about it when I come by to get Gabe."

She ended the phone call and sighed with relief, albeit irritated. Immediately she picked up the phone again; this time to share her news.

"Mother! Guess what?" Kendall shouted into the phone.

"What?! What is it?" Elena asked anxiously.

"I got an offer!" she announced — actually screamed. "And not just any offer; an out-of-this-world offer! Mom, you won't believe it. My realtor called me practically hyperventilating on the phone and said I had to come into her office to go over some paperwork. Yesterday she'd been in talks with this lawyer guy representing this mogul guy who saw my home as prime real estate. He does seasonal rentals and wants to act now because he needs it ready come fall! Can you believe it?!"

"Kendall, this is wonderful! So, what? What was the offer?" Elena asked excitedly.

"Way above asking price. Over a hundred thousand."

Elena gasped.

"Did you hear what I said?" Kendall asked.

"Kendall: I can't believe it! It's meant to be. This is all meant to be. You accepted, right?"

"Well, actually, I said I had to discuss it with my family. There's a catch. They want to close on the 13th."

"Of May?" she asked.

"Yes. Two weeks away."

"So you'd have to pack up and move out in two weeks?"

"Exactly," Kendall said.

"Dios mio," Elena mumbled, now understanding the dilemma.

"I know. So what do you think? Do you think I could do it?" Kendall asked, now pacing around her kitchen. "The packing part is a pain in the ass, but I know that can be done. But the place to live. Waiting until school? Leaving my home... Do you think — and to clarify, I'm not asking your permission — but do you think it'd make sense to move in with Anson until school starts?"

Silence.

"Mom?"

"Is he there with you now?" she asked, restrain in her voice. "Is this *his* idea?"

"No, he and Gabe are at his house, probably talking fish tanks or something."

"Kendall," Elena said firmly. "Now is that really appropriate? And I'm not talking about his questionable lifestyle choices influencing Gabriel. You have to consider your brother's feelings. If this relationship between you two doesn't work out, what happens to Gabriel's new friendship?"

"Mom, that's not fair. I don't plan to have Anson just — *poof* — disappear out of my life come fall, and you know it. I might not be marrying him, but he is important to me. If he and Gabe find a common connection? Then, so be it. Actually, it's great and we should encourage it."

Kendall could hear Elena take in a deep breath as she chewed on her thoughts.

"Moving along," Kendall continued, annoyed with her mom's reasoning... and even more so with how well they aligned with her own. "I'm not ready to quit my job yet. So, I'm thinking I can move some of my stuff into storage down south, move the necessities into Anson's place so I can keep working, then hopefully, by the end of July, I'll have found a place near the school and can move it all in there." Kendall waited a moment for a response, then added. "You can't deny the practical sense in it all."

Elena sighed heavily. "I suppose it *is* practical. I just don't want you to suddenly give up on all your dreams because you feel financially set and have this handsome doctor doting on you."

"Mo~m," Kendall nagged, suppressing her laugh. "Is *that* what you're worried about? That I'll become a Stepford wife? An ornamental doll hanging on Anson's arm?"

"Well, I definitely would understand the temptation. But when you put it *that* way... My guess is that Anson, himself, wouldn't even like that."

"Aww," Kendall sighed, smiling. "You *do* think there's good in him, too. You and Ariel. It's like pulling teeth."

"Kendall. That's enough," Elena scolded. "Well, if it's my advice you're looking for, I think you should do it. Despite all the sadness that has occurred in the last year, your acceptance into CRNA school and now the ability to pay for it completely are opportunities I would hate for you to miss out on. You've been pursuing this for years. Dan would have had it no other way and really, neither would I. Accept the offer. Move in with Anson, if you must. Take the money and run. No one can hold you back now, my dear."

***

"Good evening, gentlemen!" Kendall announced as she walked into Anson's home fully recovered from her initial reaction of Anson and Gabriel hanging out together on their own.

But for a second time that evening, she was met with silence.

"Hello?" she called out again, setting her purse down on the counter. She then heard some surround sound rumbling above and realized they were in the *man-cave*.

"There you guys are," she said loudly, opening the door to the lounge upstairs.

Both men peeked over the back of the black leather sofa at her, then returned their focus to the screen: *Star Trek Into Darkness*.

"Seriously?" she asked. "How many times have you two seen this?"

"*Star Trek Beyond* comes out next summer. We're preparing," Gabriel answered.

Anson pushed off the couch, wearing a smile too big for his face, and walked over to Kendall to greet her.

"Hey you," he said softly, pulling her into her arms and kissing her. She smiled against his lips.

"Hey yourself," she said, maintaining their close contact over a series of light, flirty kisses.

"Get a room!" Gabriel called out from behind the couch, never actually looking back at them.

Anson pulled back laughing as Kendall immediately shook her head at her brother.

"So tell me: how'd everything go with the realtor?" Anson asked eager to hear the latest.

Kendall bounced around in giddy excitement. "You won't believe it. Gabe has to hear this as well. I've got some news," she said, walking around the couch to face Gabriel. "Can we pause this a minute, bud?"

Anson paused the movie and took his seat back on the couch, giving her a captive audience.

"I sold the house today!" she squealed. "And the offer blew my asking price out of the water. School's paid for!"

Anson immediately jumped up to hug her, her effervescence bubbling over. "That's great, babe! I'm so happy for you!"

"Awesome!" Gabriel chimed in. "You're moving to Miami now!"

"Not quite yet, Gabe," she said. "I assumed it'd take longer to sell. The original plan was to work through summer. At least through July. So, uh... if your offer still stands..." Kendall smiled sweetly at Anson, her arms wrapping around his waist again. "Need a housemate for the summer?"

"You know I do," Anson said, beaming and taking her face into his hands to kiss her more deeply than before.

Gabriel groaned, both Anson and Kendall enjoying the moment immensely.

"Let's celebrate," Anson whispered into her ear.

The two headed downstairs to the kitchen, Gabriel remaining behind to finish the movie.

"What would you like? Beer, wine?" Anson asked, opening up a beer for himself. Kendall decline, however, her stomach not up to par quite yet.

"When's your appointment? I don't like how long this is going on," Anson said, taking a seat next to her at the counter.

"Thursday."

"Oh. Morning or afternoon?"

"Morning," she said.

"Would you mind joining me at a patient's funeral Thursday afternoon?" he asked almost apologetically. "It was an older gentleman. If you're up to it, of course."

"You really know how to show a girl a good time, don't you?" Kendall teased. "Of course, I will."

Anson held her hands in his. "You have no idea how happy you've made me tonight," he said, kissing her again.

"Well, it's all crazy sudden, so I'm kind of just running with it. Tomorrow the reality of it will settle in and I might not be as excited."

"The reality of living with me?"

"More the reality of leaving my home. I have to be out in two weeks. Dan and I moved into Sandalfoot just after I graduated college. It's been my home my whole adult life."

"Have you ever lived on your own?" Anson asked, reservation heard in his voice.

"No," she answered frankly. "I know. That's why it's something I've been kind of adamant about doing now."

"Stop me at any point, but uh, when did you and Dan get married?"

"It would have been five years this October. He died right before our 4th wedding anniversary. We'd been together ten years."

"Wow. And Sandalfoot was his... mother's home?" he asked, piecing it all together.

"Grandmother's," she said, a peculiar grin following. "How'd you know that?"

"Driving you home from the Hibiscus Ball," he said. "Learned a lot that night."

Kendall shook her head at the memory of her drunken debacle.

"Oh shit," she said suddenly. "That reminds me. I have a coffee date with Leo tomorrow."

"You've got to be kidding me," Anson groaned.

"No, I'm serious. I set it up last week." Kendall laughed awkwardly, pulling up her calendar on her phone. "See? *Coffee with Leo at 10am.*"

"Why the hell would you set that up? Last week? You were in the hospital last week."

"It was right when I got out. I canceled the meet-up we had last week and said I was sick and made it for this week. Anson, it's no biggie. It's all school related."

"I don't like it," he said matter-of-factly, drinking back a large portion of his beer. "And I think it's totally within my rights not to like it."

"You want me to cancel it?" she asked.

"Yes," he said. "You got into school all on your own and you don't need his assistance to help prepare you. It's just his excuse to get close to you."

"I'll cancel it if you feel that strongly about it, but you're wrong about his excuse to get close. I was the one who suggested meeting up in the first place."

"Was that before or after you hooked up at the Ball?" Anson snidely asked.

"Are we really going to do this again? Hash out *that* night?"

Anson rubbed his face and turned to face her.

"Kendall: He filled out an application for AAXLS years ago. He knows about me. I refused him a job due to the conflict of interest. He's been bitter ever since. But everyone who interviews signs a nondisclosure prior to meeting with me. I wasn't given enough information before I granted him an interview."

Kendall was shocked.

"Leo? An escort?" she asked with disbelief.

"He never was. Well, at least not with AAXLS."

She stared straight ahead, mulling over the possibility of it all for a minute.

"No," she bizarrely concluded. "I don't believe it. Not *everyone* I know is a closeted escort. At some point, I call bullshit."

Anson sighed. "He wasn't an escort. He looked into becoming one. For extra cash. That's all. The whole Johnson thing, I'll admit, is a wild coincidence. But I can't think of any other possible connections between you and my current and/or former escorts."

"DeGraff?"

Anson laughed. "No."

"Talon?"

"He wishes."

"No one else at the hospital?"

"Definitely not," he said. "Again: conflict of interest."

"Have you ever been hired by someone you knew?" Kendall boldly asked.

Anson looked over at her, putting his beer back down on the counter. "In those cases, I'd arrange for a different escort."

"So, you knew who they were, but they never found out who you were?" she asked.

"Yes. There's a screening process before they select you. Not all the escorts work this way, though. I did because of my profession. Last several years I rarely took on new clients. Just made it easier."

"Okay that's enough," Kendall suddenly announced. She smiled awkwardly.

Anson stood up from his stool, kissing her on the forehead, and walked around the counter back to the refrigerator. "Had you eaten anything tonight?" he asked. "We ordered pizza earlier. It's upstairs."

"I noticed that. But I'm good. I ate at my place. Actually, we should get going. Gabriel's got an early morning tomorrow anyway. He's going out on the boat with some friends."

"He mentioned that. So, what are your plans?" he asked casually, opening up another beer.

"You mean, now that I won't be having coffee with a friend?" she asked snootily, Anson giving her a grievous look. "I suppose the only thing left to do: pack up the house."

"I have two surgeries scheduled and then I'll be done. I'll come over afterward to help out. Don't overdo it with the packing."

"I'll leave the heavy-lifting to you," she said with a smile. "Can you believe this is really happening?"

Anson smiled. "Exactly what I hoped for."

"Movie's over," Gabriel announced as he plodded down the stairs.

"Perfect timing then," Kendall said. "We should get going. You have an early start tomorrow. Bob said he'd come over around seven in the morning."

"Yup. Early bird gets the fish," Gabriel said with a smile. He walked over to the front door.

"Hey," Kendall called over to him, getting up from her stool. "Shouldn't you say goodbye to Anson?"

"I thought he was coming back to your place," Gabriel said confused.

"Not tonight. Early day for me as well. I'll be in the OR before you even step on the boat."

"Well, in that case: thanks for the pizza, *Aces*," he said, immediately laughing.

"*Aces*?" Kendall repeated, looking to Anson. "My, oh my. Aren't you two besties now?"

"He doesn't like *Triple A*, so we had to come up with something better," Gabriel explained. "*Aces* and *G-Force*!"

Kendall laughed out loud as Anson bowed his head rather coyly. "You mean *Double A*," she said, assumingly, still laughing.

"Anson Axel All-away. Three A's," Gabriel corrected her.

"What?" she asked, quickly making eye contact with Anson.

"You told him about AAXLS?"

"Axel," Anson repeated quickly, walking over to her with hushed reservation. "A-X-E-L. It's my middle name."

Kendall's expression fell blank. "Your middle name is Axel?"

"And I didn't even tell her," Gabriel proudly pointed out.

"Hmm," Kendall mumbled to herself, lost in thought.

"What?" Anson asked, studying her expression.

"So, the business? It really *is* your pet project. Not Xavier's," she concluded. "It's your namesake. Definitely something you wouldn't give up easily, right?"

Anson's shoulders sank as he watched the wheels turn in her head. "Don't overanalyze this one, Kendall."

"I'm not. It's just an interesting observation, that's all." She moved methodically toward the front door where Gabriel stood waiting, not following their conversation at all.

"I'm curious now. What's Talon's middle name?"

"Uh... Xander," he answered. "And Gary's is Alexander. We had a grandfather named Alexander. All my mother's siblings have incorporated his name somehow into their children's names. Their family tradition, I guess."

Kendall smiled. "Oh. And they didn't want to pick *Alex* for yours?"

"My mother felt it was a nickname. Didn't stand alone. *Axel*, however, does. But it's like two first names. Two powerhouse first names. Doesn't exactly roll off the tongue."

Kendall smiled. "You've got a complex over your middle name."

Anson shrugged. "Guess we never really outgrow our insecurities, do we? So: are we good?" he asked, pushing her thoughts past the business.

"Yeah, we're good," she said, kissing him goodnight. "Thanks for hanging out with Gabe tonight."

"Anytime. Right, Gabe?"

"You bet!" Gabriel answered, meeting Anson with a fist-bump.

"Later, *Aces*," Kendall said, flirtatiously, as they exited the door.

"No. That's not yours," Anson said insistently.

"Fine. Love you, Anson."

"Love you, too, Kendall."

Chapter 17

Despite his first surgery taking an extra hour, Anson managed to leave GC General before four in the afternoon. He couldn't be sure if Gabriel would be back at Kendall's place, but he aimed to beat him there. The anticipation of Kendall moving in had him grinning like a fool. The thought of spending some time alone with her had him nearly pitching a tent in his scrubs. The need was getting desperate once again.

After knocking a few times on her front door, Anson finally opened it. Mazzy Star's *Fade into You* lazily swirled around the home, filling every corner and suffocating any semblance of foreplay he'd hoped to introduce to their afternoon. Various empty boxes were strewn about in the living room; not a single thing packed away in them. He hesitantly made his way to her bedroom, wary of getting involved. The song finished and Third Eye Blind's *Deep Inside of You* began, picking up the same heavy weight of the last one.

Kendall sat cross-legged in front of her walk-in closet with a box of memories scattered around her: letters, greeting cards, pictures, and souvenir items. Next to her was a large box of men's clothing. She was wearing an over-sized man's dress shirt, her hair pulled back in a messy bun, a letter balancing on her bare knee. As Anson came into view from around her bedroom door she looked up at him. Her cheeks were damp; her green eyes puffy and red. Words failed Anson as he switched gears.

"The first time we ever had sex was to this song," Kendall said quietly, almost with amusement. "Kind of clichéd, I suppose: *Deep Inside of You.*"

Anson forced a smile and moved further into the room toward her. He slowly took a seat on the floor in front of the keepsakes that highlighted her private relationship with Dan. There was so little he actually knew about them. He picked up a chain with a pair of dogtags and looked them over. Kendall laughed softly.

"From my bachelorette party," she said.

Anson read the tags to himself, smiling.

Firemen have big hoses.

Practice safe sex: Sleep with a firefighter.

"You okay?" he asked, putting the tags back down on the floor.

"Yeah. I'll be fine." She took in a cleansing breath. "Reminiscing. Gets me every time. I was first sorting through things, but then it ended up like this."

She picked up a remote next to her and aimed it at the receiver in the front of her room. Sheryl Crow's *Strong Enough* began and she rolled her eyes admitting defeat.

"I suppose the soundtrack is not helping," she said. She looked down at the letter on her lap and held it up. "Actually, his letter reminded me to look for something."

"Letter?" Anson asked.

She handed him the letter.

"I got this at Dan's celebration of life last month. Everyone at Station 9 writes these letters. It's their tradition. You never think you'll actually get one, though."

Anson took the letter and glanced down at it. He looked back at Kendall, as if asking permission.

"Go ahead. Read it," she said.

Dear Kendall,

"The only fire he can't put out is the one he started in my heart." I saw this bumper sticker on Jason's wife's car last week. I pictured you gagging at it. I'm fairly certain no bumper of yours will ever have this on it. And I'm okay with that. You make me laugh.

It hasn't even been a year and your dad still doesn't really know the extent of us, but I'm fairly certain I will never have to write another one of these letters to another woman for as long as I live. I could never love someone else as much as I love you right now. I've never felt something so intense. I worry about scaring you off. Proposing marriage too soon. Wanting a family with you. Frankly, it's scaring me. I'd elope tomorrow.

I hope you're at least 80 when you read this and that I died in my sleep after overdosing on Viagra, keeping you satisfied. But, in the off chance that I left you far too early and you've got a lot of living yet to live, I hope you do it. And that you do it all.

If I die before we have sex again (that's just cruel and would be sufficient evidence to denounce the existence of God), I hope you continue to have sex. And great sex. I'll never be that person that denies someone life, even in my own death. Sex makes life great. And sex with you is better than anything I've ever known.

If I die before I hear you say, "I love you," again (no sweeter words were ever spoken), I hope you find someone to say them to again. I never understood butterflies and swooning until falling in love with you. If I'm dead, you need to experience that feeling again and give it to someone else. Love makes life great. And love with you is better than anything I've ever known.

If I die before we get married (I know we will), I hope you do marry someday. You seem to want to, even though you talk about it like it's the institution. I think we'd be a pretty awesome married couple, showing everyone how it's done. It'd be an adventure. Adventures make life great. And adventures with you are better than anything I've ever known.

But whatever you might do after I'm dead and gone, make sure you're happy doing it. You deserve all the happiness — not someone else's happiness, but your own. You're not here to make sure you only do right by your mom, your dad, or your brother. Think of you. Your life should be happy. And seeing you happy is better than anything I've ever known.

I love you, Kendall. I apologize for dying on you. I'll try not to in my next life. I'll see you again. I'm sure of it.

Dan

Anson looked up from the letter at Kendall. He smiled thoughtfully. "He said it well. When did he write this?"

"His second year at Station 9, around 25 years old. He started writing letters to Gabriel that year as well. He drafted a new one to him every year. He always told me about it. But I never asked about my letter. I didn't like to think about it."

"Makes sense," Anson said.

"Funny how he never wanted to change it. Don't you think? A lot happened between the time he wrote this and the time he died. When I first read it, I was a little angry with him. Like I wanted to hear what he had to say now. You know?"

Anson nodded again. "But I suppose when you're pretty sure you said all the right things the first time around, you don't feel the need to improve upon them. So what was it that you were looking for?"

"His book about reincarnation," she said, now laughing lightly. "His last line. I'm wondering what he could have come back as if it were real. He wasn't religious. Or even spiritual, really. But he liked the idea of reincarnation."

"Do you believe in it?" Anson asked.

"Never did... But I want to." She picked up various items in front of her, looking them over briefly then putting them back down. "But during my search I fell down the rabbit hole of cards and little things we picked up at travel stops. You know: all the inside jokes we shared that only have meaning with him."

Sade's *By Your Side* now played and Anson couldn't help but laugh. "You're torturing yourself with this soundtrack."

"I know," she said, sitting up tall as if to stretch out of her brooding mood.

"Is this what he listened to as well?"

"Oh god, no," she said, shaking her head vehemently. "He definitely was an edgier alternative rock guy. Couldn't stand most of my pop hits. But he had a softer side. He was a romantic at heart. Case and point: he loved leaving me cards and poems for no reason at all. Maybe it goes with the persona. Tough guy exterior, mush interior."

"That's probably true of most men who are in love. We're all suckers in the end. So, he was a poet?" he asked, delving a little deeper into the exalted world of *Dan*.

"A *roses are red, violets are blue*, kind of poet. If he tried too hard and got all sappy, I never reacted very well. What can I say? I'm a cynic," she admitted, smiling. But then she frowned. "I'm kind of a bitch, aren't I?"

"No. Not at all. You're the classic tough exterior, mush interior. You just have a very thick exterior that takes an exceptionally long time to chip away at." Anson smiled and grabbed a hold of her hand. "I guess, guys like Dan and I thrive on that sort of challenge."

Kendall's eyes glistened as tears threatened again. "What if he never knew how much I really loved him?" she whispered.

Anson quickly gathered Kendall into his arms as she sobbed. She cried hard for a few minutes; her body shaking in his embrace and his heart swelling, then breaking with each stifled breath she took.

Suddenly she inhaled loudly, collecting herself, and pulled away from him. "What time is it?" she asked, pushing up to her knees to see the clock on the other side of the bed. "Gabriel will be home any minute. I have to put this all away."

She stood and gathered up the items, boxing them up to shelve the emotions for another day. She rapidly undressed, discarding Dan's dress shirt back into the box, and redressed in her yoga pants and tank top.

"You know what?" she then said, switching gears completely. "Actually, I'm going to go for a quick run. Nothing big. I think that's part of what's been missing for me these last couple of weeks. I run regularly and haven't done it at all. Something short. I'm feeling fine. I see the doctor tomorrow. I'll just do a couple of miles or something. Hang out here in case Gabe arrives and I'll be done in like 15 minutes. Okay?"

She left Anson with no choice of rebuttal. She was out the front door and running away down the street in no time.

***

By Thursday afternoon, Kendall had cleared out her guest bedroom. That morning she had met their mom halfway to drop off Gabriel, before heading into her follow-up doctor appointment in Broward. Once home on her own again, she was determined to plow through the next phase of packing up Sandalfoot Lane without falling apart at the seams.

AA: **Almost done here. I'll pick you up in about an hour.**

KM: **For what?**

AA: **The funeral. Still willing to go?**

KM: **Forgot about it. Cleaning house. I can be ready in an hour.**

AA: **Everything go well at your appt?**

KM: **It appears all is healing well on the outside.**

AA: **Outside? Did you ask about the nausea?**

KM: **She said my hormones are still elevated. Can be for six weeks. Yay.**

AA: **Sorry babe.**

"You really look beautiful," Anson said again just before he and Kendall exited his Porsche at the Boynton Beach funeral home. Kendall had showered and put on a simple black dress.

"Thank you. You don't need to keep doing that. I *am* fine. Yesterday was just that initial shock of moving on... once again. That's all."

131

They quietly walked through the parking lot toward the entrance.

"I'm taking you out tomorrow night," Anson said. "A night on the town, okay?"

"I thought it was my choice. Stay in or go out."

"You *want* to choose *out*. Believe me. You'll love it."

"I was leaning toward staying in. Maybe boxing up some more stuff and starting the move."

"On your birthday?" he asked.

"Well, I'm running out of time here. This weekend is busy with Ariel. Next week I have to go into work to set up my return date."

"Wait. When are you returning?" he asked, forgetting she was to get her clearance at the appointment today.

"After Ariel's wedding. I'm accepting a night shift position back in neuro ICU."

"Really? You're going back to neuro?" Anson asked with surprise. "That's great. We'll be working a little closer then. Just like before."

Kendall then stopped before they entered the funeral home. Not realizing it, Anson awkwardly turned around, smiling at a few funeral guests as he backtracked to her.

"What's up?" he asked.

"When did you exactly notice me?" she asked, her mind clicking into overdrive.

"Notice you? I'm not following."

"Talon mentioned that you noticed me before Dan died. When did you notice me?"

Anson pulled her off to the side of the walkway.

"I've always been attracted to you on some level. You're a hot nurse with a sharp tongue. There's no real secret there."

"Yes, but why would you randomly mention that to Talon?" she asked, pressing him further.

"I'm not sure what you're getting at here, but I never had a real conversation about you until after the FFN."

"Why would he have said that?"

"Because he wondered if I had any prospects at work."

"Client prospects?" she asked, clearly disgusted at the idea.

"No, no. Relationship-wise. What is this? Why is it that I always seem to be on trial with you?"

"Sometimes I feel like I'm falling into your laid-out plans a little too well."

Anson looked at her quizzically. "Kendall. I had nothing to do with Dan's death."

"For fuck's sake, Anson," she said, a little loud for his tastes. "Dan died from a building collapse. You think I think you orchestrated that?"

"No. But if you're suggesting that I was happy to hear about his death so I could make my move, you need to stop right now. You're battling another level of grief and I know it's being brought on by the house sale. But don't go down this road of pushing me away simply to feel less guilty about moving on. If you need to wait out here, I completely understand. I'll offer my condolences and be out in five minutes."

Kendall lowered her eyes regretfully. "I'm sorry," she said, exhaling. "You're right. I just get these thoughts, is all. Like you're too good to be true and things are working out so well..."

"Don't apologize." He pulled her in close, kissing the top of her head. "I understand it all. And I'll help you through it. That's why we work well together. Remember? We *know*."

Kendall took in a breath and together they walked back up to the entrance.

"So, I'm taking you out tomorrow," he concluded. "It's settled. Sometimes you need to let others just take control for your own good."

Inside the funeral home they navigated their way around; Anson holding Kendall's hand as he searched for a familiar face. Kendall felt more or less comfortable in the funeral home, considering Dan's funeral service took place at the firehouse.

A casket adorned with a folded American flag, the deceased a veteran of the Korean War, sat at the front of the viewing room. They made a quick circle, Anson entering his Dr. Allaway mode upon spotting the wife of his former patient. They spoke briefly, a sympathetic embrace exchanged, and then he and Kendall made their way out of the crowd.

"Oh god," Kendall mumbled under her breath.

"What?" Anson asked.

"It's my neighbor, Carolyn. She owns this funeral home. And another one in Lake Worth. She's crazy. Cat-lady crazy. I'm surprised you haven't met her yet, considering she makes it her job to know everything about everyone along our dirt road. Let's get out of here before she spots us."

Just as Anson pushed open the door for Kendall to escape, Kendall's name was called out abruptly, albeit quietly.

"Carolyn," Kendall said, greeting the woman with a friendly smile and quick hug. "I wasn't sure if this was your funeral home or if it was the one in Lake Worth."

"Aww, honey, we've had the two forever now. You must have known that. My brother runs the Lake Worth one and this one is all me."

"Oh. That's wonderful. I was just heading out. I came with my boyfriend, Dr. Allaway," Kendall said, stepping aside to introduce him to the woman. "He was Mr. Hubert's doctor. This is Carolyn O'Keeley. She lives two doors down from me on Sandalfoot."

"Nice to meet you," Anson said, extending a warm handshake. "I hate to cut this short, but we do need to get going, my dear." He gave Kendall's hand a telling squeeze.

Kendall smiled graciously. "Right. He's got some work to do," she added. "I'll see you on the Lane."

"Dr. Allaway?" Carolyn said curiously. "Are their multiple Dr. Allaways in this area?"

"Not that I'm aware of," Anson answered.

"So why are you moving out exactly?" she asked to Kendall.

"I sold the house and will be attending school in Miami," Kendall answered, not understanding Carolyn's line of thought.

"But you bought it?" she then asked of Anson.

Kendall began to laugh. "What? Anson didn't buy the house. It'll be a seasonal property. Some real estate mogul guy bought it through his lawyer."

"Oh. My mistake," she said, backpedaling. "I had done a little research as soon as I saw that it sold. The name that came up as the buyer was an *Allaway*. I was told he was a physician of sorts. Perhaps they just knew you were associated with Kendall. What a coincidence that would have been, right?"

Kendall turned sharply to Anson, who was already laughing at the suggestion. "I wish I'd thought of that. It is a great piece of property."

"Well, I'm sure you have something better anyway," Carolyn said with syrupy sweetness. "What kind of doctor did you say you were?"

"Gastro-guy. I do colonoscopies all day long. Look me up should you need one. Oh, I believe someone might need your help," Anson said, diverting Carolyn's attention to a guest searching for the restroom.

Anson and Kendall walked out into the parking lot together in silence. Anson, however, moved with a chipper confidence, lightly swinging Kendall's hand back and forth as they strolled along. He then brought her hand up to his lips.

"Thanks for doing that with me. Where to now? I know I have to work in the morning, but do you want to come over? Stay at my place tonight? We can do a movie and order-in. These last few nights have been kind of lonely without you."

They made it to the Porsche, Kendall noting his *AA007* tag on the *Endless Summer* vanity plate as she always did.

"How much do you make in a year?" she asked, walking to her side of the vehicle.

Surprised at the question, Anson paused before opening his door. He looked over the car roof at her. "Didn't think you were interested in that."

"I'm not, really. But clearly it's more than the average neurosurgeon, right?" Kendall got into the car, forcing Anson to follow.

He started up the vehicle, continuing the conversation hopeful to not make it into a debate. "Well, the average neurosurgeon probably has a few more mouths to feed than I, so the comparison isn't exactly on point."

"Plus you have AAXLS. That's got to be lucrative, right?" she said, looking down at her phone as Anson drove in the hot seat.

"Where are you going with this?" he asked, annoyed.

"If you wanted: Could you buy my house? Afford it no problem?" she asked, glancing over at him.

Anson kept his eyes focused on the road, contemplating his next words very carefully.

"Yes. If I wanted."

"Did you?" she asked, needing a direct answer. "Did you buy my house?"

"No. Satisfied? Will you be staying over at my place tonight? *Our* place soon enough?"

"No. I have a lot to do if I'm ever going to make this closing on time."

Chapter 18

"Actually, he's making it like a proper date. Formal, really. He's been rather insistent on the whole thing since I agreed," Kendall explained to Ariel over the phone. "Personally, I think he's overdoing it. It's not a major birthday and I'm dressed like I'm going to the Oscars and it's only five o'clock."

"Oh come on, Kendall. Everyone likes to be wined and dined every now and then. Even plain-Jane *you*."

"Of course I do. I love it. But, uh, something tells me he's trying too hard."

"What do you mean?" Ariel asked.

"Well, last week he had wanted to go to the Keys, but then this idea that that's my place with Dan got into his head. And then there was a conversation about Dan being a romantic at heart and I feel like he's trying to prove himself. Cater to the flowery side of me or something. And then..." Kendall fell silent.

"What?" Ariel asked eagerly.

"Well, the whole house sale and the incentive to move out in two weeks. Something's off about it."

"Kendall. What are you getting at? Do you think Anson had something to do with your house selling so fast?"

There was a considerable pregnant pause of thought — enough to get Ariel wound right up.

"Holy shit! He bought your house, didn't he?!" Ariel asked.

"No! Well... Actually. I'm not sure. The thought never even entered my mind until..."

"Until what? Kendall!"

"Until the funeral we attended last night," Kendall said, silently cursing herself for verbalizing her thoughts before getting any concrete evidence.

"Why? What happened?"

"My neighbor was the funeral director–"

"The nosy one?"

"Yeah, and she said a doctor named *Allaway* was the actual buyer of the home."

"No. Way."

"Yes," Kendall said, slightly annoyed now. "But he was right there because she didn't know him and he laughed it off, denying it completely. I didn't bring it up again and neither did he. We ate dinner at my place and then he left."

Ariel was silent for a moment and Kendall took it as an opportunity.

"Okay, so," Kendall continued. "You chew on that, but I have to go. He'll be here any minute. I'll give you a call tomorrow when I'm ready to head down to Miami."

She took in a deep breath and startled upon hearing a knock at the door.

Kendall opened the door, Anson looking up to see her as her figure came into view, and time stood still momentarily. Her transformation from nearly two weeks of yoga pants and T-shirts — and prior to that scrubs and ponytails — to a stunning, all-black sheath halter dress rendered him speechless for what felt like an eternity. She was breathtaking.

Surprisingly, Kendall's hesitancies vanished the minute she got caught in his stare. His attention was a nectar of the gods and she dined willingly. Instantly, she exuded the posh confidence she'd hoped to capture while wearing the dress.

"Looking very sharp there, Double O Seven. I must say, if the whole neurosurgeon thing doesn't work out, GQ will definitely take you." Kendall playfully growled, finally eliciting a response from his stunned expression.

"Kendall," he said, his voice nearly a whisper as he shook his head in awe. "Double O Seven maybe, but *you*, this dress. *This* goes beyond Bond girl. Damn." He sighed, finally looking up to meet her eyes. "Seriously, you look incredible. Gorgeous. Really. I'm speechless."

Kendall bowed her head as her cheeks heated up.

"Well, thank you," she said shyly, her modesty ultimately shining through.

"Happy Birthday, babe," he said, stepping up to her and softly kissing the corner of her mouth, careful not to smudge her makeup. He held his cheek against hers and inhaled deeply. "I almost don't want to take you out now."

Kendall smiled, then turned to lock the door, eliciting a rather conspicuous groan from Anson.

"What?" she asked, turning her head to look back at him.

He clutched his chest dramatically.

"The *back*! Or rather, *your* back. You! This dress. Kendall! You're killing me. Fuck me, I'm a very lucky man."

"Okay, *Romeo*. Let's go." She rolled her eyes at him, propelling the flirtatious force around them by dragging her finger under his chin as she sashayed out to the driveway where a black limo sat idling.

"Oh. Wow." Kendall stopped in her tracks, the sight completely unexpected.

"Told you: we're doing it up tonight."

Anson slid his hand across her exposed back and around the curve of her hip as the driver opened up the back door. Kendall carefully got in, gathering the train of her dress into the swank interior of the limo.

Once headed south on I-95, after a simple toast to the evening with the chilled bottle of champagne he'd prepared, Anson directed all his charming attention to Kendall.

"So, did I mention I like your choice of attire?" His gaze dipped down to her exposed leg along the high slit, hinting at the thoughts behind his words.

"You know what?" she replied excitedly. "We should take a picture. I know it's not the full effect since we're sitting in a car and all, but before my makeup fades and the hair falls flat, I want a picture of us looking all fancy."

She smiled at Anson and slid toward the middle to get closer to him. He obliged and stretched his arm around her. Kendall extended her arm out to frame their faces for the perfect selfie.

"Would you just smile," she demanded, reprimanding him as he conspicuously looked down at her chest several times over. "You have all night to check those out."

Immediately he laughed and she took a picture.

"Perfect," she concluded, making a move back to her side of the vehicle. But Anson stopped her, gently pulling her in closer next to him.

"Hold up. I want a pic, too." After another successful selfie and both pleased with the pictures, Anson looked at her. "That's our first picture together, isn't it?"

"I suppose it is... Well, sort of," Kendall answered impishly. "I've got a couple of my own."

"I've got a handful of pictures of you, as well. But I'm talking as a couple," Anson clarified.

"I know. I have my own pics of *us*."

"What pictures?" he asked, now very curious.

Kendall moved back to her side of the limo and smiled to herself. "You're not the only one with secrets."

He eyed her suspiciously.

"You didn't know they were taken," she admitted.

"What? You know I'd have taken any number of pictures with you."

"I know. But these were taken kind of *before* we agreed to be a real thing."

"Oh, so when I was a mere sex god to you?" he asked, his eyes teasing her.

Kendall laughed. "Sure. That phase."

"So, show them to me."

Kendall looked down at her phone and began to scroll through her pictures. Then a smile stretched across her face and he knew she'd found one. He quickly moved over, Kendall pulling the phone from his line of sight.

"What?" he asked.

"Well. I don't want you thinking I'm some sort of creeper person or that–"

"Kendall. Just show me the damn picture."

She hesitated, messing around with him until he snatched the phone from her hands. He looked down at the screen, a soft smile emerging. As he quietly studied the picture, the whole mood around them shifted. In the picture, he was fast asleep, holding Kendall against his chest in her bed. Her delicate smile, happily held in his embrace, and his peaceful expression as he slept next to her — all together it depicted something intimately greater than just sex. But sleeping over hadn't happened until after the hospital stay.

"When was this?" he asked, still respecting the serenity captured in the picture.

"That first week we really started hooking up. After your trip to Miami," Kendall said.

"So, after the *hot-spot*?" he asked, so much of their relationship now defined by that moment. He paused to think back.

"Yeah. Remember the last week in March? You came over every night, staying later and later, but I always kicked you out?"

"Maddie was staying with me that week."

"Oh yeah. That's right. That's when you almost said you loved me. I took this picture the night before."

"What? I didn't say that," he denied, smiling dismissively. "Not that week. It was too early on."

"Yes, *that* week," Kendall said insistently. "Like week one. Talk about a sap."

"More like week four!" he protested.

"We weren't making a go of any of it that whole first month," Kendall fired back, laughing.

"Well, I didn't say anything preemptively. Not that week, at least," he said, a sly smile tugging at the corner of his mouth.

"We'd been talking about your niece over the phone and when you were hanging up, you almost said you love me. But you caught yourself."

Anson's smile grew, Kendall's growing with it as he tried to recall how he felt that night. "Well, whatever. So, you took this picture, then kicked me out?"

"Pretty much," she said smartly.

"Typical. Even though by the looks of it, *you* seemed pretty smitten with me."

Kendall shrugged. "Well sure. I wanted to capture how it felt being held by the infamous Dr. Allaway... while needing to kick you out all at the same time, of course."

"Of course," he said, leaning over to kiss her hand. "So, let's see the second picture."

"Oh, well that one I didn't even take, but I'm glad I have it."

Kendall scrolled through her phone again and held it up to Anson.

"We're at work," he stated obviously. "Who took this?"

"Courtney," Kendall said. "She took it that week sometime. She already had an idea about us, but I convinced her it wasn't romantic. I guess she saw us in the hall one day talking and snapped a pic. Then she sent it to me like it was proof of a romantic relationship."

"That's pretty ballsy of her," he said irritated. "What: was she trying to blackmail you?"

"Oh goodness, no," Kendall insisted, immediately dismissing the notion. "You don't know Courtney. That's her. Innocently inappropriate. Besides. I like the picture. I have two pictures of us that really capture how we know each other."

"Sex and work?"

"You know it," she said, smiling.

Anson looked at the picture again and a proud smile surfaced. In the picture he was tenderly grasping the underside of her elbow. It did look romantic. Before he was allowed to be romantic… especially at work.

"What?" Kendall asked.

"I remember this: what I was thinking in this picture."

"You do not," Kendall said, taking the phone back to look at the picture once again, even though she'd analyzed it many times before.

"Yes, I do. I was getting a little antsy for some action."

"You're always getting a little antsy," she said dryly.

"No. Seriously. Check out my scrubs. I'm wearing OR scrubs and I didn't have any surgeries that day. And I remember that because I specifically took note of the scrub top you were wearing that day. It's the one that accentuates your tits, isn't it?"

Kendall began laughing. "Anson!"

"It is," he said confidently. "Believe me. I know."

"Maybe."

"See, I've noticed a thing or two about you for some time now, Nurse Matthews. But that day, you didn't wear your typical undershirt. You were flaunting the girls, weren't you?"

"What?!"

"You can play coy all you want, but I've studied you," he said, his wolfish grin proudly on display.

"Maybe I didn't have time to put it on that morning," she said playfully. "Someone was messing up my sleep patterns."

"Did you ever fantasize about me at work? You know: plot out a hook-up spot?" he asked, a clear thirst for answers.

"Wouldn't you like to know?"

"I would," he said, turning toward her completely. "Hey, I did all the time. No judgment from me."

Kendall rolled her eyes at him. "Says the nympho."

"Well," Anson began, settling into his story despite her resistance to exchange fantasies. "I had worn my scrubs to work that day with the sole intention of fucking you somewhere in the hospital."

Kendall's eyes widened.

"So, the thought was: scrubs would be easy to change out of if I had to. But then I saw you — and your prominently displayed tits —

and I knew: I wouldn't be satisfied until I saw my jizz covering your chest and sliding deep into your scrub top."

Her mouth dropped open at the blunt phrasing of his thoughts.

Anson grinned with salacious confidence.

"So, in this picture, I was trying to determine if you had access to hospital scrubs. I was battling whether or not I'd be able to just let the money-shot go or if I'd be okay with making you angry."

She stared at Anson momentarily, then shook her head clear. "Wait. So, the thought of, maybe *no* sex at work, didn't ever cross your mind instead?"

"After a visual like that goes running through my head? No way."

"Yeah, but we didn't do that. And I don't remember having a conversation even remotely close to that."

"Of course I didn't say, '*Let's go fuck in the men's locker room so I can come all over your tits.*' I have some level of couth."

"Do you now?"

Anson smiled at her, Kendall shaking her head and fighting back her own amusement.

"I asked you what would happen if you had to change at work," he said confidently. "You don't remember?"

Kendall eyed him closely again, then looked back at the picture. "No."

"I bet you I'm hard in the picture."

She immediately zoomed in on the crotch of his pants. "Holy shit. Really? I can't tell at this angle."

"So... what fantasy would you want to try out when you return to work?" he asked cautiously, fighting back his smile.

Kendall looked at him suspiciously.

"Come on, babe," he pleaded sweetly. "Have a little fun. Rekindle those first impressions. Fantasies at work. Tell me just one. And don't try to deny having them because you know damn well you thought the same way when we first got together."

"Well," she began, relaxing back. "Of course I thought about it a lot then. I'm the one who plotted out the FFN with you. And then it was like the night kept happening. So, there wasn't much else to think of. You're the all-powerful Dr. Allaway."

She glanced over at him. He lightly chewed on his bottom lip hungry for the boost to his ego. She had to admit: it was kind of cute.

And they definitely hadn't been addressing that side of their relationship the past few days.

"So I was fucking you at night and taking orders from you during the day," she continued. "It was kind of hard *not* to fantasize about you while at work. Sometimes I'd be charting and start thinking about you and..." She laughed softly. "Well, this one time I had to take a break to get myself back on track because I was getting so worked up. After that, I had an extra pair of panties in my bag just in case..." Kendall stopped and looked directly at Anson, his breath obviously held, desperate for her next words.

"In case of what?" he asked, never taking his eyes off hers.

Kendall laughed, her cheeks rosy with embarrassment. "You know: I always pictured you going down on me in that conference room outside the unit."

Anson's eyes lit up. "On the table in there?"

"Actually, against the door. Practically speaking, I have to plan to block anyone from entering."

"Eating you out while you stood above me?" he whispered, his mind rapidly piecing together a visual.

She nodded shyly.

Anson adjusted himself in his seat, clearing benefiting from the conversation in more ways than one.

"So you'd be sitting on my face, right?" he asked, his blue eyes sparkling with wicked delight.

Kendall looked out the tinted window, too exposed to face him straight on. She took in a deep breath.

"Were you really thinking all of *that* — a money shot and messing up my top — when this picture was taken?" she asked timidly.

"Honestly?" he asked, the amusement in his voice instantly deepening the color of her face as she whipped her attention back to him. "No. I have no fucking clue what we were talking about in that picture. But you can be damned sure: I'm thinking of a whole hell of a lot more right now."

She reached out and pushed him hard in the shoulder. "You're such an ass," she scolded, her face now beet red.

Anson erupted in laughter. "Oh Kendall, come on. Don't stop because of that. Tell me what you did that day on your break. Did you touch yourself?"

Kendall flipped him the middle finger and he laughed even more.

"Did you use that finger?" he boldly asked, teasing her further. But she ignored him completely. "Okay, okay. I'm sorry. That was a dirty trick," he said, moving closer to her side of the limo and putting his arm around her.

"*I* should be the one laughing on *my* birthday," she complained. "Did you plan that all out to get me talking?"

"Babe. There's nothing to be ashamed of. I think about sex with you, day and night. And there hasn't been much of anything lately. I'm a patient man; but after a few days I get a one-tracked mind. I'm just trying to gauge when and where I might be getting it next."

"Well, it's still not happening for a while," she said brusquely.

"I know, but once we're in the same bed together, we can start fooling around again, right? Like last weekend? When were you thinking I should book the moving van?" he asked.

Kendall looked down at her phone and took a minute to collect her thoughts on the topic of moving.

"I'm not sure yet. I was thinking of asking for an extension on the closing date," she said casually, then glanced up at him to analyze his reaction.

Anson leaned away from her to get a full view.

"Wait. What? How long?" he asked.

"Until school starts."

"That's the whole summer. Kendall: Closing dates are not like extensions on leases. I thought the point for the buyer was to get it ready to be a seasonal rental."

"That's what I was told. But really, what's the rush? It's summer, not the season at all–"

"Exactly. That's when seasonal owners do all their work on their rentals. In. The. Summer. It makes perfect sense. What about the extra money incentive?"

"What about it? Sandalfoot is also my home. Money doesn't buy that kind of memory and I'm not sure I'm ready to give it up just for a few extra thousand."

"A few thousand? It's an extra hundred grand. Kendall: the house is worth nowhere near that. It's for quick turnover. An offer like that won't come again."

"Then maybe it's not meant to be," she said sharply.

Anson sat back in his seat, reeling in his reaction.

"Financially," he began again, his voice considerably calmer now, "it makes sense to take the offer. It puts you ahead of the game. For everything. For school *and* the upcoming years ahead."

"I know. That's why I'm just *thinking* about it. I was going to make my decision on Monday."

Anson had so many questions he wanted to ask her, but he held back, fearing an unnecessary fight, resulting in a failed night out.

"My goodness," Kendall said, pushing them past the tension. She looked out the window again to determine where they were. "Where are we headed?"

"Miami," he said gruffly, although he welcomed the subject change.

"Really? Well, you should have said something. I'll be heading here tomorrow again. I could have packed my bag and stayed over."

"I was hoping you'd stay with me, though."

"Of course I will tonight. But again, a packed bag would have been nice."

"Took care of it already," he said dryly.

She looked at him, impressed.

"Hey, I'm not just another pretty face," he said, making her smile. "Kendall: Everything I'm doing is for you."

It was not long before they could see the distinct skyline of Miami reflecting in the Intracoastal Waterway. After crossing the Julia Tuttle Causeway, the amped energy of South Beach just ahead, Kendall grew noticeably anxious.

"Why are we turning onto Collins?" she asked him, shifting frequently in her seat.

"Why? Is that a problem?"

"No, but uh... this is my mom's neighborhood. So, what? Rooftop wining and dining can't happen in Palm Beach County?"

"Why do you always have to try and figure everything out? Can't anything just be a surprise? We're going to the SoBe Regia. Ever been there?"

"Regia? Very nice. I've heard good things, but never been."

"You worried your mom is staying there tonight?" he asked jokingly.

Kendall looked over her shoulder at him and rolled her eyes. "She just knows everyone. Word travels and I bet she's asked about you to everyone now. The hotel concierge will probably think I'm a client of yours."

"Kendall," he said sharply. "Don't. I've never been there either."

Kendall looked down at her silver clutch in her lap. She felt bad for making the comparison. But it was hard not to, knowing he was no novice to this type of night.

"I'm sorry," she said, reaching her hand across the seat to hold his. "It came out before I thought about it."

He shook his head, frustrated with himself more than anything. "It's fine. I should be the one apologizing. I know it's going to take time."

The driver parked the limousine in front of the SoBe Regia main entrance. Kendall grabbed her clutch and gathered her dress as Anson extended his hand to assist her out. The gesture was genuine; uncomplicated by the exchange of money or expectations of sex. He was, in every sense of the word, a gentleman. And in love with her.

Kendall stood with him momentarily as a bellhop assisted the driver with two suitcases stowed away in the trunk.

"Are one of those mine?" she asked. He winked at her and held out his arm to walk her in.

"Even a surgeon can look at the bigger picture every now and then," he said dryly as they entered the swank hotel lobby.

"Good evening. Welcome to SoBe Regia," said the receptionist. "How may I help you?"

"My name is Dr. Allaway," he answered, handing over his credit card. "I have an event taking place upstairs tonight. But first, I need someone to bring our luggage to our room."

"An event?" Kendall asked quietly, Anson remaining stoic in his expression.

"Certainly, Dr. Allaway. It is our pleasure to be of service to you. Your party guests have arrived and are currently enjoying cocktails on the private upper rooftop deck. I see you have chosen our newest amenity, the Royal Palm suite. I took the liberty of upgrading you to the Royal Palm executive suite, if that is agreeable to you." The receptionist looked up from his computer at Dr. Allaway.

"Yes, thank you," he answered without hesitation. He affectionately squeezed her hand, her energy clearly building as she listened to the exchange. She fought the urge to laugh with nervous excitement; instead mirroring their business-like mode out of fear of being found a fraud.

"Excellent choice. We will not disappoint. George, here, will take your bags up to the suite as you enjoy your evening on our rooftop. Here's your room key. Please do not hesitate to ask for any assistance at any time. Enjoy your stay with us at SoBe Regia."

"Thank you." Anson tucked the key away inside his jacket pocket. George directed them to the elevators, then took their suitcases to a separate elevator.

"A limo-ride from Lantana. A rooftop reservation for a private event. An executive suite. The Benjamins are in demand tonight, Dr. Allaway."

"All for you, babe," he said, waggling his eyebrows at her in front of the elevators.

She smiled. But her nervous energy quickly transformed into something less secure. She began to fidget — her thoughts taking over. The past week had left areas of unease.

"Thank you. For all of this," she said sincerely. "You've definitely gone above and beyond."

"It's my pleasure."

"But you should know; I've never really been good at receiving gifts. So, if there's anything more... Well, I'd hate to disappoint you when you've invested so much."

Anson simply shook his head with tired amusement. "As far as I'm concerned, my investments have paid off tenfold. We're here together, aren't we?" He stole a kiss as the elevator doors opened, then stepped inside. Kendall scrambled to catch her breath.

They remained quiet on the ride up; her arm formally draped through his — the perfectly poised couple, radiating beauty and power. It was like a fantasy, over-indulgent and enviable. But their dimpled reflection in the metallic finish of the doors hid so much. She couldn't shake the thought: *Was she being bought?*

"I've also never really been big on surprises," she commented.

"Let me guess: the lack of control has you spinning," he said smartly, glancing down at her with a smile. He looked back at the elevator doors, ready for them to open. "Not everything's a trap, Kendall. Just relax. I've got you, babe."

His words hung in the air, dangling like a carat... or three, the colorless variety. There he stood; so self-assured, so cocky, so in control. His entire demeanor already claimed the potential success of the night as his personal victory. The war to win her over had been won. Their ending had been secured. Her life was now safely in his skilled hands; his second chance finally realized. All the chivalry and glamour of the evening suddenly felt cheap; or at least refurbished and sold at a bargain price. And she was about to pay up.

Her adrenaline spiked.

"What do you call buying my house?" The question was out before she knew what she'd asked.

Anson stiffened; his eyes never leaving the gap between the doors, panic washing over them. The elevator bell chimed and the doors opened; neither budging, pinned under the weight of her question.

The punctuated silence was like a poisonous gas, permeating their moment of perfection and suffocating all hopes of a full recovery. The longer it stretched, the greater the devastation. He had to react. Finally, he spoke.

"It's called *giving you security*. Gratitude would be nice for a change."

Kendall looked up at him in disbelief, Anson steeling his stare straight ahead. He stepped out of the elevator, his arm abruptly pulling free from hers. She still could not move.

"You coming or not?" he asked curtly, his confident swagger faltering. He visibly collected himself, taking in a slow, deep breath, and looked back at her. He apologetically held out an open hand. "I love you, Kendall. That's all the plotting I had behind it."

She accepted his hand; unsure what else to do with all her warring emotions. Together they walked around the corridor to the open rooftop. Just as she regained the moisture in her mouth, still formulating the perfect rebuttal, she heard an all too familiar voice call-out her name.

"Kendall!" Gabriel shouted. "Kendall's here, everyone! Kendall's here!" He excitedly charged the couple. His hair was spiked with gel, giving his black suit and royal blue tie an added edge. Kendall released Anson's hand to warmly greet her brother.

"Gabe!" she said with stunned excitement.

Gabriel dragged her out onto the deck of the rooftop pool where she caught a glimpse of children swimming around in the changing colors of underwater lights. A DJ, pumping out pop music, sat up in one corner of the roof, waiting for the inevitable evolution into nightclub house hits. Still clinging to her hand, Gabriel rounded the large center island bar where various hotel guests gathered. Ahead she saw a short run of concrete steps that lead to an upper deck surrounded by a clear glass wall.

"Mom!" Gabriel shouted, completely disregarding the curious looks of surrounding patrons.

Kendall looked back to see Anson; he briskly followed behind them, a satisfied smile painted across his face.

"Mom! Kendall's finally here!" Gabriel shouted again.

Then all the warm and friendly faces of various loved ones in her life approached the glass wall, smiling broadly at her. Anson had planned a dinner party with her favorite people.

Chapter 19

The upper rooftop deck — the only distinguishable separation being the eight step height difference — cultivated an entirely different vibe than the lower deck. A flavorful rhythm of stringed instrument patterns layered in percussion beats hovered just above the generic atmosphere of the cabana bar below. The spicy AfroCuban jazz sailing through the sultry air by way of several tower speakers enveloped the upper deck crowd beautifully. The pulse from the streets far below and the cool air circulating high above completed the perfect escape.

In the middle of the deck was an elongated dining table covered in white linen, surrounded by fourteen dining chairs; completely in-step with the tastefully modern architecture of the SoBe Regia. Guests brave enough to stroll along the clear glass exterior wall faced the dizzying drop to the highlighted streets below. The height boasted a breathtaking view of what felt like all of Miami-Dade County. A complete bar with an attentive bartender lined the north wall next to a back stairwell that lead into the rooftop kitchen. An enormous rectangular white sectional sofa and several short glass-top tables filled the area that overlooked the lower deck. Kendall's guests found themselves circulating between this area and the three high tops along the south wall.

Anson had asked DeGraff to be in charge of GC General guests: Courtney and Rachel, along with DeGraff, made up the hospital crowd. The rest of the party guests in attendance were close friends and family: Ariel, William, Mr. and Mrs. Duval, Elena, Gabriel, as well as, quite surprisingly, Anna (Dan's sister) and her husband, Daryl. Kendall graciously greeted everyone; her face flushing deeper than a cherry red rose, but her joy obvious. Everyone quickly settled into their cocktails and small talk.

"Sorry my mom couldn't make it," Anna said, Daryl standing next to her rather restrained in his behavior. A Miami rooftop party was definitely not their style and Kendall could sense their awkwardness. "She wanted to, but the drive to and from Miami. It's just too much for her."

"I completely understand. I had no idea about any of this. So, I'm just happy anyone could make it," Kendall said sweetly.

"That's quite a dress you've got there," Anna commented, her eyes growing wider as they followed the depth of the plunging neckline. "I hope I dressed alright."

"Of course you did! You look beautiful," Kendall insisted. "I wouldn't even have this dress if it wasn't for one of my mom's events long ago. Dan always wondered when I'd wear it again, since this is definitely not something we ever did either." She laughed, almost too forcefully, needing Anna and Daryl to feel comfortable.

"So, that's the doctor you mentioned last month. Looks like things are getting serious, right? What was his name again?" Anna asked, fully aware Kendall would want her to be okay with it all.

"Anson," Kendall said, glancing over her shoulder at Anson as he circulated as the host. She sighed. "It's definitely more than it was before. But, uh, I'm not sure where it's all headed. He's a good guy, though. He's got good intentions." She paused to think for a minute, looking at Anna with reservation. Dan's family never knew about the recent miscarriage, Kendall wanting as few people to know as possible.

"It's okay to be happy, Kendall. Don't hold back because of my family. You know that's all Dan ever wanted for you."

Kendall smiled graciously, tears pricking at her eyes. "Thank you for that. It's been hard. You know how it is. Good days and bad. But, sometimes being with Anson does make it better."

Anna nodded and then smiled. "He's pretty easy on the eyes as well."

"Standing right here," Daryl piped up, swigging back his Bud Light.

Kendall laughed and immediately hugged Anna tightly, the two laughing together.

"Okay then! Time for a drink," Kendall announced.

The party continued on without a hitch. Conversation flowed and laughter seemed to fill every beat. Kendall danced with her coworkers, DeGraff gently swinging her around to every salsa beat. The numerous amount of courses served during the decadent dinner turned to a conversation all itself as everyone dined late into the night. Kendall and Anson spent majority of the night talking with others, contributing to joint conversations, but never sharing any private moments.

"So everything good between you two?" Ariel asked as she and Kendall stood alone in the corner of the deck.

"Yeah. Why?" Kendall asked unconcerned.

"You two have only exchanged looks, but not much else."

"Well, I'm not going to make Anna uncomfortable. Or my mom, for that matter. I'm having a really good time and everyone's acing the polite game of no probing personal talk. Even Courtney. Actually, I'm thinking DeGraff put a gag order on them or something (probably by way of Anson), to *not* bring up my *quote, unquote* appendectomy."

Ariel mustered up a laugh and moved her thoughts along. "So, Anson's really hit it off with Gabe it seems."

Kendall looked up at the two near the bar. Gabriel had his hand high on Anson's back as Anson engaged Anna and Daryl in conversation.

"He has," Kendall said, clearly pleased with the sight. "He's a good egg, Ariel. No matter our concerns — the red flags and all — his core is pretty golden. This need to control things around me is not done to be *in* control, so much as... Well, it's out of fear. He's trying to protect me."

"Is that what you want?" Ariel asked, but she was answered only by silence.

Kendall wore a look of uncertainty as she watched her men interact from afar. Suddenly the group laughed, Gabriel patting Anson on the back boisterously. Anson seemed fairly satisfied with his audience's response and glanced about the deck. He caught the eye of Elena and smiled. Elena nodded in icy disregard.

"Did you see that?" Kendall snapped to attention.

"I missed it. What'd I miss?" Ariel asked, looking around the crowd.

"My mom totally snubbed Anson."

Kendall bee-lined it for Elena, pulling her away from Ariel's parents momentarily.

"It's a lovely party, Kendall," Elena commented upon seeing her daughter.

"Mom, what was that? The host smiles at you and you dismiss him like you're too good for it all?"

"Kendall: I have no idea what you're talking about."

"Really, Mom? Even on my birthday you're going to judge Anson? He's clearly gone to great lengths to make this special for everyone and he's probably looking to get some sort of acknowledgement from you. Can you extend the olive branch already? At least throw him a smile. I mean, look: Gabe's in heaven, hanging with everyone again; I'm healthy and happy; we're celebrating in your beloved South Beach. What more can he do to make you realize he's not the devil himself?"

Elena let out a disgruntled sigh. "He's a performer. An actor. Comparable to a conman. How do you expect your mother to react to it all?"

Kendall groaned with petulant frustration. "He's trying, Mom. You do realize, no one's ever been good enough. Not even Dan. How many times did I have to hear it about his tattoos and smoking habits before you decided he wasn't some delinquent trying to steal the Captain's daughter?"

Elena looked off over the city lights, a small smile escaping.

"You said a man who rides a motorcycle is only looking out for himself, remember?" Kendall continued.

"*This* is different and you know that," Elena insisted, recomposing her stern expression and facing Kendall. "Besides. I thought we discussed this and you were okay taking a step back."

"I am. But that doesn't mean I want you to shun the man who is bending over backwards to make me happy right now. Even if he's missing the mark at times. He's generous and trying."

"Missing the mark?" Anson asked, approaching Kendall from behind. He slid his arms around her waist, Kendall immediately blushing and moving out to his side, his one arm kept securely around her.

"Hey there. This is above and beyond," Kendall said sweetly. "We were just saying how wonderful tonight's been. You did good, babe."

"You agree?" Anson asked skeptically, looking directly at Elena with the raise of his eyebrow and a wicked gleam in his eye.

"You've certainly outdone yourself," Elena said cryptically.

Before Kendall knew it, the guests were wishing her a final happy birthday and heading out to their respective homes. Ariel and William were the last to leave, with plans to head straight to the Miami airport for William's red-eye back to Atlanta. Anson and William were still not ready to hash out their own differences, but fully recognized they had to stay civil as long as they found themselves tied to Kendall and Ariel. They shook hands as Kendall and Ariel hugged goodbye.

Kendall exhaled loudly, slowly turning back to the empty dining table with its food stains and wine rings. Anson had stepped away to excuse the bartender from the deck. She waited, watching him closely.

As he returned to her side, his swagger fully restored, his confidence overflowing, a slower tune crooned through the speakers. Kendall's smile could not get any bigger as Anson put his moves on her. He held out his hand to her.

"Dance with me."

She willingly accepted his hand and followed him to the center of the open floor. Anson slowly spun her once before pulling her in close. Kendall laughed and fell comfortably against his chest, swaying slowly to the smooth jazz sounds of a single trumpet.

"Happy birthday, Kendall," he whispered closely to her ear. "Hope I didn't miss the mark tonight."

Kendall smiled and looked up at him. "Knocked it out of the ballpark. I don't know how you do it, but you do it every time. Thank you. For everything."

He smiled and pulled her in close again. Held against his chest, Kendall felt their energy shift as his respirations began to pick up. He stopped dancing and embraced her face with both his hands, kissing her deeply. His lips had a heat surging through them she'd never felt before. She gripped his dress shirt beneath his jacket as the passionate adrenaline surged and could feel his heart racing. It was desperately rapid and somewhat alarming. She pulled back from the kiss and looked up at him with concern.

"Are you okay?" she asked, studying his eyes.

"Kendall," he said, almost breathlessly.

"Babe? What is it?"

He took in a deep, cleansing breath, and reached into his jacket. He pulled out small, dark box, Kendall's color draining immediately.

"Oh god," she stammered.

"Kendall, I love you. And I want–"

"Anson, please don't," she pleaded quietly, shaking her head. But he shushed her.

"It doesn't have to be what you think," he said, trying to calm her fears. "Not exactly. When it comes down to what I really want —

it's simple. I want you. I want you in my life. I want you there when I wake up. I want you there when I fall asleep." Anson looked down at the box he held. He separated the outer box from the jewelry box inside; his skilled hands now fumbling with nerves over one another. "Don't call it a proposal if you're not ready for that. We don't have to get married. But I'm serious about this — about us. And I don't want you to doubt me ever."

Anson dropped down to one knee.

"Oh god. Anson," she whispered nervously, her hands in his, grazing the jewelry box as he prepared to open it.

"Kendall Elena Graham Matthews. I love you more than life itself. Stay with me. Forever."

"Wait!" Kendall suddenly blurted out, clasping her hands over the box before she saw what was inside. "Oh god, Anson," she whimpered softly, unsure how to handle him on the ground before her. "Please, stand up. You have to stand up."

Anson's eyes painfully begged her to answer him first.

"Please. Stand. Don't do this. Not now," she pleaded, her eyes welling up with tears.

His heart sank as he stood, holding her hands and never looking away.

"I'm in your life," she cried, tears dropping heavily, one by one. "And I want to remain in your life. I love you, Anson. But I can't accept anything like this right now; a permanent label just so you feel that level of commitment."

He exhaled heavily; breaking both of them. She reached her hand up to his cheek and his eyes closed momentarily.

"You have to believe that I love you. But I can't accept this," she said, closing his fist around the jewelry box. "Hold onto it until you can do with it what you intended. Don't change your story for me. If you want to marry, then you need to find someone to marry. But it's not me. I'm sorry. Not now. Maybe it will be me one day. But by then — I don't know — you might find someone else. I do love you, Anson. But this isn't meant for me."

His devastation now evident behind his serene eyes destroyed her.

"Say something," she begged.

"*Maybe I'll find someone else?*" he asked, the hurt and anger difficult to hide.

"I'm not talking now. Down the road. Anson: I'm not your forever. I've just begun to really heal and so have you. Please don't put me in this situation."

"Kendall: I didn't ask you because I hoped to find someone else *down the road*. I asked you because you *are* that person down the road. Everything in my life has led me to you."

Anson looked around the empty deck, unable to look into her eyes any longer.

"Anson," she pleaded softly, trying to embrace him.

"Let's go," he finally said, stepping away from her. "Party's over."

Chapter 20

A fine Miami morning. A white on white hotel room. A scorned lover missing. A thirty-two-year old widow plowing through.

Kendall shook her head as the events of her birthday night played over and over in her head; the outcome unchanging and seemingly worse after each encore performance. She stretched out under the luxurious pristine white duvet of the SoBe Regia. The sensation against her skin was titillating, to say the least, Anson's only packed pajama for her a short satin pink nightgown. She reached her hand and foot far across the bed, only to touch emptiness, and sighed. Anson had left the room well over an hour ago without speaking to her. She took solace in knowing his belongings were still there.

She got out of the bed and stood in front of the balcony door to look at the ocean. They'd fallen asleep on opposite sides of the bed last night, Anson actually pulling away from her attempts to cuddle him. She knew she'd done the right thing and that he'd forgive her, his ego still intact. Whether they'd truly move past it together, however, was still to be determined as it was now painfully obvious they were operating from very different perspectives.

Anson entered the room, Kendall turning to face him. He'd clearly been working out. He paused; captivated by her soft features silhouetted in the morning light. But then he disappeared into the bathroom, the start of the shower promptly following.

Kendall ambled aimlessly about the room for a minute, at a loss. She searched for her phone. But then, there on the white stand next to his side of the bed, she found something far more intriguing: the ring box. She daringly sat down by it, eyeing it, ignoring it, and cursing it — ultimately apologizing to it. She picked it up. The box was a dark, forest green with *Roberto Coin* etched in a gold font across the top. The temptations to see it, wear it, accept it — it all pulsated in her fingertips. It was practical. It was desirable. It was understandable. She *could* say yes and the world would beat on. She *could* take his money offer — his gift of love and security — and fulfill her own dreams, too. She *could* commit to him and still be Kendall Matthews — exactly what he wanted her to be.

The shower water stopped and she startled, promptly putting the box back down; her heart pounding into her eardrums.

Fuck.

She had to get them past this. He needed her like she had needed him.

Anson walked by the bed to the suitcases, his towel wrapped around his waist. He pulled out some clothes, Kendall watching him quietly from the bed. He glanced up at her, noticing her spot near the ring box and grabbed his stuff to walk back to the bathroom.

"So the silent treatment is your plan?" she asked, standing up.

He stopped, unabashedly scanning the fine material draping so delicately over her frame. "I'm fairly certain I've said too much."

"Then let's stop talking. You and me, Anson. *We know*. Remember? We can leave it all behind us like we do and just find ourselves in one another."

Dismayed, he shook his head and moved to escape again.

"Damnit, Anson! I'm here! I want you. You want me. Why can't that be enough?"

"It can't!" he yelled back, the fear in his eyes building. He threw his belongings on the dresser behind him and ran his hands through his wet hair.

"What if something happened to you and I wasn't there? Your move to Miami; the start of school; a new career... You're leaving me and I..." Each breath became more arduous than the last. His hands fell to his hips as he stilled in his own shame. "Kendall: I need you. My future does not exist without you."

With the verbalization of his fear conquered, her eyes softened with understanding and she approached him.

"Anson," she said softly, her green eyes locked into his Caribbean blues, placating his bruised heart. "I'm here for you. Use me."

The pads of her fingertips barely pressed against his abdominal muscles before he audibly exhaled. Kendall trailed her fingers further down his still dampened skin, every water bead following the deep angled line below the tempting towel line. She pushed up onto the balls of her feet — Anson's mouth opening as his eyes closed — and brought her lips to his neck. He braced himself against the dresser.

"I'm not built like you," he whispered, easing into her seduction. "You deserve to heal."

"Let me show you what you deserve," she pleaded on a moan, biting his earlobe as her hand explored beneath the towel. "Use me like you've hired me. I'm here to serve you." He hardened, then forcefully grabbed her wrist, stopping her.

"No," he said sharply. "Don't say that."

"Yes," she boldly argued back, working her hand free from his grasp, the towel falling to their feet. "Use me, Anson. *Because* I know. *Because* you see a future with me. Take it from me. Experience it for yourself. Let me love you."

She kissed his full lips and he could not hold back. Anson grabbed her ass, hoisting her up and around his waist. They locked harder onto each other's mouths, sucking and licking with fervent force. He pushed her up against a wall, his hunger dropping to her neck, her chest, her shoulder. She bit back her yelp, driving away her own physical pain as she sought to take on his. He shredded her lace panties, his hand moving with brute force beneath her.

"Christ, you're so wet," he said, panting, kissing her mouth once more.

"It's all you. You do that," she said, feeding his ego, his desire, his starved hard-on. "I want to do that for you. Let me do that for you."

"You do, baby. You do," he said, his kisses multiplying, her breast firmly pressed into his palm. "You have no idea."

He dropped her onto the bed, falling on top of her and raising her nightgown up around her waist.

Kendall quickly rolled them over and straddled him. "I need to taste you," she said, leaning down to kiss him. "All of you."

She continued her soft kisses; down his chin, over his collarbone, each nipple lightly bit along the way. His fingers weaved into her long hair as she lazily peppered her way down to his powerful erection. She firmly stroked his shaft, Anson moaning with pleasure. Before he could open his eyes to take in the view, she took him deep inside her mouth, sucking him hard.

"Oh, fuck," he exclaimed.

Kendall smiled salaciously around him, loving his response. She worked him rhythmically up and down, stimulating every sensitive area she could with her other hand. His reaction — intense and overwhelmingly therapeutic— liberated both of them. He bucked his hips up, holding on, prolonging the euphoric experience.

"Shit. Slow down," he begged, out of breath. "Christ, Kendall. Let me… *fuck*… go down… *yes, like that*… on you…"

Kendall paused momentarily, licking her lips deliciously. She looked up at him, her eyes dreamy with a thick layer of lust. "No. Just relax and let go."

Anson's head exhaustively fell to the bed again, Kendall taking him into her mouth once more.

"Okay! Okay!" he cried out, suddenly stopping her again. "You want me to really enjoy this? Then turn around so I can see your ass."

She looked up at him, her eyes lighting up with wicked amusement. "You like it dirty? I'll give it to you dirty."

She repositioned herself, straddling his chest like reverse cowgirl and took him deep into her mouth again. Anson immediately grabbed her ass, his thumb grazing over her wet layers making her tremble. She remained dedicated to him, however.

"Babe, back up a little," he begged, his fingers delicately digging deeper into the soft folds. She resisted, knowing where it would lead. But he brought his knees up and forced her back onto his face.

"Fuck me!" Kendall blurted out, Anson's hands securely held onto her hips as he ate her out from behind. "Oh god! Anson... I can't..."

But stopping was not a consideration for him. She dropped her head to his lower abdomen, the grip around his cock tightening with every shockwave of pleasure he delivered to her. She took in a breath, mustering every last bit of will she could, and took him back into her mouth, determined to finish what she started.

He cried out, albeit muffled against her clit. His rhythm against her became erratic as he seceded to her skill. He dropped his head back and braced himself.

Kendall finished him off; Anson losing all control as she slipped her finger into his ass and swallowed him down — a potent shot of pride coursing through her. She rolled off of his satiated physique and felt incredible.

Anson's abdominal muscles flexed with every satisfied pant, her hand still held around him, gently squeezing out every last drop. His eyes were closed with a tortuous satisfaction; his rampant self-hatred screeching to a dead halt.

He needed that.

She needed that.

They needed that, together.

***

"So, do you want me to call up Ariel to have her pick me up?" Kendall asked politely between bites of scrambled eggs.

They'd checked out of SoBe Regia and stopped at a sidewalk café for breakfast, their morning washing away in a sea of cordiality.

"She's not expecting you until late this afternoon," Anson commented, taking a sip of his coffee and looking over the rim at passers-by, his thoughts far from the table.

"Oh?" she asked, pausing to regain his attention.

He inhaled deeply and put his mug down. "She thinks we're in Key West."

Kendall opened her mouth to say something, then stopped herself. She quickly put together the celebratory plans he'd made… and clearly had to cancel. She took a small sip of her orange juice and smiled apologetically at him.

He shrugged. "I thought I'd finally replace those flip flops of yours."

She smiled again. "That's a lot of driving for Kinos. Another time perhaps."

"We were going to take a helicopter," he said. "It's the best way to do a day trip. I knew the plan was to be with Ariel tonight."

She felt her scrambled heart begin to digest alongside her eggs. His expression remained stoic; seeming to accept their fate and move forward like she'd commanded. But his heart was breaking all over again — even if this time it'd be for his own good.

Chapter 21

"Thank you," Kendall said appreciatively again, standing along the curb in front of the Duval home. She shifted her weight, awkwardly reticent.

Anson placed her rolling suitcase in front of her, requesting the driver give them a moment alone. He waited until the door shut before facing her. He looked kindly into her eyes; Kendall holding her breath, expecting him to lower the boom.

"I love you," he began, as if confirming the brain tumor to be malignant and requiring immediate surgical extraction. Kendall's heart shot into her throat, her anxiety getting the better of her. "I'm not going to lie. I'm hurting pretty bad right now."

She reached for him and he allowed it, her fingers locking into his to bridge the gap between them — assuaging both their fears, if only momentarily.

"I know I unfairly put you in this situation — you made it clear you weren't ready beforehand. But it'll still take me some time to really accept it," he said. "I'm used to getting my way." A faint smile emerged, smoothing the frazzled edges of their tension.

Kendall mirrored the smile.

"Okay," he said, switching gears. "So be safe tonight. Text me later. And I'll see you Monday, right?"

"Yes," she said confidently.

They kissed briefly, then Anson left in the limousine back for Delray Beach.

***

KM: **Thinking of you.**
KM: **Just hanging out with Ariel and her parents tonight.**
KM: **She told them about the pregnancy last week.**
KM: **After we pick up Will from the airport tomorrow, should they drop me off at your place?**
KM: **Let me know you're okay.**
KM: **I love you.**

Kendall had been trying to casually engage Anson for the past three hours without success. She and Ariel were both contemplating bed, both feeling less than up-to-par for bachelorette party requirements. The effects of morning sickness were hitting Ariel hard at all hours of the day now. Her other bridesmaids wouldn't be in town until later in the week anyway.

"You should probably get a prescription for Zofran or something if you want to make it through next weekend and then your honeymoon," Kendall suggested, Ariel lying on the living room couch, her mother's herbal tea now cold on the side table.

"What's it for?" she asked.

"The nausea. I'm pretty sure it's okay during pregnancy."

"My mom says it's a girl because I'm so miserable. She was the same way. She said two Duval women can't exist in the same body."

Kendall laughed. "I think that's pretty sound science right there." She looked down at her phone again, her expression turning to a frown.

"You and Anson okay?" Ariel asked, studying Kendall.

"Oh yeah. Yeah, we're fine. He's just working."

"I thought he had the whole weekend off. You know: your birthday weekend."

"He does. Or did. But then..." Kendall stopped trying. "We're fine. Just taking that step back. You know: to sort things out. After all: what's the rush?"

Ariel nodded.

"Heard from his brother lately?" Ariel asked casually, Kendall quickly looking up at her.

"No. Why?"

"No reason," Ariel said nonchalantly. "Just curious."

Kendall glared at Ariel for a few seconds longer.

"What?" Ariel asked defensively. "I was just curious. He was an interesting person."

"We're supposedly celebrating your bachelorette party right now you know?"

"Har, har, har. I know, Ken-dall."

"Picking up your fiancé and the father to your unborn baby tomorrow?" Kendall continued.

"Oh stop it. I was just curious. Can't a girl be curious?"

"Yeah. About a stranger on the street I'll never see again. Not about Anson's brother."

Ariel smiled, still curled up.

"Especially a brother with nipple rings," Kendall added, raising an eyebrow.

"I know, right?!" Ariel said, her face lighting up as she pushed up off the couch cushion.

"You totally thought he was hot, didn't you!" Kendall blurted out, almost laughing.

"Oh stop it! You did too!" Ariel shot back, fighting back her own smile.

"So we gotta get the white boys all tatted up and pierced for you to notice," Kendall teased.

"You know how I like a colorful palette," Ariel said playfully.

"You are so bad," Kendall chided, shaking her head. "Would you take Talon as a stripper for a bachelorette party?"

"Hell yeah, I would," Ariel said proudly. "And you would, too, if you were being honest."

"If I ever see him again, I'm totally telling him that," Kendall threatened, smiling even bigger.

"Wait. Why wouldn't you see him again?" Ariel asked, altering the mood completely.

"Oh, I meant in general," she explained. "He lives in California. I don't expect to see him again anytime soon."

"Is Anson coming to the wedding?" Ariel asked, completely derailing the topic.

"I think so. I mean, he intends to. Why?"

"It's a wedding. A week away. Typically, people do a formal RSVP or something to the bride."

"Oh crap! I'm sorry," Kendall said genuinely. "Things have been crazy and I guess we were just assuming you knew. But yeah — yes. He's coming. He got Saturday evening covered. He'll be at the rehearsal dinner, too. Is that going to be okay with you?"

"For sure. As long as it's alright with you. Some guests might force you to bring up things you don't want to and–"

The whistle of Kendall's phone pulled her attention away from Ariel's explanation.

AA: **I love you, too. I'm alright.**

She smiled, exhaling with relief.

"We'll be fine, Ariel. I appreciate your concern. Nearly all of your relatives know about Dan's death. It is what it is. Anson's there as my date, not Dan's replacement. It'll be a great time, no matter what the future holds. Okay? Please don't worry about it. Don't worry about any of it. You have enough on your plate as it is."

Ariel settled back down onto the couch, resting her head on the back of her hands. She stared off thoughtfully, reviewing the last few weeks and anticipating the weeks ahead.

"But in the spirit of your bachelorette party," Kendall said, a sly smirk pulling at the corner of her mouth. "I think we need to delve into the topic of Talon as your chosen stripper a bit more."

Ariel looked over at Kendall and rolled her eyes.

"Hey, did Will ever do a private show for you?" Kendall asked.

This made Ariel full on laugh.

"What? It's pre-wedding chit chat," Kendall reasoned. "We're supposed to get into the TMI girl talk of your man."

"Oh please. I think we both know way too much about each other's men to fill a thousand tell-all books. I don't want to talk about stripping and Will."

Kendall petulantly groaned, eventually caving. "Fair enough."

"I'll play truth or dare," Ariel suggested as an alternative. "I'll go first. Truth."

"Okay. You sound a bit too eager on this one," Kendall said cautiously, looking at Ariel from the corner of her eye. She thought briefly for a second and then asked: "If you could have one last fling before tying the knot, who would it be with?"

"In sworn secrecy as my maid of honor, friend for life, and the godmother to my unborn child, I'll tell you this," Ariel said, pulling herself up and sitting on the end of the couch closest to Kendall's chair. "Talon made a pass at me."

Kendall's lighthearted expression fell flatter than a South Florida topography map.

"What do you mean?" she asked stone-faced.

"You know I dropped him off at a restaurant for dinner that night on Atlantic Ave, right? Since I was leaving Anson's place, I offered him a ride."

"You didn't have dinner together, did you?" Kendall asked, still stupefied by the revelation.

"No. We were alone in my car for some five minutes and that was it. But... Before he got out, there was a spark."

"Ho-ly. Shit!" Kendall whispered harshly, moving to the edge of her seat. "What do you mean: *a spark*? Did you two kiss?"

"NO!" Ariel said, refuting the idea completely, then actually laughing. "Kendall. I'm not interested in cheating on Will by any means. Believe me. I've very much in love and happy to marry the man. I'm not going to jeopardize that. But that doesn't mean chemical reactions will never occur with someone else. It really blindsided me."

Kendall stared at Ariel bug-eyed and motionless. "Tell me what happened."

"I pulled up to the corner of the Ave and A1A and just before he got out, he took a second to look at me."

"Like looked you up and down?"

"No. To look at *me*. It was… intense."

"What were you two talking about?!" Kendall rattled off rapidly.

"I don't even remember. Small talk. Idle chit chat on the drive over. The same kind of laughter slash banter the three of us had, but it was just the two of us."

Kendall remained dumbstruck. "Okay… So, what? What happened?"

"He smiled and said, '*In our next life, I want to be the one to find you first.*'"

Kendall's mouth had popped open. "Wow," she said quietly. "That turned out to be a lot more than just a friendly ride."

"Right?" Ariel reiterated. "But it wasn't unwelcomed or awkward. It just made me genuinely hope he finds someone good."

"So, what? He just got out of the car then?"

"Basically. I didn't know what to say. I just smiled — apologetically at best. And he understood. He squeezed my hand and got out of the car."

"Wow," Kendall repeated, staring at Ariel.

"I know. He made an impression, to say the least."

"I'd say. But is that really a good impression? Doesn't it just reinforce his womanizing persona?"

"That's one way to look at it," Ariel said. "But the way it happened wasn't disrespectful or out of bounds. I don't think he was trying to get me to cheat or do something sleazy. And yes, one can argue that he never would have said it with anyone else around; so I'm sure he recognized the less than appropriate nature of it. Believe me: I've analyzed the crap out of this.

"But on another level he had to put it out there," Ariel continued. "It was the only way to make it into a defined moment, you know? Something to remember. It's either do it or live in regret. I have to respect that. He simply acknowledged the chemistry, owned it, and just like that, we moved on."

"Well, you left him at the curb," Kendall said cynically.

Ariel scornfully eyed Kendall. "Yes. I drove off and he walked away alone. But it was a conscious decision to move on."

Kendall sat there thinking for a moment. It was a lot to digest. But Ariel planted an intriguing thought in her mind.

"So," Kendall said carefully. "You're saying you felt an attraction to him before he said it out loud? A flirty connection of sorts? Like pheromones?"

"Yes," Ariel agreed shamelessly.

"And when he acknowledged it, it went away?"

"It punctuated it. Giving it its due importance, I suppose. And then we could walk away from it, knowing we both saw it and there was nothing we were going to do about it."

"Hmm," Kendall murmured.

"What are you thinking?" Ariel asked suspiciously.

"Nothing. I think that's fascinating actually. It makes sense to me."

They sat quietly for a minute, Kendall sitting back in her seat and picturing the whole scene between Ariel and Talon. Ariel found her comfortable position back on the couch. She looked up at Kendall, chewing on her thoughts, until feeling ready to dig into another secret between the two best friends.

"So, are you ready to tell me why you and Anson didn't go down to Key West together today?" Ariel asked.

Kendall smiled and shook her head. "So, that's where this whole truth or dare was going. I knew you had some sort of return confession in mind."

Ariel smirked. "You know me well."

Kendall heaved off a sigh. "I officially turned down his pseudomarriage proposal," she said. "I'm nowhere near ready. And despite what he thinks, neither is he."

"You going to be okay?" she asked.

"Oddly enough? Yes. I know I'll be fine. I'm worried about him, though. Kind of like what you said with Talon: he had to put it out there. I love him for that. But if I said, *yes*, it would have been for all the wrong reasons. And he knows it."

"But you two are still staying together. So... he's okay with it. Not bitter?" Ariel asked hesitantly.

"He once said to me that I can't have the thrill of the chase without the risk of falling in love. And then I fell for him. I fell hard. I can say the same thing to him now. He can't have the thrill of being in love and the absolute security that it'll last, right? So, he chased me down and now we're caught. But what then? We automatically get married? No! That's crazy.

"And I'm not against marrying again. I'm not even against marrying Anson. Even with every red flag — and I'm sure he's got plenty on me as well. But marriage is work and I'm not programmed to think that way right now. Of course *he* thinks that's the natural next step.

"Grace wanted to be married and he held off. Then it was too late. Does that factor in? I'm sure it does; subconsciously. But I don't think he believes it does. And, well, he needs to know — *I* need to know — that you *can* fall in love and walk away from it without tragedy ending it all. You can love and then let it go — if that's what you need to do."

"Wow," Ariel said, impressed. "You've really thought about this."

"I know. Does it sound pathetic?"

"No. Not at all. Just well thought-out. Very well thought-out."

"What else is there for me to do?" Kendall asked somewhat defensively. "If I can't work hard, run hard, or fuck hard, I'm forced to think hard."

Ariel immediately clutched her gut with laughter, Kendall enjoying it quietly.

"Oh, Kendall," Ariel said, collecting herself. "My dear, sweet Kendall. Where did all your softness go?"

Kendall sat back in her chair, her smile fading to that of a reflective state.

"Buried deep with Dan," she said much to Ariel's surprise. Kendall then looked at Ariel, giving her a quirky smile to make light of her comment. "But I'm getting it back. I can feel it from within."

Chapter 22

"So, are congratulations in order?" Talon asked immediately upon Anson answering his call.

"She turned me down," Anson said dryly, sipping on his scotch and overlooking the Atlantic Ocean.

"You don't sound too broken up about it. Did you end everything?"

"We're working it out."

"So she'll be moving in then?" Talon asked.

"That's a negative. Found out I bought the house."

"Damn. Batting zero this weekend, hey?"

"It'd appear so," Anson said monotonously.

"So…" Talon continued, contemplating which tooth to pull on next. "Are you back to casually dating her now?"

"Casual dating?"

"Well, the string-free sex and no commitment thing you had going," Talon boldly concluded.

Anson took back a large swig, his patience waning.

"Hey, if she hopes to keep things how they were when you started out, sounds like you got a win-win situation there. Just don't forget the condoms this time."

"Watch yourself!" Anson snapped, his glass knocking the railing with a clang.

"Okay, okay. Well, at least you know she's not trying to use you," Talon said, trying to backpedal a little. "You offered her everything and she's sticking to her own guns. I guess on some level you have to admire that."

"What's that supposed to mean?" Anson asked.

"She said she'd never trap herself. And buying her house from under her would appear that way, no matter how much of an Allaway spin you put on it."

"*Trap herself*? When did she say that?" Anson asked curtly.

"Last week. That day she, Ariel, and I hung out together."

"Why the hell did you not say anything?!"

"To you? Why would I?" Talon answered unapologetically. "It wouldn't have stopped you from buying the house or the ring. *A*, you were adamant on proposing to her after a few weeks of dating. You really think *I* could have said something that would have changed that?"

Anson greatly regretted answering his phone.

"Hey, listen. Don't beat yourself up," Talon continued, tempering his tone. "You're still together. Maybe she just needs more time."

"Time's working against us," Anson confessed. "She's feeling better; stronger."

"From the surgery? How's that bad?" Talon asked, confused.

"From everything," he said, defeated. "She's building up her defenses again. I can tell. Moving on. She'll replace me with school. She'll replace school with career. She'll keep her attachments to a minimum."

Talon sighed. "Anson. You know it best. You do what you have to do to get by."

"I know," he said. "I just thought she'd need me longer. What can I say? I fell for her and she fell for her independence."

"I'm sorry, man. Happens to the best of us," Talon said sincerely.

"You know what the worst part of it all is?" Anson asked. "What?"

"She's doing it for me just as much as she's doing it for herself."

California might as well have been Florida's neighbor with how close the two brothers felt during the reflective pause that followed. Anson's fated course was clear, whether he wanted to admit to it or not.

Anson sighed heavily.

"You need me to say it?" Talon asked cautiously.

"No. I know. I'll let her go… eventually."

***

Kendall remained in Miami through Monday. She and Ariel took full advantage of Mama Duval's spoiling love before her attention would be divided amongst the multiple family members flying in for the big wedding event. Kendall considered staying all week to help with last minute wedding plans, since she no longer had to pack up Sandalfoot Lane so quickly. But a call Monday afternoon changed that whole thought.

"My realtor called me and said she got the rewrite. You're offering *less* than my asking price now?" Kendall sharply inquired of Anson as soon as he answered his cell phone.

"I'm offering what it's worth," he replied, completely distracted as he attempted to finish up a conversation at work simultaneously. *"Sure. Do what you want. I'm giving you a verbal order for sixty. But I didn't order those labs. So don't call me with the results. Ask the primary for parameters."*

"But, uh… you were prepared to offer way more than that," she stated obviously.

"That was clearly an incentive for a fast closing. Did you read the contract? Since you'd rather wait until August, I had to offer a more realistic number. It leaves little time for me to hire a crew and renovate… *What? I signed off that case. Why? What's the scan show?"*

She'd have heard crickets if it weren't for the constant chatter of the hospital world behind him.

"Hey, is there anything else?" he asked quickly. "I'm sorry, babe. I'm pretty busy here."

Peeved not only by his cavalier attitude toward the entire situation he should have never been involved in in the first place, but also with his choice of a pet-name during the tension-building conversation, Kendall felt her jaw clench tighter. She looked back at the Duval house, having had escaped to the far back along the bougainvillea-vined fence. She considered how loud she'd be able to yell before her voice carried. Ultimately, she took in a deep breath and let it out slowly.

"Well, I believe it's worth more. So what do you expect me to do now?"

"You counter offer. It's business, Kendall. Don't read too much into this," he said.

"But you're basically paying me more to move in with you. How is that business? It's a total conflict of interest. I'm not for sale. It just wouldn't feel right."

She could hear his smile; his restrained chortle mocking her and all her vulnerabilities. Her blood boiled and she felt like a child.

"I've accepted a lot less for doing a lot more and still saw it all as business. If I were trying to buy you, I'd pay an infinite amount more. Babe, you can't get caught up in the personal ties of it all. If I'm not the best offer on the table, you take another one. Simple as that.

Hey look. I'll give you a call later after work, okay? I'm really swamped here."

She was stymied. She had so much more to say, but he effectively made her mute.

"Kendall? Did you hear me? Fucking reception in here. Kendall?"

"Yeah. Sure," she said numbly. "We'll talk later."

"Okay, good. Love you." He hung up the phone.

Kendall immediately went inside the house and arranged a ride home. By eight o'clock that night she still hadn't heard from Anson.

KM: **You off work anytime soon? I'm home in Lantana.**

He called her back.

"Hey," she said softly, defeated in the anger that she'd burned out hours earlier. "Thought you might come over tonight or something."

"I'm sorry. It was a long day and I drove straight home. Totally forgot to call."

"Oh," she said.

"But, uh, you're more than welcome to head on over here," Anson suggested indifferently. "I'll need my Benz back at some point anyway. So, if you want to come by, I can drop you off in the morning before work."

She actually looked down at her phone screen, curious if she'd heard him right.

"Will your guest bed be available?" Kendall asked coldly.

"What? My guest bedroom?"

"Or maybe it'd be better to just call a cab tonight so I don't trouble you at all," she countered.

Anson sighed. "Kendall: come on."

She closed her eyes, doing her quiet count, not wanting to stoke the fire any further.

"What am I supposed to do with your offer? How can I *not* take it personally when it's an insult of an offer and it's from you?"

"The first offer still stands," he said calmly. "You can always accept that one, but you'll need to be out by next week. You know I'll never recant living together. So, when you're ready... Or you can accept the rewrite. Or simply counter with a whole new one. Hell. If you'd like, you can scratch me as the buyer and wait for someone else to come along. It's no sweat off my back. I was never really in the market for a rental property anyway."

"I don't understand why you're being like this," she finally said. "I get that you're probably a little bitter toward me, but this passive aggressive animosity is not like you."

"If you want to talk about it, let's talk. But I'm not doing this over the phone. Should I expect you tonight or do we try this again tomorrow?" he asked.

"Goodnight, Anson. I'll give you a call sometime tomorrow. *If* I remember."

Kendall ended the call before he could respond. He clearly needed to lick his wounds of rejection for a little while longer.

The following day, Anson called Kendall from GC General. This time *he* was eager to hear what she had to say.

"Hey you," Anson said affectionately, Kendall's sleepy greeting warming him to the core. "You were sleeping? It's afternoon, babe."

"I was up until three," she said, yawning. "And then I had to be at my realtor's office first thing this morning. I must have fallen asleep on the couch."

"I got the call. You accepted the original offer," he said with happy surprise. She could hear the hustle of the hospital behind him again; but nothing could distract his focus from their conversation now.

"Yeah," she said quietly.

"So, you're moving out by next week? I honestly didn't think you were considering it any longer. But I'm stoked to know you agreed."

"Like you said: it's business, right? I have to move forward. Since I had stopped packing last Thursday, I stayed up late trying to make up for the lost time."

"Kendall," he said, smiling. "Don't overdo it. I'll help you out. Something tells me: if you take an extra day to clear out, the buyer isn't going to mind. This is really great. Really great. We can book a moving van Monday, after the wedding. I have to go. I love you, Kendall. I'll swing by after work."

"Okay. Love you, too, Anson," she said meekly, knowing full well her acceptance of the offer did not mandate moving in with him, despite his hopeful assumption.

Chapter 23

Ariel and William's rehearsal dinner was more extravagant than Kendall and Dan's actual wedding reception. The party took place at the Duval's palatial Coral Gable estate. The Duvals had been eagerly anticipating the day their only child, Ariel, got married since she was a young girl. The celebratory atmosphere that engulfed the bougainvillea clad Spanish-styled home — fused with its Caribbean spices and Calypso beats as the dominant Dominican and Haitian cultures of Ariel's blended family sailed overhead in a sweet symphony — lured the guests in like the songs of sirens the minute the valet attendants drove off with their vehicles.

Ariel was the clear star of the night. She stood out like a majestic swan. Her short white dress was a silk strapless cocktail gown with a sweetheart neckline; the bottom a fanciful marriage of whimsical feathers and layered ruffles. Her flawless bronze skin actually shimmered under the lights and William complimented her fairytale look in a pair of light khaki pants and a loose white linen shirt. They were a striking couple and the ambience of the evening awarded the photographers hired for the wedding weekend with more perfectly poised opportunities than a red carpet event in Los Angeles.

Kendall wore the bride's counterpart: a short black chiffon overlay dress with a dramatic asymmetrical neckline. The material gathered over one shoulder and cascaded down her arm beautifully. Her hairstyle — bunched up on one side of her head with soft curls dropping down her shoulder — left her opposite shoulder exquisitely exposed to the sultry South Florida air. Anson could barely keep his lips off this soft palette of sweet skin as they promenaded through the party.

"Stop," Kendall scolded him under her breath for the umpteenth time as Anson jumped back laughing.

"I can't help it," he said, his fingers tightening around her waist. "Have I mentioned how fucking hot you look tonight yet?"

"Yes, about a thousand times, but I need to stay focused. I'm here to help Ariel."

Kendall placated him with a quick kiss on the lips, Anson's hand immediately dropping down to the round slope of her ass before being batted away.

Their time during the week had played out as well as could be expected. Kendall drove back to Miami on Thursday and remained through the weekend in order to assist with all the festivities. But Anson had taken her out to dinner both Tuesday and Wednesday night, his affection for her only increasing as the contents of her home decreased — the height of the stacks of boxes in her living room proportionate to his smile. The plan to let her go seemed to be a distant thought chalked up to a moment of despair. Anson had his eyes once again set on building a future with her; Kendall never leading him to believe otherwise.

They exited out the back of the house through the opened French doors onto the Mexican tiled porch that overlooked the backyard. There were large white tents and strung light bulbs spanning between the branches of avocado, mango, and banyan trees. Kendall casually participated in conversation with various guests; introducing Anson, occasionally explaining the events of her last year to Duval family members she hadn't seen in years. Gabriel stood in front of the steel drum performers, watching them intently and applauding appreciatively every time they finished a set. Ariel and William circulated endlessly; greeting their guests as the gracious host and hostess that they were with kisses and hugs going out to a myriad of loved ones.

"Let's check in with Ariel and William again," Kendall suggested, looking back at Anson.

But his face had lost all robust coloring, his skin literally draining to ash right before her eyes as his expression became one of steely concern.

Kendall followed his line of vision to a well-dressed man in a khaki Armani suit and cream colored fedora, casually leaning against a high top next to one of the outdoor bar setups. He had a telling grin on his face and it looked as if he'd just raised his cocktail glass up to Anson. An exotic woman in a breathtaking backless gold gown and long black hair swept to the front, sat facing the man. She turned, noticing his interaction as he whispered something to her. She seemed to lock eyes with Anson and swiveled completely around to admire him.

"That's Xavier, isn't it?" Kendall asked, Anson's demeanor saying it all. "Ariel warned me he might make an appearance. It's fine. I'm ready. Let's get this shit over with."

180

Anson didn't respond immediately. She looked back at the gentleman who now made a move to come greet them. His swagger and smooth confidence was clearly evident as he assisted the woman off her high barstool. Together, they strutted over to Anson and Kendall.

"Yes. That's Xavier," he finally answered. "And Joice," he added, his voice falling quiet and rather distant.

"Should I know Joice?" Kendall asked, looking up at him, his eyes fixated on the approaching couple.

"Does Johnson know they're *both* here?" he asked, never looking at Kendall.

But before Kendall could respond, the mysterious couple arrived, Xavier removing his classic fedora and extending his hand to Kendall.

"Good evening. It's my greatest pleasure to finally meet you, *Mrs.* Matthews," Xavier purred, the emphasis on her married title notably intriguing Joice.

The front of Joice's dress was nearly as absent as the back — except now the draping fashion barely covering her bountiful bosom was not nearly as *breathtaking* to Kendall as she'd originally felt. Anson was obviously well-acquainted with the breasts playing peek-aboo behind the fine material. His unspoken familiarity with the woman dominated the small circle. Kendall immediately felt reduced to the roll of a prepubescent tag-along relative.

"My name is Xavier LeBeau. This is the extraordinary Joice Dossantos. Mrs. Matthews is the mysterious woman who has captivated the heart of our fine Dr. Allaway."

Xavier's eyes were rich with layers of golden caramel, harboring incredible depth — like a cat's eye gemstone. His warm smile and the soft features of his olive complexion invited her in with friendly gentility. He looked younger than his actual age of mid to late fifties. If he'd been any other man to her, Kendall may have found him attractive and rather charming. But now, finally faced with Anson's covert partner and boss — surrounded by the burgeoning tension of the awkward circle — she couldn't help it: Kendall despised the man.

Kendall politely returned his handshake, however, and extended her hand to Joice, who instead cordially nodded, excusing herself from returning the gesture by holding up her clutch and cocktail. Kendall dropped her hand, feeling foolish, and simply waited on Anson to direct the conversation.

"Don't be rude," Anson said to Joice, irritated. "What are you even doing here? I highly doubt Johnson's bride approved of either of you on her guest list tonight."

"Come on now. That's not necessary," Xavier replied grievously like a disappointed parent. "I am an invited guest and Ms. Dossantos is *my* guest. Let the past be the past. I'm sure you've had a great deal of experience with that lately, haven't you, Mrs. Matthews?"

Anson's jaw clenched down, Kendall anticipating some sort of return attack at any moment. But it never came, Anson frozen stiff in the stare of Xavier and the *extraordinary* Joice.

"Well, there's much time to catch up later in the evening I'm sure. Please do not hesitate to find me later, my dear," Xavier said to Kendall with syrupy sweetness. "I'm an open book. There's no sense in being a stranger now; we're all so intimately connected."

The corner of Xavier's lips curled with wicked delight as he positioned his hat at a slant back on his head, gliding his long index finger along its smooth brim. A chilling sensation rippled across Kendall's body as she watched Xavier and Joice stroll down the steps onto the lush grass of the Duval estate, slipping back into the merriment of the night.

Anson silently fumed.

"What the fuck was that?" Kendall chastised him, his stance during the entire exchange infuriating her.

"Did Johnson know they'd *both* be here?" he suddenly demanded again, glancing around the yard ready to hunt down the groom. "I swear, if this was something to make me look bad–"

"What the hell does that matter?" Kendall retorted. "You stood there like an ass making *me* look bad! Tell me who Joice is to you."

Anson looked over at Kendall and without an ounce of emotion, as he was wrapped up in his own anger, he replied: "She's a former client. Well, a partner. And we were once engaged. Briefly. It doesn't matter. Where's Johnson?"

Kendall stood in front of him flabbergasted.

"Did you just hear yourself?" she asked. "Did you actually just say that to me? Anson. I am your girlfriend — whom you'd like to be your fiancée — who has had to let go of a shit-ton of baggage on *your* behalf and you can't give me a minute to process being embarrassed in front of your drop dead gorgeous former sex client who you ALSO proposed to?! I must be out of my fucking mind to think an actual relationship with you is possible!"

Anson closed his eyes with annoyance before looking back at her.

"Kendall. Please. Don't start with this. She means nothing to me, so it's stupid to get focused on that when you know I love you. What's more concerning is the fact that your best friend is marrying a manipulative asshole hell bent on embarrassing me!"

"Anson!" Kendall grabbed his arm, pulling him off to the side and out of sight. "What's wrong with you? This is *their* rehearsal dinner! With *their* family and friends around you! Grow up! What is this feud between you and William?"

Anson inhaled deeply, closing his eyes again.

"I shouldn't be here. This is the kind of shit that can be harmful to my reputation and practice."

"What can be harmful? Anson. Look at me. How am I supposed to understand any of this when you continually hide it from me or give me only sound bites of information regarding your business and past?"

Anson held Kendall's face in his hands and really looked at her. Her eyes pleaded with him to be the man she needed, to fulfill those promises he'd been feeding her, to forget his past and move on.

"God, you're beautiful," he whispered. "Don't hate me. I need to head out. It's better that way for both of us. Enjoy your night and we'll touch base later."

Kendall pulled back from him; his decision like a dagger to the gut, the beauty in her eyes replaced with painful disappointment.

"If you leave now, don't bother coming to the wedding tomorrow."

"Kendall. I'll be there tomorrow. I just need to take the night."

"No, Anson. *I* don't want you to be there. You're ruining this picture perfect evening for me and I'll be damned if I let you do it tomorrow at my best friend's wedding. Leave now and we'll talk when I'm back in town next week."

Kendall turned around and walked away, not giving him a second to react. Anson watched her get swallowed by the crowd and glanced around in utter defeat. Joice's eye caught his and he immediately turned to leave the backyard through the side fence.

"She's not like us," Joice called out to him, her distinct seductive Brazilian accent now like nails against the steel of his heart.

"Thank god for that," he muttered, continuing in his pursuit to get out of there — now even faster.

"Anson-baby. Talk to me," she said, following quickly behind him. "I'm ready now — to leave it all behind. Let's do it, baby. Let's do it together. You want a new life and we–"

He whipped around and growled back at her: "I *never* wanted it with you!"

Joice stopped in shock, her alluring dark eyes growing infinitely larger as they glossed over with the threat of tears.

"Goddammit, Joi," Anson said, grabbing his head with his hand as he watched her crumble in front of him.

He stood riddled with guilt as Joice cried softly in the shadows alongside the Duval estate. Slowly he made his way back to her and brought her into his arms. They remained quiet for several minutes, the shuffle of the dampened leaves beneath their shoes the only sound outside of the distant music and chatter.

"My Prada heels are not very good for this soft ground," she commented through a sniffle, looking down at their feet.

"Well, a flat shoe would be too practical for you," he said, giving her an endearing shake of his head as their shared past slowly surfaced.

"You always wanted me closer to your waist," she murmured, looking up at him through her long lashes as she bit her bottom lip.

He looked down at her, confused; never expecting such an audacious double entendre from her in that moment. She took his pause as an invitation and brazenly dipped her hand down to the crotch of his pants.

He shoved her back, holding her out at arm's length and stared at her with disgust — until he realized it was like looking into the mirror. Everything was solved with sex. It was what they knew. And it was exactly what he'd taught Kendall to do with him.

Anson left Joice standing alone and never returned that night.

Fortunately, the evening continued on without a hitch for the others, Kendall only making eye contact with the dapper Xavier LeBeau one last time as he and Joice exited the party about an hour later during her toast to the bride and groom. The hour approached midnight when Mr. Duval began to usher the last guests out, except for

Kendall and a small handful of family guests who remained at the house overnight.

Ariel and Kendall walked William and his best man out to their car so they could return to their Biltmore Hotel suite.

"Don't go out to the Grove or anything, hoping to party it up tonight," Ariel warned, wrapping her arms around William and swooning in a long, passionate embrace.

"You're all the party I need," William whispered back.

"Okay, okay," Kendall groaned, poking at Ariel's side. "Save it for the wedding night."

"Fine. Love you," Ariel said, giggling and kissing William one last time.

The two women slowly made their way back up the drive to the house, Ariel holding onto Kendall's arm to anchor herself down as the bubbly elation threatened to lift her right off the ground.

"Everything is perfect, isn't it?" Ariel's eyes twinkled in a lovestruck manner and Kendall couldn't help but share her best friend's giddy excitement.

"It is. Princess-perfect. Tomorrow will be even better," Kendall said, squeezing Ariel's arm as they entered through the front door. "I'm so happy for you."

Kendall and Ariel went up to Ariel's childhood bedroom, still set up very similarly to when she was in high school with its pale blue and chocolate brown paisley fabrics. The only thing missing were the posters and piles of clothes. Kendall and Ariel got ready for bed as Bob Marley's *Stir It Up* played softly on repeat. Ariel rocked her hips slowly around the room with silky fluidity, Kendall shaking her head in amusement from her position on the queen-sized bed.

This had been their traditional routine when either one would get ready for a date or before going out to a nightclub along South Beach. After Kendall and Dan had moved in together, their little dance routine finally gained an attentive audience. Dan had grown so fond of the song that it played as the last slow dance at their wedding reception.

"'*And now you are here, I say, it's okay, to see what we can do, baby, just me and you,*'" Ariel crooned to Kendall as she crawled onto the bed toward her. "I'm getting married today!" she suddenly squealed.

The two laid in bed next to each other, only the glow of their phones highlighting their faces as they updated their Facebook, Twitter, and Instagram statuses. But as Ariel filled her pages with pictures of the rehearsal night, Kendall focused on the lack of any new text messages or missed calls from Anson.

The room eventually went dark, both deciding it was time to call it a night.

"Were you ever going to tell me why Anson left tonight?" Ariel asked softly, not even sure Kendall was still awake.

Kendall sighed and turned over, facing Ariel's side of the bed.

"Joice," Kendall said.

"I thought so," Ariel confessed.

Kendall sat up in the bed and reached for her bedside lamp, the room filling with a warm, yellow glow. "What do you mean? You know something about her?"

"Not much. But enough." Ariel sighed, propping her head up by her hand ready to talk. "While Will was at Tulane, he danced at a nightclub. Not XLM, but like it. Xavier had found him while recruiting since he was building a club there. I guess they got pretty close and Will helped open an XLM in Atlanta."

"Okay. Come on: Joice," Kendall impatiently demanded.

"Anyway. Well, now that I know Anson and Xavier are very close on the business side of things — your boy apparently is Xavier's right-hand man."

"Don't I know it," Kendall muttered.

"Well, I guess Anson was managing AAXLS or something," Ariel continued. "And he went to the XLM clubs in New Orleans and Atlanta to recruit studs."

"*Studs?*"

"Yeah. That's what they call them. The escorts. The *S* in AAXLS." Then Ariel paused in thought. "AA," she continued. "Those stand for Anson's initials, don't they? I never put that together until just now."

"Yes," Kendall said regretfully. "He started that side of the business. It's a shout out to himself, really. His middle name is Axel. Xavier doesn't even know that."

"Oh. Damn."

They silently stared up at the ceiling for a moment until Kendall prodded her for more.

"Keep going."

"Well, William wasn't even a dancer anymore when that all started up. Actually, he never danced for XLM, simply helped Xavier out in the Atlanta club. The whole stripper thing was only in college. But, I guess Xavier mentioned Will as someone Anson should look into recruiting or something for AAXLS." Ariel let out an aggravated groan. "I hate going over all this because I got so much of it five years ago when we started dating and then buried it deep."

"You don't have to continue. It's nearly one in the morning and you shouldn't have to think about this before your wedding. I'll figure it out later," Kendall suggested, feeling rotten for pushing it in the first place.

"No. I'm saying it all now," Ariel said insistently, sitting up in the bed. "I've wanted to have a sit down with you — and well, shit. It's happening now."

Kendall smiled with gratitude.

"So, for whatever god-forsaken reason, William was interested and he joined the whole AAXLS side of things for some six months. During that time, he met Joice and he swears up and down they never had sex. But she helped *train* new recruits — whatever the fuck that means. She herself had been an escort before becoming a very prominent client."

"Wait, what? She was an escort turned client? Anson's client?" Kendall asked, baffled.

"You're going to have to get all that from Anson because I honestly don't know it. Nor did I really care to figure it all out."

"Okay. Just tell me what you know."

"So, just before I met Will down in Miami," Ariel continued, Kendall hanging on every word. "Joice had come to him with some story of being pregnant and... and..." She took in a deep breath, her concerned look prompting Kendall to reach out.

"It's okay. I have to know, right?" Kendall said with assurance.

"Well, he supposedly forced her to get an abortion."

"Who? Will? Xavier?" Kendall asked in shock, not following.

"No. Anson. It was Anson's baby and they were engaged. Will knew they were together for at least those six months he worked at AAXLS. He said they were engaged the last two months. But Anson wanted to break off the engagement saying it only got that far because of the baby. So... they had to get rid of the baby."

The air was sucked right from Kendall's lungs. She twisted the blankets beneath her hands, stunned.

"You okay?" Ariel asked softly, touching Kendall's arm.

"Yeah," she barely answered, her look lost in thought.

"As soon as I realized Xavier's guest was Joice, I told Will they had to leave. He spoke to them before the dinner began. I'd never met her before. I swear to you. I had no idea she'd be there."

The two sat in silence for a moment longer, Ariel watching over Kendall carefully as Kendall simply stared off.

"Kendall?"

"It's fine," Kendall said predictably. "None of this is your fault. Not in the least. Or Will's. It'll be okay."

"Are you sure?" Ariel asked.

"Of course," she said. Then she sighed, reaching up to the lamp and turning it off. The room went dark. "I guess I never really considered how much more there was to know about Anson's past — other than Grace."

Chapter 24

Ariel and Kendall both stirred awake around six in the morning, simultaneously rolling over to get more sleep. But by 8:30, Ariel's mom opened the door, waking them just like she did in high school with a tray of hot morning tea and a back rub until they finally opened their heavy eyes.

"Today's your big day, child. Time to meet the sun," Mrs. Duval smiled as she sat along the edge of the bed. "You two haven't changed a bit."

Kendall pushed herself up from the bed, smiling warmly at Mrs. Duval, then looked down at Ariel as she stretched out her arms, squealing through a long drawn out yawn.

"Oh my goodness! I so needed that last couple of hours," Ariel reported, looking at Kendall with a knowing grin.

The wedding party brunch was scheduled midmorning at the breathtaking Vizcaya Gardens. Kendall and William's three sisters made up Ariel's bridal party whereas William had his best friend, two cousins, and of course, Gabriel, Ariel's honorary brother. Kendall looked forward to the gathering, hoping for a chance to really talk with William's family a bit more — last night being an overwhelming sea of people with mostly superficial interactions clouded by her distracted thoughts.

While Ariel showered, Kendall jumped at the chance to be alone with her phone. She cozied up onto the bed, sipping her tea, and powered on the phone.

One text message.

AA: **I love you. See you tonight.**

He'd sent it around 4am.

She called him up and got his voicemail, hanging up quickly. She began to type up a reply to his text, but put the phone away as Ariel exited the bathroom.

"So, I've got a blue sundress for Vizcaya, what are you wearing?" Ariel asked, a towel wrapped around her.

"That was a fast shower. Um, I have my white capris and that pink top I bought in Islamorada. Too Mother's Dayish?"

"No, that's great. I only had to freshen up. Spa stuff is later today. Come on, get up. No drama today," Ariel said with a wink.

Kendall smiled, rolling her eyes, and scooched off the bed. She sulked into the bathroom. Just before Kendall closed the door, Ariel called to her.

"Hey Kendall," she said, just like Anson so often did.

Kendall popped her head out from around the door. "Yeah?"

"He loves you. No one's perfect. We all make mistakes. But at some point, the doubt you find in him will be replaced with doubt in yourself. Don't let that happen. You can't walk away from you."

***

The gorgeous April day blazed in sunshine, the thick humidity of summer not quite upon them, but not far off. The breathtaking backdrop of the Vizcaya Gardens nourished everyone, pairing that perfect sense of spontaneity to an already meticulously planned day. Table conversations highlighted the multitude of humorous stories from William's childhood, his three sisters very animated in their impressions, nailing some of his signature gestures. Brunch concluded without a hitch as everyone separated for their grooming and preparation.

William and Ariel said goodbye one last time as singles; the next time they'd see one another face to face being at the Biltmore Hotel ready to say *I do* as a unified couple. Ariel lightly tapped the Cartier necklace adorning her neck, thanking William again for the thoughtful gift.

The charm that hung from the impressive necklace had a pair of orchids in contrasting onyx and white diamonds. William had explained to the guests that it captured their yin and yang; the balance of their personalities, taking the good with the bad, the soft with the hard, the purity of new beginnings with the contamination of the past and creating an unparalleled match in love. Ariel's hobby of growing rare and exotic orchids tied up the meaning perfectly. And of course, the classic interpretation of black and white were the themed colors for the wedding itself.

The bridal party all headed straight to the Biltmore's spa and salon to get a little pampering done before hair and makeup. Kendall relished in the light facial she selected, her worries and emotional overspill of the last few weeks drifting away. The only pronounced sad thought that popped up on occasion surprisingly centered around the absence of Dan.

However, somewhere between her teased and blown out hair, Kendall jumped the tracks back to compulsively overanalyzing the last couple months with Anson. Their entire relationship — from how it had started: out of her desperation to simply feel anything at all with another man in order to drown out her barraging sorrow; to the passion she and Anson experienced with one another purely fueled by heartbreak, carnal need, and fear; to the inevitable next step in every change of life: moving on. It all had been a series of fleeting moments and unchecked means to an unattainable end: happiness. But *that* she would only find within herself.

She sent him a text.

KM: **I'd rather you not attend. Please respect this request.**

She never heard back from him.

By the time of the ceremony, it was impossible to not get swept up in the opulence and wonder of a Biltmore wedding celebration. The ambience of the music, food, and decor radiated through every guest. The entire evening was — in a word — enchanting. Ariel and William delighted in every moment, basking in the glow of their married love through song, laughter, and shared stories. The only person missing for Kendall continued to be Dan. But with all the friends and family surrounding her, especially Gabriel jumping in as her dancing partner at every turn, the night flew by. She loved it.

Just after midnight everyone gathered outside as the couple rode off in a classic Rolls Royce headed for Miami's international airport; their red eye flight to a secret honeymoon spot set to depart in a few short hours. Only then, as the remaining few guests filtered back inside, did Kendall see Anson slowly ambling the curved drive off to the side. Every now and then he looked back toward her, standing still the moment he realized he'd gained her attention.

In that moment, she felt no resentment toward him.

"How long have you been here?" she asked, approaching him without hesitation.

"Long enough to know you didn't participate in the bouquet toss," he answered.

She nodded reflectively.

"You look amazing," he said, desperately hoping to win her over. "My outfit finally looks complete with you standing next to me. Can't be Double O Seven without a Bond girl." His tuxedo accented her attire perfectly just as they'd planned. But the compliment fell flat and

Anson drew in a long breath. "I still have the room reservation. Can we stay together tonight?"

Kendall looked behind her, a few scattered guests exiting to their vehicles. Elena and Gabriel had gone home already. She had considered using the reservation for herself, having never stayed at the Biltmore. But the thought of an exhausting night with him, potentially hashing out the details of his peppered past, had no appeal whatsoever.

"I don't think that's a good idea," she finally said. "It's been a long day. A long, wonderful day. And I know, for me, it was because I was not bogged down by the skeletons of your past. Joice and Xavier were no shows, thankfully."

"Kendall," he began, the automaticity of his fingers along her waist following — Kendall hardly noticing as it'd become so expected. "I can't stand trial for every mistake I've made in the past if I've already paid my dues. At some point you need to forget it all, just as I've done." His hand slid further behind her, pulling her in close, and she reacted.

"No!" she said sternly, shirking away his hand and stepping back. "I *can* hold you accountable for how you deal with your past here in the present. And yesterday you embarrassed me and I had to listen to my pregnant best friend — the night before her wedding, mind you — tell me how you forced Joice into an abortion–"

"That is NOT how it happened. You can't go believing every bullshit story that–"

"Damnit, Anson! You leave me no other choice! It doesn't matter if it's true!" she shouted. "It matters that I have to hear all this bullshit from someone else and you're left explaining your way out of it while I'm the histrionic fool." Then she let out a loud, exasperated wail. "I'm so sick and tired of all this fucking drama! I'm done! Anson: I. Am. Done!"

She spun around in a huff and headed back up to the entrance.

"Where are you going?" he called out after her.

"I don't know!" she yelled back, throwing her hands up in the air. "To get a room for myself, I guess."

"If I can't stay with you tonight, let me at least take you home," he offered.

"I'm going out to brunch with my mom and Gabe tomorrow. I have to stay in town."

"Kendall," he said, attempting to reason with her. "Kendall, come on. You can miss one brunch."

"It's Mother's Day tomorrow!" she shouted, stopping in her tracks and facing him. "A day *I* can never look forward to, but it's still a day I can dedicate to *my* mother — someone who is *always* honest with me!" She felt the hot tears now threaten and stormed off once more.

He caught up with her, gently stopping her, and stood right behind her in silence. He dropped his hands down her arms and weaved his fingers into hers; the warmth of his body enveloped her instantly. She closed her eyes as he leaned in just enough to drink in her scent.

"Let me stay. I want to stay with you." His whispered words tickled her exposed neckline and the heat sank deep into her bones. "Kendall, I love you. I fucked up. Let me make it right."

Her shoulders rose with a sudden intake of air as her head barely fell back before resting comfortably against him. He immediately wrapped his arms around her waist, Kendall sliding hers securely along his. His lips softly brushed the skin along her shoulder as he spoke.

"I'm taking you to our room," he said, planting a single kiss on her neck, her scalp prickling to attention.

A tear rolled down her cheek and she shook her head in mild protest.

"Yes. I'm taking you to our room," he repeated softly. "You and me. We know."

Neither spoke during their walk through the hotel lobby; simply holding hands and staying focused on this simplest form of communication. An occasional stroke of Anson's thumb along her hand was the only change in pace. Anson opened the door to their suite, allowing Kendall to enter the darkened room before he flicked on the entryway lights.

"No light," she said softly, wanting to maintain the peace she now felt.

The room warmed to a hushed glow as the streetlamps filtered through the sheer curtains, separating them from the small balcony that overlooked the treetops below. Anson strolled confidently behind Kendall, removing his tuxedo jacket along the way and placing it on the couch.

She continued through the dividing door to the bedroom where a plush, king-sized bed commanded her attention. A décor of soft creams and other soothing tones invited her further in to a place of luxurious comfort. She dragged her fingertips along the Egyptian cotton duvet, stopping along the corner of the bed.

Anson remained fixed against the door frame, watching her silhouetted figure move through the room in her long black gown. He waited.

She turned to face him.

"Come here," she said.

Before his bowtie could even hit the floor, he gathered her into his arms, getting lost in all that she meant to him.

Anson's kisses were slow and intense, Kendall's body trembling beneath each heated plea. With one tug of her side zipper, her dress slipped down into a ring of silky charmeuse around her heeled feet. He crouched in front of her, gliding his fingertips down her body, her exposed skin pebbling up from his tender touch.

He pressed his lips firmly over her panties, Kendall's breath hitching as she craned her neck back. His fingers clung to her hips, bringing her closer until he could taste her arousal soaking through. He slowly removed her underwear. His hands, then, traveled up her belly to her covered breasts, his body coming to a gradual stand. And in another moment, her bra dropped to the floor.

Kendall breathed rapidly, her heart racing along as if she'd never been touched by Anson before. If his rate matched hers, she couldn't tell — his fluid movements and soft sounds seamlessly flowed in their driven purpose.

"You nervous?" he asked, his lips tracing below the curve of her collarbone.

Curiously, she wondered if she was. It'd been three weeks since the surgery, two weeks since her ill-planned orgasm, one week since she took him on after rejecting his proposal. But it wasn't fear of pain or the risk of slower healing that spiked her adrenaline. She found herself needing to savor each moment — to know and remember every single touch and the exact response her body delivered — as if it'd be the last time Anson would touch her.

"No," she said, moving onto the bed and sliding back.

Anson looked her over in awe as he unbuttoned his shirt. He joined her, ready to rekindle the very essence of them. Before another word was exchanged, he was above her, slipping inside her velvety wet walls, and lost in love.

The push and pull of their bodies as they willingly yielded to one another; their moans and catching breaths; the soft suckle of his lips against her hips, her thighs, and back up to the sweet vanilla of her neck — they filled the room with the sultry sounds of candescent love-making and rose to new heights. Anson dug deeper, desperate to satisfy her; heal her; protect and love her. But he'd never find his fill — the taste and texture of her skin always leaving him with an insatiable hunger for more. Kendall recognized it: she'd never really be enough if he couldn't stand who he was, on his own.

As they summited the peak, an invariable set of rolling waves crashing over them, Kendall forced her eyes open — to see him, where he came alive, where he found his purpose — the moment he could not seem to live beyond.

"I love you, Anson," she cried. "I love you. I love you. Oh god! Anson, I love you!"

They made love endlessly into the night. But by the time he woke, Anson found himself in a room flooded with lonely morning light.

Kendall was gone; a handwritten letter placed on her pillow.

Dear Anson,

You once held my face in your hands and told me I was beautiful. Broken, yet beautiful. And that I would heal. Despite all the encouragement from Ariel and my mom, people who know the inner workings of my soul and knew without any doubt I would reach a place of peace eventually — only your words, your touch, and your love made me believe.

You infused a tangible love back into my lifeless body like no other person could do. Edgar Allan Poe said it best: "We loved with a love that was more than love." And because of you, my broken heart healed.

But now I need to continue this journey on my own. I want to experience life independent of your support, my family's support, and Dan's memory. I need to empower myself, love myself, and know what it is to live for myself.

And you need this, too.

My favorite little stretch of A1A is just north of the Boynton Inlet. It's a tunnel of sea grape trees. It takes some 10 seconds to drive through, but it's pure magic. I swear there's a wormhole there; some sort of time-space continuum. In the blink of an eye I experience an eternal beat of happiness. My brain grows quiet and all I feel is peace. It doesn't matter if I have music on or the windows down or if I'm distracted in thought; every single time I drive through there, I'm transported.

But that short drive on A1A only ever lasts a moment; the journey always extends well beyond that stretch. I think we experience these punctuated moments of bliss to keep us moving forward. They are the very quintessential moments that make life worth living. And their beauty lies in their greatest folly: they end — but with an impact that lasts a lifetime.

Anson, I love you. I will always love you. You have filled me with an all-consuming love. Thank you for your patience, for your words of encouragement, for your unparalleled touch. I was drowning in my sorrow and you saved me.

You saved me.

Yours always,
Kendall

Chapter 25

Kendall pulled her Jeep into her usual space on the fifth floor of the GC General parking garage. Except now she was returning to night shift; returning to neuro ICU and a very concrete plan of leaving again as soon as humanly possible. It was too early for an inspirational sunset and too late to start somewhere fresh. She closed her eyes, visualizing the 12-hour shift whizzing by without complications — an unwavering upbeat attitude and the purpose in her life restored. Her only permitted foreseeable dread in the upcoming weeks would be the unavoidably long commute home. Nothing else. Fortunately, during that first week back (Ariel and William off honeymooning), Kendall only had to drive to Ariel's empty apartment in West Palm Beach.

She scanned the parking lot below — *searching for him? For his car?* She wasn't sure. She immediately scolded herself.

It's over.

The familiar call of chaos danced about in her head as she hastily grabbed her bag and marched off to the hospital.

"Welcome back to neuro!" Cindi, one of the night charge nurses in the neuro ICU, called out as Kendall hit the floor. "We always knew you'd be back one day."

Kendall graciously smiled, settling in an area at the station to get report from the day nurse, Marie. Following report and a quick look at their two patients, Marie and Kendall returned to the nurse's station.

"So, everything's done for bed 9," Marie explained, paging through the patient's chart. "Just waiting for transport to arrive to take him to the long-term facility. I hope they come soon, for your sake, because we already heard a stroke alert called in the ED. I think you'll be the only open bed once 9 leaves."

"It is what it is," Kendall said dismissively.

Actually, she welcomed the challenge of a busy night, hoping it would make everything go by quickly. She flipped through the patient's packet, making sure all was in order to send with transport, then suddenly stiffened. Her fingers lightly grazed the ink of his signature on one of the progress notes — she knew his handwriting well.

"I heard you and Dr. Allaway were something of an item," Marie said quietly. "Is that true?"

Kendall startled and pulled her hand away from the paper — her reaction more to his name than to Marie's probing inquiry. She nervously laughed.

"This hospital loves a rumor," Kendall responded cryptically, heading in the direction of the patients' rooms. "Will you be back in the morning?"

"No," Marie said, studying Kendall closely as she walked away. "You going to be okay?"

She turned back around to face Marie and smiled assuredly. "I've never been better. Thanks for asking."

An hour later the medical transport crew arrived for the late discharge of bed 9 to another facility. After they'd left, while discarding various items in the room to prepare it for cleaning, Kendall found a patient belonging bag they'd forgotten.

"I'm going to try and catch them at the ambulance bay," Kendall announced to Cindi, holding up the belonging bag.

She jogged down the hallway and out the back where the ambulances parked. She spotted her patient and successfully returned the bag. She walked confidently back to the entrance, smiling proudly at her small accomplishment. Before she stepped through the door, she heard someone yell her name.

"Kendall!" Leonard Bautista called out to her, walking back toward the door. "It's great to see you smile like that."

"Hey there, Leo!" she said warmly, greeting him with a hug. "How are you?"

"I'm great. The question is: How are *you*? I heard you needed some emergent surgery or something. No wonder you were '*a little sick*' last month. Damn, girl!"

"Yeah. Just keeping people on their toes. You know me," Kendall joked. "I'm all good now, though. So, you just heading out?"

"Yep. I wasn't sure if that was you, running past me in the hall. Obviously you're better; which is fantastic. What are doing here? Picking up a night shift?"

"Every night shift I can until school starts," she said, smiling. "Gotta make that money. I'm back in our old stomping grounds of neuro."

"Nice move. Smart move. You're so prepared. I really admire your strength in all this."

Kendall lowered her eyes. "Thanks," she said. "You do what you gotta do, right?"

"Well, I'll let you get back to work. But call me when you're ready to set something up again... You know — should you need any help or anything."

"Thank you, Leo. I really appreciate that."

They turned to go their separate ways, but Kendall quickly stopped and called back to him.

"Hey Leo," she shouted, then falling fairly quiet. "Um... thank you for... Thank you for letting me make my own decision — about Allaway."

Leo's face relaxed, having not expected anything like that. He clearly understood what she meant, however. He walked closer to her, remaining quiet.

"You could have told me all that you knew," she continued, looking down at her hands as she chipped away at the edges of her nails. "And painted a pretty ugly picture. But you didn't. I admire *you* for that."

"It wasn't my place," he said humbly.

"I know. But a lot of people would have said something — especially considering... well, the position I put you in."

"We both put ourselves there. There's no blame."

Kendall nodded her head appreciatively. "I suppose. But I just wanted to say: thank you. It was the right thing for me. For Allaway."

"Well, you're welcome," he said kindly. "I know how hard it can be to keep a secret around here and some things are just a private matter. So, are you two... You serious?"

She took in a deep breath and shrugged, strangely unsure how to answer despite her decision to write the letter and end it. She hadn't even returned any of his calls or text messages. It seemed cut and dry. They were over.

"We were. But now... Every day I make the decision to move forward," she said. "One day, hopefully, I'll be able to include another person in that decision."

"Well, I sincerely hope you get what you want," Leo said respectfully.

***

It was around two in the morning, that her shift — and subsequently Kendall — hit a wall, as the pace and rhythm of the hospital slowed way below its resting heart rate. Kendall found herself doing laps around the unit, even pinching herself from time to time, just to stay alert. She counted down the minutes to her next entry of hourly vital signs on her one, very stable patient. The earlier stroke alert had been cancelled in the ED and none of her colleagues seemed to require any assistance. She hoped for a heavy admission, anything to keep her idle body busy. She'd never dreamed the adrenaline shot she sought would arrive by way of text message.

AA: **Where will you be staying come morning?**

Her eyes darted about the unit, paranoid. She'd avoided all communication with him in the hopes of no "accidentally on purpose" run-ins. After the Mother's Day brunch had turned into a sob session that oscillated unpredictably between heartbreak, regret, and militant anger, Elena took charge of the day; effectively turning into a frenzied moving day.

Gabriel and Kendall had been sent apartment hunting after Elena called in a favor to a friend and realtor. She then drove up to Lantana and continued the packing of Sandalfoot Lane without the sentimental harness that had held Kendall back. She and Gabriel also had stayed overnight with Kendall at Sandalfoot, and together, they'd successfully completed all the packing by Monday with the help of a moving company. So, by Tuesday, Kendall had vacated the property, having turned over her keys to her realtor and affording her ample time to take a nap at Ariel's place before heading into work that night.

Anson had left her a voicemail that Tuesday morning, calling her "abrupt amputation" of all things associated with him "expected and characteristically cruel." It crushed her. She knew he was grasping at straws to make her react. But if they'd met up to hash it out, she'd fall right back into her same patterns — their chemical attraction far too powerful to resist.

She needed time and distance — his texts were undoubtedly that proverbial gateway back.

AA: **Just answer. I know you started back at work tonight.**

KM: **What do you want me to say?**

AA: **Whoa! She's alive.**

Kendall's heart raced wildly, immediately kicking herself for engaging him in his quest for information. She tried, once again, to hold off on writing back.

AA: **Do you have a place to stay?**

AA: **It's a legitimate question.**

KM: **You need to know where I'll be staying at 2 in the morning?**

AA: **Will it be my place?**

KM: **NO!**

AA: **Then where?**

KM: **That is no longer your concern.**

AA: **It is when I love you.**

Her phone felt slick in her hand as her palms began to sweat.

KM: **That was your first mistake.**

AA: **One I'll never regret.**

KM: **It wasn't your only mistake.**

AA: **And you're perfect?**

KM: **I can't do this. I'm working.**

AA: **We can fix this. We have to talk.**

Kendall quickly put her phone away for the rest of the shift in the locker room; avoiding him once again.

As her shift came to a close, the relief trickling in through the unit doors, the pressure to escape the building increased. Fortunately, having only the one patient awarded her a quick report. She grabbed her bag and made a mad dash for the exit. But Cindi foiled her escape.

"Kendall: you've got a phone call," she said, holding up the receiver into the air as she continued her floor report to the oncoming charge nurse.

Kendall froze, unsure what to do. After a short period, Cindi looked up at her quizzically.

"Kendall? You alright?" she asked. "You've got a phone call."

"Who is it?" Kendall asked suspiciously.

Annoyed, Cindi held the phone back to her face. "May I ask who's calling?" She looked back over at Kendall. "Courtney from S.I."

Immediately the adrenaline surge flat-lined, Kendall's knees nearly buckling with relief. She ambled over to the phone, accepting it from Cindi.

"Hey there. I'm just heading out," Kendall said.

"Oh, that's fine. I was just checking in on you," Courtney said sweetly. "Saw your man this morning when I walked in. I asked if he'd heard how your first night back went. He said all he knew was you were still alive at two in the morning. That's so funny."

Kendall forced a laugh. "Yeah. Well, have a good day. I hope I can stay awake for the drive home."

"Well good thing he only lives a few minutes away, right?" Courtney said, oblivious to their situation.

"Uh, yeah. Good thing."

Kendall sped walked through the parking lot, rushed up the parking garage stairwell, and climbed into her Jeep in record time. She huffed rapidly, as if she'd just evaded an attacker. She couldn't fathom avoiding him a full two months more. Exhausted, she started the engine and routinely pulled out her phone to plug it in. His unanswered texts faced her head on.

AA: **Stay at my place today so we can talk when I get home.**
AA: **Will you think about it?**
AA: **You still have a key...**
AA: **?**

As she stared at the screen, a new message popped up.

AA: **Let me know you make it wherever safe. I'll be in the OR.**

During the entire twenty-minute drive to Ariel's apartment, Kendall went through multiple drafts of an appropriate, no frills, oneline response. As soon as she pulled into the complex's parking garage, she picked up her phone.

KM: **Home safe.**

She didn't expect a response, knowing he'd probably started his surgery. But she'd underestimated Allaway's determination to keep the doors of communication open.

AA: **My place?**
KM: **No.**
AA: **Where then?**
KM: **Don't worry about it.**
AA: **Must be somewhat local if you're home already.**
KM: **You realize you sound like a stalker.**
AA: **Maybe I'm watching you now.**

Kendall immediately looked behind her, checking all her Jeep mirrors. There were plenty of people getting into their vehicles to begin their work days. But no signs of him.

KM: **Now you just sound creepy.**
AA: **And in love?**

KM: **No. Just creepy.**
AA: **But are you smiling?**

Frustrated by how easily she played right into his game, she shoved her phone back into her bag and got out of the Jeep. She rode the elevator up to Ariel's 7th floor apartment, fuming the whole way. She entered the classy studio design — nearly barren as Ariel planned to move to Georgia shortly after the honeymoon — and heaved herself onto the bed. But on the kitchen counter, she could hear her phone buzzing from within her bag. It seemed to continue endlessly. He'd resorted to calling.

"Damnit, Anson!" she blurted upon answering the phone. "You can't do this! You know damn well our conversation would go from *I'm sorry* to *sex* in two seconds flat; bringing us right back to where we were when this all started: utterly fucked. Literally."

There was a collective gasp on his end of the receiver and Kendall froze in horror.

Anson cleared his throat. "Kendall: I'm in the OR. You are on speaker phone. I apologize for not making that immediately known. I was hoping to catch you before you went to sleep. I, uh… simply wanted to tell you I love you and hope to see you later. But I suppose I just killed any chance of that happening." He laughed sheepishly, glancing about the OR. "So, uh… Hey? I don't suppose we can just skip over all of this and go straight to the part where you move back in and this is all just a bad memory, can we?"

His attempt to make further light of their crippling humiliation was only met by silence — a painfully long stretch of silence; until the new scrub tech timidly spoke up.

"Excuse me, Dr. Allaway?" she said regretfully. "But it appears as if the call was lost."

Anson took in a deep breath. He looked up from the corner of the OR room where he stood. He'd been waiting for the anesthesiologist and surgical scrub team to finish their preparation. "That didn't go as planned. Let's hope this does. Are we about ready to begin?"

Anson rushed out of the hospital a couple of hours later after successfully finishing the case. He walked along the pond, restoring the blood flow to his heart as his body thawed from the icy temperature of the OR. He'd sworn to himself that he wouldn't do it, but his desperation got the better of him. He called Gabriel.

"Uh... Hi," Gabriel answered, somewhat uncomfortably.

"Hey man. So it sounds like you know."

"Yeah," he said sorrowfully. "Kendall said she broke up with you. She was crying. We helped her move. But my mom said these things happen. So what happened?"

Anson smiled. It was good to hear his voice.

"I'm not sure," Anson said kindly, taking a seat on a bench along the path as every muscle in his body seemed to relax. "Your mom's right, though. These things do happen. But I didn't want it to happen. I still don't. I love your sister very much. You know, I bought her a ring and everything."

"Oh. Well, did you give it to her?" "She wouldn't take it," Anson said.

"Maybe she didn't like it," Gabriel suggested. "She doesn't really wear jewelry."

"It's a pretty nice piece. Then again, she never looked at it."

"Oh. Well I can't help you there."

Anson smiled. "Well, how about other ways of winning her back. Can you think of any tips for me?"

Gabriel laughed. "You're asking the wrong dude!"

Anson joined in with his laughter. "I'm not so sure about that. You seem to have a pretty good understanding of all things Kendall. She listens to you. So when did you guys move her?"

"Mother's Day," he said. "It ruined Sunday brunch. And Monday. It took forever. I never want to move her again."

"I bet," Anson said empathetically. "Did you get a moving van?"

"Yeah. They helped. It was kind of cool. They had an electric lift."

"That probably helped with the heavy stuff."

"Yeah," Gabriel said. "We use one like it at Gold Coast Reefs. And a ramp. I'm in charge of the fish."

"I know," Anson said. "So, where'd the van take everything?"

"To Miami," Gabriel answered without hesitation.

Anson sat forward on the bench in surprise. "Miami? Really? Your place?"

"No. She got her own apartment. I helped her pick it out. It's okay. I like my place better."

Anson took a second to absorb the truth: He'd just paid an extra hundred grand to make her move to Miami faster. "But she didn't drive down there today."

"No, she's at Ariel's this week. Ariel and Will are honeymooners. Did you forget?"

"That's right. I totally forgot," Anson said, the guilty nature of his probing questions making him cringe. "My mind's been a little preoccupied. You wouldn't happen to know how to get to Ariel's apartment, would you?"

"Again: you're asking the wrong dude!" Gabriel laughed heartily.

"I'm pretty sure you were the right guy to call," Anson said. "Thanks for the help, buddy."

"Anytime, Aces," Gabriel said happily. But then he added, as if he'd been mistaken: "Well, I guess not anymore."

"Hey, listen. Even if Kendall and I don't make it work, you and I should still get together and talk fish sometime. Sound good?"

"Okay," Gabriel agreed.

"I'll talk to you later, Gabe. You've got my number. Call anytime. I have to head back into work now."

He then left Kendall a voicemail and held onto hope that she'd be open to a conversation.

"I'm sorry. I don't know what I was thinking. I thought we were making some headway with the texts and I... I wasn't thinking. I'm sorry if you felt embarrassed. I know how important your privacy at work is and I... I'm sorry, Kendall. I spoke with Gabe–"

The voicemail cutoff. It was early afternoon and Kendall had just woken up. She reluctantly played the first voicemail upon waking.

Now she quickly played the second one.

"Sorry about that. Got cutoff. Guess I'm rambling a bit. This would be a lot easier if we just spoke to one another. Like adults. Call me. I'd come over, but Gabe doesn't know where Ariel lives."

Naturally, she called Gabriel.

"Hi Barbie!" he said happily. "Guess where I am right now?"

"Where?" she asked, frustrated she couldn't dive immediately into the topic at hand.

"In a mansion!"

"Oh really? For work?"

"Yeah. The guys are measuring out a space for a custom tank. I got to come along."

"Well good for you," she said, quickly moving them along. "Hey, so… Did you talk with Anson today?"

"Yeah. This morning. I think he misses you. He said we can still hang out, though."

"I'm not so sure that's a good idea, bud."

"Why not?" Gabriel asked. "You broke up with him. But I can still be friends with him. He didn't die."

Kendall sank onto Ariel's bed, her heart aching with Gabriel's blunt response.

"You don't understand everything going on between us, Gabe; so it's best not to get involved. You know what I mean?"

Gabriel was silent.

"He's going to want to talk about me and get information out of you about me. It's only natural. Isn't that what happened? What did you two talk about?" she asked.

Gabriel sighed. "You."

"Gabriel. I know he was your friend, but right now he's just using you to get closer to me. And it's not because he's a bad guy; he just doesn't know what else to do right now. But he has to figure out his own things right now. Do me a favor, bud: Don't answer his calls. Can you do that? Maybe one day down the road you two can hang out again. But for right now, I need you to help me out with this. Okay?"

"Is he being mean to you?" he asked.

"No. It's complicated. He's confused. And if you get involved, there's a good chance you'll just get hurt."

"Okay. I won't talk to him," Gabriel agreed quietly.

"Thank you, bud. I love you and hope you have a good rest of your day in the mansion. I'll talk to you later."

"Bye, Kendall."

With seething force, she typed out a text message to Anson.

KM: **Below the belt. Do NOT call Gabriel. You are undermining his intelligence, taking advantage of his honesty, and disgusting me. Have you no character at all? This morning you embarrassed me and now you have embarrassed my brother. Unbelievable!**

Kendall's phone lit up as Anson promptly responded with a call.

"What the hell, Anson?!" she sharply demanded.

"Whoa! Calm down already," Anson said defensively. "I embarrassed you. Not intentionally, but it happened. I did *not*, however, embarrass Gabe. I wouldn't do that. I'm allowed to call him up and chat. *Yes*, I asked him where you were staying and maybe one can argue I took advantage of his honest–"

"Bullshit!" she scolded, silencing him. "Don't make this sound like you were calling him up for conversation. Did you ask him one damn question about *his* life? About what he was up to? Did you set up plans for getting together? Taking him out? NO! Your sole purpose was to take advantage and now that he knows it — *yes*, I made sure he understood that was your purpose — you *have* embarrassed him. No one likes to play the fool. Especially my brother who has had it happen to him too many times before; but *NEVER* at the hand of a man he thought I loved. *Those* men he could always trust. And now that trust is broken."

Kendall breathed heavily against her cellphone, waiting for Anson to retaliate in some form. But there was nothing; just deafening silence.

"Goodbye, Anson," she said.

"Goodbye, Kendall."

Chapter 26

Kendall was on her third lap around Miami International Airport's arrival terminal before she spotted William and Ariel. They'd been gone a week. It'd felt like a year for Kendall. William scrambled to get the luggage in the back of the Jeep while Ariel and Kendall gushed over one another. They drove off, Ariel telling Kendall all about their trip.

"You really are so tan. I seriously almost blew right past you two at the airport! Sounds like an amazing honeymoon," Kendall said, merging with the rush hour traffic of US-1. "I think after I graduate, I'm going to need a vacation like that."

"Yes! We will do a girls' trip," Ariel excitedly agreed. "William will stay home with the baby and we will sail off into the sunset."

"Uh, no," William jokingly countered. "Mama Duval will stay home with the baby and I get to go again."

"Couples trip, perhaps?" Ariel suggested.

Kendall scrunched up her face at the idea. "I think we'll leave that one alone."

"Agreed," William chimed in.

Ariel turned and looked at him scornfully in the back seat, shaking her head.

"So how's the night shift working out?" Ariel asked.

"So far, so good," Kendall said casually. "Finished a full week. Worked last night. Once I woke up, I drove right down."

"Anson off this weekend?" Ariel asked.

"Uh… I'm not sure. Hadn't asked."

Ariel looked at Kendall closely. Kendall kept her eyes focused on the road. "You two talking much?"

"Um, no. Not much. Kind of broke up with him on Mother's Day."

"Hallelujah!" William sang out behind them.

Ariel darted him an angry glare.

"So where are you staying then?" she asked carefully.

"Well, I got a place down here. But actually, I took advantage of your place for the week."

"Oh that was smart!" Ariel said happily. "I'm glad you could do that at least. You know we're driving the rest of my stuff up to Georgia this week. Should be all done by Wednesday. My lease is good through

209

May 31st, though. That gives you more than a week after we leave if you want to take advantage of it a little longer. I'm going to take my bed because it's going into our guest bedroom, but we could get one of those blow up mattresses."

"Thanks, Ariel," Kendall said genuinely. "That would really help. I'm planning to work through July before resigning. The less time I commute, the better."

They drove along quietly, Kendall eventually turning onto the serene roads of Coral Gables with their canopy tops of Banyan branches. It reminded her of her favorite natural tunnel on A1A. And now she associated that lovely spot with Anson because of her damn letter. She internally sighed and pulled into the Duval drive, parking the Jeep.

"Where are you going to go now?" Ariel asked.

"Actually back up to your place," Kendall said with amusement. "I have to empty out some things, so you can do the rest of your emptying. Then I'll be driving back down here to stay at my place. I'll call you. Lots of driving ahead. I don't work again until Wednesday night, so it's kind of perfect."

"Oh. Well, stay here for dinner and then head back to my place tonight. Will and I were planning on staying with my parents tonight anyway. Believe me. They have to hear about everything. You can stay at your new place tomorrow and I'll come by to see it before heading back up to West Palm."

"You know what? I think I'll take you up on that," Kendall said gratefully. "That sounds like a much better plan. Thank you. I could use a real meal anyway."

Dinner at the Duvals' was always the best. Growing up, Kendall tried to make it happen as often as possible. Mama Duval always made her feel like an honored guest and she soaked up the attention. She spoiled her just as she did her own daughter.

"You're glowing, my dear," Mama Duval said to Ariel, kissing the top of her head as she cleared the plate in front her. "The sun was just what mother nature ordered."

"I am starting to feel better," Ariel said, smiling. "I'm officially in my second trimester now."

"That's so exciting," Kendall squealed, handing over her plate to Ariel's dad. The two girls never seemed to clear the table, even in adulthood. Hanging out at the Duval house rendered them useless teenagers and adoringly, the Duvals wanted it no other way.

"You look like you're glowing, too," Mama Duval commented, placing a piece of sweet potato pie in front of Kendall. "Finally putting on some weight!"

"Mama!" Ariel scolded.

Kendall laughed. She swore Elena and Mama Duval constantly collaborated on what should be said to her regarding her weight.

"Well, I haven't really gained since the surgery — except for that meal I just inhaled. I'd been feeling crappy. But I will say, I am feeling ten times better now. I just have to work on getting rid of this pooch. I think two surgeries in that area has messed it all up or something."

"What pooch?" Ariel contested, standing up. "*I've* got a pooch. Did you see this?" She smoothed her top over a barely-there bump.

"All my skinny jeans are completely useless now." They all groaned with laughter.

"Well, you've got a good reason for that," Kendall said, smiling. "When do you find out what it is?"

"Next month sometime," Ariel said, raising her eyebrow with excitement. "Either way: drumroll please... It's. Going. To be. A. Jun~ior!" She announced, giving her best Oprah Winfrey impression.

"What? Seriously?" Kendall asked skeptically. "You're naming it either William Jr. or Ariel Jr.?" Ariel had always been adamant on *not* making her children carry family names. "You get married and now you're all traditional," she teased. "Is this *your* doing Will?"

"Hey, I'm just Stedman when it comes to this Queen Bee's ideas," he answered smartly, nodding back at Ariel.

"Really? You're not planning on a single one of your standalone, all-powerful, hear-me-roar names?" Kendall asked Ariel.

"Well, the names I picked still pack a punch. If it's a boy, we will name him... Wait for it... Kenneth Duval Johnson," Ariel answered, a clear twinkle in her eye. "And if it's a girl, she'll be... Daniela Duval Johnson."

Kendall stared at the two in complete awe. "Dan? Me? You're going to name the baby after one of us? Really?"

Ariel nodded excitedly. "Well, I can't only depend on this guy here to help me raise this baby. Got to give the godmother a little incentive to come to Georgia."

Kendall immediately got up and hugged both of them.

"Oh my goodness!" Kendall said humbly, still in a full embrace. "You're going to make me cry. I can't believe it!" She returned to her seat still in shock. "I have to tell my mom. She'll flip. We could finally have a real Ken doll amongst us."

"I wouldn't be so sure," said Mama Duval. "I'm calling her Daniela already. I think it's high time another heiress moves in and dethrones you two queen bees."

"Hear, hear!" William cheered, raising his glass to Mama Duval. Of course they all laughed.

At the end of the evening, Ariel and William walked Kendall out to her Jeep.

"Oh, I almost forgot!" Ariel said. "I got you something. Just something silly. Let me grab it quick. Wait here... with my *husband*." Ariel ran back into the house, laughing at herself as both William and Kendall rolled her eyes.

"Wow," Kendall said. "She really needed that vacation."

"And to get over the morning sickness," William chimed in. "It was probably around day two when she really noticed she was feeling pretty good. Plus all the stress of the wedding was gone and well..." He shuffled around on the drive, pushing a stone away with his barefoot.

"What?" Kendall asked.

"Well... you seemed happy at the wedding. That was really important to her. She needed to see that. You guys are linked too much."

Kendall sighed through a smile. "She's my blood, Will."

"Don't I know it," he said, shaking his head.

"Can I ask you a question?" Kendall asked, twiddling around with her nails before peeking up at him.

"Oh no. Here we go."

"No, no. Nothing major. Well... yes: Anson related. But not anything long and drawn out."

William sighed, rubbing his face and looking back up to the house to gauge Ariel's return. "Okay. Shoot."

"Do you hate him because of what happened with Joice? Or is it something else?"

"Not major?" he chided, shaking his head.

Kendall offered up a sympathetic shrug.

He then groaned and wiped his face again. "I got involved in what I got involved in, to make money. Nothing else. He's in it on a whole other level. It was nothing I could ever identify with. I got along with Xavier and gravitated to the business aspect of things, learning what I could to manage a business of that size. Allaway came from money and had money on the horizon as a doctor. But he still chose AAXLS above everything else. His motivations were clearly something different."

"So... his ex? Joice?" Kendall asked hesitantly.

"I only got her side of the story," he said reluctantly. "Listen: She was a hustler just like him. They were two of a kind and did what they had to do to get ahead in the business. If he has a different story than hers; well, let's just say I wouldn't be that surprised."

Kendall nodded her head thoughtfully. "Well, thank you for being honest. I'm still trying to piece things together. For myself."

"Is that why you broke up?" he asked.

"Among other things. I don't know. It was moving all a bit fast for me."

"He's only ever had that one speed," William commented casually, looking back at the front door as Ariel bounded out.

Kendall looked up at him with intrigue, but didn't push it, knowing Ariel didn't need the stress of her stress any longer.

"It was all the way at the bottom of my one suitcase," Ariel exclaimed exhaustively. "My goodness. I was going crazy trying to find it."

She handed over to Kendall two small items wrapped in a generic blue convenient store plastic bag. Kendall took it, eyeing Ariel's eager expression suspiciously.

"I found it at our layover airport last week," Ariel admitted, laughing. "I don't know. I thought you could put them on your refrigerator or something."

Kendall pulled out two square magnets. One had Ariel's favorite quote that Kendall had adopted as her mantra:

"One must still have chaos in oneself
to be able to give birth to a dancing star."
Friedrich Nietzsche

The second one made Ariel start laughing before Kendall even fully registered what she'd read:

Work Hard. Play Harder.

But if you're hard for more than four hours,
seek out medical attention.
I am a nurse.

"You found this at an airport?!" Kendall asked in surprise.

"You like it?" Ariel asked, biting her lip in an attempt to hold in her laughter as Kendall shook her head with begrudging amusement. Kendall narrowed her eyes at Ariel.

"Oh come on!" Ariel said, pushing Kendall back. "Remember what you said to me before the wedding? About working hard... among *other* things? Hmm?"

"Okay! Okay!" Kendall said, flushing a brilliant red and immediately glancing at William who simply shook his head at the two friends.

"It's just a fun joke," Ariel said, smiling.

"I know, I know. I'm teasing," Kendall said in surrender. "Thank you. I will proudly display them on my Miami apartment refrigerator and never invite a single soul over."

They all laughed, Kendall wrapping the magnets back up in the bag and hugging Ariel once more. They made plans to make arrangements with one another the next day and said goodbye.

As Kendall drove back to West Palm, her mind wandered back to her conversation with William. She'd never given Anson a chance to explain anything. But then again, he'd never seemed willing to do so, either. Whether it was the hour left in her drive or the fact that she'd felt completely restored in her relationship with Ariel despite knowing she'd be moving in a few short days, Kendall decided to call Anson.

"Hey," he answered somewhat perplexed. "Uh, how is everything? You working tonight?"

"No. Just leaving Miami. Picked Ariel and Will up from the airport. They're home from their honeymoon. I had dinner with them and her parents. It was really nice."

"Oh. That's right. It's been a week, I suppose."

"Yeah," she said sullenly.

Their pause of silence reeked of obvious clumsiness, both incapable of small talk when it came to what truly occupied every space of their thoughts — and hearts.

"So, uh... Did you need something?" he finally asked.

"Well, I was just thinking as I drove–" she began.

"Dangerous territory there. Aren't there enough distracted drivers in South Florida without adding one more to the mix?"

"Funny," Kendall sardonically replied. But she smiled, grateful for his continued ability to put her right at ease exactly when she needed it. "Anyway. I never gave you a chance to explain your side of the Joice story. I was wondering if you wanted to."

Anson heaved off a sigh, wishing he could just keep the mood with her light and forgiving; his past always casting such a dark shadow.

"Why now?" he asked.

"Because I struggle with the idea that I was so blinded by you that I never really saw you."

"So, this is for you to feel better about yourself," he said flippantly. "To either make me not the monster you think I am because how could you have fallen in love with such an asshole in the first place. Or to make that monster realized; then at least you know you made the right decision last week — your only fault being that you hadn't done it sooner. Am I right?"

"You know what," Kendall said with exasperation. "Never mind. I'm sorry I called."

"No. I'll tell you," he said arrogantly. "I want you to have that peace of mind you so desperately seek.

"Joice was never pregnant to begin with. Yes: she told me she was pregnant and I jumped the gun. But I was also helping her get a green card. I'd known her for years and she never judged me. I suppose we're cut from the same cloth. It was going to be a marriage of convenience. She wanted to keep working like we were doing. I forbid it because of risk. She never gained weight. I got suspicious. It ended. I moved to Florida shortly thereafter and dropped our joint clients. She agreed to stay away. I guess she said what she thought she had to say to salvage her reputation.

"So? Tell me: am I the monster or are you just holding my past over my head?"

Kendall cruised robotically amidst the sea of red backlights lit in front of her on I-95. She didn't know how to respond, unsure how she even felt. If anything, she suddenly had more questions — none of them particularly appropriate to her own assessment of their breakup. *Joint clients? Ménage à trois style?*

"I... uh... I-I don't know," she stuttered. "Why didn't you tell me any of this?"

"It's nothing you want to hear. And I'm not proud of any of it. Not when it's said out loud to the woman I love. It's in the past and shouldn't matter to you."

"Well, of course it matters," she countered. "On some level everything in our past matters. All our actions have consequences. You can't run from them forever."

"I'm not trying to run from them. I'm trying to be done with it. Kendall: I'm not ashamed. But at what point do I get a new start? I've changed. For you! But it's not good enough."

"Anson: you can't change for anyone, but yourself," she said firmly. "If this isn't who *you* are, then don't change. Not for me. Not for anyone."

"You're the one unwilling to change now — to move on in your life and see me as an integral part of it. I wouldn't have changed if I wasn't willing to. You were simply a catalyst to my change."

Right then: his choice of words hit him harder than anything she'd spelled out in her letter to him. She heard his sharp inhale as the word *catalyst* echoed repeatedly between them.

"You do realize," Kendall began cautiously, almost guiding him along in his own thoughts. "The role of a catalyst in a chemical reaction is to initiate change, and then... leave unchanged."

"Yeah. I gathered that," he said. He sighed; a deep, foreboding weight adjusting across his chest as he attempted to reconcile their anger toward one another. "Listen: I know much of what I've covered up about myself has hurt you. I understand your reasons to walk away from this, even if I don't exactly agree with them. You need to know, though: I never meant to hurt you. It was the last thing– No. It was never even a thought. Everything I did — *everything* — I thought I was doing it for you. For us. For a future we both deserved, but got cheated out on."

Kendall took in a long, quiet breath away from the phone receiver as a few isolated tears broke through, rolling down either side of her cheeks. She could feel the pull of his voice begin to toy with her heart, tempting it to play with the spark she knew could easily ignite between them if she allowed it.

"But everything grows in its own time, right?" he said poignantly, then laughed at himself. "Hey, can I change my analogy and say you were the fertilizer instead?"

Kendall chuckled, wiping her tears away, and quickly collected herself.

"Sure. I'll be your horse shit if that makes this easier on you," she quipped.

"I can't win, can I?" he said, his smile shining through.

"Well, if I remember correctly: *you remind me of my Jeep.* I don't think analogies are exactly our forte."

Anson laughed, Kendall eventually joining in. She felt light, comforted, loved. She missed that feeling of simplicity and wished it hadn't been bogged down by all the complicated emotions of their past. She wanted to cherish this moment with him and hoped for more like it; a natural progression of growth rather than depending on the constant adrenaline rush of it all.

"I miss you," he said suddenly, casting her fleeting thoughts of whimsy out the window.

"Anson," she pleaded weakly.

"I know you don't want to hear it, but it's the truth."

"I know," she said. "And maybe one day we can be friends."

Anson audibly groaned, Kendall immediately sensing an ominous turn in their phone conversation.

"Anson. It's been a week. Just give it time to–"

"I've given it a fucking decade, Kendall! Ten fucking years! I'm not looking to give it anymore time."

Kendall's respiratory rate immediately picked up; that rampant surge of adrenaline working her tirelessly over once again. And all because of him.

"And I haven't had that same luxury," she said. "Thank you for talking with me tonight, Anson. Goodbye."

Chapter 27

"As I live and breathe," Mark DeGraff dramatically called out across the hallway as Kendall walked toward GC General's back entrance. "I was beginning to believe you were some kind of apparition around the hospital corridors. A lonely nurse soul who still longed to push all the IV *roc* she could; leaving every unsuspecting heart gravely paralyzed in her wake."

"DeGraff: You missed your calling," Kendall replied, feeling obliged to walk over to him and engage in conversation; although the decision made her wary.

"I tried to join the theatre, but they said: *go be a nurse* — I was too dramatic for their tastes. How *are* you?" He gave Kendall a warm hug.

She'd been leaving the hospital through the back doors all in an effort to avoid the probing eye of a certain neurosurgeon who she'd been told had stopped by the unit during shift change on several occasions, looking for her. He hadn't called or texted since that last phone call on the way home from Miami. It'd been a week of silence. As long as she could keep the distance, she knew she could keep going.

But DeGraff was a direct connection to him... even if he was supposedly her friend first.

"I'm doing well. Working the night shift. You in charge today in SI?"

"That I am. Just grabbing my morning cup of Joe before heading back in there," he said, raising his paper cup of vending machine cappuccino. "We miss you in SI. Just isn't the same without our Kendall."

"I'm sure you're getting by just fine," Kendall said, smiling. "Besides. I heard Julia already moved into my day spot."

"Well. She did," DeGraff admitted. "But it's not like it was. You. Me. Rachel. The team is fracturing."

"It hasn't been that way ever since Rachel went per diem and I took leave. Plus: the whole last month I was there was like the twilight zone. It was time for something new."

"Time for something new, or *someone* new? Got a call from a certain gentleman the other day looking to hang out and catch the fight at a downtown bar. Ordinarily this would have been a normal Friday night outing. Until a certain woman entered his life. I hadn't heard much from him during that time. But now he's back. Interesting, isn't it?"

"Well maybe he finally decided to add a little *handball* to his bag-of-tricks and you should take him up on the offer," she said boldly, seeing right through his playful ploy to extract some information on her relationship with Anson.

"Point taken. Too personal. I'll keep my musings to myself."

"I have to get going," Kendall said, heading to the hospital exit.

"Well, I hope you don't remain a complete stranger. Cutting all your ties to the past, unless they caused undo harm, never seems to do anyone any good. That level of harm hasn't been done, has it?"

"Did he send you, Mark?" she asked, turning back to face him.

"No," he refuted sincerely. "But he is crushed. And he is my friend. I thought I could…"

"What?" Kendall asked brusquely. "A clean cut can be far better than small little slices over time. You and I both know that. February 27 through May 9 — that was our run and it's done now. It was exactly what I needed to jumpstart my life again. He knew where I stood from the very beginning."

DeGraff looked at Kendall sympathetically. He couldn't blame her. "Well, I don't know. Maybe I can just give him some sort of positive feedback or something."

Kendall snorted; his statement ironic to say the least.

"Well," she said, a mocking overtone emerging. "I'd give him five stars in all services, through and through. Unfortunately, I'm just too jaded to pay extra for the lifetime warranty."

She dropped her air-mic and left the hospital.

Kendall immediately called up Ariel. Quick phone calls on their ways in and out of work had been the favored form to stay in touch since Ariel's move to Georgia. Unfortunately for Ariel, Kendall always seemed to call when Ariel was rushing out the front door.

"I'm avoiding Anson like it's the plague and it's beginning to burn a hole through my stomach," Kendall rattled off the second Ariel answered her phone.

"Okay. Hold on just a second," Ariel said. "I'm putting on mascara… Okay. Go ahead. You're on speaker phone. Hole in your stomach…" Ariel had accepted a summer teaching position at a university with the potential of becoming a full-time position by spring. It was a perfect arrangement since she'd be out late fall with the baby arrival.

"What am I going to do? I can't keep this up. Eventually I'm going to run into him. Then what? Hope I've gotten over it?"

"Have you?" Ariel asked, keeping pace.

"I don't know. For the most part, I think I have. You know: out of sight, out of mind. But who knows what could happen if I actually see him again — face-to-face. If we *talk*. The thought alone is enough to give me an ulcer."

"Then quit your job!" Ariel reasoned. "If it's causing you this much stress, just freaking quit already. You've got your school money. You've got your apartment ready. Just move and take some time off to prepare for school."

"I can't do that," Kendall said, shaking her head as she drove along. "First of all: I'm committed to the hospital. Second of all: I'd go stir-crazy. No. I made my bed and I'll sleep in it."

"I don't recall much sleep going on in that bed."

"Okay you. Pipe down."

"Seriously, though. All joking aside," Ariel said, donning her voice of reason. "You're moving out of my place in a few days. The commute alone might make your decision for you."

"That's true," Kendall agreed. "Driving all the way south at this hour of the morning will be murder. Well, I'll let you finish getting ready. Love you!"

"Love you, too!"

Kendall pulled into the parking garage of Ariel's old apartment complex and exhaled with relief. Another shift survived without Anson. She entered the room and collapsed onto the bed; restless sleep promptly following.

The aerodynamic design of the home blows Kendall's mind. She finds herself slip-sliding up and down the walls like an amusement park ride. Then suddenly she's air-born; over the living room, over the countertops, flying free through the air, until landing safely in the kitchen. Everything shines in chrome and reflective black mirror. Ultrasleek and modern.

"What is this place? A space room?" she asks.

"My latest design," Talon answers.

"It's incredible!" she praises him, taking another quick spin around the slick surfaces. "Is it meant to be a ride?"

221

"Well, it's a home. A family lives here, Kendall," he explains. "Only you are riding the walls. No one else has done that."

"Are you kidding me? No one else has ever thought to slide and fly in here? Not even the children?"

"It's not the purpose of the design," he said matter-of-factly.

"Yes, but it certainly can be used this way. I'll need to show them what they're missing out on."

"Haven't you done enough damage already?" he asked sternly.

"I didn't mean to damage anything," she said regretfully.

"You can't go and change people's designs without them getting pissed."

"What are you talking about? It's still the same design. I just made it better!" she argues.

"But how can I sell it as a family home when it's actually an amusement park?" Talon shouts back with frustration.

Suddenly the entire structure flips upside down and Kendall only sees the Milky Way strewn across the black sky. She lies on her back and finds herself utterly alone.

"That was a cheap parlor trick," she says to no one as her stomach finally flips right-side up. "Anson? Are you there?"

A hand holds hers, grasping it lovingly.

"I'll always be here," Dan says.

Kendall turns her head to see his face and only finds emptiness. But the Milky Way shines bright.

"I love you," she says.

"I know," Anson answers.

***

Kendall staggered out into the GC General parking lot, the blinding light of the South Florida summer morning scorching her and all her exhaustive thoughts. With only two shifts down that included the Miami commute, the end of summer couldn't come soon enough. She dreaded every horn that blared point three seconds after a light turned green, prompting her to gun it; every state trooper that guarded the HOV lane, delaying her commute; every bumper to bumper accident that backed up I-95 for five miles because of gawkers taking it all in, forcing her head to bob incessantly as she fought off sleep. Something had to give and she knew: it had to be this job.

"Hey girly!" Courtney shouted from the parking garage, Kendall never even noticing her as she stared off mindlessly.

"Oh, hey there, Court. Did you oversleep or something?" Kendall asked.

"No. Apparently they're pretty desperate today. I agreed to come in... after I slept in a little." Courtney laughed. "You back tonight?"

"Yes," Kendall said with disappointment. "This commute is killing me. But fortunately after tonight I have a few days off."

"Your commute? You're not at Allaway's?"

Oh shit.

"Uh... we're not together anymore," Kendall said despite every fiber in her body telling her to just run the hell away.

"Oh?! You broke up?" Courtney asked in shock. "You two looked so good at your birthday party. I thought things were getting pretty serious."

"Well, you know. Not everything works out. We're just on different pages."

"Oh... I guess that kind of explains his comment the other day," Courtney said.

"What comment?" Kendall asked, unsure whether she actually wanted to know.

"DeGraff said something about needing another ICU night out. You know: to a bar or something. Allaway was at the station and I asked if he'd come again. He said something like he hadn't still recovered from the last time we all went out. I didn't think anything of it. But, uh... That was when you two got together, isn't it?"

Kendall nodded slowly. "I have to get going. My place is in Miami now. I'm all ready for school in the fall."

"Wow. Well, drive safely."

"Thanks, Courtney. Have a good day today."

"Thanks. And Kendall: Don't be a stranger!" Courtney said, smiling.

Kendall began her long commute, stopping for a drive-thru breakfast just to keep her occupied along the way. She then called Ariel once on the highway.

"I'm just pulling into work," Ariel said. "You're calling a little later than usual. All okay?"

"Yeah," Kendall said. "I'm tired. This commute is for the birds."

"Told you that might be the deal-breaker for you. Just quit. No one will bat an eye."

"*I* will," Kendall protested. "Plus: what does that say? I can't handle the stress of working with him?"

"No. That you don't want to commute an hour and a half for a night shift job. *That's* what that says."

"But I'll know the truth."

"Who the hell cares, Kendall," Ariel argued. "Why is this eating you so much?"

"Because I left him high and dry and I'm not sure it was the right thing to do," Kendall confessed.

"It wasn't the easy thing to do, but for what you've been battling in your gut? I think it was the right thing."

There was a shared silence as the two thought about it for a minute.

"I'll let you go," Kendall finally said. "Thanks for putting up with me this year."

"You know I'd have it no other way."

"Love you."

"Love you, too, babe," Ariel said, then hung up the phone.

Chapter 28

"Kendall: radiology's on the phone," Cindi called over from the opposite end of the nurse's station. "You ready to take the patient down?"

"Uh, hold up," Kendall replied, covering the receiver for the phone call she was already knee deep in. She looked at the unit secretary, Dante. "Call Patel again. This is ridiculous. He needs to make a decision." Then she immediately switched gears back to her current phone call. "What do you mean they don't have the specimen? I sent it there, so I *know* it's there. Look. Harder." She forced the phone back into its cradle, releasing a disgruntled groan and stormed back toward her crashing patient's room.

"Radiology's still holding," Cindi called out apologetically. "Line two."

"Shit... Hey, it's Kendall. I'm waiting on respiratory to set... What do you mean they can't set up the vent down there? Broken? Well, we can't wait. They'll just have to bag him right before the scan. I'll head down as soon as they arrive." She ended that phone call and hustled back into the room.

For the moment, she'd been able to stabilize the unfortunate thirty-year-old frequent flier of the neuro ICU. He suffered from a recurring malignant brain tumor, among other areas of metastasis, and his functional decline was compounded by the multiple craniotomies performed over the past five years to alleviate the pressure caused by the tumor. The hospital staff knew him and his family well. Although everyone hoped for a miracle, the nurses who cared for him wished his young wife would reconsider her stance on Hospice.

"Lab's on the phone again," Dante said, signaling to Kendall.

"It's Kendall," she said gruffly, labeling some specimen tubes of fresh blood. "You found the blood but it's clotted. Figured as much." Kendall shook her head with disgust. "I'm sending down some new specimens and an incident report will be written."

She hung up again and growled. "Why can't we ever depend on them when we need to?!"

Cindi offered a sympathetic shrug. Dante volunteered to courier the specimen down and headed out with the blood.

"And make sure they do it stat this time!" Kendall called after him.

The phone began to ring at the desk, but Kendall ignored it, heading right back into her patient's room, prepping for transport once respiratory arrived. Cindi picked it up, but, of course, it was for Kendall.

"It's Dr. Patel."

"Oh right!" Kendall called out. She finished spiking a new bag of an IV drip to balance out the patient's blood pressure and rushed out of the room... right into her very own pressure-altering drug.

"Anson," she said on a gasp, quickly regaining her composure. "Excuse me. Um... Dr. Allaway. I, uh, didn't realize you were here in the hospital covering."

Anson took the phone from Cindi and spoke with Dr. Patel. He kept it brief, then hung up the phone and turned to Kendall who was still frozen outside the patient's room.

"I happened to be in-house. I'm very familiar with the case. What's going on?" he asked, walking into the patient's room — and right past her without pause.

Kendall fell in line.

"He's declining. I've stopped his sedation and he's not rousing at all. Mild posturing. Ventilator settings had to be adjusted. Earlier in the shift I got some decent responses when turning down the sedation. I think he's herniating. It's not a typical presentation, though."

"ICP?" Anson asked, walking over to the patient's monitors. "Has it increased?"

"No. Not at all. That's why I'm confused." Kendall looked at Anson, hoping he'd have the answer.

"Did you call the wife?" Anson asked, meeting Kendall's eyes. "She should know."

"I did," Kendall answered, now saddened, realizing he did not have the answers. "She's on her way."

They looked at one another, a marked kindness shared between them — soon the wife would be in their unfortunate club. The patient's wife was only 27 and their whole marriage had been through the revolving door of the hospital.

"You agree he's herniating? You can't decompress the pressure or anything? He's still a full code. If it happens..." Kendall stopped, looking down at the unresponsive young man knowing he couldn't possibly endure one more surgery. She instinctively held his hand. "I know it's futile, but the wife…"

"It was evident during surgery. Hardit said he evacuated a new hematoma twice in the OR. His wife was aware. That's why the surgery lasted so long."

"Don't you think she'd want you guys to go back in? She's never been receptive to a DNR or anything like it," she said.

"No," Anson replied, shaking his head slowly. "She decided this would be the last surgery no matter what. Hardit– Dr. Patel, rather, even clarified that before the surgery, discussing this very scenario. It was a last-ditch effort."

Kendall looked up at the room entryway as Karen, the night respiratory therapist entered.

"Everything ready to go?" Karen asked.

"Yes. Let's get going," Kendall answered, then looking back at Anson. "You coming?"

Karen disconnected the ventilator and began bagging the patient as the three of them, Dr. Allaway included, maneuvered the large ICU bed out of the unit and to the elevators.

While Karen and the CT tech settled the patient up on the table, Anson and Kendall stood inside the darkened control room, watching through the large window.

"Had you received my first page for Dr. Patel?" Kendall asked, curious as to why he'd been in-house.

"No. He's on-call, I just happened to be here," he replied, glancing back at her from the corner of his eyes. "Thought I'd check in."

"Oh."

It'd been two weeks of total silence between them. But it'd been over three weeks since seeing one another. And now here they were: together, yet apart. Kendall mistakenly drew in a deep breath through her nose, flooding her mind with memories of skin-to-skin contact.

"Ever see that movie *Eternal Sunshine of the Spotless Mind*?" Anson asked seemingly out of nowhere, still focused on the patient beyond the glass plate.

Kendall looked right at him. She'd seen the movie forever ago, vaguely remembering the main theme: a former couple erasing the memories of their relationship, yet still finding one another afterward.

He turned his head when she didn't respond and read her quizzical expression.

"Smell," he stated plainly. "It's one of the biggest triggers of memories."

The CT tech and Karen then entered the control room, breaking his concentration on her. They both backed up from the control desk as the tech took his seat and began the scan. Kendall moved to the back wall and Anson hovered over the computer to see the images as they came across.

What the hell did he mean by that?

"Right there," Anson said, pointing at the screen and breaking Kendall's ruminating thoughts. "Those bleeds could be corrected. If those were it, he'd still be salvageable. But *that* right there" —he pressed his finger sternly against the screen at a blurred out area— "*that* can't be corrected. He's done." He smacked the counter with alarming force. "He's done."

Anson swiftly moved to the door, but then turned to Kendall. "We already had him on high dose steroids, right?"

She nodded.

"Damn," he said, shaking his head with disappointment. "I'll talk to his wife."

Back in the unit, the patient's vital signs continued to rapidly decline. His wife and parents were now at the bedside, the DNR status agreed to and forms signed. They'd all been ready for this prior to surgery, yet still hoped for the best until faced head-on with the possibility. The neuro ICU mood deteriorated right along with the patient's status. He'd been in the hospital already a week as they debated and prepared for the risky final surgery. The family regularly provided coffee and food for the hospital staff, showing their appreciation for all that they did. The loss of this patient would be difficult for everyone involved.

Kendall hadn't taken a break all night, despite having just the one patient. The hour approached five in the morning. Cindi encouraged her to take at least fifteen to simply recharge before her shift ended. Reluctantly she agreed, concerned she might not be there for the patient's family when his heart stopped.

She hadn't seen Anson since he left the radiology department, but her thoughts couldn't leave his comment. She swiped her badge to enter the private counseling room just outside the unit doors. The room was dark and windowless, a perfect spot for a catnap — and overanalyzing. Just as she flipped the lights on, she caught the light scent of his cologne and then saw him.

"Shit!" she shrieked, startled. "Anson, you have to stop scaring me like this."

Anson had made a makeshift cot with the chairs. He straightened up quickly, rubbing his eyes.

"Sorry. I was just dozing. Alarm is set on the phone. Did he die?" he asked.

"No. Still hanging on. Barely," she answered, standing motionless in front of the door unsure what to make of the encounter. "Started seizing. He'll go soon. The sedation is high. Cindi's watching him."

"Did you need the room? For the family?" he asked, standing up.

"No. I was just going to take a quick break and didn't want to be in the lounge. Little more isolated in here. But I suppose that's why you're here... Actually, why *are* you here? Why haven't you gone home?" Kendall walked further into the room, placing down her lunch bag on the round table, Anson positioned behind it in the corner of the room.

"I was visiting a friend upstairs," he answered. He looked exhausted, but kept his gaze steady on her.

"I'm sorry to hear that. Hope everything's okay."

"Thank you. She's fine. Elective surgery. Didn't take well to anesthesia. I told her it was a stupid idea."

"Oh," Kendall said, crossing her arms. *Elective surgery as in plastic surgery as in a boob job that he's probably going to fuck in a few weeks.* "And she needed a visitor in the middle of the night?"

"It was Maddie, Kendall," he said, as if reading her thoughts.
"Madison? My niece?"

"Oh." She looked down, feeling ashamed, but also relieved. "Well, you said *friend*, not family. Not that it should matter... Is she doing okay? Why'd she come down to Florida for it?"

"You going to sit down or do you need me to leave?" he asked, irritated.

"No, I'll leave." She picked up her food from the table. "You're right. It's none of my business. This is all a little too weird for me anyway."

"Why?" his tone almost accusatory. "If you want to be here. Be here."

"I can't be here with you," she admitted with exasperation.

"Why not?! Are we simply never going to speak to one another again? Is that your plan?"

"No! No... But when you ask shit like that in cat scan–"

"I'm trying to get you to talk, Kendall. I'm not going to ask about the fucking weather and pretend you're simply a nurse I've always worked with."

"That's our reality now!" she shouted, completely disregarding where they were. "We're colleagues and nothing else. Not anymore."

He shoved the chairs abruptly out of his way and moved around the table to her, Kendall reflexively backing up and away from him. Her stance stopped him dead in his tracks.

They entered a staring contest, his eyes burning with a mix of fury and desire. "Damnit. I still want you," his words heaved from his mouth as if they'd been a vice around his heart. "And I can feel it from you — this buzz. You still want this, too."

"Anson: Don't do this. We can't keep trapping ourselves like this."

He took another brazen step toward her.

Her back found the wall and she had nowhere to escape. She breathed heavily, her body a warring frenzy of emotions.

"We can't keep creating this codependency on one another," Kendall began, the same old arguments always ready at hand. "Bound by grief and all the bullshit that goes with it, where we hope sex is enough of a high to make us grow. We need time apart — or more accurately, time alone to understand–"

"Would you *please*: Just shut up. For once. Please," he begged with desperate exhaustion.

Stunned, Kendall's mouth popped open in protest, but his eyes dropped to her heated lips, throwing her from her game. He wet his lips, his energy building as he contemplated his next move.

The crackling current pulsating between them instantly caught fire. Her heart rate soared as she interpreted his heady stare.

He watched her swallow — a look that nearly choked her dry.

230

"Don't look at me like that," she pleaded on a whisper, her knees already weakening with the kick in adrenaline.

"Why?" his voice now low and seductive.

"It's disarming and you know it."

"Tell me you don't want me," he boldly demanded, crowding out the air she breathed.

She stood speechless. *This could not be happening.*

"Tell me to go." He rolled his bottom lip in slowly, wetting it, his gaze fixed on hers. "Stop me if you want."

And then his fingers grazed her tightly knotted fist, still clinging to her plastic lunch bag. Obediently, every muscle in her hand relaxed; she never even heard the bag hit the floor.

There was only him.

"Kendall."

Her name reverently spoken from his lips pushed her over that self-imposed line. She no longer had the strength left to fight the force that pulled and tore at her when near him. She needed to feel it all again. At least once. She closed her eyes and lifted her chin up to his, her lips parting. Wanting.

***

Anson's mouth crashes into hers and she's gone.

Oh. My. God. Strike me dead now.

His large hands greedily tear into her scrubs, seeking out skin, flesh, life — anything that makes her real to him once again. His fingers dig hard into her curves with blistering force, pinning her between his grip and hips. He barely pauses to taste her as his lips ravish her throat.

And as he devours her desire for him, she prays he never finds his fill.

He moves faster than her thoughts, suddenly dropping to his knees and stripping her pants and underwear down just far enough to expose her unruly, dark hairs to the room. The room spins in a blinding blur of shooting stars and bursting flames.

This can NOT be happening!

He splays his fingers over the coarse patch, his hand pressing into her and separating her luscious folds. She drips with juiciness, an invariable honeycomb of succulent syrupiness against his tongue. He plunges in as he inhales her deep into his lungs.

"Fuck yeah," he groans, his words muffled against her. "Oh baby," he cries, besieged, his tongue swirling over her slick surface like a last meal.

The manner in which he conducts himself — his desperation: completely uninhibited and shameless — it's unnerving. His fervent pace is beyond sexually charged and undeniably carnal.

He needs her in order to survive.

But it's like heroine. Toxic and overpowering.

Kendall covers her eyes with one hand while the other holds steadfast to the crown of his head, her hips rhythmically bucking against his mouth. He positions his head further beneath her, forcing her legs wider apart as he stabilizes each thigh on the palms of his hands, his thumbs exploring and kneading into her groin.

"Oh god, Anson! I can't, I can't. Oh god. Anson, please! Fuck me," she whimpers as an orgasm rips through her, her knees nearly buckling.

Anson immediately stands and pushes her satiated body to the table, Kendall collapsing over top and her arms spreading far out along the smooth surface like a spilled drink. Without a word, he's suddenly inside her; deep inside her, filling and stretching her, her body's muscle memory squeezing against him reflexively, celebrating his return.

The strange stillness of the room quickly fills with guttural utterances punctuated by the rapid slapping and sucking of skin against wet flesh as he plows into her from behind. The table rocks forward, skipping on the polished wood until knocking into the chairs on the opposite side. But Anson remains relentless in his pursuit of release.

He forcibly yanks back on her hips one last time, Kendall's nails chipping into the varnished surface as her body climbs to unimaginable heights, and together they come. Anson slumps over her with exhaustion, panting. Kendall's heated breath fogs the surface of the table.

"Goddamn," he growls with each spasm as she internally tightens against him. And with unexpected affection, he kisses the back of her scrub top, his heated breath soaking through the material and deep into the fabric of her soul, and whispers: "I love you. Always."

***

Anson's forehead fell to hers, each breath longer and more languished than the last, a hand softly settling to her hip.

"What I'd do to know your thoughts right now." The grit in his voice melted her insides, her lips aching for more than the heat of his words. "To fulfill your fantasies. To feel how *wet,* you are. For me. And only me. To come inside you. One. Last. Time."

She waited; holding her breath, her knees ready to give, her heart ready to explode. Any second she'd experience it all over again: the heat, the passion, the incomparable erotic euphoria. She wanted him to take her hard and not hold back. Just for old time's sake. Just to feel it again. *Just...*

And then he pulled back.

He loosely looped a lock of her hair around his finger, letting his palm brush against her cheek. Her adrenaline rush betrayed her as tears breached the seal of her eyelids and rolled down her face. Anson wiped them away with his thumb along the side of her cheek.

"Now you understand the frustration my clients felt when I left," he whispered impudently. "Fucking someone else hardly seems worth it when you've already had the best."

She opened her eyes with a start, his smug expression proudly greeting her. She waited again, shocked by his unwavering nerve. Then, without a second thought, she smacked him hard across the face and stormed out of the room.

***

"I almost kissed Anson last night," Kendall said matter-of-factly into the phone to Ariel.

"Wait– What?! Where? How? You're talking again? What do you mean *almost*?!" Ariel fired in rapid succession as she tried to make sense of Kendall's confession.

"At work. Actually, it was this morning. I don't even know how it happened. Suddenly he was there and saying he wanted me and I couldn't think. But he did it to prove a point. He wasn't himself. He was hurting. I could tell."

"Where was this? The stairwell? What point is he proving? You're going to make me be late for work!"

"No. In a room. Like an office. I left the room as soon as I realized it was a game. Maybe he wanted to make me squirm or something. To prove he still has that effect on me. I heard a rumor at work that he was taking some time off. We didn't talk much, but there was a detachment there, like he'd already checked out from his job."

"Wow. Maybe that was the closure you two needed," Ariel offered, unsure of how else to analyze it.

"No. I don't know. It was strange. A patient of his practice died earlier this morning and there was a lot going on. Anyway. Thought I'd share. I have a doctor's appointment now in Broward, so I'm heading there before going home. It's my follow up to make sure everything's healing properly. I'm betting they'll have to do a D&C. The bloating and weight gain is getting worse. I just don't feel like myself yet. It's a constant reminder of him and needs to be over with already."

"Call me afterward," Ariel requested.

"Will do. Tell baby Ken slash Daniela that Auntie Kendall loves loves loves him/her."

Ariel laughed. "He/She heard you. Love you!"

Kendall waited patiently in the gynecologist's office, still draped in her paper gown after her vaginal exam. She was nodding off to sleep exhausted from her shift when there was a knock at the door. A moment later an ultrasound tech entered.

"Excuse me. Hi. Mrs. Matthews?" she asked as she peeked around the door.

"Yes," Kendall answered sitting up.

"My name is Tami. Dr. Douglas wants you to have an ultrasound. So if you could go ahead and get dressed. I'll take you over to my room."

"Oh sure. Is something wrong?" Kendall asked, moving off the table.

"She just wants to check out everything," Tami answered with a smile.

Kendall now laid flat on Tami's examination table as her belly was prepped with the cool blue ultrasound jelly. She stared at the photographs taped to the ceiling: a series of swirls and colors like cosmic pictures taken by the Hubble telescope. Then Tami stood up from her stool and informed Kendall she'd be back in a minute.

Kendall waited again, her scrub pants pulled down and the gel still coating her lower abdomen. She shifted around trying to angle herself to see the screen that'd been turned away from her. But then Tami reentered the room with Dr. Douglas.

Dr. Douglas took a hold of the ultrasound wand and began to slide it across Kendall's belly again.

"Is something wrong?" Kendall asked. "I need a D&C, don't I?"

Dr. Douglas smiled, took a deep breath, and looked directly at Kendall. Her face was warm and kind — and in a word: unnerving.

"What is it?" Kendall asked, panic rising.

"I know your history well, Kendall, and I don't want to create false hope; but it's not just elevated hormones you've been experiencing. You're actually pregnant my dear."

"Like fetal tissue? So I need a D&C, right? What are you trying to say?" Kendall pushed up slightly, trying to see the monitor.

Tami reached over and turned a knob on the monitor as Dr. Douglas turned the screen to face Kendall. Immediately the room filled with the rapid, rhythmic sounds of fetal heart tones.

"This is your baby, Kendall," Dr. Douglas pointed to a black and white image of curved, blurred lines bending and flexing on the screen. "And as of right now, it looks like a healthy 13 to 14-week fetus. You're in your second trimester."

The fast beating sound suddenly stopped as Kendall sat straight up in a state of shock.

"What?! I don't get it. I don't understand what you're saying. I can't have babies. How is this possible?"

"Kendall. Listen to me," Dr. Douglas said, encouraging Kendall to lie back down. She put the wand back onto Kendall's belly, the ultrasound image reappearing on the screen. "This is a very rare occurrence. The baby appears to be in a good position within your uterus. I have no reason to believe that this baby can't be carried to full-term. You've had what's called a heterotopic pregnancy. You were pregnant with twins. One was ectopic and the other is in the uterus. We only saw the ectopic one. You are still pregnant and barring no complications, you will have a baby in some 25 weeks — Most likely via c-section due to your surgical history."

Kendall stared at the screen gobsmacked. And then tears flowed to the surface as she smiled appreciatively at Tami and Dr. Douglas.

"I'm going to have a baby," she said with more conviction than anything else she'd said that entire year. "I'm going to have a baby."

Chapter 29

KM: **Are you home?**

It was nearly one in the afternoon. Kendall sat in her Jeep in the parking lot of the gynecologist's office stunned. She looked at the small seats behind her and assessed where a baby seat would go. *What about school? The rental in Miami? Does the lease include a baby?* She was wired. She had to tell him. No matter the state of their personal relationship, Anson had to know.

She waited. The chime of her phone made her jump.

AA: **Yes.**

KM: **We need to talk.**

AA: **My door is open.**

After pulling up into his drive a half hour later, she quickly looked herself over in the mirror. Still in her scrubs and feeling fairly disheveled — her sleep and shower long overdue — Kendall attempted to tamp out the puffy pads beneath her eyes.

This is it, she thought to herself. They'd now be forced to continue to know each other in every other way, *except* sex, and it was all *because* of sex.

They were going to have a baby together.

Together, they'd be parents.

She rehearsed every possible way to tell him the news as she walked up the pathway to his front door. Just as she settled on the sudden-death method of just blurting it out, she heard the thump of a bass coming from inside his home. She didn't bother to knock, opening the door up to a blast of pounding music.

Anson's dark and brooding side was home.

Kendall headed up the stairs, assuming he'd be in his lounge getting an early start to his day with a drink. After all, she did slap him. Hard. And he'd acted like an asshole. But then the clink of weights coming from the gym room caught her attention — the bumping remix serving as his motivational soundtrack: *The Hills* by The Weeknd featuring Eminem.

Anson was working out. And oddly enough, she'd never seen him do it before.

She entered through the gym door and first noticed the sprawling view of the crisp turquoise Atlantic Ocean through the wall of windows. She missed that view.

Then she heard him: grunting — and found him hidden behind another piece of exercise equipment, finishing a set. She quietly moved to get a better vantage point; then watched... in awe.

This view she missed even more.

He was gorgeous; drenched head-to-toe in sweat as he benchpressed what seemed to be a ridiculous amount of weight above his perfectly sculpted chest. The choppy hiss of air he exhaled as he forced the loaded bar high above him was nothing short of inspiring. And intoxicating. Clearly his body did not come easy.

She admired him: his work ethic, his stamina, his results. He worked harder than anyone else she knew.

And then she realized — as she stared and studied the mastery of his physique — she could no longer objectify him. It felt wrong. This stunning, Adonis of a man was the father of her child. And without any doubt, she knew: he'd make an excellent father.

He locked the bar into its cradle with a loud clang and lay spent, breathing heavily on his back. She didn't say a word, the epiphany of the moment captivating her more than she'd expected.

But then the words of Eminem's rap registered with her: "*So no complexities, just sex. And don't lecture me, just accept.*" Anson sat up on the end of the bench, his back to her as the thunderous bass dropped and The Weeknd sang out the chorus with its haunting frankness. By the second run through, Anson's body swayed into a rhythm, his head bobbing with the beat.

> *I only fuck you when it's half past five.*
> *The only time I'd ever call you mine.*
> *I only love it when you touch me, not feel me.*
> *When I'm fucked up, that's the real me.*
> *When I'm fucked up, that's the real me, babe.*

The tempo slowed way down as the ethereal sounds of the singer's falsetto voice bridged the song. Anson stood up, grabbing his towel hanging on some nearby equipment. He saw Kendall in the mirrored wall and immediately spun around to face her.

"What–" he began, then immediately stopped, finishing the question with his eyes.

He hadn't actually expected her to drop by. She mustered up a shrug, the innocence in her subtle smile further throwing him. He regretted his earlier comment and knew he'd have to apologize at some point. But now she stood in front of him as if she'd already forgiven the whole thing. In those thirty seconds of the sweet layered harmony caressing them — the lyrics enveloping them, tempting them, locking all thoughts onto one another — the spark, once again, caught fire.

The burn singed deep and before The Weeknd finished his melodic call, "*Only you to trust,*" Anson made his move.

He crashed into Kendall, the telling chorus rolling in, reverberating like thunder beneath their skin. Her body willingly surrendered to all he commanded. Immediately she was off the ground, supported by his strength, and pressed against the back mirror, her thighs squeezing him with desire.

Their mouths, starved for the taste of the other, clashed with lustful need. The music continued; trapping them, teasing them along almost on a dare. In another half minute — now filled with rampant fury where their physical actions outpaced all semblance of thought — Anson sunk in deep, Kendall gasping as a streak of stars shot across her vision.

Oh god. This is happening.

The music slowly dropped to the background as it drifted off into its final meditative chant. Then the speakers fell silent. Nothing followed — except the restrained sounds of forbidden sex echoing in the gym.

One and a half minutes. That's all it took — the extent of their impulsive moment — then Kendall's spark extinguished as the thought of their baby drifted to the forefront of her mind.

"Please put me down," she whispered, her voice choked — torn.

"Baby." Anson filled her mouth with his tongue, her request not heard at all in his thoughts.

But she pushed back against his shoulders.

"Anson: Put. Me. Down."

He snapped out of his blinded pursuit and looked into her eyes. Immediately he set her down and took a step back. He was breathless and confused.

"What's wrong?" he asked, adjusting his gym shorts around his hips.

She stood there dumbfounded, her scrub top awkwardly out of place without its matching counterpart that had been casted off to the side. She shook her head at him and snatched her underwear and pants from the floor.

"What?" he asked again, now irritated. "Kendall: You came over here. What the hell?"

"I can't do this, Anson. This isn't how I see you. Not anymore. I came here to *talk*!" she said in a huff, tying her pant cords in a frenzy.

"*You came here to talk*," he muttered sardonically. "Kendall, come on. You wanted me to fuck you this morning and I would have, except... I pissed you off. Yell at me for that: for making you angry. But don't go pretending you don't agree with it; as if you see me in any other way than the best fuck you've ever had. You and I both know why you're here. And at least I'm man enough to be okay with it. This is us, Kendall. You and me. This is who we are."

"Is *that* what you really think?" She stopped in her mad dash for the stairs and returned to him. "You think I came over here to get fucked and that *that* is the only thing we will ever be to one another? As if we're incapable of any other role in one another's life? Seriously? Seriously, Anson?! Well, fuck you!"

"Wait. What?" he called out confused, while following after her, and wrongfully amused by her outburst. "Kendall. Come on. Fine. I take it back. Kendall."

She continued to rapidly descend the stairs, forcing him to follow after.

"Damnit, Kendall," he snapped, grabbing her arm before she got to his front door. "Stop. What? Talk to me. Why did you come over?"

She looked down, the adrenaline of anger still surging. She didn't want to lash out again. She waited; Anson watching her closely.

"I'm listening," he said, exhaling heavily. "But I'm not a masochist; so if you came over to just bash me–"

"That wasn't fair — what you said at the hospital. I've never tried to hurt you like that," she argued. "To pull you in only to shoot you down. That was a pretty malicious move; even for you."

"You're right. It was below the belt," he said indifferently.

"But you're not sorry?" she asked, frustrated.

He took in a breath, running his hands through his hair and pacing in place.

"Of course I am," he said reluctantly. "But sometimes you get so tired of being the *bad guy* for no apparent reason that you end up doing something to make the image fit."

Kendall studied his face, all the hurt held behind it now painfully visible.

"I figured" —he threw his hands up in the air— "if that's how you saw me, I could see you that way too."

"Is that how you really see *me*? The best *fuck* you've ever had and that's it?" she asked, working to prevent her voice from cracking.

"No! Of course not... Well. In a way you are..."

Kendall's eyes narrowed with contempt.

"Well, that doesn't sound exactly right," he said quickly, somewhat flustered. "Kendall: you won't even see me now. It's been weeks and every time I'm around in the unit, you're gone. *On a break, down in radiology, called in sick.* Your colleagues have endless excuses. It kills me to know how much you hate me. How much Gabe must hate me. I can't handle it."

"Anson," she said in disbelief. "I don't hate you. I could never hate you. And don't worry about Gabe. He's just following me. And that's my doing. He's loyal. Not a hater. The whole reason I came over here was to take our first steps toward friendship."

"Then why do you treat me like shit?" he asked, his frustration overflowing.

Her shoulders sank. "To make it easier on myself. You have to have known that. Otherwise: why even try to embarrass me like you did this morning? I don't know how to be your friend without getting mixed signals. That's why I'm here. I want to try. There has to be a way without all of this... this angst. Don't you think? Is it even possible?"

"I don't know," he said, shaking his head. "I really don't know."

Kendall looked deep into his eyes, almost in awe — his vulnerability uncanny.

"It has to be," she said with conviction. "Anson: I can only offer you my friendship right now. And I really want yours. Is that something you can give to me?" She studied him: his breathing, his posture, the crease between his brow. He looked away, knowing she could read him too well.

"Do you really believe what you said upstairs?" she continued. "Because I don't. I think it's fair to accuse me of it, but I could never see you as just that. Never."

Anson closed his eyes as he pinched the bridge of his nose, the pressure of the moment hitting him all at once. He purged the air from his lungs and opened up to her.

"Not too long ago I thought I might spontaneously combust if I didn't have sex with you for a couple of days," he said lightheartedly, their tension instantly easing up a bit. "Call me an addict. I don't know. But it was all-consuming. Now it's been some six weeks or more and we've had actual sex– what? One time? Well, one and a half if you count just now."

Kendall begrudgingly smiled.

"On one level: Yes. I meant every word of what I said," he admitted, lifting his eyes to look at her straight on. Kendall remained unnerved, however, knowing he had more to say. "But you know me better than anyone else. I've got the persona I present to protect myself and then there's the one only you know.

"Kendall: I'd be your friend in a heartbeat if I knew how. But it's going to be pretty hard to separate you from sex and everything I experience with it... only with you. The bottom line is: I want you in my life. So, talk to me. I'm listening. Where do you think we should begin?"

She now sighed heavily, looking up at him with surrender.

"Six weeks," she said, Anson not quite following. "Today was my six week follow up from the surgery. I went straight after work."

Anson's entire body stance changed as he took a step back and sat down on his foyer steps, letting out a guilty groan. He rubbed his face, running his fingers back through his hair.

"Fuck. I really can't get anything right, can I? I completely forgot. Should I have been there?" he asked with genuine concern.

"No. God, no. It's like a pap smear. I didn't want you there at all," she quickly answered reassuringly. "It was fine. Everything was fine. Great actually. Fittingly, she cleared me for sex."

Anson groaned again, now through a forced smile, and stood back up. "I'm sorry. I suppose a friend would have called at least."

"It's fine. You were under no obligation to know or keep tabs on my doctor visits. And we weren't friends... yet."

He returned her smile, locking onto her eyes once more. With his brawny chest still aglow from their upstairs romp, Kendall instinctively moved to touch him, then stopped herself.

The tension switch felt misplaced, not at all like the moment upstairs.

It was respectful, not sexual — and entirely unfamiliar.

Neither knew how to proceed; the strong desire to embrace pushing both of them, but the barraging mindset of their current situation causing restraint at the same time.

"Well," Kendall suddenly said with a side-jab to his arm. "I better get going." She smiled broadly and turned around to open the door.

"Wait. That's it? That's all you wanted to tell me? That you're cleared for sex? Kendall: Come on now. What did you want to talk about?"

She opened the door a crack and then paused. *He has to know.* She looked back at him.

"I wanted you to know… to know that… Well, it turns out, I'm still…" But she couldn't.

Everything in her said to wait — that it wasn't the right moment. They had a moment and used it up in a fit of passion and now they needed the moments between moments to recuperate.

"You know what?" she said. "Another time. We just had a whole crazy thing happen and I think we need some time to… sort through it. Don't you think?" She began to ramble rapidly, swinging open the door. "So, I'm sure I'll be in touch with you soon; but for now, everything's great. We just needed to get it all out of our systems. Now we're good. Moving forward. Keep healing and growing. Forward on, right?"

Kendall, now halfway down the front pathway, turned back to see Anson. He remained on the front step, listening to her prattle on from afar, and shook his head in amusement.

"Whatever you say, Kendall," he said, smiling. "Like I said to you before, my door's open."

"Okay then. So, I'll be in touch?" she said, deciding for the both of them.

"Actually, how about you come over for my birthday next month," he suggested innocently. "Talon and DeGraff are throwing a party here. It's more like a going away party. I'm taking leave for a bit. We'll be surrounded by people — it'll be safe." He smiled.

"I heard about that: you taking some time," she said. "Good for you. I'll think about it."

"Kendall, I want you to come — as my friend... To my party! Get your mind out of the gutter!"

She full-on blushed, Anson's smile too big for his face now. He always loved it when she squirmed.

"We definitely need to practice our friendship phrases," she said, walking further away. "Or more importantly: *you* do. But why not? A crowd is good and friends do go to each other's parties. So, I'll try and stop by."

She moved quickly to her Jeep, looking back only once. Anson waved goodbye, his perma-grin of confidence making her unravel completely.

"Aaaaaaaaahhh!" Kendall screamed, scolding herself, as she drove back home. "What the hell is wrong with you?!"

She pulled in front of her apartment complex and rested her head onto the steering wheel. She'd been awake a full 22 hours and had very little sleep in the last 72 hours. She was overly tired and overly wired all in one.

She had to call someone to let them know the news. Someone who wouldn't go ballistic and ask a million questions, yet still would be excited to know. Someone like Gabriel.

She flopped onto her bed, unable to even undress, and called her brother.

"Hey Kendall!" he answered, prompting Kendall to smile into her pillow.

"Hey Gabe."

"What's up?"

"Well, I just got home after a long night of work, so I'm really tired. But I had a doctor's appointment so I couldn't go to sleep yet."

"You sick?"

"No, just a check-up. And guess what?"

"What?" he asked.

"You're going to be an uncle," she said, smiling and knowing it'd take him more than a minute to understand.

"Ariel had her baby?" he finally asked.

"No," she answered, laughing. "No, she's still pregnant. But you're going to be a *real* uncle now. I'm going to have a baby too."

"Really? When?"

"November. Just before Ariel."

"But I thought you couldn't have babies."

"I thought that, too. Turns out, I can have just this one. So it's pretty special."

"Awesome! This is awesome! Is it a boy?"

"I don't know that yet!" Kendall said, laughing. "It's still real small in my belly. I guess I'll find that out next month or something. I'll be going to the doctor a lot to make sure everything's fine, but yeah. I wanted you to be the *first* to know."

"I'm the first to know?"

"Yup. You're a pretty special uncle."

"Wow! Even before Mom?" Gabriel asked doubtfully.

"Yes. Even before Mom. But you can't tell her, okay? Not yet. I'll be the one to tell her. But right now I really need to get some sleep. Maybe I'll come down to see you guys tomorrow, okay?"

"Okay. That sounds like a good idea."

"Promise you won't tell Mom?" Kendall asked.

"I promise," he said.

"Great. I'll see you tomorrow. Love you, bud."

"Love you, too."

Kendall was just about to end the call when she heard Gabriel again.

"Hey Kendall?"

"Yeah?"

"Who is the dad?"

Kendall took in a deep breath and closed her eyes. "Anson."

"Really? Are you boyfriend and girlfriend again?"

"No," she said quietly. "But he's still going to be the dad."

"Oh. Okay. He'll make a good dad."

"Yeah, that's what I think," she said.

"I guess you better tell him," Gabriel concluded most appropriately.

"Yeah. I will. When the time is right."

"When's the baby coming again?" he asked.

"End of November."

"That gives you some time."

"I hope so," she said even softer.

"Do you want him to be the dad?"

Kendall opened her eyes. She hadn't even asked *herself* that question, and here Gabriel was probing the deepest corridors of her heart. She thought about it for a moment before responding.

"I do," she said clearly. "I really do."

"So do I," he replied, now really taking Kendall by surprise.

"Okay Gabe. I have to go to sleep now."

"Okay, see you soon. Congratulations on your baby."

"Thanks, bud."

Kendall ended the call and turned off her cell phone. She barely placed the phone on her nightstand before falling asleep.

***

Kendall curls herself into a ball on the floor in the corner of the dark, cramped room. She cries and cries. But it's too late now. The moment is gone.

Through her blurred vision, she watches as Anson walks away down the street holding hands with his amazing wife and their small child. Their teenager is a few paces ahead, pushing a stroller with their twin infants inside. His wife turns, pregnant with another baby, and Kendall sees that it is Joice. He's married Joice and they're happy. As they walk, more children appear, running up to him and shouting, "Daddy!"

She never doubted his ability to be a great dad.

Kendall curses herself for not telling him when she had the chance. She strokes her belly, still 14 weeks in with her precious pregnancy, and now there's no daddy available to claim.

Anson fades away happily, moving forward just like she instructed him to do, oblivious to Kendall's sobs.

She blew it. Maybe she could have salvaged their relationship and made it just that: an actual relationship. But he's moved on with Joice, having babies across the world, and will never know of his one, special child — with Kendall.

Chapter 30

"Anson and I had half-sex and I'm still pregnant," Kendall said in her usual dry fashion upon answering Ariel's phone call the next morning.

There was a sputtering of sound following by a few expletives as Ariel reacted to the comment.

"Did you get that? Anson and I? Sex? Still pregnant?" Kendall repeated, a wry smile tugging at her mouth as she pictured Ariel right in that moment.

"You bitch. I spit my tea all over the steering wheel and my skirt. I am officially late for work. I need to call you right back." Ariel hung up the phone, Kendall immediately erupting in laughter.

"Hello?" Kendall answered hesitantly a few minutes later as Ariel stayed true to her word. "Is it safe to speak?"

"I just told my new job I had a family emergency and I'd be a few minutes late for work. William is out in the Georgia morning heat cleaning out my car. You better start talking and you better start talking fast."

Kendall fought the urge to not laugh out loud and began to tell Ariel everything that had happened since they'd spoken the previous morning. The two squealed and cried and planned and laughed. The feeling was nothing short of euphoric. They'd be having babies together.

"No, she doesn't know yet. I'm going over to their house to tell her today… if Gabe hasn't let the cat out of the bag yet," Kendall said. "I still can't believe it either. It's awesome and exciting and crazy and nerve-racking."

"But you're happy, right?" Ariel asked quickly.

"Ecstatic," Kendall said confidently. "I want this more than anything. I just have to figure out how to tell him now."

"Well," Ariel said, letting out a fast exhale. "This certainly changes everything between you two. I was originally going to ask whether you gave your two-week notice, but uh, your topic was way better. Definitely worth all the spray of tea."

"You know I was thinking about that, as I drove up to Anson's home yesterday — quitting the job. Now that I know this, and all the stress I've already put this baby under unknowingly… I want to put in my two weeks now. Just take it easy before school. Get myself in a super good spot for everything. My doctor assured me all looks well, but I don't know. I wasn't on prenatal vitamins or anything and I–"

"Kendall," Ariel said sweetly. "Your baby's perfect. If you want to take the time off, take the time off. But don't go down that road of *shoulda*, *woulda*, *coulda* thought. You didn't start the baby off on the wrong foot, okay? Everything's going to be fine. Your body knows what to do."

"My body's never known what to do," Kendall said quietly.

"But now it does. And it's going to do a damn good job at it."

***

Kendall slid back into the plastic dining chair of the nurse's lounge, instinctively resting her hands on her happily growing belly. It was after midnight and she'd just enjoyed a potluck meal courtesy her nightshift coworkers. Tonight was her last night at Gold Coast General. She managed to keep her pregnancy a secret as her work scrubs hid it all very well. She looked about the lounge, thinking of when she'd first left it for the SICU a few years back. She'd left in order to get more experience prior to applying to CRNA school. And now she was leaving for CRNA school. She felt incredibly proud in that moment. Damn proud. She'd come so far.

The door opened and Anson peeked his head around the frame, Kendall immediately dropping her hands to her side and sitting straight up.

"Hey. Didn't mean to startle you," he said kindly, his smile sincere.

"What are you doing here so late?" she asked.

"Thrombectomy on the new patient in three," he said. "Someone mentioned food and your last day. I hadn't realized."

Her stance softened as he remained glued to the door handle, waiting for her approval.

"I haven't really kept up on my end of the friendship bargain, have I?" she asked, offering up an apologetic smile.

He moved into the room and picked up a homemade egg roll from a platter. He dipped it in the duck sauce, took a bite, and smiled. "Not bad. Ami make these?"

"I think so," she said, returning his smile, her arms now crossing over her abdomen in an attempt to cover it.

"Well, you made it mid-June. Impressive. I would have bailed on that commute day one. My last day is July 3rd. You still considering the party at my place on the eleventh?" he asked between bites.

"Sure. But there's something I need to tell–" and then the door opened up behind him, Ami walking in.

"You like those?" she asked, gesturing to the egg roll in his mouth. He raised his eyebrows playfully as he bit in. "Secret family recipe." She giggled and his smile that followed lit up the room.

It was all fairly innocent, but Kendall immediately felt uncomfortable. She stood up, Anson looking over at her with question. She took in a breath, smiled bravely, and exited the room. He followed behind.

"So, Kendall," he said before she made it into the open of the unit.

She turned, her arms covering her midsection. "Yes?"

"When does this friendship start?" he asked.

"It already has," she said, smiling sweetly.

"So if I text you sometime?" he asked curiously.

"I'll answer." She smiled again and then turned to walk away, unable to look at him any longer knowing the secret she kept from him and how desperately he'd want to know it. But then she turned back to him, Anson still standing there watching her.

"I know I'm awkward," she said bluntly. "And I appreciate your friendly approach... as awkward as it is. But you do know it's nearly one in the morning."

"Sometimes I work at this hour," he said honestly. "I can't help it. Nature of the job."

Kendall nodded her head in agreement.

"Maybe we can get together before the party sometime?" she suggested.

He responded fairly quickly by shaking his head. "Not such a good idea. You want us to learn friendship, we'll need to learn it in a crowd. I just wondered if I could check in every now and then via text. Especially considering you'll be in Miami full-time now. Believe me: the distance is a good thing."

"Oh," Kendall said, a little surprised. "Sure. I better get back to work."

"It was good to see you," he said genuinely. "I hope to see you again next month."

"Okay. Sounds good." She walked back to her patients' rooms beyond baffled.

***

"What? What?! Tell me!" Kendall said excitedly into the phone.

Ariel and William were at their second ultrasound appointment, trying to find out the sex of their baby. Kendall waited on the speaker phone and could only hear muffled squeals of elation from Ariel.

"I'm sorry to say, but you will be the only Ken doll around–" Ariel began, abruptly being cut off by an ear-piercing scream.

"Aaaaaaahhhh! It's a girl! Daniela! Princess Daniela! Oh my goodness! I knew it! Mama Duval knew it! Daniela Duval Johnson!"

The anticipation of her upcoming pseudo-niece was the perfect distraction before Anson's upcoming birthday party that loomed overhead. She'd been suppressing the anxiety of the event, playing the whole thing down to Ariel. That was the only way she knew Anson was really getting under her skin once again. But now it was because of their own baby; their own potential growth; their budding friendship being fostered through the briefest exchanges in text messages.

"Okay," Ariel said immediately. "So now tell me what you're having."

"I put the card in the mail," Kendall said. "You'll know soon enough."

"You know this is breaking all sorts of friendship rules, holding out on me like this."

"Believe me: I'm hearing it from my mom every single day. But I will see Anson tomorrow and tell him. He has to be the first to know something. I owe him that much."

"I can't believe I'm saying this," William jumped in. "But I agree with Kendall. I'm married to you *and* at every appointment for this baby *and* still feel like I don't get to be as involved. It's just not the same being the man. And I can't imagine being the dad and not knowing anything."

"Especially if you're a man who wants to be the dad," Kendall added. "And I know Anson will want to be involved... It's just *how* involved he'll want to be that has me worried."

"You're going to accept his help, aren't you?" William asked.

"Financially? Emotionally?" Kendall said. "Of course. I know he'll have it no other way. But I just don't want him to give up the direction he's heading in, for us. We'll still be here after he takes his break."

"Where's he going and for how long?" William asked.

"Still not sure. Guess I'll find out more tomorrow. Oh shoot. I'm getting another call. I'll talk to you two later. Love you and baby Daniela!!!" Kendall switched lines on her phone.

"Hey DeGraff," she said.

"Hello to you Ms. Matthews. You still on for tomorrow? I'm finalizing the guest list."

"How fancy. Do I have to dress up?"

"Beach party attire, I suppose," DeGraff said. "I wouldn't recommend a bikini, but nothing formal."

"Oh believe me. I will not be in a bikini. More like a tent." She laughed.

"Trying to make yourself unappealing?" he teased.

"No. Just less curvy," she said cryptically.

"I thought you were a fan of curves."

"Sure. In the right places when people expect them."

"I'm not following, but I suppose I will find out more tomorrow."

"There will be much revealed tomorrow," Kendall said suggestively.

"Oh? Is there something going on that I'm not quite aware of? I will say, our man has seemed fairly upbeat lately. I chalked it all up to his new move, but perhaps you have your own news to share?"

"Move? Is he moving?" Kendall asked quickly.

"And now our conversation will end," he said smugly. "What exactly do you two talk about when you say you're keeping in touch as friends?"

"We don't talk. We text. And it's just a *hello* here and there. I think it's all we can muster at this point. But it's something."

"What do you hope to accomplish tomorrow?" he asked.

"Accomplish? I'm not going on a mission," she refuted. "Well… not exactly. We're both working toward a friendship. It's not easy, given our history, but it has to be possible."

"*Has* to be?" DeGraff asked.

"There's a lot at stake," she confessed.

251

"Hmm... And to think Talon thought this party might be dull."

Kendall ended the call and smiled. The sun's heat soaked deep into her skin; the chatter and roar of the Atlantic Ocean keeping her mind occupied from her own cyclic thoughts. The sound made from her toes crunching into the sand traveled beneath her towel all the way up into her ear. She couldn't deny it: an afternoon at the beach was another perfect idea of Elena's.

Elena eased onto her towel next to Kendall and smiled.

"So? Did they find out this time?" Elena asked.

"Daniela. She's having a girl," Kendall said extremely pleased, the shine in her eyes even evident beneath her sunglasses. "Ooh, quick! Give me your hand! The little one is waking up."

Elena stretched her hand across Kendall's belly, Kendall holding it snug against the spots she'd felt the movement. Suddenly her hand jumped.

"Did you feel it?!" Kendall said, sitting up slightly.

"Yes!" she said, immediately tearing up. "Amazing, isn't it?"

"It is wild," Kendall agreed. "Hey Gabe! Want to feel the baby?"

"Wait until your whole belly rolls like an incoming tidal wave," Elena said with awe. "You look truly beautiful, my dear. I don't think I've ever seen you more beautiful than this." Kendall sat up and looked at her mom.

"Oh, Mom. Thank you," she said.

Kendall wore a red bikini, proudly showcasing her baby bump. She found herself truly embracing the added size, clearly excited by the life behind it. She'd continued to run, Dr. Douglas encouraging her fitness routine since Kendall had always done it. The time off between work and school seemed to be exactly what she needed to find her balance once more.

Gabriel sat down next to Kendall. She guided his hand onto her belly and they waited.

"I don't feel anything," he said.

"You have to give it a minute," Kendall said.

"Does it hurt?" he asked.

"No. Not at all. Feels like a rumble in my belly. That's all."

"But later on," Elena added, "it'll feel like a good punch to the lung."

"Great," Kendall said sarcastically.

Suddenly Kendall looked at Gabriel excitedly. "You felt it, didn't you?"

"That was a kick?" he asked.

"Yes! The baby said hello to you!" Kendall said, beaming.

Gabriel laughed, Elena smiling proudly at the two of them.

"When do we get to know what it is?" he asked.

"When I tell Anson about the baby tomorrow," she said.

"Why do we have to wait?" he asked.

"Because it's important to include him," Elena explained, Kendall immediately looking over at her mom and smiling. They'd come a long way in the last few weeks, recognizing the importance of Anson's role in all their lives at this point.

"Do you like him again," Gabriel asked to their mom.

"Well," Elena said with a sigh. "It's not that I didn't like him. I just wanted to keep Kendall protected. And you. That's my job as your mother. But I also know: Anson will do a very good job protecting his child. My grandchild. We all take our own pathways in life, don't we Gabriel?"

"You always say weird things, Mom," Gabriel said, laughing. He got up and walked back over to his fish pole casted in the surf.

Elena looked at Kendall. "You'll have your own dose of that loving reality soon enough."

Chapter 31

Kendall pulled slowly through the open entry of Anson's driveway, disappointed the wooden gate was already hidden behind its coral pocket. She mocked herself, feeling possessive of the gate, now curious if anyone else at the party even appreciated it like she did.

Their child would like it.

The circular drive was teeming with vehicles. A man dressed like a valet attendant rushed up to her Jeep.

"Sorry ma'am. This is a private party."

"Oh, yes. I know. I know Anson. Anson Allaway. It's his birthday party," Kendall rambled on awkwardly. "I'm his... a friend. I'm a friend of his. Well, more than a friend. We used to date, but then we broke up. He asked me to move into this place. I was going to live here. We're still very close. Well, not really, but we will be. We're trying. Not because I want him back or anything."

The young valet looked up from his clipboard squarely at her, Kendall immediately experiencing an unwelcomed wave of reticence.

"Your name?" he asked brusquely.

"Kendall."

"Kendall...?"

"Matthews. Kendall Matthews. I should be on the list. Mark DeGraff confirmed it yesterday. But maybe I didn't get added. I could call DeGraff qui–"

"Here you are. We'll take your vehicle and park it down the street. Here's your ticket," the attendant said, handing her a valet ticket through the window, then immediately opening up the car door as another young man jumped forward to boot her from the driver's seat.

Kendall hesitantly stepped out as if she was just dumped from her life raft.

"Oh... but... Well, I'm not sure how long I'll be stay–"

The Jeep door closed, forcing Kendall to jump back. The thick tire tread squeaked along the concrete as the attendant sharply turned the wheel, taking her Jeep back out onto A1A.

"You can enter right through the front door there," said the gentleman with the clipboard, pointing up the pathway. "Enjoy your evening, Ms. Matthews."

Kendall stood frozen for half a minute, second-guessing the whole cockeyed plan to become friends again. Oh... and announce her pregnancy. She adjusted her top, perfectly masking the bump, and hiked her pants up one last time.

The front door then opened, Kendall stiffening in anticipation. But it was no one she recognized, a partygoer stepping out for a cigarette break on the front step.

"You coming in?" the party guest asked her, pausing in his decision to close the door behind him.

"Yes," Kendall replied, quickly walking up to the door. "Thank you."

She stepped into the slate stone entryway and was immediately met with a shiver. It took a hot minute for her eyes to focus on the faces of those ambling about in the living room and kitchen; their shadowed outlines contrasting against the back wall of sun-lit windows. She took in a deep breath and eased her way up those four steps into his home.

Acid reflux burned in her throat. She didn't see a soul she recognized, but hoped to blend in with the crowd before catapulting herself into a platonic *happy birthday* wish and *you're going to be a daddy* surprise. She balled her fingers into fists at her sides, sheer will propelling her feet forward.

The house appeared stylistically unchanged, yet somehow felt different — emptier despite the crowd. Kendall idly wondered if Talon had switched up the feng shui of the home. When she saw him, she'd let him know he was getting it wrong. All wrong. Anson's home had a pulsating presence within her and it was notably absent.

She saw a small group of women near the fireplace, gesturing at the handcrafted vintage surfboard that hung above it, and Kendall figured they looked like a safe group to join. She needed a vantage point to search for Anson.

"So, after this is taken down and the old floats and pilings are removed" —the one woman leading the discussion animatedly waved her arms about— "I'll bring in some real color to make the place pop. I'll admit, Talon did an amazing job honing in on Anson's tastes. But I do declare: It is time to bring a woman's touch to this sterile concrete slab. Am I right or am I right, ladies?"

The women nodded in agreement to the Debutant's assessment, their arms casting figurative brush strokes, sopping with intrusive colors, across the canvas of Anson's home. Suddenly, Kendall caught on.

What?

"And then I'll work on disassembling that liquor lounge upstairs, making my daddy roll over in his grave, for sure. Since the oversized fish tank won't be moving anytime soon, I'm picturing a South Hampton escape," she said proudly, the women *oohing* and *ahhing* in agreement.

"What?!" Kendall asked abruptly, never actually intending to engage in the conversation.

All four women spun around to see *who* or *what* could possibly be traipsing all over their interior design conference.

"You can't do that," Kendall said, before she had the chance to mentally gag herself.

"I beg your pardon?" asked the lead Debutant, her southern drawl more heavily pronounced.

Kendall's mouth went dry, despite the bile churning even more now. She had an urgent need to fight for Anson's tastes. After all, it was *his* birthday and *his* home. Even if he'd hired this woman to create a new style within the place, Kendall believed her audacity to be far too brazen, teetering on reprehensible.

"Well, it's just that... that... Well, Anson loves that surfboard," Kendall stated, hoping to explain her way out and do it quickly. "It sets the tone for the whole room. It's one of the many things that makes this house *his*. He would never go for anything that included taking it down and replacing it with some glitzy storefront art piece. His colors are from the beach — his backyard *is* the ocean! I mean, it's in his eyes, for heaven's sake! Every mood he experiences — his eye color is straight from the Caribbean, the Atlantic, and even the Gulfstream that runs through them. This is simply who Anson is. You can't just change his whole style simply because you want to add a woman's touch."

The women stared at Kendall in stunned silence, the ring leader stepping forward.

"Honey. If Anson wants to keep the surfboard, he can keep the surfboard. But if I'm moving in here, I will decorate this place as I see fit. Last I checked: happy wife, happy life. So, this hunk of wood and the tired, overplayed ocean theme it's surfing upon? Well, they don't exactly factor into that equation, now do they?"

Kendall was knocked metaphorically on her ass. *Wife? WIFE?!!*

"And who might you be, with your fierce analysis of Anson's dreamy blue eyes?" the woman asked, looking down her nose at Kendall.

Shit.

"Kendall Matthews," a male voice suddenly announced from the sliding glass door, drawing the attention of all the women, but most importantly, a grateful Kendall.

"DeGraff!" Kendall called out enthusiastically, quickly moving away from the gaggle of ladies and into his welcoming embrace.

"As I live and breathe. Here you are," he said predictably in his overindulgent manner.

"God, it's good to see you," Kendall whispered, exhaling over his shoulder with relief. "I was beginning to regret my promise to come."

DeGraff greeted her with a tight squeeze, then immediately stepped back, holding her at arm's length to look her over. Kendall quickly dropped her arms, blousing out her loosely cut satin top.

"So I've gained some weight," she announced, unable to maintain eye contact.

"I'd say," DeGraff boldly agreed, his eyes fixed on her belly. "But it's all pretty localized."

"Don't," Kendall warned.

"Thought you said you hadn't seen Allaway in a while," he teased, slowly drawing his attention back up to Kendall's face, a distinct arch in one eyebrow.

"Jumping right into the topic at hand, I see," Kendall replied.

"I believe you jumped in the minute you walked through the front door."

Damnit, DeGraff.

"Well, I guess you're right with that," she seceded. "There's something we have to talk about before he takes that leave from work. But please tell me his *wife* is not the reason he's leaving work," Kendall said, looking back over her shoulder at the woman. "Is it like a green card thing because she does not seem his type at all. And I'll admit: the *South* does seem like a whole other country at times. Where is she from?"

DeGraff immediately began to open up in laughter, walking between people to make his way into the kitchen. Kendall quickly fell in line behind him.

"What?" she hissed. "Tell me."

"Do you honestly think *that* could be Allaway's wife?" DeGraff asked, lifting his nose in the direction of the woman. He pulled a Heineken from the refrigerator and popped the top. "*I* have a better chance of marrying him than she does." He laughed heartily again, a wave of relief washing over Kendall.

"Well, she's moving in and changing the whole setup, apparently. How should I know? Anson and I are total strangers to one another now."

"Oh dear Kendall. Give your time together a little more credit, would ya? And it's been weeks; not years since you've really sat down with him."

It feels like years.

Kendall sneered at him and smacked his arm. He laughed.

"So, get a drink and find Allaway out on the deck."

"I'm not hanging out long. Before I talk with him, tell me what's going on with that woman and his move."

"Didn't you come here to talk with Allaway? Or were you planning on catching a glimpse of the man through everyone else's eyes tonight?"

"You're still so evasive when it comes to your boy, aren't you? I swear; he's probably paid you to just drop lines and pique my interest when I'm least interested. I'm working up to our conversation. Give a girl a hand."

"Working up to it? Since when have you had to work up to anything? If you want him as your friend, mend your old bridges and throw water under them. Catch up on each other's lives. A lot has changed for both of you in the last couple months. And by the looks of it, there might be a whole hell of a lot more to catch up on than he realizes." DeGraff looked down at Kendall's belly again.

"Don't. Finish. That thought," Kendall said indignantly. "It's not out there until *I* say it's out there. *You* convinced me this was a good idea, so either help me out with my nerves or I'm heading out and he'll have to settle for an impersonal bill in the mail a few months from now."

"A bill for what?" came a voice behind her, one that resonated deep within her.

Kendall spun around and there Anson stood, his enigmatic smile throwing her completely. He maneuvered in between her and

DeGraff's private conversation and opened up the refrigerator, grabbing himself a Heineken. The very essence of him sunk deep into her lungs as she drew in a breath.

Holy hell, this was a bad idea.

Anson stepped back through them, creating a triangle, and snapped off the Heineken top with a bottle opener he had conveniently placed in his pants pocket. He winked at her, while placing the cap and opener back into his pocket, a collection of caps clinking inside. It was definitely his party and he had nowhere else to be.

He wore off-white Bermuda shorts with a navy blue polo shirt and a canvas belt. His shirt draped his sculpted physique like silk, softly following the contour of his body, yet still loose against his skin. The front of his shirt was tucked into the waist of his shorts, drawing Kendall's eyes down and inviting her mind to a dreamier place. She quickly brought her eyes back up as Anson raised the bottle to his lips, drinking back half the beer. Even the stretch of the shirt fabric around his beautiful bicep made her mouth water.

Fuck.

"Happy Birthday!" Kendall immediately said, moving the moment and her distracting thoughts along.

"Thank you. You look great. Nice to see you wearing something other than scrubs," Anson spouted off, barely looking her over and never permitting himself to lock onto her eyes.

"Uh, thank you. You seem well," Kendall answered nervously, glancing at DeGraff who offered no help. He remained statuesque and actually, rather stunned by Kendall's surreptitious admission to her pregnancy. And clearly, Anson had not a clue.

"I am," Anson said, smiling.

Kendall smiled kindly, again looking to DeGraff for guidance.

"So, Kendall thought Brenda was your wife," DeGraff suddenly mentioned, as if *this* was the line to get the conversation going.

Anson immediately began to laugh, looking about the room to see where Brenda and her crew were now. Kendall's cheeks blushed with heated embarrassment. His carefree laugh, however, was like hearing heaven.

"What gave you *that* idea?" Anson asked, still laughing.

"Uh… She was talking about redecorating and moving in, so I just thought…" Kendall said, cursing the whole shit-brained idea to get reacquainted while a crowd surrounded them.

"Definitely not my wife. But you did hear right. She is moving in — with my cousin, her husband. Poor bastard." Anson took another swig of his beer, chuckling to himself. "He just signed a contract with GC General. He's a thoracic surgeon."

"Oh wow. That's great. And very nice of you," Kendall commented, smiling — and beyond relieved.

"Well, the place was going to be empty otherwise, so it made sense," Anson explained, his eyes continually shifting about the area avoiding prolonged eye contact with Kendall. "They're from South Carolina. So, it gives them a year to find a place or decide if it's not for them."

"Oh. So, what will you be doing? You're not moving into Sandalfoot, are you?" Kendall asked.

"No," he said, laughing. It was fucking adorable. And irritating. "I'll be traveling. Overseas actually. Taking a yearlong sabbatical. Doing some medical work abroad," Anson said nonchalantly. "Well, maybe longer if it suits."

"Really? Oh wow. I, uh, had no idea it was a *move* overseas. For a year? Wow. Wow…" she said, her voice trailing off as she began to rethink all her plans of her pregnancy announcement.

"Well, yeah. I think that's the minimal amount of time necessary to really immerse myself into a new culture while teaching." Anson now looked more closely at Kendall, then to DeGraff as he gathered the distinct feeling of something being amiss in the group.

"Teaching? You're going to teach? This is really great, Anson. Really great. Where exactly are you going?" she asked, her blood surging with a mixture of genuine excitement for him and complete dismay for herself.

"Well, I'll still be doing surgeries, so not exactly academic teaching. First I'll head to China. After that, though, I'm not sure. It's wide open. Not ready to sell this house yet, but who knows what I'll want in another year. Nothing's really keeping me here, so…"

"You have two properties here," DeGraff commented.

"Definitely don't need to be local to maintain them," he responded.

"Plus, you have family here now," DeGraff countered. "Did you know his niece, Madison, moved into Sandalfoot?"

"Oh, that's wonderful," Kendall said, with far too much exuberance.

"Yeah, for now. It should good. We'll see," Anson answered, a little amused by Kendall's awkward behavior. "But again, I can still visit. Who knows? Maybe I'll start my own family overseas."

As soon as he said it, he felt uncomfortable; his laugh making it obvious he never considered the possibility. He looked down at the floor as he shifted around, drawing Kendall's attention to his flip flops.

"Kinos," she stated, recognizing the brand of sandals. "You got some."

"Yeah, went ahead and picked up a couple of pairs last month when I was down there. Figured I'd see what all the hubbub was about. Actually, I got you a pair. To replace those ones."

The energy in the triangle shifted as memories surfaced.

"Oh. Thank you. That was really thoughtful of you," Kendall said, smiling. "You didn't have to do that."

"I wanted to," he said. "It's what friends do."

The world around Anson completely blurred. So much centered on him now without her ever intending it.

"So what do you have there, Kendall?" DeGraff asked, pointing at the greeting card envelope she'd been turning over and over in her hands.

"What? Oh, um, a birth card... Day! Birth*day* card," she chirped, severing her trance on Anson's distant look. "Just something I thought you should know... or *like*, rather. Or maybe not. I don't know. Um, just something I had to give you." Kendall shook her head as if to scold herself and hesitantly handed it over to Anson. "But don't open it now or anything. Later. By yourself. Well, I mean, it doesn't have to be by yourself, it's just that... You know what? Nevermind. I shouldn't have come over here today. I'll have to just call you up–"

"Hey! Kendall!" Talon called out from the other side of the kitchen. "You made it. She met mom and dad yet?" he asked, bounding over toward her and completely disrupting her debacle of an escape.

"Your parents are here?" she asked in a panic.

"Don't worry. I won't subject you to any of that," Anson said quietly.

"So how's my girl, Ariel? Still pregnant with little Jameson?" Talon teased, engulfing Kendall with the warmest of hugs. She tried desperately to prevent any contact against her belly, but he nearly picked her up off the floor. Then he put her down abruptly and stepped back stunned.

"What is going on with your–" he began, Kendall swiftly cutting him off.

"Talon! It's great seeing you, too. Ariel's great. Very happily married now and she's having a little girl to be named, Daniela," she rambled off rapidly, overdoing it completely. "I was just heading out, but I'm so glad I got to run into you as well. It's like one big, happy reunion, isn't it?"

Talon looked at her quizzically and then over to Anson who was clearly annoyed with Talon's overtly friendly hug.

"Well, okay then. How about you? That top is… very loose," Talon strangely concluded.

"For fuck's sake," Anson barked, punching Talon in the arm. "You're such an ass sometimes."

Talon laughed, but didn't flinch. "What? Did you hug her? What is it that you're wearing?"

"Her perfume?" DeGraff suggested slyly.

"Huh?" Talon was now sufficiently confused by the complete disregard for Kendall's swollen belly.

"I agree. She smells great. What is it? Chanel?" DeGraff continued on in his tactful tangent.

"It's not a perfume. It's a lotion," Anson said with irritation. "A body butter, actually," he muttered, then pounded the rest of his beer. He gruffly moved through the group to open up the refrigerator again. "Kendall? Can I get you anything? You sticking around now?" he asked from behind the fridge door. Several other people stepped around into the kitchen, taking advantage of the open access to cold beer. Anson shuffled around, exchanging small talk briefly.

"What the hell is happening here?" Talon whispered sharply to Kendall and DeGraff. "You're wearing a fucking maternity top and no one's saying anything?"

"And that's my cue," Kendall announced, stepping back from the social ring as Anson reentered it.

"Sorry," Anson said courteously. "What did you want? Or there's a cocktail bar out on the deck if you'd prefer something like that instead."

Kendall's heart resided in her throat as her stomach imploded. This was no longer a search and rescue mission of their faltering friendship. She'd missed the boat entirely and was now drowning in her lack of strength. He was moving forward just like she'd always wanted him to do. She needed to step back and let it happen.

"No thanks. I need to head out," she said calmly, ignoring the burning stares of both DeGraff and Talon. "But, in case of anything... Like sharing some news with you... Or whatever. How will I contact you?"

"Oh. Well, I'm here through next week... if you need anything," he said, a curious look upon his face. He looked at the three of them. "Did I miss something here?"

"Damn right you did!" Talon blurted out.

"Maybe I'll drop by next week, if that's okay. To get my Kinos," Kendall suggested, ignoring Talon.

"Sure. I can grab them now, though," Anson replied, still wondering what happened.

"Not necessary. Gives me an excuse to come by again and say hello," she said, forcing a laugh. "So, I'll see you all later."

"I'm walking you out then," Talon quickly added.

Kendall looked at Talon with sheer venom and marched away to the front door. But he quickly caught up, opening the front door for her and stepping out right on her heel. The sun beat down on them, the July heat radiating off the paved stones, and Kendall felt as if she'd stepped into the stifling space of an interrogation room.

Talon pounced.

"You're pregnant!" he reamed into her. "Is it his?"

"Talon! That's a bold accusation just because I've gained some weight," she said with disgust, trying to escape down the path to the valet.

"Drop the act. You lied about having a miscarriage with Anson and got pregnant by someone else? Who does that?"

"I never!" she growled back, whipping around to face him. "We lost a baby together. It wasn't a fucking act."

Talon's eyes steeled over. "How could you go out and betray him like this? After all that?"

"Talon: go back to the fucking party and leave me alone. You have no idea what you're talking about." She turned away to leave.

"Does he know?" he asked, his tone softer now. "Kendall: answer me. Does. Anson. Know?"

"No. And he doesn't need to know. Not now."

Talon shook his head grievously. "You're right. He's in a good place right now; finally, moving on. This would only mess with him. It's better to just forget you."

Kendall's eyes welled up. *Did he really just say that?*

"He will know soon enough," she said, her back to him. "I just want him to pursue his dreams without factoring in the needs of someone else for once."

"So, you were going to ask for his *help*?" Talon asked repugnantly. "Now *that* is a bold move." He shook his head with disgust, clearly misinterpreting the entire situation. "You're really hitting some new lows here, Kendall."

She stopped and turned around, shouting: "It's. His. Baby!"

Stunned silence.

Then Anson opened up the front door.

"What the hell is going on out here?" he asked Talon who just stood there, gaping with an open mouth. Kendall's expression followed suit. Anson looked between the two shocked faces with frustration. "Answer me!"

He hadn't heard her. It was still her secret to tell.

"I... I," Talon stammered, then held up his hands in surrender. "You two need to talk. This is now well beyond my skillset."

Chapter 32

"Can we go somewhere private?" Kendall asked. Talon had quickly reentered the house, smartly avoiding the detonation that was about to go off. The was no escaping now.

"I've been drinking and I think this is as private as I want it to get with you," Anson said frankly. "Besides, the house is swarming with people. What's going on, Kendall?"

Her entire brow glistened in sweat. Her clothes were beginning to cling to her in all the wrong ways. She need to just get it over with; so *both* of them could move on.

"I need to get into the shade," she said, walking further down the pathway toward the canopy of banyan trees.

Left without a choice, Anson followed after her, irritated. A valet attendant began to walk toward them, Kendall promptly waving him away.

"Listen," he said, gaining an immediate upper-hand. "There's a reason I asked you to come to this party. It was so we could just hang out among friends. And be friends. Get to know each other like that. No drama. No privacy. None of *this*." He pointed around them and the isolation they now had from everyone.

"I know. I wanted that, too. I get it. You don't trust me and—"

"Kendall. I don't trust *me*," he said, interrupting her. "Shit. No matter how disconnected I force myself to feel from you, there's still this pull. And if I need to move across the entire fucking planet to break it" —he shook his head at himself with pathetic amusement— "then so be it. But you have to help me out here. *This* — right here — is something I need to avoid. I'm trying my best to get over you. But when it comes to our chemistry? We need distance. It's how I'm built."

She took in a breath.

"I'd rather walk away right now and let you go off to China, blissfully unaware. I'd rather you leave South Florida, knowing you were going to do important and wonderful things for your own personal growth and not be tied to any obligations."

Anson looked at her, confused.

"What are you talking about? That's what I'm trying to do," he said exhaustively. "So, what am I missing here?" he asked, pushing her for answers. "Kendall: Are you okay? Should I be worried?"

"I... I..." she fumbled along, his eyes fully engaged, locked in and holding the keys to her future. She grappled with her desire to just melt into him; telling him the news one word at a time — punctuated between their smoldering kisses — and ultimately trapping him into everything she could no longer offer, not now at least.

"Here: I put it in this card," she suddenly said, offering him the sealed envelope.

Anson looked at her cynically, but took the card anyway.

"You want me to read this. Now? In front of you?" he said, raising his eyebrow of disapproval. "The last time I had to read something from you... You know I had to pay the Biltmore for damages — more than tripled the bill."

"What? *Damages*?! Oh shit. What happened?" she asked, committing to the digression and the reprieve it brought to their space. He always had a knack for diffusing their tension, even if just for the moment.

"The bedside lamp was the closest thing to me after I read it," he said matter-of-factly. "Apparently it wasn't the lamp that racked up the bill, but the gilded mirror it smashed. Who knew?"

"Anson! Oh my goodness!"

He shrugged as if she should have expected that sort of reaction from him.

"I, uh... I'm sorry. It felt like the right thing to do at the time. For both of us. I was feeling trapped and I needed–"

"Kendall. Stop," he said reassuringly. "There's no need to apologize. It's done and over. No need to rehash it. So: this card? It better not be your way of telling me you have some sort of brain tumor that I need to operate on."

Kendall laughed nervously. "Well, not exactly."

Anson's eyes darted up at her and narrowed as if attempting to read her thoughts. "Kendall," he said with warning. "You're okay, right?"

"Yes! Yes. I'm fine. Believe me. I'm healthy and well. I plan to *live long and prosper.*"

He shook his head, smiling, and ripped open the envelope. He pulled out a folded card that Kendall had designed. Printed on the front of the card was the poem by E. E. Cummings, *I Carry Your Heart with Me*. Anson began to read it to himself, then stopped.

"Kendall," he said regretfully. "I can't. This is not what I need from you right now." He reached out to hand the card back to her.

"No," she said insistently, trying not to laugh. "No, it's not of romance. Or even necessarily of you and me." Kendall held out her hands to him. "Give me your hands."

"Kendall," he said, shaking his head. "I can't do this again. Not again. Losing you was... I won't go through it again." He began to shuffle back and away from her.

But she took his hands into hers anyway and he immediately stilled under her touch. She gently pulled him toward her, placing his hands upon her firm, round belly. Anson snapped to attention as a bolt of understanding shot through him. Almost in a panic, he searched her eyes for an explanation.

"The poem is about *this*," she said, smiling. "Not you and me. But *us*, as parents, and *this*: our baby. Anson: I'm still pregnant."

"But... Wait: what? When did this... How?" he stuttered in shock.

"It was a heterotopic pregnancy. I miscarried the one, but somehow, the other survived safely. We're having a baby, Anson."

His eyes glossed over. The pure joy he found in her words surged through his veins like a rush of adrenaline he'd never experienced before. He immediately dropped to his knees, and without a moment of hesitation, he pressed his lips against her abdomen.

Tears threatened, forcing Kendall to look up toward the canopy above. Her hands hovered over his sandy brown hair, unsure where to put them or how to accept his affection. She knew the answer was *not* to do what felt natural: to get her fingers tangled up in his hair, eventually pulling his lips up and over her body, only to lock them onto hers. Anson clung to her hips even tighter and finally Kendall embraced him softly.

And in the moment she let go of her thoughts, they both felt peace.

Anson kissed her belly adoringly, one, extended time; then finally stood, moved beyond belief.

"This is amazing," he said. "I'm... I'm, uh... Speechless. I don't even know what... Is this really possible? Well, obviously, but... I had no clue. It's incredible. Amazing really. How are you feeling? Were you just as shocked? I just... I can't believe it. Listen to me!"

They laughed out loud, wiping their tears away. They shared the same ridiculous Cheshire grin plastered across their faces, and couldn't shake it. Anson grabbed her into a hug.

"God, I'm so happy for you. For us," he said, over her shoulder. He kissed the side of her head repeatedly in rapid succession, then stood back. "Congratulations."

"To you, too," she said through a laugh. "I was so hesitant to say anything because I wasn't sure how you'd react and if it'd make you think you have to stay here like we were back together–"

"Hold up. What?" He looked at her sternly. "Kendall: Of course I'm staying. This is my child you're having. I'm not leaving you two behind."

Kendall's smile faded. "No. That's why I didn't want to say anything. Anson: you need to still go to China... or to wherever."

"Are you out of your mind? Kendall, think about what you're saying."

"I am. And I *have*. For weeks now. And I think we have to–"

"You've known about this for weeks? Well, obviously. Look at you" —he gestured to her belly— "What are you, about halfway through already? Why wouldn't you have told me?! Kendall. I had a right to know!"

"I tried to tell you six weeks ago! But you wanted to fuck me instead!" she shrieked.

Anson stepped forward and reached for her, briefly glancing over at the valet attendants. He ushered them further into the shadows.

"Okay. I'm sorry," he said softly, his arm wrapped around her. "I hear you. So... what now? What were you thinking in all of this? You still want me to leave?"

"Don't patronize me. I'm pregnant; not a child," she muttered, taking in a breath and shirking his arm off her shoulder. "I've thought about this. *A lot*. Believe me."

"Okay. Okay. So, talk to me."

"Well..." she said, pausing to collect her thoughts. "Yes. You should still leave and move abroad. Go find what it is that you're searching for... even if it's starting a family elsewhere. Of course, I want you to be a part of our child's life — and you will be — but I want you to just focus on you."

"Damn. Do you ever get tired of hearing yourself talk?" he asked, running his hands through his hair. "Listen to what you're saying. You sound so patronizingly generous. Politically correct to a fault. As if I'm the goddamn child here. Kendall: I'm a grown ass man and if I'm having a child with someone, I'm going to be there to be a dad... *Dad*. That's something else, isn't it?"

Kendall smiled. "I know. It's wild. No more AA007. Now it'll be Double A-Dad."

Anson raised an eyebrow at her with intrigue. "I like the sound of that," he said, Kendall immediately rolling her eyes at him. "Okay," he said, moving them along with a snap of his fingers. "So when are you due?"

"Well, we're basing it off the March 7th conception date. So that makes it end of November. But, Dr. Douglas said I'll go earlier than that. Planned C-section. She's insistent, considering the previous surgeries."

"Of course. I agree," Anson said, donning his Dr. Allaway hat. "No sense in risking anything."

"Personally, I think it would be more like a V-BAC and totally within–"

"Kendall."

She rolled her eyes at him. "I already agreed, so moot point."

"Good. So, mid-November. Obviously, I'll be back for that. If I'm in China–"

"*When*," Kendall said, correcting him. "*When* you're in China. There are no *ifs*."

"Fine. *When* I'm in China, I should finish up my initial commitments in Shanghai by the end of December. After that, things were still in the air, so I can easily move back then."

"I thought you wanted to do it for at least a year? Anson, I really think–"

"Are we negotiating our terms here?"

She shrugged. "I guess, kind of."

"Okay then. So, I will leave next week and return for good in December. It's settled. Next item: Have you withdrawn from school yet?"

"No! Are you crazy? I'm going to CRNA school come rain or shine or baby."

"Kendall. Is that even possi–"

"Anson, are you really ready to argue with a 20-week pregnant feminist out in your front yard in the muggy South Florida heat of July on whether or not she will finish graduate school because she's pregnant in the 21st century?"

"Point taken."

"Thank you. So... We're good." Kendall smiled like the greatest weight had been lifted from her shoulders. "Right? We're having a baby and you're still traveling and I'm still going to school and we're not falling into a pile of crazy, sexual impulses? It's all good, isn't it?"

"So... we don't try to make us work?" Anson asked, fairly certain of her response, but needing his answer nonetheless.

Kendall inhaled, shaking her head as she exhaled.

"No. This will be our common core. Not sex. Not a relationship. Only our baby. One thing at a time."

Anson laughed, then nodded his head in agreement. "I suppose you're right on that. One thing at a time. Okay then. It's all good. We're having a baby. Holy shit. This is crazy."

"And we will be apart, yet still together," Kendall added, as if needing to make perfect sense of it all.

"Yes. It would seem so," he said with a smile. "Anything else you want to wash away in this endorphin high? Past grievances? Now's the moment."

Kendall's cheeks hurt from how big she was smiling. She was so proud of him. So proud of them. So proud of how far they'd come, how much they'd healed, how strong they'd be for their child on that day adversity would come knocking and they'd handle it with ease. Together, they could do anything.

"Want to get into the last name territory?" she asked, a sly smile pulling at the corner of her mouth.

Anson's face went blank. "Not *Allaway*?"

"Uh, try again. The baby's going to take my last name."

"Graham?"

"You know damn well that's not my last name anymore. *Matthews*, of course."

"Kendall, come on. It's not his..."

She looked at him closely, almost daring him to say it.

"Well, it's not," he said assertively. "It's my baby. And I don't know, call me old-fashion, but uh, shouldn't the baby take the father's name?"

"Uh… No."

"Well, what?" he continued. "You want to hyphenate it? Matthews-Allaway? The poor kid'll get teased on the playground for having a combined last name."

"Maybe we'll blend it. Like maybe, *Mattaway*. Or *Allahews*. Or just the beginnings: *Mattalla*." Kendall began laughing. "Or *Allamatt*."

Anson remained poker-faced, not wanting to give into her amusement.

"Fine. Be a dull, uncreative dad," she jibed, poking her tongue out at him. "But it *will* be Matthews until further notice."

Anson crossed his arms, fighting back his smirk. "Whatever. We'll tackle that topic later. Anything else we need to get out of the way?"

"You want to know the sex?" she asked, her playful grin lighting up her face once again.

Anson's smile fell flat once more; now frozen with wonder. "You know?"

She nodded, bouncing in place. "Found out a couple of weeks ago. Go ahead and read the card."

I Carry Your Heart with Me
i carry your heart with me (i carry it in
my heart) i am never without it (anywhere
i go you go, my dear; and whatever is done
by only me is your doing, my darling)
i fear
no fate (for you are my fate, my sweet) i want
no world (for beautiful you are my world, my true)
and it's you are whatever a moon has always meant
and whatever a sun will always sing is you
here is the deepest secret nobody knows
(here is the root of the root and the bud of the bud
and the sky of the sky of a tree called life; which grows
higher than soul can hope or mind can hide)
and this is the wonder that's keeping the stars apart
i carry your heart (i carry it in my heart)
-e.e. cummings

Anson read through the poem, his smile growing gradually as he read it now from the perspective of a soon-to-be-father. He looked up at Kendall, a slight glistening in his striking blue eyes.

"This is it, isn't it? This is where I lose it. That's your plan?" he asked, his endearing smile making Kendall swoon in anticipatory excitement.

Anson opened up the card and saw a fetal ultrasound image printed inside — a clear black and white profile view of their healthy baby filled the area of the card. Anson brought the image closer to his face, marveling at the features.

"That's incredible." He looked at Kendall, then back at the picture. "Think that's my nose?" He analyzed it a little longer, mesmerized. "So, am I supposed to tell from this?" he asked, looking closer at the area between the legs.

"No. I don't think you can on that one," she said eagerly, biting her lip wanting to blurt out the answer so badly. "But, check out the back."

Anson flipped the card over and along the bottom Kendall had cleverly printed a personalized logo.

This card is brought to you by one fierce little female.

He smiled broadly. "I knew it," he said, shaking his head. "I knew it. Holy shit. We're having a girl."

"Yup. A baby girl. Scared shitless now, aren't you?" she asked, lightheartedly.

He laughed, running his fingers through his already disheveled hair. "Maybe so, but it'll be great."

"I don't know, Anson. I can picture it. She'll have you wrapped so tightly around her little finger, driving you insane as you try and meet her every demand. You thought you had girl problems before — just you wait."

Kendall giggled to herself, his foregone look amusing her to no end.

"Having second thoughts?" she teased.

Anson looked directly into Kendall's eyes, his sincerity captivating her.

"Never," he said, emphatically.

She smiled. "Good. Because I know I can't do this without you. I need your help."

He put his arm around her and they began to walk back toward the house.

"I'd have it no other way. You've got me, babe. I'm not going anywhere."

"But I haven't trapped you, right?"

"No! Not at all," he said, stopping them in the middle of the pathway. He placed his hands on her belly once more. "Whatever happens between us doesn't change the fact that what we've done, right here, is perfect. This is exactly what I've always hoped for, but never dared to think I deserved.

"Kendall, no matter what: you will always have my help. Maybe it'll feel like we're tied to one another at times and can't escape. But that doesn't mean we're trapped. Our daughter? She's our future — our freedom. Kendall: this is the moment where forever begins."

The End

More to Come

I hope you enjoyed the second book in my Gold Coast Romance series. Find out what's next for Anson and Kendall in the third, and final book of the series, *Make Me Yours Forever*. Stay up-to-date on all my latest musings through my website www.ellegmraz.com. Thank you so much for reading!

Love, Elle

About the Author

Elle G. Mraz has several not-so-secret love affairs: peanut butter *M&Ms*, sweet champagne, and writing run-on sentences. She merged all three one day in 2014, continuing off and on, until completing her first romance novel, *Love Me Back to Life*.

Elle met her Canadian husband in Guatemala and got hitched in Las Vegas. Together they laugh, dream big, and ponder life's great mysteries ("When did our junk drawer become a junk room?") while raising their two children, a couple of odd rescue cats, and two evenodder rescue greyhounds. While she's done her fair share of traveling and has lived abroad, Elle was raised along the briny Atlantic coast of South Florida, which she'll always call home.

Writing spicy dramas for others to enjoy is a welcome distraction from Elle's real on-the-job drama as a full-time registered nurse at a South Florida hospital. When she's not working, spending time with her kids, or paying a bit of attention to her main man, she tries to squeeze in some writing and reading time — preferably on the beach with a mimosa.

Contact the Author

Thank you for reading my book! I'm truly honored you took the time to read it. If you have more time, please take a moment to review the book and let myself and others know what you think. Feedback helps me greatly, making me better at my craft. THANK YOU! If you have anything you want to ask or share with me, please feel free to get in touch. I love hearing from readers and will gladly write back!

ellegmraz@gmail.com www.ellegmraz.com
www.facebook.com/ellegmraz
@ellegmraz on Instagram
@ellegmraz on Twitter
Elle G. Mraz on Goodreads.com

www.ingramcontent.com/pod-product-compliance
Lightning Source LLC
Chambersburg PA
CBHW060304260626
47160CB00007B/2498